WHAT LIES BENEATH

Other young adult books by Marissa Doyle

Evergreen
Between Silk and Sand

The Leland Sisters series

Bewitching Season
Betraying Season
Courtship and Curses
Charles Bewitched

WHAT LIES BENEATH

MARISSA DOYLE

Published by Book View Café
304 S. Jones Blvd., Suite# 2906
Las Vegas, NV 89107

ISBN: 978-1-63632-003-8

www.bookviewcafe.com
www.marissadoyle.com

For Scott
You know why

·CHAPTER ONE·
MALCOLM

Late May 1917
Cape Cod, Massachusetts

A t four in the morning, it wasn't always easy to remember why the hell I was trudging alone down a deserted beach in the gray murk of pre-dawn, the sand cold on my bare feet, my kit bag heavy in my hand.

But the relentless rhythm of the waves to my left — slapping the shore then hissing and foaming in retreat — reminded me what I was doing down here today and every morning for the past few weeks.

They were out there, somewhere, hiding in the dark waters. The enemy.

And it was my job to find them.

The United States had been at war with Germany not quite two months, but there were already signs that Germany would very much like to bring the fight to our side of the Atlantic. We'd seen U-boats skulking just offshore since April, slipping in close to the beaches then darting away. Just trying to frighten us, maybe. Or scouting the coast in preparation for putting a more sinister scheme in motion.

The thought made me walk a little faster.

By mid-summer, the ports of Boston and New York would

commence sending ship after ship of soldiers and supplies and food to our Allies in Europe, and the prowling U-boats would be on those ships like the wolf-pack they'd been likened to, torpedoes at the ready. There was a brand-new navy installation here on our island, set to guard the sea lanes leading to those ports, but the aviators with their seaplanes and dirigibles could see only so much from their bird's-eye view.

That's where I and my friends came in.

I swung my bag as I strode down the firmer sand just above the water-line. This had all been my father's idea originally. I think he came up with it as a way to keep me from high-tailing it up to Boston to enroll in officer training. My going off to fight on another continent was not something he would countenance; doing nothing wasn't an option as far as I was concerned. But guarding our home against the threat of attack was acceptable — mostly — to both of us. Father was nothing if not clever.

In the growing light, I spotted the scrubby beach rose thicket at the top of the beach, near where the dunes began: the place where we left our clothes when we were going for a swim. It was far enough from my family's hotel that guests almost never wandered near, but out of sheer habit, I paused to take a long look and listen. Good, I was alone. I hurried up to the thicket, dropped my kit bag and took off my sweater, then got to work unbuttoning my shirt.

It had taken me a week or two to forgive my father; at first, I was just plain mad that I wouldn't be joining Mitchell, Chambers, and the other men from my college crew team to go to war. But I felt better about staying once I started recruiting my friends here to help, and even more so when the commanding officer of the air station, Captain Abbott, enthusiastically welcomed our help when Father and I approached him. Once his initial shock wore off, that is. I grinned, remembering his expression as he'd watched me demonstrate exactly how we would guard the shore. Good thing he didn't have a weak heart.

The eastern sky was brighter now, the deep blue beginning to fade into that strange colorlessness that would resolve into the gold of sunrise. I stood still for a moment to watch the subtle blooming of the light, then quickly finished taking off my clothes and dropped them on the sand. I took another look around to make sure I was still unobserved, then bent to my kit bag and pulled out a length of sleek, dense fur, warm in my hands, before bundling my clothes away and—

"Gods, Malcolm, what's taking you so long? We're waiting for you!"

I lifted my head and looked down the beach. My friend Luthais stood waist-deep in the water, a length of fur like the one I held tossed over his shoulder, hooked casually by one finger. When he saw me looking, he waved.

I smiled to myself and yelled back, "I'm coming already!"

I shoved my bag into the thicket, then went quickly down to the water's edge. The sand behind me was just warming from gray to tan as I slipped my sealskin over my head and shoulders and sank into the waves, to join my fellows in watching for the U-boats that threatened my other home.

·CHAPTER TWO·

EMMA

Late May 1917
Boston, Massachusetts

Dad and I watched a stream of laughing, jostling young men pour onto the platform of South Station from the New York train. A few of them were already in uniform. They were bound for basic training at Camp Devens, a couple of hours west of the city…and after that for France to join the fighting, I supposed.

"There must be hundreds of them," I said, raising my voice so that Dad could hear me above the clamor of voices and trains. The boys looked sturdy and so blithe, as if they would dance rather than march into battle. "Do you think they've all enlisted?"

"I expect so. Almost all my students have," Dad said. He himself was wearing a brand-new uniform with the insignia of a captain; tomorrow it would be his turn to get on a train. "I hope Helen was able to get a seat."

Or hadn't missed the train altogether. Or changed her mind about spending the summer on Cape Cod with me. For heaven's sake, *I* wasn't sure I wanted to spend the summer on Cape Cod. But Dad didn't have to know that.

"I hope we'll recognize her," I said. "It's been—what, six years since we saw her? Seven?"

A passing youth lugging a duffel bag caught my eye and winked. I felt my cheeks grow hot and looked away, then wished I hadn't—civilians were supposed to be *supportive* of our soldier boys, even if they weren't yet in uniform. I hoped I hadn't hurt his feelings.

Dad squinted after him in the afternoon sun slanting through the frosted glass ceiling over the platforms. "Maybe I should go with you after all. Two young women traveling without a chaperone—"

"Yes, and you'd miss your train to Washington and be declared AWOL and get clapped in irons, and then what good would you be?" I took his arm and squeezed it, to belie my scolding tone. "Helen and I will chaperone each other. And Gran's already arranged for a wagon to meet us in Mattaquason and bring us to the ferry. We won't have to lift a finger." I nodded toward my trunks stacked on the platform, marked with my and Dad's identical initials, ELV—Emmeline Laura and Ernest Lowell Verlaine.

Dad sighed and examined his watch then slipped it back into his pocket. "I can't help worrying even though you are a young lady now. I suppose I'd better get used to it if you're going to college in the fall."

I pretended I hadn't heard him—which wasn't hard in the din of the station—and resumed scanning the crowds. "Oh! Is that her?" I gasped.

Before Dad could respond, I darted into a mass of people. I'd spotted something all right, but it wasn't my cousin.

I wormed my way around more boys carrying everything from carpet bags to cardboard suitcases, trying not to lose sight of my goal—a Red Cross booth near the far door to the main waiting room, adorned with a big, eye-catching bouquet of red roses and festooned with posters. It was one of those posters that had caught my eye: "FIVE THOUSAND BY JUNE" it read, above an illustration of a calm-looking, beautiful nurse in cap and cape. "GRADUATE NURSES YOUR COUNTRY NEEDS YOU." I wasn't a graduate nurse, but surely they would take trainees. Five thousand was an awful lot of nurses, after all. Here was my chance — and the reason why I didn't really want to go to Cape Cod.

I'd had one goal since April, when we had entered the war: find some way to be a part of it. If I'd been a boy, I would have joined up immediately. Since I wasn't, the next best thing I could do to help us beat the Kaiser was to become a nurse and take care of the boys who were fighting.

I hadn't said anything about it to Dad, because I knew he wouldn't agree to let me go. I'd more or less spent my entire life with him in the Geology Department at his university, playing with his rock specimens when small and doing lessons with my governesses in an empty office after that. It had been a cozy, secure way to grow up. But now that I was older, I felt like one of those specimens, wrapped in cotton wool and tucked into a box for safekeeping.

Tomorrow he was leaving for Washington to do some kind of secret war work — something to do with cartography, I'd guessed — and, irony of ironies, all I wanted to do was go with him so that I could find my own war work to do. Instead, I'd probably be more securely wrapped in layers of cotton wool than ever on Cape Cod with my grandmother and, in the fall, at a select women's college.

But if I was old enough to be sent off to college, I didn't see why I shouldn't be old enough to go to nursing school instead. I'd sent away for a catalogue for a nursing correspondence course I'd seen advertised in the back of a magazine and had it packed away in my trunk. As soon as I got to Gran's I would enroll — I'd held off because I'd hoped my cousin Helen might want to take it with me, so we could study together. I figured that if I did well on this course over the summer, the Red Cross would have to take me. But maybe a more direct approach would work, here and now.

I was thrilled to see that one of the women in the booth wore a nurse's cap and pinafore in addition to her Red Cross armbands. I paused to straighten the jacket of my new gray-blue linen suit, pretended I had a steel yardstick in my spine as my second governess, Miss Hayter, had taught me—she was very strict about posture—and approached the booth with a firm step.

"Good afternoon!" I said brightly to the two women there. In addition to the nurse there was an older woman in an asymmetrically swooping hat like a swan's wing, just like the ones in this month's *McCall's Magazine*. "I'm so glad to see you here—how is the membership drive doing?"

The woman in the fashionable hat smiled at me. "Very well, my dear. Would you like to become a member?"

I opened my purse and fished around in it. "Oh, I've already joined, thank you, but I'm happy to contribute again." I slid a couple of quarters into the collection box, and hoped the coins' satisfying jingle would soften them up for the rest of what I was about to say. "Actually, I was hoping you could help me."

"Oh?" she asked. The one in the nurse's cap said nothing, but narrowed her eyes as she looked at me.

"Yes. I..." I swallowed and tried not to show that her silence had rattled me. "I will be taking a nursing correspondence course this summer and hoped that come fall, instead of going to college, I could look forward to being engaged by the Red Cross for overseas duty. I understand this particular course has been very highly recommended—"

"Which one?" the nurse interrupted me. "The National School for Nurses, out of St. Louis?"

"Yes, that's the one!" If she'd heard of them, they must be good. "They even set up your hospital experience for—"

"How old are you?" she interrupted again.

I glanced at the lady in the swooping hat, who was gazing at me with limpid blue eyes, and sighed to myself. "I'll be eighteen in March. The National School—"

The nurse snorted. "They're rubbish. They keep getting shut down and reopening under new names. That's their latest—a few months back they were the American Academy of Nursing Science, and before that the Professional Nurses' School of the

United States. And even if they weren't a sham outfit, you're far too young. The Red Cross is only taking graduate nurses over the age of twenty-five. We can't be sending children over there."

Twenty-five? Why, the war would be long over before I was *that* old. "But—but the army is taking eighteen-year-olds for soldiers if their parents agree—"

"That's different," she said quickly.

"How is it different? Why are eighteen-year-old girls less acceptable than eighteen-year-old boys, if they both want to serve their country?" My temper was starting to rise; I hoped my voice hadn't shown it.

"Boys are much more mature at that age than girls. As is being made plain by this conversation." She looked down her nose at me—not very successfully, as I was taller than she. "If—and I repeat, *if* you are still interested in nursing when you are twenty-five, the Red Cross will be prepared to consider you." She turned away, ostensibly to adjust a poster affixed to one of the booth's supports, but I still caught her muttered, "Stupid romantic girls, wasting our time…"

I couldn't help it—the tears started to my eyes. I lifted my chin, and turning on my heel, dove back into the crowd milling beyond the booth. Fine—maybe the Red Cross wasn't willing to take young, inexperienced nurses. But did she have to be so—so condescending about it?

"Miss—my dear child, wait—" A hand touched my elbow, and I turned. The other woman from the booth was there beside me. "I'm so sorry about Miss Richards," she said hurriedly. "I think headquarters thought having a real nurse at an enrollment booth would attract people, but honestly, I think she's scared more people away than brought them in. She wanted to go overseas, she told me, but they wouldn't take her—some health thing, she said—and I think she's bitter about it."

I knew she was trying to make me feel better, but the scorn in the nurse's face and voice had burned too deep. "Thank you—it's nothing—"

"No, it's not! She could have said the same thing much

more kindly." She put her hand on my arm again and fixed me with a sincere, sympathetic look. "You may not be able to go overseas, but there are still things you can do for our boys over there—important things! The local chapters all need our help and support. Do you knit? The Red Cross has promised to send a million and a half pairs of socks to our overseas troops. You'll be doing a real service if you could complete even *one* pair of socks."

My last governess, Miss Nutting, and I had joined the Red Cross the day after war was declared. I'd been knitting socks every spare moment I had and rolling bandages at our weekly local meetings. But I couldn't wound this woman the way her colleague had me. "Socks—yes, ma'am, I can do that."

"Thank you, dear. I know we can count on you." She patted my arm, gave me a sunny smile, and went back to the booth.

"There you are!" Dad had caught up with me.

"I'm sorry I ran off—it wasn't her after all." I hoped my hat brim shaded my eyes sufficiently to conceal any tell-tale brightness.

"I didn't think it was. I believe she's over there." He pointed.

I stood on tiptoe to follow his finger. A petite, dark-haired young woman was stepping out of the train, followed by a stout, middle-aged man who struggled with a pair of large valises, a basket, two umbrellas, and a newspaper. I forgot my upset and dashed toward my cousin, dodging and weaving between groups of soldiers.

"Oh, thank you, sir," she was saying in a clear, carrying voice to the stout man. "I don't know how I should have managed without your help." She took the basket and one each of the valises and umbrellas from him. He opened his mouth as if to reply, but at that moment Helen spotted me. "And there's my cousin and her father come to meet me!" she cried, managing to wave gracefully despite her burdens. "Emma! Cousin Emma!"

The stout man looked nervously around him at that, and by

the time I reached her, he had melted into the crowd shuffling toward the main waiting room.

"Helen!" I wanted to hug her but suddenly felt shy, so instead I took her valise and shook her hand warmly. "How was your trip? Who was that man you were talking to?"

She grimaced. "I'll tell you later. I'm fine—now let me look at you! How tall you are! I can't stop thinking of you as little Emma with the straw-colored braids and torn stockings."

"Oh, pooh." I could feel myself blushing. "You're making yourself sound ancient." I remembered her eyes, big and brown and ringed by long, thick eyelashes. But her once-chubby face was now fashionably rounded, framed by waving, almost black hair. Her skin was smooth and creamy and her lips a lovely rose. She looked like an advertisement for Ivory soap in one of the fancier color magazines.

"Believe me, I feel years older. Hello, Professor Verlaine." Helen smiled shyly as Dad joined us. "Thank you so much for taking the trouble to meet me, sir. I'm very grateful." She tucked her arm in mine. "Won't we have fun? You and I always got along when we were kids, didn't we?"

"We sure did," I said. Helen and I *had* been great chums the times all the families were together. I'd always longed for an older sister, growing up, and would have liked one just like her: she was so pretty and always seemed so smart and sure of herself. Maybe this summer I'd finally have that sister.

Dad took Helen's ticket and went to see that her luggage got transferred to the Cape train. I took advantage of our being alone to ask her, "Who *was* that man who got off the train with you? A friend of your father's? It was nice of him to look out for you—"

"Oh, Emma." She shook her head. "I'd never seen him before in my life. He saw me traveling alone and tried to…you know. He wanted me to come to his hotel with him when we got to Boston."

"Oh!" I hoped my shock didn't show on my face, but it probably did. Dad always said I should avoid playing cards because I'm terrible at hiding how I feel. It was something I'd planned to work on this summer for when I went to nursing school. Nurses were never supposed to show disgust or fear when working with patients, so I needed to start practicing now. Of course, if Nurse Richards had her way, I'd never get any-where near a wounded soldier—

"It's all right." Helen smiled mischievously. "I pretended not to have any idea what he meant and told him that as soon as I saw how much he looked like my papa, I *knew* he had to be terribly good and kind. It stops them every time."

How horrid! The man had *looked* perfectly respectable. "So…um…you've had this happen before?"

"Yes." She shrugged. "At least he kept any of the boys from bothering me. They can be harder to deal with than the old ones. Poor Emma, I *have* shocked you, haven't I?" She patted my hand. "Let's talk about something else. What fun we'll have this summer! Picnics and boating and sea-bathing! I've never been sea-bathing—have you?"

"No. I haven't been to the Cape since I was born." Not that Gran didn't invite us every summer. But Dad never wanted to go. Perhaps it would have reminded him too much of my mother. And he and Gran…they were always cordial toward each other, but there was something bubbling underneath the polite surface that I'd never been able to figure out.

"Since—you mean you've never visited your grand-mother?"

I shook my head. "She comes to Boston to stay with one of my uncles and see us a few times a year. But I can swim. I learned in New Hampshire on the lakes."

Further conversation was halted by the conductor's shouting, "All aboard!" We hurried over to our train and boarded it, Dad fussing over whether we had our baggage tickets. And then when everything had been taken care of, he stood in the aisle by our seats and held my hands in his. Even his neatly-clipped beard looked sad.

"My dear child," he began, and then fell silent. I wasn't sure if he didn't know what to say or had too much to say and couldn't decide where to begin. Probably the second, because I felt the same way. I squeezed his hands and swallowed the lump in my throat.

"If there had been any other way…" he continued. "I tried so hard to make them let me bring you to Washington with me."

He'd tried to bring me? The lump in my throat got bigger. "It's all right, Daddy. Gran will take good care of me."

His face sort of crumpled. "I wish to God I didn't have to send you down there! Maybe your Uncle Robert—there's still time—"

"Dad!" Stay with Uncle Robert, whom even Gran, his own mother, called the most boring man in Boston? "We can't change everything now. If I can't go with you, I'm going to Gran. With Helen."

He fell silent, staring at me pleadingly, and I relented. I didn't care that we were in the middle of a crowded passenger car—I gave him a fierce hug. The realization that I wouldn't see him for *months* hit me like an express train.

"She'll be fine," Helen said kindly, when we finally let go of each other. "I promise I'll take good care of her too, sir. Why, Aunt Dorinda wrote that she's even gotten a telephone. We can call you immediately if we need to."

He didn't appear reassured; his mild blue eyes were clouded with something that I couldn't at first identify. "Yes, yes. But Emma, please—"

I glanced behind me. The conductor was coming through the cars, politely evicting all non-passengers. "What, Daddy?"

"Please…be careful. If anything happens, I'll come right away, Army or not."

I finally figured out what I was seeing: *fear*. "Dad—?"

Then the conductor was there, and my father was giving me one last kiss and making his way out to the platform. I waved as long as I could see him, until the train slid out of the bright station and headed south out of town. Oh, Daddy…but no, I wouldn't cry. How could I, when all those boys in the station

had been so cheerful even though they were heading someplace
much less pleasant than a visit to their grandmothers?

I sat back in my seat and pictured my father going back to
our house before he caught his own train tomorrow. It was
closed and dust-sheeted, the icebox emptied and Mrs. Keegan,
our cook-housekeeper, gone to do war work. When would I see
it again? And then I had to laugh because I would certainly see
it that fall, if only to pack up my winter things before going to
coll—to wherever I'd end up.

"Funny that your father never remarried." Helen's voice
interrupted my thoughts. There was an odd, speculative note in
her voice that I didn't understand.

"Is it?"

"Well, most men would, with a small daughter to care for."

"I guess we were too comfortable together to want to
change things. In the summers I used to go with him and his
graduate students on his rock-collecting trips in New
Hampshire." Now that I thought of it, I was glad that he
wouldn't be trying to clamber around the mountains this
summer; his health hadn't been the best over the winter. A nice
quiet desk job wouldn't leave him gray-faced and short of
breath and groping for the little nitroglycerin pills that the
doctor had given him.

"What a pity we're at war now—you could have had a
marvelous time with them." Helen winked.

"I suppose," I said dubiously. Honestly, they'd been more
like overgrown schoolboys than serious scholars. But speaking
of college students—"Helen, maybe you can help me. My father
is determined that I should go to college in the fall if the war is
still on—probably Bryn Mawr since it's closer to Washington
where he'll be. And I don't want to go."

"Why not? Are you afraid college would be too hard for
you?"

"No! Dad made me sit for the entrance exams already, and I
did fine. But it...well, it seems like such a waste of time. This
war is probably the biggest thing that will ever happen in our

lives, and I want to be part of it." I tried to put the scornful look on the Red Cross nurse's face out of my mind. "I'd thought about applying to nursing school."

Helen took out a small brass compact and examined herself in its mirror. "That's very patriotic, but if you became a nurse, you might be taking a job from some other girl who needs the money. Going to college—what an opportunity! Besides," she continued, "the last I heard, you had to be at least twenty-one to go to nursing school."

"Twenty-one! But surely they need a *lot* of nurses now that we're at war—maybe they'll make exceptions..." I saw her skeptical expression and sighed. All right, maybe they wouldn't. My dreams of being a nurse were getting more remote by the minute, but I wasn't going to give up yet. "Would you go to college if you were me?"

Helen dabbed at her nose with the compact's puff, then snapped it shut. "Like a shot. But I have five younger brothers and sisters, and they all need shoes and coats and things. So no college for me, and no nursing school either. In fact, when I go home I'll be starting out as a career girl."

"Really?" Now *that* was brave; very few females worked, though Dad had said he wouldn't be surprised if that changed what with the war taking young men away.

"Mm-hm. There's a job waiting for me as a secretary at the office of a friend of my father's. The girl that's there leaves in September to get married, and I'll be taking her place. It'll relieve the money situation at home a bit, and maybe make it possible for one of my brothers to think about college. Isn't that great?" She smiled sweetly at me.

Poor Helen! I knew that her family wasn't wealthy. Helen's grandfather—he'd been Gran's youngest brother—had run away to New York as a boy but hadn't prospered there. I cast a surreptitious glance at my pretty cousin. Only now, on closer examination, did I see the scuffed-though-carefully-polished shoes, the not-quite-this-season hat, the inexpensive frock. Helen was setting aside her dreams and taking a job to help her family make ends meet. It was perfectly splendid of her.

The train, which had been clacking along at its usual rhythm, suddenly slowed, then squealed to a stop. A murmur of consternation arose from the other passengers.

"What is it?" Helen asked. "Is everything all right?"

"I don't know." I leaned over to peer out our window.

"There's an express coming up from Fall River," a conductor passing through our car told us twenty minutes later. "We can go as soon as they're through. Trains on war business get right of way."

The twenty minutes had lengthened to more than an hour before we were on our way again, but we finally chuffed into the station in Mattaquason. It was a small, gaily-painted building heavily adorned with gingerbread trim and looked like it had come straight from a storybook illustration. While Helen took care of our baggage, I went in search of our ride to the Monomoyick ferry. I found a weathered old wagon waiting out front, harnessed to a somnolent-looking horse. On the wagon's seat was an equally weathered old man with fearsomely bushy whiskers, sound asleep.

"Sir?" I said, hesitantly.

"Won't wake him if you whisper like that," said a man in a peaked cap—the stationmaster, maybe?—who emerged from the station just then. He paused and looked at me. "You Dorinda Wetherell's granddaughter?"

"Yes, I am."

"Heard you were coming. Remember your mother. You look like her."

Oh. I knew I did—Dad had said so—though my eyes were brown while hers had been blue. But I hadn't expected *this*—that there would be people who'd known her. It gave me an odd feeling of belonging in this place I'd never seen. "Really? I wish I—"

But the man had already turned away. "HEY ABE," he shouted, and slapped the side of the wagon with the flat of his hand. "YOUR FARES ARE HERE."

Mumbling, the old man slowly sat up and glowered at me. Fortunately, Helen appeared just then with a porter who loaded our trunks into the back of the wagon. The stationmaster helped us up into the seat behind the driver and shouted, "THE FERRY, ABE."

"Thank you, sir," I said. Thank goodness he'd been here. I wasn't sure I'd have been able to wake our driver.

"Don't mention it." The stationmaster pulled his watch from his pocket and frowned at it, but just then the horse leaned into the traces with more energy than he'd seemed capable of, and we lurched and rumbled out of the station yard and onto the dusty road. After a few turns and a mile or so past scattered cedar-shingled houses washed gray by the ocean wind, it took us onto what must be the main street of Mattaquason. Three or four white clapboard churches with short steeples and two neat rows of shops lined its sides, but all were closed, with drawn shades in their windows.

"Is it always this quiet, do you think?" Helen murmured to me.

"I don't know." Compared to Boston, it looked like a ghost town. If there hadn't been a handful of people out on the street, strolling casually about, I would have been tempted to tell our driver (if I could shout loudly enough) to take us back to the station because there must have been some mistake.

I pulled Gran's last letter out for reassurance. Yes, the livery wagon had been waiting for us—now all we had to do was catch the ferry (the *Never Late*, a very encouraging name, I thought) for the short ride across the channel separating Monomoyick Island from the mainland.

At the end of Main Street was a sprinkling of small warehouses and disreputable-looking buildings. When we reached them we turned right again onto a rutted road that ran parallel to the shore, half-heartedly paved with some sort of white material like smooth, flat gravel. A collection of docks and shacks draped with drying nets crowded the water's edge, and a strong fishy scent pervaded the air. Boats—mostly fishing boats—rode serenely at their moorings. A group of sleeker (and cleaner) pleasure boats, both sail and motor, clustered together at one end of the harbor, like a group of gossiping society matrons. It was as quiet as Main Street had been.

A short dock with a slightly better-maintained shed stood at the end of the road. Mounted on the shed's roof was a cheerfully painted sign reading NEVER LATE. I breathed a sigh of relief...but something didn't seem right. The dock was deserted, and the shed's ticket window was tightly shuttered. When I climbed down and knocked on it, no one answered.

"I don't understand," I said, turning back to Helen.

Abe, who'd remained silent throughout the drive, let out a sudden harrumph. "Last boat's at five now with the war, ain't it? No lights showin' at dusk. Ferry'll start half-past eight to-morrow, fer the churchgoers down island to git to town. Both of 'em," he added with a sardonic chuckle.

"But we were supposed to catch the five o'clock boat. Gran said—" I began.

"Oh!" Helen sat up straighter. "The train was delayed—remember?"

I thought of the stationmaster looking at his watch as we'd left the station. No wonder the town had been deserted; everyone was probably at home having supper. "Why didn't you say anything?" I demanded of Abe. "You knew we were catching the ferry."

He shrugged. "Didn't ask me, did ye?"

I restrained the impulse to call him some very bad names I'd learned from Dad's students a few summers ago and walked to the end of the dock to stare across the stretch of water, barely a mile, to the island. Gran was probably there, wondering what had happened to us. Funny how the war could affect our lives, though it was happening thousands of miles away.

I heard Helen climb down from the wagon. "We could call Aunt Dorinda from the post office, couldn't we?" she asked hopefully, coming to stand with me.

"Except that the post office will be closed, too. I guess we could go back to the station and use their telephone." I shaded my eyes and squinted at the water. A small boat appeared to be coming toward us from the island, rowed by a solitary figure.

"Do you think he'll take us back there?" Helen nodded toward Abe. "There might be a hotel in town we can stay at—"

"May I be of assistance, ladies?" called a voice behind us.

I turned. A young man was walking up from a smaller dock where a shiny mahogany runabout was tied, a few dozen yards from where we stood. He was nattily dressed in a dark blue blazer and white duck trousers.

"Umm...." I said, remembering the man who'd tried to pick Helen up on the train. He wasn't trying to do something similar, was he? Abe would be no help if he were. Should I scream or hit him with my purse?

But Helen had no such fears. "Oh, I hope you can!" she said, taking my arm. Her other hand she let flutter before her in a pretty gesture of helplessness. "Our train was delayed and we've missed the last ferry. We're on our way to stay with Mrs. Wetherell—she's my great-aunt...that is, she's my cousin's grandmother," she added, giving my arm a little shake.

The young man took off a dazzlingly white yachting cap as he halted before us, revealing a head of sleek blonde hair parted in the middle. He had wide-set green eyes, a handsome, straight nose, and a firm chin. Only his mouth seemed somehow wrong. One of my governesses, Miss Ayers, had been obsessed with reading character from facial features. We spent hours in the Museum of Fine Arts looking at portraits of historical figures and speculating what personal traits the sitters must have had. It was nonsense, of course, but I still found myself doing it sometimes.

"Wetherell?" he said, smiling at me. All right, I'd probably imagined the pout; he had a nice enough smile. "Are you any relation to the Boston Wetherells?"

"They're my mother's family," I said. "Do you know them? My grandmother lives here now—she left the Boston house to my Uncle Robert when Grandfather died."

The young man raised an eyebrow. "Uncle Robert being the president of Wetherell Capital? My father banks with them. You've missed the ferry, you say?"

I nodded. "I don't know what we're going to do—maybe you know of someone with a telephone we might use?"

"I can do better than that. I can take you over on my boat." He smiled at me.

Helen dropped my arm and clapped her hands. "Your boat? How wonderf—" She stopped and looked abashed. "But we couldn't ask you to go out of your way like that."

"Not at all. I'd be happy to be of service to a Wetherell." He gave the name a sort of verbal caress. "I hope you're here for a good long visit?"

"All summer," Helen said quickly. "Do you live on the island too, Mr.—?"

"No. My family's house is on the bluff, up from the lighthouse." A note of pride had entered his voice. "And I haven't introduced myself, have I? I'm George Osborn." He looked at me expectantly, as if I should know who he was.

I opened my mouth, hoping something sensible would emerge from it, but Helen was already replying. "How do you do, sir? I'm Helen Sutton, and this is Emma Verlaine. We'd be happy to accept your offer if it isn't too much trouble. Wouldn't we, Emma?"

I hesitated. If Helen didn't have any concerns about the idea, then it was probably all right. But still—"If—if you're sure..."

"It'll be a pleasure, Miss Verlaine. Just give me a moment and I'll have the *Fast Lady* here directly." He smiled at me, then turned and walked quickly back toward his boat.

Helen waited until he was out of earshot then poked me triumphantly. "Ooh, this is much better than the ferry! Isn't he handsome? I think he likes you, Emma."

"Oh, pooh." I laughed nervously, then said, "Do you think so? How can you tell?"

Helen smiled. "Oh, I can tell."

This was probably another one of the things I'd missed out on by not going to school. But I wasn't sure I wanted this Mr. Osborn to "like" me, even if he was being nice enough to bring us over to the island. For one thing, why hadn't an able-bodied young man like him volunteered for the army, like the ones we'd seen in South Station—oh! "Helen! Our trunks!"

Helen glanced over her shoulder at the wagon. Abe and the horse seemed to have dozed off again. "Don't worry. Just say something about our bags and blush as prettily as you did a minute ago, and he'll have them unloaded and on his boat in no time. I can never blush when I need to; it's such a useful skill."

I blushed again, to my chagrin. "I didn't do it on purpose!"

She poked me again. "I was only teasing. I'm sure he'll be glad to take care of them for us."

She was right. When Mr. Osborn came putt-putting up to the *Never Late*'s dock and tied up his boat, I hesitantly mentioned our luggage. He looked at the wagon and may have winced—I couldn't tell from where I stood—but squared his shoulders and went up to Abe. "I say, good man—lend me a hand with the ladies' trunks, will you?"

Abe opened one eye. "Cain't," he wheezed. "My rheumaticks are kickin' up something fierce. And b'sides, that ain't my job. I jist drive."

I looked from our things piled on the wagon to Mr. Osborn's boat. "I don't think we're going to be able to fit everything in anyway—"

"Hello! Are you here to visit Mrs. Wetherell?" someone called. I felt something bump into the dock and turned.

A dory—the one I thought I'd seen crossing the channel?—had drawn up alongside us. A young man was seated at its oars, holding onto the edge of the dock and looking up at me with a quizzical half-smile. His brown hair was tousled and he wore a shapeless cotton jersey, sleeves rolled partway up his tanned forearms.

"Yes," I said. His eyes were light brown, almost amber-colored and startling in his tanned face. There was nothing off about his mouth, I couldn't help noticing; Miss Ayers would definitely have approved. "Did she send you? Our train was late so we missed the ferry."

He nodded. "She guessed something like that had happened and asked me to come see if you'd arrived. I can bring you right over."

"That won't be necessary," George Osborn said, coming to stand by me. "I'll bring the young ladies across. You can see to their baggage, boy." He dug into his pocket, pulled out a dime, and flipped it toward the boat.

"But—" I looked at the young man in the dory. After all, Gran had sent *him* for us.

The young man didn't move, but watched the coin bounce off one of his oars and fall into the water. Then he smiled, a soft, curious smile.

That smile caught me, just as his eyes had. The corners of his mouth quirked with humor and a certain wickedness that made me wish I could hear what he was thinking, though after Mr. Osborn's condescending behavior, it wasn't hard to guess.

"It's all right," he said to me. "I'm happy to oblige your grandmother in whatever way's needed. You go."

It took me a minute to realize Mr. Osborn was trying to catch my attention. I tore my gaze away from the young man and let him help me into his boat. He settled Helen on the bench seat next to me, cast off the lines holding us to the dock, put the engine in gear, and turned us toward Monomoyick.

I looked back and was surprised to see that Abe had evidently forgotten his rheumatism and was helping the young man load our trunks into the boat. Gran's friend was evidently very persuasive. When they were done, he took up his oars once more and pulled them with long, easy strokes that propelled him swiftly across the channel behind us. Considering how much lower the dory rode in the waves with our belongings on it, he must be extraordinarily strong. If only I'd thought to ask him his name—

Something round and sleek and brown poked up suddenly

from the surface of the water, not far from the boat. I blinked at it for a few seconds before realizing what it was. "Helen, look!" I pointed. "I think it's a seal!"

Mr. Osborn glanced casually at it. "Oh, yes. There are a lot of them around here. Smelly things. The fishermen think they steal their fish."

I frowned. That hardly seemed fair—after all, the seals had been here first. Wouldn't the fish more properly be theirs?

Helen made a face. "It gives me a turn, seeing animals wandering around free like that. But then, I'm a city girl."

I think Mr. Osborn said something in reply, but I was too interested in watching the seal to pay attention. It seemed to be looking at me...and there was another, its whiskered nose pointed inquisitively toward our boat.

"Hello," I said softly, though there was no way they could hear me. Their dark, shining eyes seemed to gaze directly into mine. I had a sudden urge to jump in and swim over to them.

Gran was waiting on the *Never Late*'s island dock as Mr. Osborn cut the engine and eased alongside it. "There you are, girls!" she said, tossing a line to Mr. Osborn. "Was your train late? I thought I saw Abe's wagon over there and sent Malcolm to look for you. Did you see him? Helen, my dear, it's lovely to see you again."

So the young man in the dory was named Malcolm, was he? I was up on the dock before Mr. Osborn had quite finished tying his boat to it. "Yes, we saw him, Gran. He's bringing our trunks across. I'm so glad we're here!" I took Gran's outstretched hands and kissed her cheek.

Gran was as handsome as ever, though it seemed funny to see her in a light spring frock and cardigan rather than the tweed suits she always wore when visiting us at Christmas. "Well, all's well that ends well," she said briskly. "Thank you, young man—?"

"Gran, this is Mr. Osborn, who was kind enough to bring us over," I explained as he helped Helen onto the dock. She'd waited nicely for him to do so, as I probably should have.

He removed his hat. "It was my pleasure, Mrs. Wetherell. I'll say, though, that it's nonsensical of them to stop the ferry at five when it's May and no one needs running lights on till after seven. We wouldn't be aiding and abetting the Germans, if there are even any out there. But I can't complain about the rule, at least not right now." He smiled at me. "And please, Miss Verlaine, call me George. 'Mr.' is too formal for Cape Cod."

Gran cleared her throat. "Nonsensical or not, Captain Abbott has asked us to comply with it for the duration."

"Who's Captain Abbott?" I asked.

"He's the commander of the naval air station here on the island—didn't I write you about it? It opened just before we declared war. They have seaplanes and dirigibles to help guard the approaches to Boston Harbor and Nantucket Sound against U-boats."

An air station! Now that I thought about it Gran *had* mentioned it, but it hadn't really sunk in. Since my nursing school correspondence course didn't seem to be all it was cracked up to be—though I wasn't sure that horrid Miss Richards hadn't made it all up just to spite me—maybe I could get work at this air station. Dad's secretary in the Geology Department had showed me how to use a typewriter, and Dad bought me a book on teaching yourself shorthand because he thought it might be useful for me to learn for note-taking in college. He couldn't be upset at me doing war work if I were living with Gran, could he? This just might turn out to be a better summer than I'd expected.

Gran was still speaking. "It isn't easy to keep over three hundred young men in order on a remote place like this. I think the captain's curfew has something to do with that." She looked at George Osborn. "You're not an islander, young man."

It was phrased as a statement, but he took it as a question. "No, ma'am, but I hope to spend more time here, especially if the Ocean Hotel is still holding its dances."

Dances? I looked at Helen. She raised an eyebrow at me and said, "I hope you do. Emma and I will be put out if you don't come and make sure we aren't wallflowers."

"You aren't likely to be," Gran said drily. "Mr. Galbraith at the hotel is doing his part to help keep the men from the station entertained, so you'll have more dance partners than there are dances."

They continued chatting, but I couldn't help turning back to look out at the channel. The dory with our baggage was nearly across. "That was fast," I murmured to myself.

Gran heard me. "There's no one faster than Malcolm with a pair of oars in his hands," she said, smiling fondly. Evidently they were friends. "He's been a tremendous help, with the ferry being on reduced hours."

"Lucky for him. He can save up for a motor boat with the extra work he's putting in," George commented.

Gran laughed. "He doesn't charge us. Why should he? His father owns the hotel." She tilted her head to indicate a horse and wagon waiting near the end of the dock, which couldn't have been less like the one we'd been picked up in by the bewhiskered Abe. The wagon was painted glossy sea green, with "The Ocean Hotel" emblazoned on its sides in royal blue and gold. "And he loves rowing too much to use the hotel's motorboat. He rowed for Harvard, after all."

George's face reddened. I thought of the coin he'd tossed to Malcolm and Malcolm's smile as he watched it drop into the water and turned away in embarrassment. It was more pleasant to watch the boat skimming across the channel toward us.

"That looks like fun," I said, mostly to myself.

"Get Malcolm to teach you to row. He'd be happy to, I expect," Gran said.

Hmm. "Maybe I will," I said.

·Chapter Three·
Malcolm

After Abe and I finished loading the young ladies' cases and trunks in the dory, I pushed off. It felt good to be on the water, if only for a little while; I'd been stuck indoors all day at the front desk, training our new desk clerks. My shoulders opened as I settled into the rhythm of rowing, and my muscles stretched and yawned like they'd just woken up and were eager to get to work. Not the same as an eight on the Charles with the crew team, but a good feeling nonetheless. It would have felt even better to put on my skin for a swim, but I'd be out on patrol tomorrow morning bright and early. Besides, I liked Mrs. Wetherell and was happy to do her a favor.

I'd liked her granddaughter, too, and not just because she was stunningly pretty. I'd been caught by that little worried frown she'd given me before she got onto the boat with the fellow in white trousers; I'd wanted to make that worried look go away. And the white trousers...*white* trousers! Did he think that runabout of his was a yacht?

The growing strip of water that separated me from the mainland glowed silver in the early evening sun. I was partway across it when a dark head surfaced from the water. I nodded to it. "Hello, cousin. Is all well?"

The seal looked past me, toward the island. I glanced behind and saw the motorboat was just tying up at the

Monomoyick dock. "Yes, more boats and more people. It's that time of year. What about them?" Apart from the fact that one of them was such a beautiful girl. This summer might turn out to be better than I'd expected.

Another seal surfaced. It too looked over to the dock, then back at me. I was able to catch just a flavor of its thoughts: *like us.*

I looked over my shoulder again. "Of course they like you. You're very likeable."

The seals continued to gaze at me. Something was troubling them, either about the boat or its occupants. I wished I had my skin with me so I could get in the water and hear their thoughts more clearly. Maybe I'd do that after I got the Wetherells taken care of, if Mother didn't mind me missing supper. "It's all right. You don't have to worry."

The pair looked at me again, and it finally hit me that they weren't worried. Deeply interested, yes. And excited. I'd have to look into this—along with the seven hundred other things on my "to do" list.

Another dozen strokes brought me close to the dock. I gave one last pull, then let the boat's momentum take me alongside it, right to where Mrs. Wetherell waited. "Thank you, Malcolm," she called.

I grinned up at her as I shipped my oars. "Aw, I just did it because I had to, Mrs. Wetherell. You know how much I hate being out in boats."

Mrs. Wetherell snorted, then grinned back at me. "Smart alec. Come and meet my granddaughter and grandniece."

"One moment, ma'am." I secured the dory at both bow and stern before climbing up on the dock. "We've partly met," I said, looking at the blonde girl.

"But not entirely. Emma, this is Malcolm Galbraith who so kindly came to your rescue." I saw White Trousers scowl. "Malcolm, my granddaughter, Emma Verlaine."

Emma. I'd always liked that name. "I hope you'll enjoy your visit here, Miss Verlaine," I said.

"I'm sure I will," she said, and then grinned as impishly as her grandmother had. "However did you get that Abe to help you load our things?"

I laughed. Abe liked to put on his yokel act for the "dam turrists," as he called them, but all I'd had to do was mention my mother, and he'd been out of the wagon in a heartbeat. He'd worshipped her ever since she nursed him through a bout of pneumonia some winters back.

"You just need to know how to ask him nicely," I said. Behind Emma, White Trouser's scowl deepened.

"And this is my great-niece, Helen Sutton," Mrs. Wetherell was saying.

"How do you do, Mr. Galbraith?" the other girl said, giving me a wide smile. I supposed she was pretty enough, but there was something about Emma that just made me want to keep looking at her.

But looking at Emma wasn't going to get her luggage in the wagon. I turned back to the dory and unloaded it as quickly as I could, then hefted one of the trunks to my shoulder. We got everything loaded—even White Trousers pitched in, though he didn't look happy about it—and I dragged my dory back to its place on the beach and went to Mrs. Wetherell, standing by the wagon. "All set, ma'am. May I help you up?"

"I suppose I'd best be going before it gets any darker," White Trousers said. "Don't want to break your Captain Abbott's precious rules." He smiled at the girls. "I hope it will be all right if I pay a call in a day or two?"

"We would be delighted to see you," the cousin purred, but I saw that White Trousers was looking at Emma as he spoke, which kind of set my back up for some reason. And what was his problem with Captain Abbott?

"Um, yes—do." Emma didn't sound very enthusiastic about the prospect.

As White Trousers turned to go, a sudden impulse grabbed me. "Say, boy?" I called after him, reaching into my pocket.

He stopped in his tracks, then turned, glaring at me. I found a quarter and flipped it toward him. He caught it.

"Thanks for bringing the young ladies across. It saved me a second trip." I nodded to him, then turned back to the wagon, hiding a grin. I heard him stomp away down the dock to his boat.

"What was that all about?" Mrs. W. asked, eyebrows raised.

I shrugged. "Just returning a favor, though I probably should have restrained myself." After all, he probably couldn't help the fact that he was an idiot. Even though I'd given him fifteen cents more than he'd thrown at me.

I untied Sally and climbed into the wagon, and we ambled past the handful of shops and houses that was Monomoyick village. Some minutes later we passed the granite pillars and glossily painted signboard on the left that marked the drive up to the hotel.

"Is that your family's hotel? It looks delightful," the cousin — what was her name? — said.

I glanced down the long road at the large building with its two deep wings, all covered in silvery cedar shingles and surrounded by extensive lawns and gardens, Mother's especial pride. White-painted shutters trimmed each row of windows across the face of the hotel, three rows on the main building and two on the wings. Beyond it the open Atlantic was a dark, cold-looking blue. "We think so," I said, trying to sound off-hand. "I expect we'll have a busy season again this year, since no one's going to Europe on holiday."

"That's true." Emma sighed.

"Are you all right, dear?" Mrs. Wetherell sounded concerned.

"I expect she's tired. We both are," the cousin said sympathetically. "Emma, your hands are like ice. You should be wearing your gloves."

I glanced behind me. The cousin was rubbing one of Emma's hands. She withdrew it, a little sheepishly. "I know, but I hate gloves. The seams always chafe between my fingers."

"I hate 'em too," I said. Emma looked at me and gave me a

small smile.

"Well, it was chilly enough on the water that I was glad to have mine," Helen—that was her name!—said. "Oh, Aunt Dorinda, you won't guess what we saw from Mr. Osborn's boat! Seals!"

My ears pricked up. "There are a lot of them around here."

"Mr. Osborn said that the fishermen don't like them because they steal the fish."

Before I could make a sharp retort, Emma said, "I thought they were sweet. They were looking right at me with such expression in their eyes—I was waiting for them to swim up and say hello and invite me in for a swim."

I wished I weren't driving, because I wanted to turn again to look more closely at Emma. Was *she* why the seals had been so excited?

We passed a handful of houses, big, solid saltboxes, classic Cape Cod cottages and a few Victorians separated by thickets of scrubby cedar and jack pine and bayberry and beach rose. Mrs. Wetherell's house was another half-mile through the cedar and bayberry thickets. I turned the wagon into the short U-shaped drive, leading up to a sturdily handsome Queen Anne Victorian sided with the same silver-gray cedar shingles as the hotel. A deep porch wrapped around its side to the back, and the scent of lilacs wafted from tall hedges to either side.

"Lilacs?" Emma said. "At the end of May?"

"Everything blooms later here," Mrs. Wetherell said. "It's the ocean. It freezes later in winter here, too, so I still get roses in December some years. Here they are, Josiah," she called. "They missed the ferry, but we all managed."

Josiah Barnes, who'd always reminded me of a beanpole topped with graying brown hair, was just coming around the side of the house. He'd worked for Mrs. Wetherell as long as I could remember. He came up to the wagon to help her down then froze, staring past her. "Miss Laura," he whispered, his face paling.

"I warned you, you great lummock," Mrs. Wetherell said,

but not unkindly. "Girls, this is Josiah Barnes. I'm afraid you're going hear a lot of the old-timers here telling you how much you look like your mother, Emma dear."

"Hello, Mr. Barnes," she said, politely. "Gran's often spoken of you."

Josiah's face took on a little more color as he continued to stare at her, then shook his head. "Pleased to meet you, Miss Emma. I—well, I was awful fond of your mother, once." He shook his head again and helped Mrs. Wetherell down.

We all unloaded the wagon; I offered to carry the trunks upstairs, but Josiah bristled at the suggestion that he might need any help.

"Thank you, Malcolm," Mrs. Wetherell said. "What would we do without you?"

"I expect you'd do just fine, but I'm always glad to help. Old Sally here is probably wanting her supper, so I'll say good night."

I climbed back onto the wagon seat and picked up the reins, but something made me pause and look back. The others had already gone inside, but Emma was still on the porch stairs, half-turned, to watch me. Her head was a little tilted to one side and her lips slightly parted as if she'd been about to call out to me. Our eyes met, and something just seemed to fall in place inside me, something I didn't realize I'd been waiting for.

"I—I wish we could have gone in your boat," she said. "It looks more fun."

"I'd be happy to take you out in it some time," I said immediately. And meant it. "As soon as you're settled in."

"I'd like that," she said.

It took an impatient snort from Sally to make me tear my gaze away from hers. "Good night," I said, and set Sally toward home.

·CHAPTER FOUR·
EMMA

I stood in the driveway, watching till Malcolm disappeared from sight, and tried to figure out why I felt like we already knew each other. I had to be imagining it, but *still*. He'd been at Harvard, just over the river from Dad's university; might we somehow have met before, somewhere in Boston?

No. I definitely would have remembered if we had.

"Coming, dear?" Gran was back out on the porch. "I'm sure you'd like to freshen up before supper."

"Yes, Gran." I climbed the stairs to join her, not letting myself turn again to see if Malcolm was still in view. "Gran, that Mr. Galbraith—"

"Malcolm. As your Mr. Osborn said, 'Mr.' is too formal for Cape Cod," Gran said teasingly.

"He's not *my* Mr. Osborn." I wrinkled my nose at her. "But Malcolm—he…" I floundered into silence.

"What about him? Malcolm is a charming young man. All his family is, though they can be reserved around strangers, like most native Cape Codders."

"Are they natives?"

"About as native as you can get, without being an Indian. His grandfather started the hotel, but they've lived on the island since—since forever, practically. Local legend has it that the first Galbraith on Monomoyick arrived while Queen Elizabeth was on the throne—a sailor washed off a Scottish fishing ship who managed to make it to shore and survive."

"My goodness." I linked my arm through hers and we went into the house. The front hall was large and airy, with white painted woodwork and Chinese wallpaper. The newly installed phone sat in solitary glory on a console table next to the stairs to the second floor. To either side I caught glimpses of a library and a sitting room, but Gran had let go of my arm and was already heading up the stairs.

"You can see the house later," she said over her shoulder. "Let's get you settled first, shall we?" At the top of the stairs, she paused and looked down at me. "I've put you in your mother's old room. Is that all right?"

A sudden lump rose in my throat. I nodded.

Gran led me to the end of the hall, to a room on the back side of the house. "You can see the water from here," she said, going in. "Laura liked that."

I hesitated on the threshold, feeling as if I were intruding on someone else's private space. "Is this how she had it?"

There were the usual bureaus and bedside tables and a wardrobe with a mirrored door. Two large windows with a cushioned window-seat looked out over the back lawn and an expanse of salt meadow leading down to a low dune and the ocean beyond. I went to gaze out at them. Night was finally starting to fall, and their colors were muted yet beautiful in the soft dusk.

"The furniture is hers." Gran touched the wardrobe gently. "The rugs and linens are new, and the curtains—everyone on the island has been asked to use black curtains, so no light is visible at night in case there are German U-boats out there. Make sure you have them drawn well before dark or one of our zealous blackout watchers will report you." She joined me and pulled the heavy black curtains closed, checking that no crack showed between them, then drew the blue-and-white toile curtains over them. I was sorry; the view had been entrancing.

"I was thinking just now," I said, not looking at her. "No

one's ever told me much about my—about Mom." It was hard to say the word; when had I ever needed to use it? "Dad never talks about her."

For a while when I was younger, I used to lie in bed before going to sleep and make up stories about her, stories of impossible adventure where we'd travel to India and ride elephants or rescue orphans from Ottoman slave-traders who turned out to be long-lost princesses (the orphans of course, not the slavers.) Despite the heroic bravery and cleverness I endowed her with, my mother remained a shadowy figure. I stopped doing it eventually.

Gran put her arm around my shoulders. "I've wondered about that," she said, sounding sad. "I don't like to criticize your father, and I would never have said this to you before, but you're almost an adult now. I think it's wrong that he's kept her from you because remembering would cause him pain. I'll try to help you get to know her while you're here." She gave a soft chuckle. "You should ask Josiah about her. He thought the sun rose and set on your mother. I think he was more than a little in love with her, though he would never admit it to me."

"Who's in love?" Helen was standing in the doorway. "Oh, how nice your room is, Emma! Come see mine—it's just as pretty. I can't thank you enough for inviting me, Aunt Dorinda."

Gran smiled and gave me a squeeze. "You're welcome, dear. I'd better tell you about the curtains, too."

Helen's room was across the hall and down a little from mine, all in buttercup yellow with touches of green. She'd already begun to unpack her valise but came to examine the black curtains. "My goodness. It makes the war seem so much more real, doesn't it? Even more than the ferry stopping early. I hope that nice George Osborn got back all right. Are private boats not allowed out at night too?"

Josiah came in, hoisting a trunk. He let it down with a thump. "He'll be all right, so long as he doesn't have any lights showing in that fancy runabout of his."

"Oh, do you know him?" Helen asked.

"Know his boat," Josiah said. "Flashy, but I wouldn't want to be out in it when there's any kind of sea running."

"Don't let Josiah fool you." Gran winked at us. "He knows all the gossip about everyone here. Men always do. Who are the Osborns, anyway? I don't think I've met them."

"New people with new money—pots of it, from all accounts. They're from up Lowell way." He made it sound like deepest Siberia. "The old man started out as a mill boy in a factory and now owns the place. Built one of them big houses up on the north bluff last year and thinks he's king of the hill."

"Good for him," Gran said. "Don't be such a snob, Josiah. There's nothing wrong with new money—it has to start somewhere. I ought to call on them to thank your Mr. Osborn."

Helen brightened. "Would you? Oh, thank you, Aunt Dorinda! When will you go?"

Under cover of their discussion, I slipped out after Josiah who was already halfway down the stairs. "Er—Mr. Barnes?" I called.

He stopped and looked up at me. A smile softened his craggy features. "It's just Josiah, Miss Emma."

"And it's just Emma, please. I feel like I already know you, Gran's talked about you so often. Thank you for being here for her."

He didn't actually blush, but his ears reddened a bit. "I've worked for her since I was a boy. I don't plan on stopping any time soon."

"I'm glad to hear that." I hesitated. "I was wondering...do—do you know the commander at the naval station? Captain Abbott?"

"Enough to pass the time of day with. He's a good 'un, from all I hear. Why?" His smile faded. "You aren't thinking about messing with none of those navy boys, are you?"

"No! Well, not exactly. I hoped you might be able to put in a word for me with him if I..." I trailed off as his face grew downright stern.

"You don't go setting foot anywhere near that station. It's

no place for a properly-brought-up girl to be even thinking about going."

"But I only want to—"

"Didn't your grandmother tell you to keep away from there?"

"No, she didn't." Honestly, Gran had barely had a chance to say *anything* yet.

"Well, I'm telling you now. You don't go near that station, do you hear?"

I took a deep breath. "Josiah, please. All I want to do—"

"What?" He scowled at me.

"All I want to do is ask for a job there, to do my bit for the war," I said in a small voice. "As a secretary, maybe. I can type and all."

I waited for him to explode, either in anger or laughter. He did neither. Instead, he rubbed his jaw and looked at me. "Just like your mother, ain't you?" he finally said, almost gently. "She'd have wanted to do that, too. Thing is, though, they won't hire you. They got their own secretaries—enlisted men who they can trust."

"I'm trustworthy!"

"But they don't know that." He shook his head. "I'd give up the notion."

I looked away from him so that he wouldn't see the disappointment in my face. "Are you *sure* they won't hire civilians?"

He sighed. "Well, not entirely. But I never heard of any non-navy folks working there. I'm sorry, chickie. But there's still things you can do for our boys—the churches are all doing Red Cross work for the duration, and I know they're always looking for help. Your grandmother's already doing that—"

"Thank you, Josiah." It was the Red Cross lady at the train station all over again. "I—I'll look into that."

"That's good." He nodded, then looked at me for a long moment. "Just like your mother," he said again, but to himself this time, then went down the rest of the stairs.

I watched him go, suddenly feeling better. After all, he'd said he wasn't *sure* that they weren't hiring civilians, hadn't he? Miss Richards-the-nasty-nurse had merely given me a temporary set-back; I'd find my war job yet.

·CHAPTER FIVE·
MALCOLM

4:00 a.m. patrol duty. Again.

You'd think that since I was the one drawing up the schedule, I'd have given myself a more civilized shift — say, from noon to four. But Father needed me at the hotel during daylight and also had pointed out that I shouldn't expect others to do what I wasn't willing to do myself. As much as I liked to grumble about it, I knew he was right. So here I was, a mile off Monomoyick and heading east toward open ocean, where U-boats might lurk.

There were a few benefits to taking the 4 a.m. shift. For one thing, it put a damper on my sister Isabel's attempts to pair me off with one or another of her friends so that we could "get to know each other better." She hadn't listened when I'd reminded her that patrolling wasn't a social activity. Fortunately, most of them weren't so eager to get to know me that they were willing to commit to being up this early every morning. But a few were, alas.

It was mostly my parents' fault. Recently Father had started to hint that it was time I found a nice girl and settled down to take on more management of the hotel, so he could spend more time and attention on his other job, which was being one of the elders of our people on Cape Cod. Of course, he meant me to settle down with a nice girl like us — a selkie girl. Hence Izzy's matchmaking efforts—but I knew it would never work. Ironically, that was Father's own fault.

My great-grandfather had been one of the first selkies in New England to choose to pose as human; his son, my grandfather, had opened the Ocean Hotel back in the 1870s. Running a fashionable resort hotel in our own backyard, so to speak, gave us the perfect cover to keep a finger on the pulse of the human world. Father wanted me to go to college to get to know it even better, to make connections with important people in case we ever needed their help. I was fine with all that—*but*.

I hadn't said anything to them about it, but sending me to college had— well, kind of ruined me. Now I had feet in two worlds, the one of my birth and the human one. What's more, I *wanted* both worlds. I had lots of human friends now and liked doing human things. So how could I ever be happy with a selkie girl who knew and cared nothing about the fascinating human world…and how would she ever be able to help us with the hotel, knowing little about humans? Father glowered when I pointed that fact out. Mother would sigh and agree with me; her own adjustment to posing as human when she married Father had been a hard one.

On the other hand, how could I marry a human? We selkies told no one what we were. But I could never court a human without letting her know that her prospective husband could put on a sealskin and turn into a seal whenever he wanted: that wasn't a secret you kept from someone you love. Besides, the rest of our people would not happily countenance a human who knew our secret—it was too dangerous. We'd certainly been known to dally with humans, but human-selkie marriages had never worked well.

It was, in short, a conundrum.

That was why I'd schemed to go out alone this morning. I usually sent patrollers out in twos, but Dugal hadn't shown up, and I was able to pair Isabel's latest protégée, giggly Màiri, with my friend Luthais. The look he'd given me as they swam off probably should have killed me—he loathed giggling girls—but the chance to be alone with my thoughts for a few hours had been too tempting. With summer at hand the hotel was starting to fill up, and Father expected me to be really *there* and attending to guests, not brooding about my problems.

Not that Emma Verlaine could be considered a problem. But I hadn't been able to get her out of my head all night—her mischievous smile, the light in her clear brown eyes when she'd looked at me back at the ferry dock, head just a little tilted as if she were asking me a question. But most of all I'd been caught by the sound of her voice when she talked about seeing the seals. I'd never met a human girl who'd reacted to them the way she had; most of the hotel guests who tried to flirt with me pretended to be terrified of them, which just made me roll my eyes. Emma, on the other hand, had *liked* them.

So yeah, I'd been more than a little taken by her, but that wasn't the only thing that had kept me awake, thinking about her. Was she what had excited the seals yesterday? If so, why? I would definitely invite her to go rowing in a day or two, both to see what the seals did and because I wanted to see her again, have a chance to get to know her even if she was a human who shouldn't interest me this much—

I suddenly realized that I'd been hearing a low, whirring hum, edged with a high-pitched whine, for the last couple of minutes. I swore and stopped swimming to listen, and the fur on the back of my neck bristled and my heartbeat quickened because there was only one thing that made a sound like that.

Another German U-boat was nosing around my home.

Damn it! I wished there were a rock nearby, so I could bang my head against it. How could I have let myself get so lost in my thoughts that I'd not paid attention to my job? I'd have torn into any of my patrollers who did the same thing.

I made a quick trip to the surface for a deep breath, then dove. I had to figure out where the invader was. Sound carries much farther underwater than it does on land: that was why we selkies were out here in the first place, listening for U-boats when the humans at the air station couldn't look for them from the air. I hung motionless about ten feet down, and listened.

I was maybe a mile and a quarter from the beach by now; the U-boat sounded like it was east and south of me, pretty far off—but that still put it uncomfortably in range of the air station itself. What was it doing? There wasn't enough light at this early hour for it to navigate easily, but there also wasn't much light for an aviator to scan the sea surface for invaders. Maybe that was it—it could be testing the waters, seeing how close to shore it could creep...

I needed to do something. Now.

I could go find the U-boat, though it wouldn't be easy—selkies were not like the whales who could use sound to "see" by. I could follow it and watch what it did, get its number and any other information about its condition and behavior that might help the Navy track it. Or I could get back to shore as quickly as possible, throw on my clothes, and run back to the hotel to telephone Captain Abbott, using our pre-arranged code to communicate the approximate location of the U-boat. He'd send out one of the air station's seaplanes to track it down and maybe drop a bomb or five on it.

Except it would take at least three-quarters of an hour to do all that, and by then the U-boat could have slipped away—or completed whatever nefarious business it was here to do. We didn't just worry about the Germans attacking the air station directly, though that was a major concern: a well-launched shell could blow the base's hydrogen storage tank—and the rest of the island as well—sky-high. No, we also worried about U-boats landing spies on one of the Cape's deserted beaches, just as they tried to do in England...and I understood the huge, stupid mistake I'd made. *This* was why I always sent my volunteers out in pairs: if we spotted a U-boat, one could follow the enemy while the other went to report it to the air station. I should have called in a replacement to go with me when Dugal didn't show, but I'd been so intent on a chance to be by myself that I'd broken my own rule. Damn, damn, *damn*.

I hesitated, then surfaced again and took a look around. The day had dawned gray and sunless, the sky heavy with low sullen clouds buffeted by an east wind that felt more like March than May. That decided me: visibility would be poor today, even from a scout plane—just the kind of weather that might embolden a U-boat to creep in close to shore. All I could do is hope that one of my other patrolling teams had heard this U-boat too and sent someone to the hotel so that Father could telephone the captain. In the meanwhile, I had to follow it. I took a deep breath, dove, and headed south toward the hum.

This was the fifth U-boat we'd heard since the beginning of the month. For three of those, we'd been able to get word to the air station in time for Captain Abbot to send up seaplanes to chase them, though no hits had occurred. But it showed our patrolling could make a difference. In time, I had hopes that selkie patrols would operate from here to the Maine coast, so that Boston shipping could be protected, at least near shore. Every U-boat we took out close to shore meant one less wolf in the wolf-pack out at sea.

I stopped swimming to listen and make sure I was still headed toward the U-boat. It seemed to moving north, traveling parallel to the coast. Scouting out landing spots farther up the Cape, now that the air station had made the southern end too risky? I could picture it slicing through the waves, conning tower just above the surface, from which steely-eyed men peered through binoculars at the beach. I altered my course a little and kept on swimming.

What if it turned west and went into shore to drop off spies? There wasn't much I could do, without human clothes to cover myself—or a weapon to halt them with. The thought made me grind my teeth in frustration: another reason to never be out alone again—

A different sound drew my attention. I slowed to listen, then darted up to the surface, where a seaplane roared directly over my head. Its bulbous pontoons hid the cockpit but I knew what I would see if I could: a spotter with binoculars, sweeping the surface of the waves. The knot of tension in my midsection loosened; one of my teams had reported to Captain Abbott. If this was like any of the previous experiences we'd had with cruising U-boats, the enemy would turn away from the coast into deeper water as soon as it spotted the plane. We wouldn't see any more of it today.

I sighed and watched the plane till it shrank into the distance, then looked around me at the gray, choppy waves. There wasn't much point in my staying out here. I'd already proved to myself how stupid I'd been to try to patrol alone. Of course, I could just declare myself off-duty and enjoy a few hours of solitude...

Or...or I could stop being such a selfish bastard, go back to the hotel to get cleaned up, and help Father. This time of year, we were usually busy training new employees, so he'd probably set me to working with one of the new desk clerks. How long would this year's crop be around before they decided to enlist and we had to find new ones? It used to be that we turned applicants away; they liked to train at summer resorts before trying for positions at hotels in Boston and New York. Now, all the young men were flocking to the war.

But even though we were at war, people still wanted to take their summer vacations, and since the war had broken out in Europe in 1914, they were taking them here in the states. Business had been booming these last three years and would probably continue to boom this year. I sighed again, took one last look at the morning, and dove back under the waves to make my way home.

When I got to shore, my sister Maggie was waiting.

"Did you get it?" she demanded, dancing around me as I trudged up the sand toward my bag in the thicket.

"Get what?"

"The U-boat!" She sighed impatiently. "Why can't I go out on patrols too? I bet I could chase all the U-boats right away from Monomoyick."

"How? By showing them your knees and scaring them off?" Maggie's knees were generally covered in bruises and scabs. She was an incorrigible tomboy.

"Malcolm!" She launched herself at me and started pummeling me. I dropped my sealskin and grabbed her wrists, swinging her off me, then round and round in a circle, until her shrieks changed to laughter. "Stop it! I'm dizzy!" she finally howled.

I slowed until her feet touched the ground, let her go, picked up my skin, and continued up the beach.

She staggered along beside me. "I think I'm going to throw up."

"No you aren't. You love it when I do that. Except you're almost getting too big for it."

"If I'm getting too big for that, then why can't I go on patrol?"

I opened my mouth to tell her why not—and then got a brilliant idea. Isabel couldn't foist her friends on me if I was training Maggie to patrol, could she?

"Maybe you *are* old enough. But Father and Mother will have to decide that," I added, because I didn't dare start taking her without their permission. "And it's not all fun and games. Most of the time we don't hear anything, and it's pretty dull."

My warning flew right past her. "Really? Promise?" She launched herself at me again, this time intent on a hug. I tried to dodge, but she managed to wrap her arms around my neck in a stranglehold and give me a sloppy kiss.

"Yes, if you don't choke me first. And I'll bet if they say yes, it can only be on weekends until school is out." I tickled under her arms, and she stopped trying to strangle me and collapsed again.

"That's okay," she said, beaming up at me from the sand. "It'll make school end quicker." Maggie hated school.

I pulled my clothes on quickly and folded my skin into my kit bag. We were three-quarters of the way back to the hotel when a sudden thought occurred to me. "How did you know I heard a U-boat today?"

She rolled her eyes. "You must have, because I heard a seaplane flying out this morning when they don't usually go, and then Captain Abbott telephoned. He wants to see you. So I figured something must have happened and guessed it was a U-boat."

I swore and broke into a run. "Blast it, Maggot, why didn't you tell me he'd called as soon as I got to shore?"

She kept up with me easily. The kid was fast. "Because he said not to come till this afternoon, and anyway, you got me all excited when you said I could go out patrolling with you."

"I said *maybe*," I grumbled, but slowed down.

"You'll tell Father I'm ready to learn, won't you?"

It was on the tip of my tongue to say no, but I remembered Isabel—and my own longing to be doing something for the war, even if this wasn't the form I'd thought it would take. "Yeah, all right. But next time, tell me immediately if Captain Abbott phones or anything like that, or I won't train you."

She appeared suitably chastened. "Aye-aye, sir."

·Chapter Six·
Emma

I was awakened Sunday morning by a knock on my door. "C'min," I yawned and turned to my bedside clock, picking it up to peer at its face in the dimness. Eight-fifteen! But why was it still so dark?

Helen came in. "Good morning, sleepy-head!" She crossed to the windows and drew back the curtains with a flourish. The sky was cloudy and gray, but the morning light should surely have woken me by now. Then I remembered the blackout curtains.

I sat up and regarded her doubtfully. "You're not one of those people who are excessively cheerful in the morning, are you?"

"Why, Cousin Emma! Aren't you?" Then she laughed. "Not at all. But I'm too excited this morning to lie abed. Didn't you sleep well?"

"I slept fine." I had, once I'd been able to calm my racing thoughts about air stations and being in my mother's room. Though I'd somehow, even in my sleep, been acutely aware of the ocean so close to us. It had moved restlessly through my dreams, surging and foaming and hissing. Funny—back at home in Boston I'd lived only a few miles from the Atlantic, but it had never haunted me the way it had last night.

"What are you so excited about?" I drew up my knees and

clasped my arms around them. "Was there something you wanted to do today?"

"Oh, I don't know. Explore. Pay a visit to the Ocean Hotel and see what all the fuss is about. You'd like that, wouldn't you?" She gave me a knowing smile. "I got the feeling that you and Mr. Rowed-for-Harvard found each other interesting."

How *did* Helen know these things?

As it turned out, Helen got her trip to Mattaquason. Gran wanted us to attend church in order to introduce us to her friends, so we all piled into Josiah's lovingly polished Pierce-Arrow so he could drive us there.

"Her trim's not anything to write home about. It ain't easy keeping her looking as she ought in the salt air," he grumbled as Helen and I exclaimed at the automobile's spotless appearance, but I was sure he was blushing under his eternal tan.

"Keeping her polished keeps you out of trouble, young man," Gran said. She made it sound like Josiah was still about seventeen.

The tires of Josiah's car crunched as we drove. I'd had a chance to examine the road surface and discovered that it was paved with pieces of broken shell. "Thank the Navy for our new road," Gran commented. "They need it to be in good repair. We can't complain about them as neighbors."

Josiah grumbled something about "navy boys," but she ignored him.

We drove directly onto the *Never Late,* which turned out to be a sort of motorized floating platform that could hold four cars, if they parked close. It was a curious feeling to sit in the car while feeling the sway and dip of the waves and watching the sun sparkle on the channel.

"No seals today," I commented to no one in particular. "I wonder why? There were several of them around yesterday."

Josiah harrumphed. "You keep away from them seals, Miss Emma!"

I stared at him in astonishment. If anything, he sounded even more vehement about my keeping away from seals than he had about navy boys.

"I believe they can be unpleasant if you get too close," Gran said into the silence that followed. "If they feel threatened, they might bite."

"I wasn't going to go anywhere near them. I just find them interesting. I'd never seen one before," I said, trying to sound as dignified as possible. Josiah tried to catch my eye again in the mirror, but I refused to look at him.

Gran's acquaintances all seemed to be lying in wait for us after the service. "Just what we need," said one sweet-faced lady with a steely glint in her eye, as we stood outside the church. "Some nice young hands for our Red Cross work."

"You'll have to bring them to the meeting this week, Dorinda," added another.

Gran smiled at them. "I'm sure you can count on them, Agnes."

"We wouldn't *dream* of missing it," Helen said. "Would we, Emma?"

I nearly gaped at her. She hadn't seemed very enthusiastic about war work on the train yesterday, but she certainly looked sincere about it now.

"Oh, er, no," I agreed. "I'd do anything for the war." It wasn't *too* much of a lie. If I could manage to get hired at the air station, I'd be helping the war effort plenty—only it wouldn't involve bandage rolling and sock knitting.

"So much like her mother, that Emma. Spitting image," I overheard one woman comment as we were making our way back to the waiting Pierce-Arrow, where Josiah had napped while we were in church. A chorus of agreement followed, and I couldn't help feeling a warm little glow. My mother. I'd had just one parent for so long, and now suddenly I had two—well, sort of.

"Let's hope not too much," someone else said. "Remember how *she* ended up."

I almost stopped walking in surprise and looked at Gran, but she was far enough ahead that she evidently hadn't heard.

What could that have meant?

When we were home again and Josiah had gone to put the Pierce-Arrow in the old barn, I waited while Gran unpinned her hat in the front hall mirror. "Gran, something happened back at the church—I don't know if you heard it." I told her, and she sighed.

"They may be my friends, but most of them are far too fond of gossip," she said. "Did you see who said it?"

"I didn't turn around. And, er...I don't think I caught everyone's name anyway."

Gran smiled but sighed again. "It was probably Millie Tanner. She was always the most vocal about it, probably because she was trying to distract attention from that son of hers. Your mother had a reputation for being...well, a little wild."

"Really? Was she?" It was exciting to have a mother who'd been a little wild.

"No, not particularly."

"Oh."

"You sound disappointed." Gran went to the stairs and sat down, patting the treader next to her. "Unless you consider tomboys wild. Then yes, Laura was a little wild. She never liked girlish games and manners. When we were here in the summers, she always preferred to be out in a boat or setting crab pots in the marsh or climbing trees for wild grapes. At first, she tagged along after her brothers—your uncles Robert and Samuel. When they'd outgrown such things, she kept it up with Josiah, who was a year or two younger than she. Your grandfather would scold sometimes, but I think he secretly was proud that she was just as adventurous as her brothers had been. She and Josiah would sneak out at dawn with a bag of sandwiches and not be home till supper, which got poor Josiah in trouble with his mother as he was supposed to be fetching wood and pumping the water tank full and weeding the flower beds. It didn't stop, even late in her teens, which of course shocked the ladies of the town."

"I wish I could have done that too," I said wistfully.

"Maybe. I don't think you have quite your mother's disdain for womanly interests." She touched a fold of my dress, one of my airy new summer ones in the latest style. "Half the time I had to force her to put on a frock and clean stockings for church—when I could find her on a Sunday morning, that is. She was even spotted wearing a pair of Sam's old trousers, which of course was a very shocking thing in those days. It's different now—no one would faint if you were to put on a pair of trousers in order to spade over the garden."

"How did she and Dad meet?" I couldn't picture this trouser-wearing girl at a debutante dance where it seemed most girls and boys met, according to the stories I'd read. My second-to-last governess, Miss Blunt, had been an avid novel reader, though she'd not let me read all of her collection. I'd had to exercise a bit of subterfuge to get a peek at *those*.

Gran's expression grew a little grim. "Right on the island. Your father was here with one of his classes, studying something about glaciers—we're evidently sitting on what was left after a glacier melted—and met your mother while he was gathering sand samples. She offered to show him a gravel outcrop down island, and he was smitten. They were married six months later. He was so much older than she—he was already teaching at his university, in his early thirties, and she was barely twenty. I think she liked him because he wasn't shocked by her tomboyishness. And he thought he'd found a wife who would take an interest in his work and be willing to accompany him on his expeditions in the summers."

"Didn't she want to?"

"Yes, she did—but he was only a junior professor, and his department head would not allow him to bring her, no matter how helpful she might be. So she always came back here in late May when he left on his trips, and then..." She trailed into silence.

And then she died, giving birth to me. "How sad."

"No," Gran said firmly. "Sad is the last word you should

use when thinking about your mother. She was always so full of life."

"I mean sad that Daddy's professor wouldn't let her go with him. That couldn't have made him very happy — or her, either."

"No, it didn't." She stood up abruptly. "Well, shall we see about lunch? We usually clean out the icebox at Sunday mealtimes in summer, so it's catch as catch can."

I was disappointed that confidences appeared to be over, but I stood up obediently. Could this be the source of Gran and Dad's coolness toward each other — the fact that he'd left my mother alone all those summers? Then I remembered something I'd wanted to ask. "Gran, wait. Do they ever have visitor days at the air station? You know, for people to see what they do there?"

"As a matter of fact, they will, soon — on alternate Sundays this summer, starting in June. We can go to the first one — it'll be next weekend. I didn't know you were interested in airplanes." Gran looked at me with raised eyebrows.

"Oh — well, who isn't these days?" I said, trying to sound offhand. "And to have an air station practically next door... where is it, anyway?"

"Just down island, another mile and a little bit down the road." She hesitated. "Josiah told me you were asking about it."

Why, the big tattle-tale! "Well, I am interested in it."

"That's fine. But please, Emma, keep away from it unless we're there on a visiting day. There are over three hundred young men there, and while they may be perfectly nice boys individually, the sight of a pretty girl might encourage them to not behave in as — as gentlemanly a way as usual. You'll be doing Captain Abbott a service if you keep away."

"But I thought you said they would probably be at the dances? Are we supposed to avoid them then as well?"

"When they're at the hotel, they'll be on their best behavior. It's at other times that you'd best keep out of their way." She shook her head. "I wish your father hadn't kept you quite so sheltered. I expect Helen might be more sophisticated," she added, mostly to herself. "I shall have to speak with her—"

"It's all right, Gran. I understand. You don't have to talk to Helen." Bother! How was I going to get to the air station and apply for a job now, when everyone seemed intent on keeping me away from it?

Happily, the morning's clouds gave way to a sunny after-noon—just perfect for a walk. When I went to invite Helen to come with me, I found her in her room in a chair by the window, industriously sewing.

"Busy for the Red Cross already?" I asked her. "Will your conscience let you stop for a little while and go exploring?"

Helen grimaced. "Those ladies this morning were terrifying. I am the world's worst knitter, so I hope they don't have a sock quota for members. No, I'm just catching up on some mending I didn't have time to do before. You go on. We'll do our tea at the hotel in a day or two, once all my stockings are darned."

I didn't press her; this was too good an opportunity to miss. I wouldn't venture actually *onto* the Monomoyick Air Station, but I could at least go see where it was. That wouldn't be disobeying Gran, would it?

I almost skipped down the stairs and along the drive to the shell-paved road. The ever-present wind tugged at the brim of my straw hat, and the air was fresh and cool off the water, but the warmth of the golden afternoon sun on my shoulders through the thin cotton of my dress hinted at summer. I had changed into one of my old frocks to walk in; it wouldn't do to ruin one of my new ones if I should—oh, maybe, happen to end up leaving the road and walking cross-country through the scrub to have a closer look at anything. After all, it wasn't as if I was likely to meet anyone I knew.

·CHAPTER SEVEN·
MALCOLM

I watched Captain Abbott pace back and forth in the small space behind his desk, six steps each way. He was neatly uniformed as always, but his pleasant face was frowning and his hair disheveled where he'd rumpled it in frustration. I'd come to the air station in the afternoon as he'd requested.

"Do they know why the bombs didn't explode?" I asked.

It turned out that the plane I'd seen had this morning while out on patrol found the U-boat and dropped two bombs near it—both of which had failed to detonate. The U-boat had been able to slip unharmed into deeper water and get away. The thought of it made me furious, but probably not as furious as it made him.

The captain gave a short bark of a laugh. "Because the Mark IVs are duds? We're not the only station reporting that they're not exploding, from what I've heard on the grapevine. We could have taken out at least three U-boats by now—U-boats that your people spotted for us." He shook his head. "You're giving us great leads, and we're wasting them, and meanwhile ships are suffering."

Another two fishing boats had been torpedoed by U-boats off Provincetown, I'd learned. What would happen when troop transports started leaving Boston in a few weeks? Unless we could get the U-boat raids under control now, more young men—a *lot* of them—would die before being able to fire off a single shot at the Germans.

"I wish there were something we could do, sir."

He stopped pacing to look at me, and the steely expression in his eyes softened. "You're already doing everything you can, son. I didn't know what to think, back at the beginning of the month when your father came to see me. But I'm more grateful than I can express to your people. It's a shame there isn't some way I can acknowledge what you're doing for your country."

"It's a nice thought, but we'd rather you didn't do any acknowledging." I grimaced. "The best thing you can do is make sure the next bomb you drop on a U-boat actually blows it up."

"Believe me, I'm working on that." He sighed. "I've been giving your patrols some thought. Would it be possible for you to have watchers out on moonlit nights? Word is there's the possibility of the enemy wanting to land individuals on shore, and the full moon is prime time for that sort of thing."

I didn't ask how he'd heard that—one didn't. But it made my blood run cold: U-boats dropping off spies to sneak into Boston or New York, or worse, groups of saboteurs who could spread terror and destruction. "The next full moon is on the fifth, right? I'll start them four days before and keep them four days after."

"Four days on either side should cover it." He glanced at his watch, one of the new wrist ones that aviators had been enthusiastic adopters of. "I've got another appointment coming in. Keep in touch, and let me know if there's anything I can do."

"I will, sir." We shook hands. I left his office, past the curious looks of the staff in his outer office—they weren't quite buying the "islander liaison" excuse for my frequent visits to their boss—and headed toward the station's main gate and on my way back home.

Captain Abbott wanted night-time patrols—which meant I would need more patrollers. At least I'd have good reason to ask Father to let me start training Maggie. I'd have to go further north to talk again to the families there and ask them to participate more; most of my present patrollers were our own local selkies. And I'd have to ask my own friends to take more shifts. Captain Abbott had asked for more than he realized: selkies often lived solitary lives, ranging around the coast by themselves. The full moon was the night we liked to meet on a beach somewhere and socialize and dance and flirt together. Well, if I had to take those nights myself, I would: it would be another excuse to keep away from Isabel's friends —

The sound of a voice coming from over the first rise in the road halted me — the voice belonging to the person I'd had in my head all night.

"It's a nice day for a walk," Emma Verlaine was saying in an *I have no desire to talk to you so leave me alone* tone that was quite clear — at least to me.

It evidently wasn't to whomever she was addressing. "Didn't know there were any fair damsels on the island, or I woulda gone for a walk before this," a male voice said.

"As I've only just arrived, we would not have met." Emma sounded positively frosty now. "Now, if you'll excuse me —"

"I'll bet she's staying at the hotel. Summer visitors must be starting to come in now," someone else said, and then I knew who they were — sailors from the air station, no doubt off duty and on their way to Mattaquason...and probably pinching themselves at their good luck in meeting a pretty girl on the road only feet from the station.

"When's the next dance there, anyway?" the first one said. "Will you save me a two-step, sweetheart? What's your name?"

Right — I'd heard more than enough. I strode up the last of the rise. "The next dance for enlisted men at the hotel is in three weeks, and she's my cousin," I said loudly, hoping Emma would catch the verbal rescue-line I was tossing her.

The pair of uniformed young men — yes, definitely from the air station — jumped. Emma did too. She looked different today, no longer wearing her chic suit and hat but a dotted green frock that made her look a lot younger. She was a little pale and flustered-looking, but then her chin rose.

"Why, Cousin Malcolm," she said. Good girl! "If I'd known you were walking this way, I would have waited for you."

"Who're you?" said the first young man, scowling at me.

"Aw, it's only the captain's pet civvie, from the hotel," the second one said. "You must have seen him around the skipper's office. Hey Galbraith, when're you going to enlist? You're on the station enough."

I ignored them. "Grandmother sent me after you. She was afraid you'd get lost. Afternoon, gentlemen," I said dismissively to the pair.

"I don't know how I could possibly get lost on an island," Emma said as she walked toward me. The two men were forced to step aside. "And it's such a lovely afternoon for a walk."

"You know she worries about you," I said. We began to stroll back toward the station; after a moment, I heard the pair continue on their way, grumbling. I waited a minute or two, then said in a low voice, "Are you all right?"

"I'm fine. Just—mad. They were being frightfully rude," she said, then let out a long breath. "Er, did my grandmother really send you?"

"No. But she would have, if she'd known. It's not a good idea for young women to walk alone down this end of the island, Miss Verlaine. Didn't she tell you that?"

"No." Her chin rose again, but then she sighed. "Well, not quite. She did say I shouldn't go near the station. But I didn't know I was that close to it."

"Fair enough. But you are." We'd topped the rise and come a little way down, and I halted. There, spread before us, was the Monomoyick Naval Air Station.

Dozens of buildings—some of them huge—and radio towers, and the great circular hydrogen tank that fed the dirigibles were surrounded by a high barbed-wire fence. A gatehouse with armed sentries guarded the entrance. A seaplane, floating on its pontoons, was tied up at a ramp that led up into a large building, and a dirigible's nose poked from an enormous hangar nearby. Men scurried everywhere, like industrious ants around their hill.

Emma shaded her eyes with her hand. "Oh." A pause. "It's larger than I thought it would be. And so busy, even on a Sunday."

That made me smile. "The war doesn't take time off on Sundays. Shipping still has to be protected and patrols flown."

She flushed. "Of course they do. I just thought — since those men were off-duty — "

"There are enough men on station to keep things running smoothly around the clock. There has to be."

"Yes, I can see that." Her gaze swept over it again, up and back. "Then maybe it isn't impossible," she murmured.

"What isn't impossible?"

She bit her lip. "Promise you won't laugh."

"I promise," I said immediately.

She looked at me and seemed to make up her mind. "I want to work at the air station," she said, turning back to gaze at the shiny dirigible being eased out of the hangar. "I've done plenty of bandage rolling and sock knitting for the Red Cross already, which is all very good, but anyone can do that. Now it seems I'm too young to apply to nursing school, and by the time I'm old enough the war will probably be over. But I want to do something to help *now* — something meaningful. I can't enlist and fight, but I can do other work on a place like this. I was going to ask those sailors if they knew about any positions open, but — " she wrinkled her nose. "If the Navy *really* needs people doing things around the clock, doesn't that make it more likely that I could find work here?"

I didn't laugh. For a moment I was reminded of Maggie, and then of my own disappointment that I couldn't enlist with my friends. "I understand. I truly do. But you must see, after what just happened, that it isn't a very realistic proposition."

"But those two boys were off-duty. Surely when they're on base they'd behave very differently..." She trailed into silence as I shook my head.

"Maybe, but not necessarily. It could be very uncomfortable

for you. And bad for discipline. How would it be possible to maintain order if every boy on base is constantly trying to find an excuse to stop by whatever office you're working in to flirt with you? And incidentally, not paying enough attention to things like flying airplanes and making sure equipment is properly maintained?"

She looked like a dirigible that had been deflated. "It's not fair! Women are Americans too. We care just as much as men do about serving our country, but all we can do is knit and sew and cook because men don't think we can do anything else and won't respect us enough to let us try."

"Are you for women's rights?"

"Yes, I am!"

"I am too."

She brightened. "You are? Truly?"

I looked at her. "Yes, I am. I've always thought it's ridiculous to regard women as the weaker sex, considering you're the ones who bear children. Wouldn't nature make you stronger and more enduring, precisely because of that?"

"Oh!" Her eyes shone. "I wish more people thought as you do. Like my father."

"Your father doesn't want you doing war work?"

"My father doesn't want me doing *anything*. I'm amazed he even let me come here, except they needed *him* to do war work." She sighed.

I'd never want Emma to be exposed to any danger—but I understood what she was feeling. It *wasn't* fair that women couldn't work for their country just because they were women. "All right. I'll see if I can set up an appointment for you with Captain Abbott. I'm almost positive he'll tell you what I did, but at least you'll have had a chance."

She gasped. "Oh! Could you do that? That's—I—thank you!"

"Don't thank me yet. I can't promise he'll see you."

"I don't care. Thank you for…for taking me seriously and not laughing at me."

"I would never laugh at you for wanting to help." On the contrary, I liked her even better for it. I smiled at her and was a little stunned by the smile she gave me back—her brown eyes practically glowed, and her mouth was curving and soft. I tore my eyes away from it and said hastily, "This is your first visit to Monomoyick, isn't it? That's what your grandmother said."

"It is, but it isn't. I was born here, actually."

"You were?" Funny that Mrs. Wetherell hadn't mentioned that. "So how do you like it?"

"I love it. I had no notion of how beautiful it would be." She gestured. "I like the color of the sun on the dunes. The quiet's a little strange—I'm used to living in the city—but I think I like that too. And the water—it's beautiful, but so—so big. It scares me a little. But I can't stop looking at it. It draws me whenever I'm outside or even near a window."

Here was my chance to get her near the water and see what the seals had been excited about. "You don't ever have to fear it, Miss Verlaine. Can you swim?"

"Yes. I swam all the time in lakes in New Ham—"

"No. Lake swimming and ocean swimming aren't the same thing. You really shouldn't go in the water here until someone's seen how strong a swimmer you are. Like me," I added, shamelessly.

She turned slightly pink. "Oh, you don't have to do that—"

"Yes, I do. We—er, we don't want anyone getting into trouble in the water on our island. It might give the hotel a bad name." That had been a good bit of quick thinking. "Promise?" I added.

She laughed. "All right, I promise. Is that why you're at the air station a great deal? Are you giving the aviators swimming lessons?"

She didn't miss much, did she? "I teach people sometimes at the hotel, but the Navy's on its own for that. My father's the island's unofficial civilian liaison to the station. But he has the hotel to run, so I do a lot of his leg-work. I'm there pretty frequently."

"Oh. I'd—I couldn't help wondering why you hadn't enlisted. But what you're doing is kind of a war service, I suppose. Do you help with the hotel as well?"

"Of course." I turned away from the station and started to walk slowly back the way we'd come, so that she had to follow. "It's my family's business. We all help."

She fell into step beside me. "Do you have brothers and sisters?"

"Two sisters. One's married and lives…off-island." I'd nearly slipped there and said something about Isabel having gone back to the sea. Talking with Emma was dangerously easy. "My little sister thinks she helps."

"You're lucky," she said wistfully. "I wish I had two sisters."

I made a face. "Come and meet mine and see if you still think so. Maggie's enough to make anyone swear off sisters."

She laughed. "She can't be that bad! How old is she?"

"Eleven, although she can act anywhere from three to forty. I don't know which extreme is worse."

"She sounds darling."

"Don't say I didn't warn you." I hesitated, then said, "Actually, my mother wanted me to invite you to call. She can't get out much during the day—the hotel, again—but she's very fond of your grandmother and wants to meet you. Can you come tomorrow afternoon?" It wasn't much of a fib. Mother was sure to want to meet Mrs. Wetherell's granddaughter at some point.

"Can I come Tuesday instead? And bring Helen? She'd love to see the hotel."

"Of course." I'd forgotten about her cousin. I supposed she'd have to come too. But I mostly wanted Emma to come.

We were almost back to Mrs. Wetherell's by now. It had been comfortable walking with Emma; I liked the free and easy way she moved.

"Thank you for coming to my rescue," she said when we reached the house.

"Don't mention it. I'm glad I happened to be there. I wouldn't want you to form a bad opinion of Monomoyick on your first full day here. See you Tuesday?"

"Don't worry, I won't. Er, haven't. And yes, Tuesday."

I sketched a salute at her, and whistled all the way home. I was liking her more and more—she was funny and smart and seemed to care about all the right things, and was completely not like most of the young ladies who stayed at the hotel with their parents. I wanted my family to meet her so that they could see that not all human girls were so bad. That at least one of them was—well, really pretty wonderful.

·CHAPTER EIGHT·
EMMA

At breakfast next morning Helen asked, "Might I go shopping in Mattaquason today, Aunt Dorinda? I could take care of any errands you might have there."

Gran smiled at her. "Feeling island-bound already?"

"Not a bit. Manhattan's an island too, remember?" She smiled back. "But I'd like to buy a bathing suit. If I'm going to be here for the next few months, I ought to learn to swim, don't you think?"

Helen would be beautiful in a bathing suit. I thought about mine with its droopy drawers and — oh, horror — *frills*. It would be nice to have a sleeker, more grownup suit. Especially if Malcolm was serious about vetting my swimming abilities.

So after breakfast Josiah drove Helen and me to the ferry. A pair of seals swam companionably alongside us in the *Never Late*, but I didn't bother pointing them out. I'd decided they were mine and didn't want to share. I liked the air of friendly curiosity about their pointed snouts and the way their heads tilted as they returned my gaze, and I gave them a little wave as the *Never Late* bumped into its dock.

We strolled up the road to Main Street. I stopped at the pharmacy to buy a few magazines in hopes of finding a better nursing correspondence school listed among the advertisements. I wasn't ready to give up on *that* just yet, in case Malcolm couldn't arrange a meeting for me with Captain Abbott. Which reminded me… "Helen, you said something the other day—how do you tell if a boy is…you know…*interested* in you?"

Helen didn't laugh, thank goodness. "It's not hard. They make themselves as obvious as possible, so that you have to pay attention to them. Or they'll do or say something mysterious so that you do the pursuing, just to find out what they mean." She looked at me sideways with a small smile. "Let me guess. You weren't alone on your walk yesterday."

I flushed. "How did you guess?"

"Oh, feminine intuition. Tell me about it." I gave her an edited version of my meeting with Malcolm. She nodded as I spoke. "It will be instructive to see how he behaves tomorrow. With his looks he must be mobbed by girls during the summer when the hotel is full of guests, so he's had plenty of time to refine his technique."

"His technique? Do you think so?" Somehow he hadn't felt like that kind of young man. I remembered the way he'd chased those sailors off, not brooking any nonsense. And the way he'd looked at me as we walked and talked. The thought of him being mobbed by girls—well, it wouldn't surprise me if he were. But it wasn't a very pleasing thought.

The first store we stopped in didn't carry bathing suits, but two dress shops did. We dithered back and forth between them until Helen finally chose a chemise-style suit in white-striped blue sateen with a square collar and matching bloomers. I found one I liked in green jersey. It was sleeveless and much sleeker than my old one. Best of all, I was able to pay the clerk for both of them before Helen could stop me.

"You shouldn't have done that," she said as we left the shop. She sounded almost angry.

"Why not? Dad gave me more pocket money than I could

ever spend on myself. It's my way to say thank you for coming to spend the summer with me. I'm sure you had plenty of other things you could have done instead." I took her arm and gave it a squeeze.

An odd expression flitted across her face, but before I could identify it, it had vanished. "No, there's no place I would rather be this summer than here," she said. "Thank you, Cousin Emma." She placed a swift kiss on my cheek. "Now, shall we go to the soda fountain up the street? My treat."

"No, *my* treat, ladies." George Osborn had materialized on the sidewalk next to us. He took off his hat and smiled. "That is, if you don't mind some company."

"Why, Mr. Osborn! We'd love some company." Helen smiled as if she were genuinely glad to see him. I smiled too, but wished I could slink away and leave the two of them to go without me. Something about George Osborn gave me the creeps.

The soda fountain was all pink ruffles and twisted white wrought iron. It was surprisingly busy at this hour, with several tables of older women with their heads close together over pots of tea. Eyes followed us as we made our way to the counter, and I was sure I heard "Wetherell" whispered more than once.

I thought I was being clever when I managed to get a stool on the opposite side of Helen from George, but soon realized my mistake: he ordered us all chocolate malteds and then began to talk to me *across* Helen. "How do you like Monomoyick so far? A little dull, I guess, after Boston. And your Uncle Robert, is he well?"

"Er, as far as I know." I didn't much care for Uncle Robert, who had inherited all of Grandpapa's self-importance and none of Gran's sense of humor.

"He was a guest of honor at the opening of our new factory in Lawrence in March. We make muslin for aircraft wings. Business is booming now that we're at war."

"How wonderful that you're making such an important contribution to the war effort!" Helen said admiringly.

That reminded me. "Do you have brothers, Mr. Osborn?"

"Please, do call me George—and yes, two brothers. They're still in school."

Hmm. Then he wasn't the only son after all. The services weren't keen on taking only sons as soldiers if they could help it, which was probably part of why Malcolm hadn't enlisted. But George had no such excuse. "Were you planning to enlist?"

He shook his head. "I wish I could, but father needs me at the company or I'd be off to France like a shot. I've just joined the firm as a junior partner," he added. "They need me since production is ratcheting up so much."

Helen seemed impressed. *I* wanted to ask him why he was in a soda fountain in Mattaquason on a Monday morning if the pressures of work in his father's factory were so great, but Helen was asking him about how airplane muslin differed from regular muslin, and I didn't want to draw his attention back to me. So I tried to make myself invisible and sipped at my chocolate malted (which was too sweet) until a voice—one of the ones I'd heard say "Wetherell" as we came in—caught my attention.

"—*just* like her mother, don't you think? Gave me a turn, seeing her at church with Dorinda."

Another voice snickered. "Too bad she doesn't look just like her father, so we'd finally *know* who he was."

Both voices tittered. I was clearly the topic of conversation, but what in heaven's name did they mean about my father? I was just about to turn around to find the owners of the voices, but an exclamation from Helen stopped me.

"We'd *love* to! Wouldn't we, Emma?" she said.

"We'd love to what?"

Helen kicked me in the ankle, but George only smiled and said, "I'm inviting you two ladies for lunch later this week. I'll come for you in the *Fast Lady*."

I didn't need to look at Helen to know how to answer. "Yes, thank you." When she kicked me again I added, more enthusiastically, "That would be delightful!"

We left a few minutes later as Helen and I had to catch the

ferry back to the island in time for lunch. I looked carefully around to see if I could tell who had been talking about me, but everyone in the shop suddenly seemed very absorbed in their teacups.

"Thank you for a lovely treat," Helen said to George as we stood outside the shop. Thank goodness she was there to do the talking; I was too rattled by those women.

"My pleasure. I hope you'll let me know the next time you're planning to come into town—"

The cheerful blare of a car horn drowned the rest of his speech, and a large black Marmon sedan with "Ocean Inn" emblazoned on its door pulled up next to us. "Drawn to the bright lights and bustle of downtown Mattaquason already?" Malcolm asked, leaning over to look out the passenger window at us.

"We came to buy bathing suits." I suddenly felt better. "We're on our way home."

"So am I, now that my sister has the lunch pail she seems to forget once a week. Want a lift back? Good morning, Miss Sutton. Osborn." He nodded pleasantly at them.

George scowled in return. "Not a very good reason to waste gasoline when our Allies in Europe need all the fuel they can get."

Malcolm shrugged. "Since I also had to drive some guests to the station, I figured a short detour to the school wouldn't lose us the war."

I tried not to frown at George. Didn't his silly motorboat use gasoline too?

"We'd love a ride, if you're on your way back." Helen turned her smile on him. "We were having such fun that I'm afraid time got away from us and we'll be late for lunch."

"See you Thursday?" George put in.

"We wouldn't miss it. Thank you!" And before I'd had a chance to move, she'd whisked open the door and climbed into the front seat next to Malcolm. George hastened to open the back door for me and I thanked him grumpily. I'd thought *I'd* sit in front next to Malcolm.

"It was sweet of him to treat us like that," Helen said over her shoulder to me. "And it's most kind of you to give us a ride," she added to Malcolm. "Do you do a lot of the driving for the hotel? That must be fun!"

All the way to the ferry (all right, it was only about five minutes but it *felt* longer) she kept up a bright stream of chatter and questions for Malcolm. I sat silent in the back, not sure if I should try to get a word in edgeways or not. I hadn't minded at all when Helen chattered at George but was less delighted now…until I glanced up in time to meet Malcolm's eyes in the rear-view mirror. They crinkled at the corners and the right eyebrow was ever-so-slightly raised. I let myself smile at him, really smile, and relaxed into the comfortable cushions of the seat once again.

While we made the crossing, Malcolm nodded his head toward the side of the *Never Late*. "Did you notice?" he said, interrupting Helen and looking at me in the mirror again. "Your friends are here." There was a slightly strange note in his voice, or maybe it was just the thrum of the car's motor combining with the ferry's engine.

"Oh, yes," I sat forward to look out the window. A pair of seals swam alongside the ferry, much as they had this morning. I smiled to see them. "I wonder if they're the same ones I saw this morning? Why do they like to follow the ferry?"

"Sheer nosiness, mostly. They're as bad as cats when it comes to curiosity." He was looking straight ahead now, as we were about to dock.

He brought us right to Gran's house, which was nice of him. Helen thanked him effusively for the ride and climbed out of the car. I'd just done the same and was about to thank him when he abruptly asked, "What are you doing with Osborn on Thursday?"

I paused. "He invited Helen and me to meet his parents and have lunch," I said, surprised.

"Both of you?"

"Yes."

"Hmmph." But his expression lightened just a little. "See you tomorrow, right?"

"That's right."

He nodded and continued around the drive onto the road, tooting his horn once and waving. I waved back and followed Helen into the house.

After supper I went up to my room to think about what I'd overheard in the soda fountain that afternoon. I suppose I shouldn't have been surprised that we'd be a source of gossip: any new faces in a small town were bound to be, according to all the novels I'd read with Miss Blunt. But this was different: there was evidently history behind it, like it was a continuation of an old story the town had whispered about for years. It sounded like people thought that my mother had been less than faithful to Dad, and I was the result.

The more I thought about it, the angrier I got. What basis did they have for such a story, apart from my mother's not being a conventional girl who liked to stay indoors and stitch samplers? If she'd been able to go with Dad on his summer trips, she would have. It wasn't her fault she'd been stuck here without him. If Dad ever heard about any of this, he'd be devastated—and then I wondered if he already had, and that was why we never came down here all the years I was growing up.

I made sure my lights were off—couldn't forget the blackout—and went to sit in the window seat and gaze out at the growing dusk over the dunes. It made a calm and beautiful picture, but even its peace couldn't cool my ire. I thought about going to Gran and pouring it all out to her. But she'd seemed uncomfortable talking about Dad and my mother the other day on the stairs. Besides, it was probably her friends who were doing the whispering. She'd probably tell me not to listen to the old biddies, but we were expected to go to their Red Cross and Ladies' Aid meetings every week. Even if they behaved themselves, I was sure I'd still have to put up with incidents like this morning's in the soda fountain.

All the more reason, then, for me to get a job at the air station. With any luck I could avoid having to go into town much at all if I did.

I was glad I had on one of my smart new frocks when Helen and I entered the lobby of the Ocean Hotel the next afternoon, or I would have felt dreadfully out of place. It was gorgeous—all sea green Persian rugs and brass chandeliers and polished cherry furniture. Malcolm, who came from around the front desk to meet us, wore a beautifully-cut gray suit and tie and immaculate white shirt rather than the casual clothes I'd seen him in before. I wasn't sure which I preferred; he was awfully good-looking in both.

"Hello," he said cheerfully. "You look nice. Mother is waiting for you."

"Thank you. Helen and I were wondering—where do you live? I thought you might move from room to room like indoor nomads, but Helen didn't think so."

He grinned. "My parents let me and my sisters do that occasionally when we were younger and the hotel was closed for the season, just for fun. But we have a very nice apartment here." He led us to a door by the front desk, where a dark-haired man now stood. He looked like an older version of Malcolm.

"Father, here are Miss Verlaine and Miss Sutton," Malcolm said to him.

Mr. Galbraith nodded. I tensed, waiting to be told how much I looked like my mother, but he only said, "Pleased to meet you, Miss Verlaine. Welcome back to the island."

"Thank you. Though I can't say I remember much from the last time I was here."

Helen sidled forward. "The hotel is beautiful, Mr. Galbraith. I hope we can have a tour."

Mr. Galbraith smiled briefly. "I'm sure Malcolm will be glad to show you around—"

The door behind Malcolm jerked open. A girl with long brown braids and Mr. Galbraith's dark eyes stood in the doorway, trying to look as if she hadn't been listening, then gave up. "I'll give them a tour. Malcolm always leaves out the good parts."

"Like the laundry chute and the pastry cupboard," Malcolm said. "In case you hadn't guessed, this is my little sister, Maggie, and yes, she has a habit of listening at doors."

"Only when there's something I want to hear. Come *on*, we're waiting for you." She looked at me, head to one side. "You're Emma, aren't you?"

"Margaret." Mr. Galbraith said it quietly, but Maggie looked abashed.

"I mean, Miss Verlaine? I'm right, aren't I? I only called you Emma 'cause that's what Malcolm called you and so that's how I think of you now. But I guess I have to remember to call you Miss Verlaine." She looked at Helen. "Who're you?"

I was sure I was an interesting shade of pink by then and was very aware of Malcolm standing next to me. He'd talked about me to his family. Did that mean he really did like me and wasn't just practicing his "technique", as Helen had said?

Fortunately at that moment the door opened wider and a slender, dark-haired woman appeared. She put her hands on Maggie's shoulders, steering her gently aside, and said, "Thank you, dear, that will do," then smiled at us. "Won't you come in? I'm Elizabeth Galbraith. Maggie was more than a little excited to meet you—"

"I told my teacher she had to let me go home early today 'cause I didn't want to miss anything *good*," Maggie interrupted. She squirmed out from under her mother's hands and danced down a short hall ahead of us.

"Did she let you?" I asked her. I hadn't spent much time with younger children apart from Uncle Robert's and Uncle Samuel's grandchildren. They were all just toddlers and not very interesting, whereas Maggie seemed to be very much a *person*.

"No, the old meanie. I had to ride my bike like anything to get to the ferry early. Do you have a bike? The roads on the island kinda stink for bike-riding, but—"

"Why don't you go see if the kettle has boiled, Maggie?" Mrs. Galbraith interrupted. "If it has, you may warm the pot and I'll be in to make the tea."

This evidently met with Maggie's approval: she disappeared through a doorway, bellowing, "I'll be right back! Don't say anything interesting while I'm gone!" over her shoulder.

We were now in a sitting room, not as grand as the lobby but as handsome. Mrs. Galbraith said, motioning to a sofa and chairs by a fireplace, "Won't you sit down, girls? Malcolm, your father said he can spare you for an hour or two; the new clerks need to practice being on their own anyway. Excuse me a moment; I must make sure Maggie doesn't eat all the cookies before the tea is ready." She glided away after Maggie.

I perched on the edge of the sofa, feeling self-conscious and aware of my feet as I tried to dispose my limbs gracefully. Helen, of course, looked perfectly elegant as she sat in a chair and removed her gloves. Malcolm took the chair next to me. We sat silently for a moment, and I scrabbled desperately for something polite and grown-up to say...and then came to my senses. I didn't have to pretend to be a grown-up to Helen—and to Malcolm, well... "I like your sister. So much for your dire warnings."

"Try living with her for a week, and then we can discuss it again. She's mostly a good kid, though. She just tends to be overenthusiastic. About everything."

"Is the hotel full?" Helen asked quickly, before I could

respond. "I never thought about it, but running one must be a very busy job."

"Not full, but filling. It's just the beginning of the season. Most of our clerks from last year enlisted, so we have to train new ones. I'm afraid these will enlist too, and then we'll have to start again. Father doesn't want to, but we may have to hire women clerks."

I bristled. "What's wrong with hiring women?"

He looked at me, and I was sure he was remembering our discussion of women's rights. "Nothing at all. But our guests aren't used to them. At a hotel like the Ocean, the front desk staff have always been men."

Maggie came back in carrying two plates of cookies, followed by Mrs. Galbraith with a tea tray. She set it down on the low table in front of the sofa and sat down next to me. Maggie, suddenly docile, put down the cookies and distributed the cups of tea her mother poured, then parked herself on the floor at my feet, strategically close to the cookie plates.

"Don't eat them all," Mrs. Galbraith said. "Someone else might like one."

Maggie promptly offered me the plate. "Those are the really good ones," she said, pointing. "I helped make 'em."

It was clear what was expected of me. I took two and she beamed, then got up to offer them to Helen.

"You're very kind. Maggie can be overpowering," Mrs. Galbraith said, smiling a little ruefully while Maggie was instructing Helen on which cookie to choose.

"I like her," I said again. "I wish I could have had sisters or brothers."

"I wish you could have too. I knew your mother a little—not very much, as I was older than she and busy with my children and helping with the hotel. But enough to know she would have been a good mother."

That of course raised a lump in my throat. I took a sip of tea to help swallow it down.

Mrs. Galbraith went on as if she hadn't noticed. "I know

your grandmother is very happy you're here. Will you stay all summer?"

"As far as I know," I said, and explained about Dad's going to Washington.

She nodded sympathetically. "It must have been hard to leave the city. Malcolm missed it dreadfully after he graduated last year. He still misses it, I think."

"But he decided to come back here."

"Well, our family has been on the island for a very long time. I don't think we could live anywhere else. Would you like to see the hotel now? Malcolm?"

Maggie jumped up. "Can I give them the tour? Please?"

"We'll all go," Mrs. Galbraith said firmly.

We filed out into the lobby, where a few guests were reading newspapers in the sitting areas around the edge of the room. Mr. Galbraith glanced up from behind the desk where he stood with a young man—one of the new clerks, I assumed. Mrs. Galbraith led us across the large space to a set of double doors and opened them.

The room beyond was filled with tables covered in crisp white tablecloths. A handful of black-suited waiters were laying out place settings, and an elderly woman was arranging flowers in vases. She paused and examined us curiously as we clustered around the door. A row of French doors across the back of the room looked out across a deep veranda toward the water.

"This is the dining room, of course," Mrs. Galbraith said. "There's also a pair of smaller dining rooms to that side for private parties. And over here"—she led us to the right, to another set of double doors—"is the ballroom."

"Where the dances for the air station are held," Helen said. I looked at the beautifully kept parquet floor with a raised stage at one end for the orchestra, the polished chandeliers, and the sea-green silk drapes at the windows, and wondered if Malcolm danced.

"That's right. It seems the least we can do for those boys— there's not much else around here for them when they're off duty. We used to have weekly dances anyway, during the season, so now we'll have two—one just for guests on Saturdays and one for everyone, including the air station, on Fridays."

"Do you know how to dance?" Maggie was at my elbow.

"Yes. I went to dancing school all last year." My last governess, Miss Nutting, had herself scorned things like dancing—her passion was Eastern religions and peculiar health diets—but she had strong family feeling and got Dad to send me to her sister's dancing school in Newbury Street.

"Will you teach me? *Some* people think I'm too young to learn"—she cast an accusing look at Malcolm—"but if I don't start now, I'll never be able to. I'm awful clumsy. It's gonna take me *years* to get it right."

"I love to dance. I'd be happy to teach you," Helen said, smiling at Maggie.

She shook her head. "Uh-uh, not you. I want Emma to teach me."

"Maggie, you're being—" Mrs. Galbraith began.

"No, it's all right. I'd be happy to." I sent Helen an apologetic look. She shrugged.

"Goodie! We've got a Victrola and records and everything. We can start on Saturday." She smiled up at me happily. I glanced at Malcolm, waiting for him to protest. He opened his mouth, then closed it and didn't say another word.

Mrs. Galbraith showed us the card room and the library, the gentlemen's smoking room and the ladies' salon, the billiards room and even an indoor ninepin alley. There were also a supervised children's playroom, a barber shop, and a beauty parlor.

"Feel free to come here if you don't want to have to go over to Mattaquason for a haircut," Mrs. Galbraith said. "Your grandmother often does in summer. Our hairdresser is from New York—she calls this her summer vacation."

"Thank you. I just might do that." My hair was still long. I wore it braided and coiled on the back of my head but had been thinking about getting it fashionably cropped, like Helen's that curled so becomingly about her face.

We went out onto the veranda next, which held several groups of cushioned white wicker chairs and lounges. I went immediately to the railing to stare out at the water. Beyond a wide strip of beautifully green lawn scattered with clumps of hydrangea bushes and lawn chairs was the beach, already dotted with little sea-green-and-white-striped tents for guests who preferred to sit out of the sun and wind.

"They're great for when we play capture-the-flag." Maggie was back at my side. "Wanna go see?"

I hesitated; Mrs. Galbraith was already leading Helen toward stairs leading off to the side, where I could see a glimpse of a garden with a gazebo and tennis courts beyond it.

"I'll show her the beach," Malcolm said, and looked hard at his sister. She stuck out her lower lip in a belligerent pout, then sighed and scampered off after her mother.

"How did you do that?" I would swear that they'd held an entire conversation in that brief exchange of looks.

He grinned. "While my mother showed you the library, I told her not to make a pest of herself or you'd change your mind about coming on Saturday. And neither of us wants that." He started down the stairs, and I followed after him, feeling a little fluttery.

At the edge of the lawn, he led me to a pair of chairs near stairs that went down a steep bank to the sand. "I don't think you want sand in your shoes. Why don't we—"

"Hi, Malcolm!" a girl's voice called. A pair of young women in bathing suits and beach robes were coming up the stairs.

"Were you looking for us?" The second girl tossed her head coquettishly.

"Did you have a pleasant afternoon?" he asked politely, but I saw the way his shoulders stiffened.

"We hoped you'd come down and sit with us." The first girl was carefully ignoring me. "We *waited* for you."

"I've been on the front desk. Maybe another day." He turned deliberately to me. Both girls glowered as they passed us on their way up the lawn.

"I imagine you get a lot of that," I said when they were out of earshot, keeping my voice neutral.

"More than I'd like," he said shortly.

I took the chair he indicated. Hmm. So much for Malcolm's technique. Maybe Helen didn't know everything about boys after all. Or at least this particular boy. I stared out across the broad beach. "The tide's nearly out, isn't it?"

He didn't even glance at the water as he sat down. "It'll be dead low in another forty-five minutes."

"I thought so. It's funny, but I seem to have developed a tide clock in my head over the last few days."

"All islanders get one after a while. It's just part of life here. I still always knew what tide it was even when I was up at school."

I remembered what Mrs. Galbraith had said. "Do you miss being at college?"

He was quiet for a moment. "Yes. I miss a lot of things about it. My friends, mostly, and the crew team. I'm still rowing here, but it's different—different boat, different conditions. Rowing on a team isn't like going out on your own. They're both good in their ways, but I miss being in an eight on the Charles on a chilly October morning. I miss the dinners we used to have after regattas. And I miss Bailey's in the square."

"Bailey's ice cream?" I sat up. "Oh my gosh, I love Bailey's! Chocolate ice cream hot fudge sundaes!"

He shook his head. "Too much chocolate. Coffee ice cream is better for sundaes."

"There's no such thing as too much chocolate. Besides, my governesses would never let me get coffee ice cream." I sat back in my chair. "What else do you miss?"

He told me—about snow muffling the paths between the old brick buildings in Harvard Yard, or the lights on Cambridge Bridge glowing eerily in a fog at dusk, or the crowds of people that the first warm, bright day in late March would bring out all over the city, turning their pale winter faces up to the sun.

"Don't you want to go back?" I asked when he paused for breath.

His expression darkened. "I do go back, for visits. But this is where I belong."

There was something so firm and final in the way he spoke that I knew it was the truth. Mrs. Galbraith had sounded the same way. "But you went away to college anyway."

"A college education will be useful here. The Ocean Hotel's almost a small city, really. Father's more like a mayor than an innkeeper."

"And you're his deputy." I wished I had a place I felt as rooted in; our house in Boston was nice, but it wasn't—it wasn't like *this*.

I sighed and stared out at the water too. It seemed lately that whenever I caught sight of the restless water, whether gleaming like molten silver in the afternoon sun or bright blue in sunshine, it transfixed me. "When can we swim?" I heard myself ask.

I could feel him looking at me. "Another few weeks. It'll be too cold for you now."

Huh. Did he think I was a total softie? Some of those New Hampshire lakes I'd swum in had been *frigid*. "Is it too cold for you?"

"No. But I grew up here. Do you want to swim that badly?"

I tore my gaze away from the water. "Yes."

He leaned back in his chair and smiled at me—really smiled. "Maybe we can try on Saturday," he said. "It might be warmer near your grandmother's house—that's the sheltered side of the island."

We left shortly after that; Maggie came to fetch us because Malcolm was wanted back at the front desk. Helen was waiting for us on the veranda. She was quiet during our walk home, which struck me as a little unusual—Helen didn't seem to much care for silence—but suited me perfectly as it let me think.

I *was* in great danger of making a fool of myself over the first boy I'd ever gotten to really know, which made me feel somewhat cross. How...how clichéd of me. Miss Blunt, my novel-reading governess, would have said it was narrative imperative that I do so. But I wasn't going to let myself behave like some silly goose of a girl in a romance who swoons whenever she sees the strong, manly hero. I was a *modern* young woman.

Bailey's. He liked Bailey's. I felt a silly grin begin to stretch across my face and firmly ordered the corners of my mouth to behave themselves.

·Chapter Nine·
Emma

I had a great deal less to smile about on the day of our lunch with George Osborn. As promised, he picked us up in the *Fast Lady* to bring us to the mainland, where a car and driver were waiting to take us to his house.

"We could have just taken the ferry," I blurted. Really, it was ridiculous to have made such a fuss about coming for us in his boat.

Helen kicked my ankle. I was going to end up with a permanent bruise there by the end of the summer if I didn't learn to guard my tongue. "It was lovely of you to come get us," she cooed as George finished tying up the boat and helped us onto the dock. Well, it had been a nice trip—a large, handsome seal had accompanied us across the channel, gazing at me with lustrous, soulful eyes—but *still*.

Helen looked marvelous—so smart and yet so dainty in a primrose-yellow summer frock. I'd checked to see what she was wearing so I could choose something less pretty. I wanted to make sure she got all the attention today.

Mr. and Mrs. Osborn were waiting for us in the drawing room of their enormous house—yes, they called it the "drawing room." I'd snorted and earned a frown and an elbow in my side from Helen when the maid opened the door to us and announced that fact.

Mrs. Osborn was a small, pretty woman—George must have gotten his good looks from her—but her elegant clothes had more personality than her greetings. Mr. Osborn was obviously the dominant member of the family. He wasn't much taller than his wife but possessed a nervous energy that filled the space around him. I could understand how he'd gone from bobbin boy to mill owner.

"Miss Verlaine!" he exclaimed in a voice like a melodious foghorn. "It's a pleasure to meet you!" He peered into my face. "Yes, I can see you're a Wetherell. How's your Uncle Robert?"

"Actually, I haven't seen him in a—"

"Fine man, Robert. Like your grandfather. If I'd known your grandmother lived here, we would have called on her long since." He glared at his wife, as if it were her fault that they hadn't.

We were summoned to lunch then, which was a relief; I'd been afraid that poor Mrs. Osborn was about to burst into tears. I was seated between Mr. Osborn and George, to my dismay. So much for letting Helen be the center of attention—but as it turned out, Mr. Osborn assumed that role. My Uncle Robert had the same fondness for holding forth at family gatherings, but I think Mr. Osborn had him beat. And unfortunately, his favorite topic was the war and how it was being run—or botched, according to him.

"When our boys get over there, they're going to be slaughtered," he said, slicing with great gusto into a lamb chop. "Slaughtered, I tell you. The Kaiser runs a much tighter ship than we do. When's the last time we had a good war? Our boys won't know what hit 'em."

George nodded his agreement. I stared down at my plate (lamb chop, potatoes Anna, new peas swimming in butter, and two kinds of bread—evidently the Osborns didn't subscribe to the voluntary food-saving measures that the government was issuing) and bit my lip to keep from saying anything as an image of the boys we'd seen in South Station—so lively, so *alive*—flashed into my mind. I put it firmly aside and wished I could do the same to Mr. Osborn's words.

Helen was braver than me. "Oh, how can you say that, Mr. Osborn? And with our own air station so close by, keeping us safe—"

He gave her a fatherly smile. "Keeping us safe from what? The Kaiser is busy enough on the other side of the Atlantic. He's not going to be bothering with anyone on Cape Cod. All we'll have is a camp full of young men spoiling to get into trouble when no Germans turn up. Thank God they aren't near Lowell, or they'd be sparking riots just for the fun of it. I would sleep more soundly, Miss Sutton, if that station *weren't* there. I hope Mrs. Wetherell is keeping her doors locked."

That was so unfair that I opened my mouth to refute it— and caught Helen's eye just before I sputtered an indignant rebuttal. At least she couldn't reach my ankle for a kick.

Almost as soon as dessert was over (banana ice cream and profiteroles—definitely not on the government's food conservation list) George took us for a spin on his boat before he brought us back to the island. I was happy to get out of the house though I'd calmed down enough to say polite good-byes to Mr. and Mrs. Osborn. My mood improved even more when another seal—or was it the same one that had followed us before?—appeared near the *Fast Lady* and seemed intent on following us as we meandered north up the coast a little way, then back toward the island.

"You were very good," Helen said after we'd waved good-bye to George and were walking back up the road to Gran's. "I thought you were going to explode."

"Gosh, Helen, I sure wanted to. What a horrid man! How could he say those things about our boys? I'm never going to set foot in that house again if I can help it."

Helen's face fell. "But if we're invited, I can't go without you."

"Would you want to?"

"Yes. Mr. Osborn wasn't that bad, really, and Mrs. Osborn seemed very nice—"

"She's downtrodden, like Mr. Osborn's workers in his factories probably are."

"Oh, hush. He was probably just trying to get a rise out of you. Some men like to do that."

"Well, he can do it to someone else," I said, and then sighed. "I'm sorry, Helen. If we're invited, I'll go with you. But wouldn't it be nicer if George invited just *you*?"

"Emma!" She laughed, but a blush spread across her cheeks.

"Aha! So you do like him!"

"He's a very nice young man," she said primly. "I enjoy his company."

"Uh-huh." I grinned at her. "Sorry, Helen. But if you really do like him, then why pretend otherwise? Wouldn't it be fabulous if he decided to fall madly in love with you and asked you to marry him?"

"You're being ridiculous, you know," Helen said severely, but that lovely rose color had crept further north.

I didn't say anything more. I'd found another mission for the summer besides getting a job on the base: I was going to do everything I could to see that Helen and George spent plenty of time together. If I could actually get him to propose, that would be even better.

On Friday Gran, as promised, brought Helen and me to the Red Cross work meeting at the Congregational church hall after lunch. The large room was full of women, some of whom we'd met and more we hadn't—the chapter encompassed all the churches in town. Rows of tables had been set up, and women were busily cutting pieces out of gray flannel or white cotton while others sewed them together. A few sat at sewing machines that had been set up near a window, and their treadles made a gentle rhythmic clatter that punctuated the hum of conversation in the room. That hum faltered slightly as we came in, then escalated.

Gran led us to one of her friends, who was frowning at a clipboard. She examined us with narrowed eyes and said, "Bed shoes, till we see how good your sewing is."

I blinked. "I beg your pardon, ma'am?"

She sighed impatiently. "You two can start piecing flannel bed shoes—on that table there. Or we can put you on hemming—I assume you can sew a hem?"

Helen stepped in before I could open my mouth. "Yes, ma'am. Bed shoes sound like fun!" She took my arm and propelled me toward the table.

"You can probably sew circles around her, and I'm perfectly capable of plain sewing, thank you very much!" I muttered. Miss Tortill, governess number seven, had me making her petticoats when I was eleven.

"I know," she said soothingly. "Some ladies don't like to think that we girls are as capable as they are."

"Balderdash," I said, but didn't dare say any more as we were being watched by multiple pairs of interested eyes. We sat down at one of the bed shoe tables, let the ladies there explain how they were pieced, and got sewing.

At first Helen and I chatted a little, but my attention was soon drawn to a discussion at the table behind us. From the snatches I caught, I guessed it was about me—and my mother, of course. I sewed away, my attention apparently fixed on my work, and eavesdropped shamelessly.

"—hardly surprising, after all, when you consider how she used to run around like a hoyden," murmured one voice.

"Did you ever meet the husband? College professor or something like that, I hear," said another, just as quietly.

"No, I didn't. They married in Boston, but I think they met here. He's some kind of scientist. Never came here together after the wedding—what does *that* tell you?"

An elaborate silence followed.

"I don't think Dorinda's got a photograph of him, at least

that I've seen in her parlor," another voice said thoughtfully. "Too bad. It might make it easier to see if there's any resemblance."

I felt suddenly hot, as if my eyeballs were shriveling in my head, and almost got up and left. I managed to grit my teeth for the next two hours though it was a near thing, especially when the afternoon ended with tea, cookies, and a handful of harpies vying to corner me near the tea urn.

"So lovely to have you visiting, dear! It's a pity your papa didn't come as well," said one of them. I recognized her voice from the group I'd been eavesdropping on.

"Since he was called to Washington, it wasn't possible for Ernest to come." Gran had come to my rescue. Had she overheard any of the unpleasant gossip too?

"Washington!"

"Commissioned a captain," Gran said sweetly. "We miss him, but duty is duty, after all. Emma dear, Josiah's waiting, and you know how he gets."

I was a model of demure American girlhood as we said good-bye till next week, and I quietly followed Gran and Helen out to the Pierce-Arrow. Once we were in the car, though, I exploded. "I can't believe that really happened. Those women are *poisonous*."

Helen sighed but didn't say anything.

"Well, aren't they?" I demanded.

"Emma—" Gran began.

"Did you hear what they were saying—or not saying, about my mother?" I slid down in the seat and covered my face with my hands. No wonder Dad never wanted to come here. He must have had some inkling of what was being said about her—and him. "She's dead," I said fiercely. "Why can't they just leave her alone? Gran, they're supposed to be your *friends*." My voice broke on that last word. "How can you stand them?"

"That's your grandmother's business, missy," Josiah said sternly.

"No, Josiah, Emma's question is a valid one." Gran sounded

tired as she turned around in her seat to look at me. "Believe me, right now I'm not proud to call them my friends. But I have to live here with them, which means I have to accept that at times they can be small-minded and cruel. I also know that if any trouble were to befall me, they'd be the first ones here with a hot meal or whatever other support they could offer. Good people can sometimes behave badly. It doesn't mean they're all bad."

We drove onto the ferry in silence. I stared at Josiah's hands on the steering wheel and wished I could drive, because right now I wanted to be anywhere but here—at home in Boston, say, or taking care of the wounded in Belgium. That would get me away from the horrid Red Cross harpies—except I wasn't allowed—

A sudden idea drove the thought of those women right out of mind. They wouldn't let me be a nurse, but if I could drive, then maybe I could get a job as an ambulance driver! If I could just get Josiah to teach me how…could I convince him? It was worth a try—*anything* to get away from the local Red Cross and do some real work was worth a try.

When we got back to the house, I dawdled behind when Gran and Helen went into the house, then pounced on Josiah when he came out of the barn after parking the Pierce-Arrow. I'd thought about trying to ease into my proposition with chit-chat and flattery, but guessed that would be the wrong approach to take with him.

"Josiah, will you teach me how to drive?"

He stood still and frowned at me. "Why?"

"Because I want to learn."

"I'd guessed that. Why?"

"Don't you think it's a useful skill for someone to have?"

"Emptying a mousetrap is one, too, but I don't see you asking me to teach you how to do that."

"Ha ha, very funny. I already know how. Josiah, please will you teach me? Then I can drive Gran places this summer so you can go fishing if you feel like it." I'd thought that up on the spot and was rather proud of it.

"What in? I wouldn't trust you in my machine."

I stifled my groan of frustration. "Josiah, *please*?"

"Not unless you tell me why."

There would be no getting around him, would there? "I want to learn to drive so I can apply to the Red Cross to be an ambulance driver, since they won't take me as a trainee nurse," I said, all in one breath.

He opened his mouth, closed it again, then took off his cap and scratched his head. "You want to go to Belgium, just to get away from the Mattaquason Ladies' Red Cross Committee?"

I felt myself flush. "That's not the only reason why."

He went and sat down on the wrought iron bench under the lilac hedge next to the barn. I followed and stood in front of him, willing him to say yes.

"And?" I finally asked when I couldn't stand it any longer.

He fetched a heavy sigh. "For all the fancy governesses you had growing up, didn't none of them teach you a lick of common sense?" He ignored my sputter of protest. "You can't be an ambulance driver for the same reason you can't be a nurse or pretty much anything else: you're too young and too pretty, and you're a girl, and this war is a man's business."

"Except when you need bandages and pajamas," I said bitterly. "So half of the human race gets to sit there and rot when we could be doing something useful, because the war is a 'man's business.' Why not just follow that argument to its logical conclusion and say that it's a man's world, and that women might as well just lie down and die once we've delivered our sock quotas?"

"What do you think would happen if they did let you go be a nurse or drive a damned ambulance?" he demanded. "You'd be in trouble in five minutes flat—"

"Because you men can't treat us like fellow human beings who just want to work alongside you for the same things," I shouted back. "It's not *fair*."

We stared at each other, me breathing hard. Josiah wore a strange expression—anger, but also sadness.

"You're right," he said in a quieter voice as he stood up. "Life isn't fair. I learned that myself at about your age. I'll teach you to drive if you want, Miss Emma. But you may as well get used to the fact that you won't never see Belgium, at least while the war's on."

He brushed past me and went into the house.

I was glad that I was already supposed to be going to the hotel on Saturday afternoon to give Maggie her dance lesson, or I would have had to find some other excuse to get away from Gran's house. No one was angry or cold or even the least bit stiff with me after what had happened yesterday; I was the one who felt awkward, though I still stood by everything I'd said to Josiah.

I was putting on my hat in the front hall mirror when the door knocker made me jump. I opened the door. George Osborn stood there, resplendent in a striped summer blazer.

"Hello, Emma. That was prompt," he said, taking off his straw boater and smiling at me.

I took the hat-pin out of my mouth and jabbed it into my hat. "Not really. I just happened to be by the door. I'm on my way out."

His smile faded. "But I've come to see how you're settling in."

Fortunately, Helen came down the stairs just then. "My cousin will be happy to tell you," I said quickly. "It was nice to see you, Mr. Osborn."

"Wait—it's George—" he began, but I whisked out the door and past his roadster parked in front. *Nothing* was going to keep me stuck in the house with George Osborn this afternoon.

Maggie was at the start of the hotel's drive when I got there, sitting atop one of the tall granite pillars and grinning down at me.

"How did you get up there?" I asked, since it was obviously expected.

"Malcolm figured out how to climb it when he was twelve. He showed me how, to annoy our sister. She's kind of bossy sometimes." She twisted around and launched herself off the pillar, landing like a cat in a patch of tall grass, much to the detriment of her frock.

Malcolm had mentioned his other sister. "Maybe she wasn't annoyed—just afraid you'd break your neck."

"Naw. You don't know Izzy." Maggie paused to pull up her sagging socks. "She'd have thought it only justice if one of us cracked our head open. Wanna try climbing it?"

"Maybe another time. This dress is new, and I don't want to tear it." Or show my underwear to the world as I tried to shinny up the rough stone.

She examined me critically. "Yeah. It's too pretty. C'mon."

To my disappointment, one of the new clerks, not Malcolm, was at the front desk when we came into the lobby. He pulled a hideous face at Maggie by way of greeting, which she cheerfully returned; then he saw me and turned bright red. I smiled sweetly at him and asked Maggie, "Um...isn't your brother here?"

"He went to the station to pick someone up. He does that a lot on weekends," she said offhandedly.

Of course he did. He had a job to do. I couldn't expect him to be hanging around waiting for me, could I? Besides, I was here to teach Maggie how to dance, not moon around after her brother. "So where shall we practice?"

She looked surprised. "Why, the ballroom, silly. I set up the Victrola in there."

We had it all to ourselves, for which I was grateful. I knew how to dance well enough but had realized that teaching it would be another matter completely. For one thing, I'd have to take the man's role and lead rather than follow my partner. At Miss Nutting's sister's school, I'd usually followed.

Maggie went to the Victrola, which she'd set up on the

orchestra dais. "Will you teach me how to tango?" she asked, waving a record at me.

"Why don't we start with something a little less ambitious?" I said. Besides, I didn't know the tango. I shuffled through the records.

"What about the Grizzly Bear? Or the Turkey Trot or the Duck Waddle? I like the name of that one." She was winding the Victrola energetically.

I wrinkled my nose. "No one does those any more. We'll try a one-step." I put a record on the Victrola and set the needle down. "Here—put your left hand near my right shoulder—like that—and take my other hand with your right." I held out my hand to her.

She reached out, then paused. "Your hands look like mine," she said slowly.

"Most people's do. Five fingers are the usual number—" I started to say, then stopped as she held her hands out for inspection.

I'd always thought my hands were—well, kind of weird. They were large and capable-looking rather than slender and dainty; the weird part was that the webbing between my fingers was much larger than usual, going partway up toward the first knuckles—which was the source of my dislike for wearing gloves. No one I'd met had hands like that: I'd paid attention during dance classes last year.

Maggie also had long fingers with deep webs, even deeper than mine. We both gazed down at hers, then at mine. Maybe it wasn't so uncommon after all. I smiled at her. "You're right, they do. Maybe we're related."

She drew in her breath and looked up at me. "I'll bet we are." She took my hand—and her eyes widened. "Emma?" she whispered.

"What is it, Maggie? Are you all right?" I peered down at her over our joined hands. She'd gone white, and her mouth was open. She stared me hard for the space of another several seconds.

"Maggie?" I said again.

Her mouth abruptly closed and she dropped her gaze to our hands once more. Then she shook her head and straightened her shoulders. "Umm, what is it I'm supposed to do with my other hand?"

I got her hands placed correctly. "You'll start with your right foot and go forward while I go backward, and we'll sort of dip sideways as we take four steps. But let me start the music again."

I went to the Victrola and moved the needle back, my thoughts racing. What had that been about? I glanced at her, but she'd folded her lips together and had a determined look on her face. Malcolm had said she could be a funny kid. But I liked her kind of funny. Some of the girls at the dancing school had brought younger siblings to watch, and many of them had been horrid, sniveling little brats. I doubted Maggie would ever snivel.

She was a quick learner. I put a different record on the Victrola and we practiced that one-step variation for a while, and then I taught her another so that she could start learning to read her partner's signals. We were working on the waltz when I heard a door gently shutting and turned. Malcolm stood next to the ballroom door, watching us. He wore a suit again today, and looked every inch the junior partner of a prosperous, upscale hotel.

"Let's show him," I said to Maggie, and swept her into a turn, then another as Malcolm applauded. I lengthened our stride so that we managed to finish our circuit of the room directly in front of him just as the music came to an end.

Maggie grinned at him. "Told you I was old enough to learn!" she shouted, and launched into the waltz again by herself, embracing an imaginary partner and swooping off into circles.

"You dance well," he said after we'd watched her for a minute. "I'm rusty as anything. I try to avoid it."

I remembered the girls on the beach the other day. "You

mean it's not part of your job to keep female guests happy by dancing with them on Saturday evenings? I would have thought that would be one of the amenities provided by the hotel."

He grimaced. "You're as bad as Maggie. Thank you for coming to teach her, by the way," he added in a lower voice when she circled closer. "She was over the moon about it. She doesn't have a lot of friends on the island—there aren't many her age here—and the girls at school don't always come up to her standards. She's kind of...different."

"Maybe that's why I like her. She sounds like me."

"Oh?"

I swallowed. "I'm 'kind of different' too. I never went to school. Dad brought me with him to the university when I was little, and the department secretaries used to take care of me. When I was older I had governesses—a new one every year, because Dad thought I'd learn better that way. So I never had a lot of friends either—a few girls who lived near us, and that was all. I'm just beginning to realize what I might have missed."

Malcolm was watching Maggie again. "Why didn't your father send you to school?"

"I'm not sure. He's always been protective of me—maybe because of my mother's dying. This is the first time I've been without him for more than a couple of days."

"You must miss him," he said gently.

"I do. But I'm also glad. Is that wrong? It's—I can't be his little girl forever, can I?"

I hadn't ever said any of this aloud but it was a relief to tell *someone*, though I wasn't sure why that someone was Malcolm. Except that I just felt so comfortable with him. I stole a look at his face. It was thoughtful.

"By the way," he said. "I talked to Captain Abbott about you today."

"What did he say?"

"He said that he was looking forward to meeting you. There's a visitors' day at the air station tomorrow. You ought to go."

"We're planning on it. Oh gosh, do you think he has a job for me?" That would mean I'd never have to deal with the awful Red Cross ladies again.

Malcolm hesitated. "He didn't say. But go. You never know what might happen."

"Oh, I will." I was so happy, I could barely keep myself from kissing him. And then blushed when I thought of actually doing so, so that I had to keep my face averted till I was sure my cheeks had cooled.

"There," Maggie said, galloping up to us as the record on the Victrola wound down. "Aren't I good, Malcolm?"

"Yes, because you didn't have a partner just now with feet for you to tread on. I'll bet Emma's are black and blue." He glanced at the door. "I should get back to work. Father will be wondering where I am."

Maggie grabbed his arm. "Malcolm, wait. Look at Emma's hands. They look just like ours. Show him, Emma."

I obediently held my hands out for his inspection. "I always thought mine were strange, but it seems they aren't all that uncommon."

He looked at them. Surprise flickered in his eyes. "Yes, I…see."

"But Malcolm—" Maggie began. He looked at her, and after a moment she closed her mouth and nodded.

"You keep doing that!" I blurted out. They both looked at me. "How do you manage to hold conversations without saying a word?"

Maggie looked puzzled. "Do we? I…well, I guess we do." She grinned. "It's just because Malcolm and Izzy are so bossy that I always know what they're going to say."

"If you weren't such a pest, we wouldn't have to be bossy," Malcolm said, looking down his nose at her.

They were joking now, but it was true. I was sure I'd felt something going between them just now—and I'd sensed it before, when I'd been here the other day. I wished I could be so close to someone that words weren't necessary between us. As close as my father and I were, he was too buried in his glaciers and outcrops. Maybe they spoke to him instead.

"Will you be at the air station tomorrow?" I asked Malcolm before he left.

He shook his head. "But I'll call in a day or two to see how it went. I could take you out for a row, weather permitting. I promised you one the day you arrived, remember?"

Malcolm in his favorite element. "I'd love to."

Maggie clutched at my arm. "Don't do it, Emma! He always throws me overboard when I go rowing with him."

He sighed. "Because you ask me to, Maggot."

"Not that time last summer when we were going to the picnic—"

"That time it was because you deserved it."

She made a face at him. "Go away. We girls are busy now."

I ended up staying for a visit with Maggie and Mrs. Galbraith and promising to come again the following weekend to practice dancing with Maggie. To my relief, Mrs. Galbraith didn't try to dissuade me as I half-feared she would; she seemed willing to accept that I'd enjoyed myself. And I had. I felt more cheerful than I had since—well, since Helen and I had come for tea here.

When I got home, there was no sign of George. Helen was on the side porch, reading a magazine. She put it down and examined me as I came up the steps. "Did you have a good time?"

I sank into the rocker next to her. "Yes. Did you? Did he take you driving?" I picked up her magazine and began to leaf through it.

"No. I wish he had. It might have taken his mind off having his feelings hurt."

I looked up at her; her tone had been distinctly icy. "Helen, what's wrong?"

"George was upset at how you ran out the door when he arrived to see you."

I couldn't help noticing she'd called him George, not Mr.

Osborn. That surely must be a good sign. "He didn't come to see me—he said he'd come to—"

"He came to see *you*, in case you haven't figured it out. All he wanted to talk about was you—for an entire hour and a half."

"Oh, Helen! I'm so sorry!" How awful—but I was still glad I hadn't been there. "It's dreadful that you had to sit through that. I ran out because I didn't want to be late, and besides, I thought that if I weren't around, he'd pay attention to you."

"It was a nice thought, but it didn't work." Her voice was still cold.

"I guess it didn't. I—" I looked down at my hands in my lap. My strange, Maggie-and-Malcolm hands. "I know it's not nice to say so, but I don't want him to like me."

"You like Malcolm Galbraith better."

I felt myself turn about six shades of pink. "Yes. But even if there were no Malcolm, I'd still wish I could undo whatever it is that makes him like me."

"A lot of it seems to be who your grandfather and uncle are."

"Which is just plain ridiculous."

"Not to George. His family may have money, but he wants to be associated with more than just that."

"So he fancies me because of my family." I pretended to pout. "And here I thought it was my exquisite face and witty yet profound conversation."

She snorted.

"Really, Helen," I went on. "I told you the other day that I want him to fall in love with you, and I meant it. I'll do anything I can to make that happen."

"Oh, Emma." Helen's voice had thawed. "You're a dear. I didn't mean to snap at you."

"You just wait, Helen. I'm going to find a way to make him like you before the summer is much older."

She sat back in her chair and started rocking again. A small smile played about the corners of her mouth. "I hope you do," she said.

·Chapter Ten·
Malcolm

I was mostly expecting it, but Maggie's *"MALCOLM!"* blasted inside my head like a steam whistle about ten seconds after Emma left the hotel. Something had happened while Emma was here—something to do with her hands.

A bare instant later, Maggie tore into the lobby like a small tornado. "Malcolm, we *gotta* talk! *Now!*"

Unfortunately for her, Father was standing right behind me at the front desk, just out of her view. He stepped forward. "Margaret, is the hotel on fire?"

She skidded to a halt. "N-no, sir."

"Then is there another reason for you to be shouting like this within walls?"

She looked at me desperately, and I could feel her whirl of thoughts—again, something to do with Emma's hands. Even in our human shapes Maggie and I could usually communicate thought-to-thought, as selkies did when wearing their skins, pretty well. But just now she was too excited to do more than project pure emotion.

"Please, Father—it's—it's urgent that I talk to Malcolm *right now,*" she managed to get out. Which was pretty good for her—when Maggie's over-wrought, she often can't manage more than stammered phrases. My little sister was growing up.

Father looked at his watch. "It is just before five. You know that the front desk will be busy until guests begin to go upstairs to dress for dinner and that I need Malcolm here until Elmer has had his supper and can take over."

Maggie opened her mouth to protest. I cut in before she could. "Later, Maggie. It can wait."

She gave me an agonized look. "No, it can't!"

Father frowned at her. "What is so important that you need Malcolm now?"

She gulped and began to sidle away. "Nothing. I—I'll talk to you later." Before he could say another word, she'd turned and fled out the door to the veranda.

He gazed after her in bemusement. "What was your sister so eager to discuss with you?"

"I'm not entirely sure," I said. After all, I wasn't, *entirely*.

"No?" He gave me a shrewd look.

I should have known he'd see through that reply. "I'd guess it's about Miss Verlaine, who was here to give her a dance lesson." I tried to sound as off-hand as possible. "If there's anything wrong, I'll tell you at once. But you know how dramatic Maggie likes to be. I expect she's just excited about learning to dance."

"Hmmph," he said, and went back into his office.

"Hmmph" summed it up for me, too. Yes, Maggie could be dramatic—but I'd rarely felt her get this agitated before. I wished I dared sneak out to find her, but I couldn't.

When our new clerk Elmer finally came back to take the desk at 6:10, I didn't bother stopping to change out of my suit but went directly outside to find my sister.

"*Maggie*," I called, and hoped she wasn't far.

"*Beach*," she answered.

I should have guessed.

I found her at our changing spot three-quarters of a mile from the hotel, sitting with her knees drawn up to her chin and arms clasped around them. When she saw me, she launched herself up like a released spring and threw herself at me. "Malcolm! Emma—her hands—I felt her! But how can she be one? It doesn't make any sense!"

"Maggie, calm down and tell me what happened," I said, trying to sound like Father.

She shook her head. "I'm calm. I'm—I'm—Malcolm, Emma's a selkie—I *know* she is!" She began to talk faster and faster. "She held out her hand and I saw what it looked like, and then she took mine and I could feel it—I could feel *her*. But I tried to talk to her and she couldn't hear me—"

"Whoa! Slow down." I sounded a lot calmer than I felt. "Tell me again what happened. Every detail."

Maggie shook her head in an agony of impatience. "I *told* you. You saw her hands. They're selkie hands. And when I touched her, I knew she was one of us."

Emma, a selkie? It was impossible. My parents had been acquainted with her mother, and they would have known if the Wetherells were selkies. Mrs. W., as much as I liked her, was certainly all human. And Professor Verlaine—from what Emma had told me, her father never went near the sea. There was no way Emma could be a selkie.

Still, I couldn't help the rush of excitement that flooded me. What if, somehow, Maggie was right? I ignored the fact that I was still wearing good clothes and sat down in the sand next to my sister. "But you couldn't talk to her in her mind."

"No, but..." She scowled, then sighed. "Why couldn't she hear me? She's a selkie, I know she is. I wish you'd touched her too—you woulda known she was. We've gotta go see her tomorrow. Or right now. You have to see—"

"I can't just walk up to Emma and grab her," I said, even though that was exactly what I wanted to do.

"Why not? This is—it's more important than anything!"

"Don't you think I know that?" I took a few deep breaths to calm myself. "Listen, Maggie. We have to be careful. Above all, we can't do anything strange that would frighten a human—"

"But she's not a human!"

"We have to assume she is until we know otherwise." I thought for a minute. "We have to be quiet about this. Don't say anything to Mother and Father. I work tomorrow and Monday, but after that I'll find a way to see Emma." When she looked mutinous, I added, "Don't you think I want to find out too?"

She didn't look happy, but nodded. "Do you like her?"

I almost pretended I didn't know what she meant, but this was too serious a matter to pretend to brush off. "Yeah, I do. I like her a lot."

That satisfied her. "And you promise you'll talk to her as soon as you can?"

"As soon as I can do it without being noticeable."

"All right." She sighed. "I like her too. I want her to be a selkie."

So do I, Maggie. So do I. I stood up. "We should get back to the hotel before we're late for dinner."

It was still mostly dark the next morning when I slipped out to go down to the beach, swinging my leather kit bag as I made my way down our private path to the sand. Most Sundays Father wanted me around in case departing guests needed to be driven to the station in Mattaquason, but today we had no departures until well after lunch, and only one of those needed a ride to the train. I could stay out on patrol as long as I wanted. I'd convinced him I was especially needed today because the air station would be busy with its visitors' day and we would be taking up the slack. It was a point of pride that Captain Abbott had come to trust us enough to ask us to cover for his men.

Thinking about the visitors' day made me think of Emma. She'd be there today, and unless I missed my guess would try to talk to Captain Abbott about getting a job on the station. I was almost certain of what his answer would be; I just hoped she wouldn't be too disappointed. But she needed to have the chance to ask. She was owed that much.

Oh, Emma. I hadn't slept well again last night, thinking

about her. Letting myself think about what would happen if it turned out she really were one of us. Did she already know it? Did she have a sealskin hidden away in one of those trunks I'd ferried to the island for her? I'd never met a blonde selkie before; would her sealskin be golden as well? I thought about swimming with her, showing her our home waters—

Damn it, why hadn't she been able to hear Maggie?

As I neared our changing spot, I thought I saw someone sitting in the sand just below it in the pre-dawn dimness and my steps slowed. A hotel guest out for an early morning constitutional? That happened sometimes, though not usually this far down the beach. When it did, it made getting out of the water after a swim in selkie form impossible. But a moment later I knew who it was.

"Morning, Izzy," I said as I came up to her, dropping my bag. "I didn't know you were patrolling today."

To my surprise, my sister ignored my use of the nickname she'd demanded years ago we stop using. "I'm not. I wanted to talk to you. Sit." She pointed at the sand next to her.

I sat, warily, and watched her as she fidgeted with her sealskin draped over her knees. Isabel never was one to expend any effort on such things as asking how anyone was or other polite inquiries. "Foolish human time-wasting," she called it, which hadn't made her popular at Mattaquason High School despite her good looks and might have had something to do with why she'd decided to turn her back on human life and return to the sea to live as a selkie. Her husband Muirfinn almost never took off his skin to walk on land. It had taken a lot of convincing to bring him to the hotel for their wedding, but Father had insisted they have both a human and a selkie joining.

"What did you want to talk about?" I finally asked. "I'm due out on patrol in a few—"

"Who is this girl I've heard about?" she demanded.

"What girl?"

She sighed irritably. "This human girl you're so smitten with. Maggie told me about her a few days ago."

All right, I wouldn't murder Maggie yet; she'd evidently told Izzy about Emma before we knew — er, suspected — what she might be. I thought about pretending not to know what she was talking about, but that wouldn't accomplish anything. "Are you talking about Emma Verlaine? What about her? She very kindly gave Maggie a dance lesson yesterday —"

"A *human*." Her voice dripped scorn. "I knew Father's sending you to college would be the ruin of you. I've tried to introduce you to any number of nice selkie girls who are willing to overlook the fact that you spend so much time on land. In fact, there's a friend of mine named Osla who wants to start helping with your patrols — she's lovely and dying to meet you."

I realized I was gritting my teeth. I un-grit them and said, "They'd better think twice about 'overlooking' how we live, because whomever I eventually marry is going to have to live this way as well. Our family are the ones who pretend to be human so that other selkies can stay in the sea and live as we always have without worry, remember? Are any of your nice selkie girls willing to do as Mother did when she married Father and live as a human most of the time?"

"But how could you sink so low as to fall for a *human*?

"You know what, Iz? Honestly, it isn't any of your business."

"Malcolm!"

"Don't 'Malcolm!' me. You may be my older sister, but we're both grown now. You don't have the right to intrude in my affairs any more than I do in yours. Do you see me scolding you and Muirfinn for not coming to see Mother and Father often enough, even though I know they'd like to see more of you? Now if you don't mind, I need to get ready to go on patrol. You're welcome to join us, if you'd like." I stood up and began to unbutton my shirt.

"Well!" She stood up too and glared at me. "Whatever else you learned at Harvard, it wasn't manners!"

Any number of retorts came to mind but I bit them back. She was still my sister, even if I sometimes wanted to pretend otherwise. "Come on, Izzy. You're just mad because you've gotten a taste for matchmaking since you introduced Iain and Seonag, and I'm not cooperating. I'll bet you'd like Emma if you met her."

She glowered at me for a moment longer before a reluctant smile tugged at one corner of her mouth. She was opinionated and didn't have much of a sense of humor, but she was usually fair, I would say that for her. "I hate it when you're right. All right, then, I'll meet her. But I still think you're wrong to fall in love with a human."

We don't know *that she's human,* I wanted to say but didn't. And wondered if she would notice that I didn't contradict the falling in love part. I finished undressing, folded my clothes into my bag, and picked up my skin. "Come patrol with us?" I invited again.

She shook her head. "Some other time. When shall I meet your human?"

I restrained myself. "Come to the dance at the hotel next Saturday. You can slip in and out for a little while, though I'm sure Mother would love it if you stayed overnight."

"We'll see." She walked with me down to the water, put on her skin, and was gone. Saying good-bye was not a selkie custom. I'd decided it was because we didn't have homes the way humans do—since the sea was home to all of us, farewells just didn't make sense. But it was an example of how different humans and selkies were—and just how divided I was between the two worlds, because I noticed the differences.

I waded a little further out and put my skin over my head and shoulders. There was that moment of in-betweenness, of shifting and rearranging, stretching and compression and an overall shiver, and then I fell into the water's embrace, in my other shape. I would never admit it to my sister, but I had missed this desperately when I was living in Cambridge—being able to put on my skin whenever I pleased and take seal form. I needed both of my worlds—there were things to enjoy in both. I could never understand why Izzy had so resolutely turned her back on one of them. Sometimes I wondered if Maggie would do the same, because I knew she was often unhappy at school. Maybe Emma's giving her dancing lessons and just being her friend would help her see that the human world wasn't all bad.

A second later, I felt someone—no, several someones—approaching. *"Malcolm!"*

"I'm here."

A few minutes later, we met—at least twenty selkies of all ages, though many of them were close to me in years. We touched noses as they clustered around me—fortunately, there was no sign of Izzy's latest protégée. *"Are we all here?"* I asked.

"Iomhair and Struan are not yet come," my friend Luthais said, butting his head into my side—the selkie equivalent of a human's friendly clap on the shoulder.

I returned his greeting. *"All right, we'll wait a little longer."*

"You can tell us about your new girl while we wait for them." He swam around and nipped playfully at my tail flippers.

I swatted him away just as playfully, but my heart sank. *"What new girl?"*

"This human your sister was talking about. The one you're in love with." He swam alongside me. *"Come on, Malcolm. Tell us about her."*

Unfortunately, it probably wasn't possible to kill Maggie twice for the same offence. But I could always try. *"And you're going to listen to my little sister about anything?"*

"'Twasn't Maggie who told us. It was Isabel," said another of my friends, Eachann.

Ah. No wonder she hadn't wanted to come on patrol just now. I surfaced to grab a breath, buying time to think of an evasive answer. Damn Izzy! I wasn't ready to talk about Emma yet—for a lot of reasons. To my relief, Iomhair, followed by Struan, shot into our midst just then, trailing apologies, and gave me an excuse to end the conversation. I waited until they'd been greeted, then rose to the air and slapped the surface with my tail to get everyone's attention.

"Since we're all finally here"—Iomhair and Struan

ostentatiously pretended to ignore me – "*then let's go. Those of you with regular routes can get started.*" Three-quarters of the group swam off in different directions, in pairs, to patrol their usual stretches of water, watching and especially listening for unfamiliar engine noises. "*The rest of you, I want to head further off-shore. Listen for U-boats, but also listen to what the whales are saying. They might have heard something in deeper waters.*" Now was the time humpback whales came to feed and raise their young in the fish-rich shallows off Cape Cod. I'd just thought a few days ago how we might enlist their help and was eager to see if we'd hear anything from them. I gave my remaining patrollers an area to target and watched them swim away.

"*And?*" Luthais had hung back to partner with me. We'd been friends since we were pups, but today I almost wished he'd gone with someone else.

"*And?*" I repeated. "*I thought we'd head off-shore as well to listen to the whales. I don't know if it's a completely crazy idea or not, but today seemed a good day to try it out.*"

"*That's not what I meant.*"

I knew that. "*What, Luthais?*"

"*What's going on with this human? Isabel said –*"

"*Isabel has no idea what she's talking about,*" I said, perhaps more sharply than I should have. "*She's never even laid eyes on Emma.*" I turned away with a flick of my tail and shot out toward open water.

Luthais was beside me in an instant. "*You're in love,*" he said accusingly.

"*What makes you think that?*"

"*Because I've never seen you get this way about a girl.*"

That gave me pause. "*Get what way? I've never even talked about her.*"

"*Don't be an idiot. How long have I known you? You think I can't feel the shape of your thoughts when you say her name?*"

Was I that obvious? I kept swimming. "*Maybe I am. I'm not sure yet,*" I finally said, because this was Luthais and I couldn't just tell him to mind his own damned business.

"*Enough to want to take her as your mate?*"

"*No one's said anything about that. I've barely gotten to know her.*" I paused, then said, "*But why not, in a couple of years?*"

"*Because...a human? Your family's important, Malcolm. Your father's one of our leaders; we trust him. You're following in his wake. You know the humans better than any of us ever have—I don't understand how you stood it, all those years living in a city—and we need you. But this—*" I could feel his doubt like a heavy, cold fog. "*If you're going to be one of our leaders someday, you can't be married to a human.*"

"*I don't see that it's anyone's business whom I marry,*" I said shortly.

Luthais knocked into me sideways. "*Idiot. Of course it's everyone's business. If you're married to a human, it will seem like you aren't one of us anymore. Some will think you've gone over to their side.*"

"*What? That's ridiculous.*"

"*I know that, but listen to me. There're those here and there who don't trust your family because you're posing as human—yes, I know you're doing it to protect us. But they don't understand that we need that protection—now more than ever, or we wouldn't be out here listening for their wretched engines. If they think you've gone over to the humans, it'll...*" He hesitated, then said, "*It will very possibly tear us apart.*"

I started to scoff, then stopped as an image of Izzy and her husband Muirfinn came into my mind's eye. He was probably one of those who mistrusted us—he'd married Izzy in spite of, rather than because of, her family, and only because he was so head-over-flippers in love with her that the entire selkie population around the Cape had snickered over it. If he thought I'd married a human, he would take Izzy and leave for Maine or Fundy rather than stay and be infected by humankind—and others might go with him. I bristled for a minute at the thought of anyone thinking of Emma as an infection, then sighed to myself. Father would be devastated to lose their trust.

"*And do you really think that you could be happy forever with a human?"* Luthais was still talking. *"It just doesn't work. It never has. I know you spend a lot of time at the hotel, but the heart of your life is still here in the sea. She'd never be able to share that with you, and you'll both be unhappy."*

But what if she could? I wished I could tell Luthais about our suspicions about Emma, but I couldn't. Not yet. Not till I knew.

·CHAPTER ELEVEN·

EMMA

Almost before lunch was over on Sunday I was looking at the clock, checking to see if it was time for us to go to the visitors' day at the air station. It was a cloudy day with rain threatening, so Josiah drove us. I expect he would have anyway, to guard Helen and me from the potential ravages of three hundred girl-starved young servicemen.

Actually, as we drove through the station's gates past saluting sentries, I couldn't help a small feeling of uneasiness. The boys on guard looked at us so intently that my heart sank a little. Josiah scowled at them.

"You'll crack the windshield if you keep making faces like that," Gran said. He scowled at her too, and she laughed. "The girls are perfectly safe. Don't be such a mother hen."

Josiah parked the Pierce-Arrow where a sailor directed him, and we joined the crowd of visitors gathering under the flagpole in a sort of square near a group of buildings that Malcolm had pointed out as the station offices the day we'd walked over here. A group of young ensigns waited there, accompanied by an older man in a dark blue double-breasted jacket with rows of gold braid around the cuffs, greeting visitors as they arrived.

I had to restrain myself from making a beeline for the older man; it *had* to be Captain Abbott. He was nice-looking, with laugh lines at the corners of his eyes and a firm jaw. Miss Ayers, my physiognomy-studying governess, would have thought him trustworthy.

"Welcome to the Monomoyick Naval Air Station," one of the ensigns said, elbowing his fellows out of the way to greet us.

"Are you an aviator?" Helen asked, wide-eyed.

"One of 'em," he replied. "So are the rest of these fellows." He indicated the group around him. "Though none of them are as good as me."

"Bite your tongue, Hutchinson," said another young man, grinning. "Who nearly banked into the observation balloon last week, coming in to land?"

"That was Ballard," the first ensign said imperturbably.

"Who conveniently isn't here to deny it," said another. "Good afternoon, ma'am," he said, taking off his hat to Gran. "Would your party like a tour of the station?"

Gran said yes, and after a brief squabble about seniority, two of the young men detached themselves and started to lead us away.

I looked back longingly over my shoulder. "Was that Captain Abbott?" I asked one of our guides.

"Yes, ma'am, that's the old man." He looked at me curiously.

"I'd...um...kind of hoped to meet him," I said.

"I'll make sure you do when we're done with the tour. I promise," he added gallantly.

I smiled at him. "Thank you, Mr. — er — "

"Ensign Gray, ma'am."

Ensign Gray and his fellow aviator, Ensign Hewitt, turned out to be very nice; not even Josiah, who watched them in suspicious silence throughout our tour, could complain about their conduct. They showed us the enormous hangar, big enough to comfortably house one of the station's two dirigibles, and the equally enormous seaplane hangar, answering our questions with good-humored patience. We saw large barracks for both enlisted men and officers, and at least a dozen other buildings, from a mess and recreation hall and a dispensary to a machine shop and a hydrogen-generating plant. There was also a huge storage tank for hydrogen for the dirigibles and observation balloons, one of which hovered several hundred feet above us, tethered to the ground. Ensign Hewitt explained that they'd worked hard to clear out the scrubby beach growth and plant grass over the base; it provided better footing for the dirigible crews and would not strike sparks or hold static electricity — important features when there was so much explosive hydrogen around.

True to his word, Ensign Gray steered us back toward the flagpole at the end of our tour. I could feel the mist turning the escaped ends of hair under my hat into a halo of undignified curls and wished we'd been able to meet Captain Abbott first thing, while my hair was still tidy.

The ensign caught the captain's eye. He immediately came over to us. "It's a pleasure to see you here, Mrs. Wetherell," he said to Gran.

"It's a pleasure to be able to see the work you're doing close up," Gran said politely. "I know the islanders are sleeping better knowing you're here."

I thought of Mr. Osborn and his supposed insomnia for the very same reason. But at that moment, I realized that the captain was looking from me to Helen with evident interest, and a small flock of butterflies took wing in my stomach. Malcolm *had* spoken to the captain about me — and he obviously remembered. I opened my mouth to say something — I wasn't sure what, but hoped it would be good — but Gran beat me to it.

"May I present Emma Verlaine and Helen Sutton, my granddaughter and great-niece? They're visiting me for the summer. Girls, this is Captain Abbott," she said.

"How do you do, captain? Your air station is fascinating," Helen said. "And terrifying. I can't imagine going up in one of the airships like these boys do."

He looked at her and hesitated, and I realized he wasn't sure if she were the grand-daughter or the great-niece. "Oh, I don't know, Helen. I wouldn't mind trying it," I said quickly. "If you ever give aerial tours to guests, sir, I'll sign up."

"Over my dead body," Josiah muttered from behind me. I ignored him; I was too busy hoping the captain had figured out which of us was which.

He had. "I applaud your bravery, Miss Verlaine. There are days when *I* wouldn't go up there, but I'm a deepwater man myself. I leave the aeronautics to my boys." He hesitated again as if about to say something else...and that was the moment the lowering clouds decided it was time to drop their watery burden on us.

Josiah swore and Helen squeaked in protest. Gran calmly raised the umbrella she'd been carrying.

Drat this rain! "Malcolm Galbraith said he'd spoken with you," I blurted out to the captain.

He nodded. "I hope we might have an opportunity to talk soon."

"Gosh, that would be great! When—"

But Gran had come to hold the umbrella over me, Helen crowding under it as well. "Come along, dear. Josiah's gone to start the car—rain makes it temperamental." She took my arm.

"I hope my hat isn't ruined," Helen fretted as we moved away from the captain in an awkward little huddle. I glanced back at him and saw that Ensign Gray was hurrying after us. I pulled away from Gran and waited for him. Maybe the captain had changed his mind and wanted to talk to me right now—

"Told you I'd make sure you talked to the Old Man," he said. "You owe me one."

"I *what?*" I said in what I hoped was my most quelling voice. Miss Gregson, governess number ten, had a wonderfully forbidding scolding tone that I did a spot-on imitation of.

"Sure you do. You have to promise me a dance at the Officers' Dance next Saturday. Will you be there?" He took off his cap and smiled at me, rain running down his hair and over his face.

I couldn't help it: I laughed. "All right, you horrid thing. I promise."

Naturally I was disappointed that I hadn't been able to *really* talk to Captain Abbott. But it had been a start. He knew who I was; the fact that he and Gran were acquainted could only help. Now I just had to figure out my next step.

I decided that a note would be the most direct and professional-appearing way to go, so I penned one reminding him of who I was and asking for a meeting. Gran had asked me to run an errand for her, so I'd stop at the little Monomoyick post office in the village and mail it.

Before I left, I went to Helen's room to invite her to join me, but she wasn't there. It was too bad—we hadn't had a chance to talk about the visit to the air station…or a lot of things, I realized. I'd cherished the hope that we could be—well, not sisters, because she already had two of those. But best friends, talking endlessly about everything that happened to us, the way I imagined girls at school did. Except we hadn't. I hoped I hadn't done anything to offend her.

The rain had stopped sometime during the night and it was a lovely, cool day, perfect for a walk. I went through the village, mailed my letter, and proceeded down a rutted lane to the isolated little cottage Gran had directed me to.

It was all weathered gray, built on a small sandy bluff above the beach. But there was a flower garden in front hinting at a riot of color to come in the summer, as well as neat rows of fledgling vegetables in a small fenced plot. Before I could knock, the door opened, and a white-haired woman in an apron and long brown dress stood looking at me. "Yes?" she said.

"Good afternoon, Mrs. Goslin," I said. Something about her seemed familiar. Had I met her already? At church, maybe? "I'm Dorinda Wetherell's granddaughter—"

"Yes, I thought you were. Come to pick up her shirtwaists, are ye? Come in, come in." She stood aside and motioned me in.

I hesitated, not wanting to have to put up with another

nasty-nice interrogation like the one I'd escaped from at the Red Cross meeting on Friday. But she didn't feel like those ladies with their glistening, avid eyes. I went in.

The cottage's main room also doubled as her work room. A large table strewn with pattern pieces and pins was drawn up under one window, and a sewing machine under another. Shelves held boxes overflowing with thread and ribbon, bolts of fabric, and cards of buttons. It was spotlessly clean, but other than the sewing supplies, almost bare of anything more than the most necessary furniture.

"Sit down while I get your waists. I'd just hung them up for a bit after pressing them, to let their lines fall into place," she commanded, whisking into the kitchen. There was a burr in her slightly creaky voice—Scottish, maybe?

"Thank you, Mrs. Gos—"

"Nobody calls me that. I'm Annie. Would ye like a cup of tea after your walk? I've just put the kettle on." She poked her head out the door again. "It's peppermint and spearmint, from my own plants. And the honey's from my own hives."

I suddenly remembered where I'd seen her before. "You were at the hotel last week, arranging flowers in the dining room," I said, taking a seat in a corner of the room that seemed to be set up as a sitting area—at least, there was a pair of Windsor chairs with a braided rug before them and a small table with a reading lamp.

She smiled. "Yes, that was me. I saw you too. Och, there's the kettle." She vanished back into the kitchen but kept on talking. "It was Mrs. Galbraith's idea to have me come in a few days a week to do the flowers, kind soul that she is. It's hard for seamstresses to make ends meet these days, what with all the ready-made clothes in the shops for people to buy."

"The flowers were beautiful, so I don't think it's a completely one-sided deal," I said.

She emerged from the kitchen carrying both a tray and a pair of white shirts on hangers suspended from her thin wrists. I jumped up to take the tray from her.

"Thank you, dearie. You've a kind soul yourself, I can see." Annie carried the shirts over to her worktable and started to wrap them in tissue paper.

I set the tray down and waited for her. "No, not really," I said. "I can be just as unkind as the next person, probably." The hideous Red Cross ladies came to mind. I could be *very* unkind to them, given the chance.

Her shoulders shook as she bent over her work. "Aye, well, you're an honest one, then. There you go; I hope your grandmother will be pleased." She brought the wrapped shirts to me. "Now, will ye pour for us, then?"

I poured the tea into the two mismatched cups, added honey as she directed, and handed her one. A heavenly scent of mint rose up as I lifted mine. "Oh, that's wonderful," I said, and took a sip.

"It was a good year for my mints. Other years havena been so good. I've seen enough of them, now."

"Have you always lived on the island?" I asked. I knew what I was getting myself into: I was probably about to hear her life story and then some. But I'd been lonely often enough growing up to recognize a fellow sufferer. Besides, I liked the sound of her voice.

"I wasna born here, as ye might have guessed." Her eyes twinkled very blue, like the ocean outside her cottage. "I married young and came here with Mr. Goslin. And that's about it. No children, because Mr. Goslin rejoined the Merchant Marines and disappeared a year later."

"I'm so sorry. Was...was he lost at sea?"

"Ye might say that...though I expect he found himself pretty quickly again in Rio or Caracas, the wee bastard!"

I choked on my tea. Annie laughed and leaned over to pound my back.

"And you decided to stay here rather than return home?" I asked when I could talk.

"*This* was home. I was better off here as a widow—well, a grass widow, anyway—than I was back in Aberdeen. Too many people there, pressing all around me. My neighbors here don't expect me to live in their pockets or try to live in mine. Though I do enjoy a cup of tea with a visitor I like." She lifted her cup to me. "And besides, I have my protector." She nodded at a shelf near the door. To my surprise there was a large, pearl-handled revolver there, resting on a stand.

"Good heavens! Can you shoot that thing?"

"Well enough to keep the groundhogs out my garden. I feel safer, knowing it's there. There's plenty of oddities about, even on this wee island. Up at the hotel, for one thing, when I do the flowers. Some of the guests..." She shook her head. "I prefer the oddities you see in nature. I've looked out my kitchen window and seen lightning storms that make ye want to hide under your bed, if they weren't so beautiful, and shooting stars that light up the whole sky. I've seen waterspouts out to sea, and prayed they wouldn't come any closer. I've seen whales puffing and blowing or even jumping out of the water, though I can't imagine why they'd want to do that."

"Neither can I. What about seals? Do they do odd things too?"

She smiled. "Seals? Aye. They do odd things, especially when they're not seals."

"When is a seal not a seal? It sounds like a riddle."

"When they're selkies, of course. Haven' ye no heard of selkies? I was surprised to see them here when I came; I knew of them from home though I'd never seen one—you don't, living in the city." She must have seen my puzzlement, for she continued, "They're seals sometimes, and live in the sea. But they can take off their skins and walk on land, just like you or me. As I said, they live in the seas around Scotland and Ireland. But they're here too. Some must have come over here at some time from the old country."

I blinked. Magical beings? That was unexpected. "And you've seen them here? How do you know that a seal is a selkie...or that a selkie isn't just a person?"

"Ye can't always tell if a seal is a selkie. But I've seen them often enough when the moon is full, come up on the beach to take off their skins and dance together in the moonlight —"

I laughed. "You've *seen* that?"

"I told you I've seen odd things here, didn't I?" she said, unperturbed.

"Maybe you just saw people from the village..."

"Our village? Och, I canna see the ladies from the Congregational church havin' *that* interesting a social life."

I laughed, but examined her while taking a long sip of tea. She wasn't trying to pull my leg, as far as I could tell. I didn't think she had that kind of sense of humor. "Do...do selkies always live as seals? Or do some of them live on land?"

"A few do...that is, I expect that they do." She bent to lift the teapot. "More tea?" She refilled my cup and hers, and began to speak of her garden again.

I got up to leave not long after. Annie came out with me to say goodbye. "And ye'll come again to see me, won't ye?"

"I will," I said. "I want to hear more about the selkies. I love the seals here and the way they follow boats around. Malcolm Galbraith says they're nosy."

"Aye, he'd know." When I looked at her, she said, "Well, he's out in that boat of his often enough. I see him rowing by almost daily."

"I suppose you would." From here in her garden you could see the *Never Late* chugging across the channel as well as fishing boats coming in and out of Mattaquason's little harbor. "Captain Abbott down at the air station should appoint you to observation duty here to look out for Germans."

"That's what he has his station for." Annie's mouth tightened. "I'd rather see ten waterspouts than a U-boat any day."

I would too. Waterspouts didn't carry guns and bombs. "I'd rather see a selkie," I said, to lighten the moment. "Isn't the moon almost full? I should go down to the beach at Gran's and look for them."

"I wouldn't do that, dearie. They like their privacy, same as anyone." Her dried-apple face was unsmiling.

The moon *was* full the next night. I went out onto the front porch with Gran and Helen to watch it rise, since all the blackout curtains were already drawn.

"Next month we'll go to the hotel," Gran said. "You can watch it come up out of the water from their veranda. I'm surprised Mr. Galbraith doesn't schedule dances around the full moons. They'd be a boost to business."

"That would be romantic," Helen said.

I thought about watching the moon rise from a chair on the hotel's enormous porch...maybe with Malcolm. That *would* be romantic...

I didn't linger, though. I had a letter from Dad to reply to. Poor thing, he was sounding pretty forlorn now that the bustle of settling into his new job was past...and of course, he missed me. I missed him too, but I think I was probably enjoying myself more than he was.

So I wrote him a long, chatty letter, telling him all about the air station and the seaplanes and dirigibles and my visit to Annie—especially the story of her wayward husband and the tales of the selkies she'd told me. I didn't say much about Malcolm, though I had mentioned him in other letters I'd sent. I couldn't write about him without feeling dreadfully self-conscious, and I didn't want Dad to get the wrong idea. Not that there was anything to get the wrong idea about, but *still*. The air station and Annie were much more likely to make him smile than moonlight and Malcolm.

I finished Dad's letter and got ready for bed, sneaking a quick look out of the edge of my blackout curtain. The cool moonlight illuminated the lawn and the beach beyond it so invitingly that I was tempted to go down for a walk. Maybe the dancing selkies Annie had told me about would invite me to join them. The thought made me smile. I changed into my nightie, got into bed, turned off the lamp, and went to sleep.

It was hardly surprising that I dreamed that I had indeed gone out into the moonlight to find the selkies dancing on the beach. It was one of those dreams where you know you're dreaming, and yet you can't—or won't—stop. I couldn't have stopped this one if I wanted to, though; I had to hurry, or they wouldn't wait for me. The night and the moon were too delicious to wait for anyone.

But instead of flitting to the beach behind the house, in my dream I set out down the road. Somehow I knew that the selkies would be on the other side of the island, facing the open ocean. I wished they weren't—the shell fragments of the road, glowing preternaturally white in the moonlight, were much less kind to my bare feet than the grass of Gran's lawn would have been.

All was clear and sharp as I hurried down the road: I could see the gingerbread trim along the tall, pointed front gable of the Hammetts' house almost as plainly as day. I could cut through the Milleys' yard a bit farther down, then across the—

"Emma?"

Who said that? I frowned; this was not how my dream should go. I kept going without even bothering to turn to see who it was.

"Emma!"

Wait—I did know that voice. I turned. Ah, it was perfect for Malcolm to be in my dream—hadn't I been thinking about him and moonlight? I smiled at him. "Do you want to come with me? We need to hurry—they're waiting for us."

"Emma, wake up. You're dreaming."

"What?" Something wasn't right...and then the world seemed to slip sideways, and— "M-Malcolm," I stuttered.

He was looking at me with his brow furrowed, a flashlight in one hand, and I realized that I was feeling bits of shell pressing into my cold bare feet because they really were. I was here, really *here*, in the middle of the moon-drenched road.

I'd been sleepwalking.

I stared at him, too shocked to speak. He turned off his flashlight, stuck it in his pocket, and held out his hands to me. I took them because I couldn't think of what else to do. His hands closed over mine—and he drew in a sharp breath.

"Wh—what is it?" Even in my befuddled state I could sense the sudden, almost electrical tension thrumming through him as he gripped my hands hard—and harder.

"Emma," he said, and then he let go and put his arms around me and pulled me hard against him. "Oh, Emma," he murmured into my hair. "It's all right. Everything's all right."

Without consulting me, my body relaxed into his. It evidently knew what I needed better than I did, and right now, I needed to be held and told that everything was all right.

In a few minutes, it actually *was* all right. I felt safe and…and content, like I could stand there for hours, no matter how cold my feet were, because the rest of me felt so warm and cherished. I buried my face against his neck and felt the pulse there, beating hard and fast, and breathed in the scent of his skin and hoped he wouldn't move.

He didn't. If anything, he held me tighter. It wasn't until my conscience pricked at me—I standing in the middle of the road, in the middle of the night, in my nightgown, being hugged by a boy—that I reluctantly lifted my head and backed away an inch or two.

"Thank you," I mumbled. I felt a lot better, but I wasn't sure that I could look him in the eye yet. "I can't believe I sleepwalked."

"I don't think it's something anyone has much control over." He sounded calm—unsurprised, almost.

"I know, but I've never done anything like it before." I thought sleepwalking was one of those things that only happened in Miss Blunt's juicier novels. "What are you doing out here, anyway?"

"Filling in on blackout watch for a friend. Not that there's a lot of need for it on a night like this. You gave me a bit of a shock, I'll admit." There was a smile in his voice. "I thought you were a ghost, and I wasn't sure what the correct procedure was for accosting spirits."

"You'll have to ask Captain Abbott," I said, and suddenly shivered.

He took off his jacket and put it over my shoulders. "Come on. Let's get you home before you freeze."

"I'm not really cold," I said, but didn't argue when he put his arm around me and began to lead me back up the road.

"It must have been quite a dream," he said after a moment. "Or was it a nightmare? You didn't seem scared, though."

"No, not a nightmare. It was—" I paused. He wouldn't laugh at me, would he? "I dreamed I had to go to the beach to dance with the selkies. They were waiting for me."

He almost stopped walking. "Selkies," he said after a moment. "Where did you hear about them?"

"I had tea with Annie Goslin yesterday. She told me that they come onto the beach on the night of the full moon to take off their sealskins and dance. It must have stuck in my mind—I was writing to my father before I went to bed and told him some of her stories to cheer him up. I've never had such a vivid dream before. I was so *sure* I could feel them calling me. I can't explain—"

"You don't have to." He gave my shoulders a squeeze.

"But what if you hadn't stopped me?"

"You'd have woken up eventually. Probably as soon as you left the road and walked into a tree."

He sounded cheerful and sensible...but I don't think I would have walked into a tree. I'd seen everything so clearly— the trim on Hammetts' house, the white road, *him*. Thank heavens he'd found me—but what if it happened again and he wasn't there to stop me? Would I go all the way to the beach? Would I have sense enough not to keep right on going into the water?

"Anyway, you've saved me a trip again," he was saying. "I was going to stop by in the morning and see if you wanted to try a swim in the next day or two. Tomorrow, if you're up for it—I have a couple of hours free before—"

"Yes."

I swear I could *hear* him smile. "That was a quick answer. I'll be over around ten, then. Well, here we are."

We were at the bottom of Gran's drive. I slid Malcolm's jacket off and gave it to him. "Thank you," I whispered. It wouldn't do to wake anyone right now. "Um…I'd rather my grandmother didn't know about this."

"I won't say a word." He looked down at me, and I felt uncertain again. "I'm glad I was there to find you," he added, and reached out and touched my cheek. His fingers were warm. "Don't worry. Everything will be all right."

We stood there staring at each other, and I felt myself leaning into his touch. He leaned closer too…and then drew back.

"I'll see you in the morning," he said, and turned away, heading back down the road the way we came. I watched him until my cold feet drove me back into the house.

It took me a long time to fall back asleep again when I regained my bed. I was almost afraid to sleep: what if I tried to get to the beach again? Beyond that, I wasn't sure which had me more agitated, the sleepwalking or Malcolm.

Everything will be all right, he'd said in that assured way of his. I wished I could take some of that assurance for myself. I felt anything but that, about everything. Including him.

What was a girl supposed to do when she liked a boy and thought maybe he liked her too? Miss Blunt's novels would have me swooning in Malcolm's presence, falling into his arms like…like a limp dishrag. But I had no interest in being a limp dishrag. When I went into his arms, I was going to go there under my own power and of my own free will, thank you very much. And I certainly would not be doing any swooning; I didn't want to miss a second of it. Tonight didn't count; that had been a comforting hug, not a passionate one. I wondered what a passionate one would be like, and lay awake longer, trying to imagine it.

·Chapter Twelve·
Malcolm

Walking away from Emma was one of the more difficult things I've ever done.

Thank the gods I'd been out to make sure my patrollers had actually gone out to patrol; they hadn't been happy about missing a dancing night, and I'd had to swear on my skin that they would have the next moon off before they'd agreed to go tonight. I'd been on my way home to grab a few hours of sleep when I'd found Emma in the middle of the road.

It was true: she was a selkie. I'd felt it as soon as our hands touched — the sense of kin, the feeling of belonging. No wonder Maggie had been practically incoherent with excitement.

A selkie. I wanted to shout my jubilation to the moon. Emma was a selkie.

A selkie who didn't know she was one. She'd had no idea why she'd wanted to be on the beach tonight, but she must have felt the excitement that always buzzed among us on the night of the full moon and had to follow it, even in her sleep. Funny that she'd felt that, when she hadn't heard my calling directly into her mind when I held her.

Emma was a selkie.

When I got back to the hotel, I avoided the front door and skirted the south wing so that I could get to our apartment without having to explain to the night desk clerk where I'd been.

I had to talk to my parents, but they were out—gone to one of the gatherings on the beaches to see and be seen, if anyone needed them. So I settled on our private section of porch to wait for them and stared up at the moon. Gods, Emma had felt good in my arms. I'd wanted to hold her tight against me so that I could feel every warm inch of her, head to toe...but also to soothe away her confusion and fear. I had to do *something* to help her find out what she was, so that she wouldn't have to suffer that again.

Mother and Father got back about an hour later; I heard them coming up the path and stood to greet them.

"Malcolm!" my mother said, pausing on the porch stairs. "Shouldn't you be asleep? You have early morning patrol duty, don't you?"

"Yes. But something's come up. Father?" I took a breath. "Your counsel is sought, *mo triath*."

I'd addressed him as a selkie elder because that was the tradition. But Mother was just as respected as he, and I'd need her help just as much, if not more.

"Oh. Oh dear." Mother sat down in the rocker next to me. "What happened, Malcolm? Are you all right?"

"What counsel do you seek, *mo mac*?" Father said, in the old ritual way.

"I'm fine." And then I couldn't help it: I jumped up and started to pace. "Everything's wonderful, in fact." I turned and faced them, grinning. "It's just that I've found out that Emma Verlaine is a selkie."

Mother drew in a sharp breath.

"How do you know this?" Father asked.

I told them about Maggie and about what had happened tonight. "We're not the only ones," I added. "The seals knew as soon as they saw her. They kept saying *she like us, she like us*. I thought they meant she was fond them. But that's not what they meant at all."

My parents looked at each other. I could feel the speech flying between them but kept my attention respectfully focused elsewhere. Then Father said with a frown, "I do not understand how can this be. Where is she from? We've met her mother and her father. Neither was one of us."

"Perhaps we were wrong," Mother said slowly. "Malcolm, you were too young to be aware of it at the time, but there was…gossip in town about Emma's mother."

"What about her?" Gossip was the number-one pastime of the ladies of Mattaquason.

Her eyes went distant, remembering. "She was enough younger than me that we weren't more than acquaintances. She used to spend the summers here while her husband was away — he's some kind of scientist, if I remember rightly. She became pregnant, and some of the busier bodies in town counted months and had a great deal to say about the fact that he hadn't been visiting at the correct time and wondered whose baby she was carrying. She shook her head. "I have to wonder if the gossips weren't right after all."

"You think that Emma's father was a selkie?"

"He would have to be," she said simply.

Then it made sense for her to be what she was. "I don't think she knows it, though — what she is. She couldn't hear me when I tried to reach out to her. At least, she didn't seem to."

"That doesn't surprise me, if she's been brought up as a human by her father — by the man she knows as her father, that is," she amended. "She doesn't know how to listen inside as well as out. Or it could be that as a half-breed, she lacks that ability."

"It could be that as a half-breed, she will not need to be told what she is. If she does not have a skin, she will never be a true selkie," Father said.

The thought of Emma being half selkie yet unable to claim that side of herself was too painful, so I shoved it aside. Did she have a sealskin? If so, where was it? Should I just come out and ask her, "say, you weren't born covered in fur, were you?" Somehow I couldn't see that working very well.

"If Malcolm could tell she is selkie, then my guess is that she was born with one," Mother said, and I wanted to hug her.

"What might have happened to her skin if she's been raised human? Her father—you don't think he destroyed it, do you?" The very thought made me feel ill. "And even if he didn't, he must have realized that there was something different about her. How could he deny her what was hers? It would be like taking away half of someone."

"We don't know that he did anything of the sort," Father said mildly. "This skin of hers is just conjecture, Malcolm."

"No, we don't know," Mother said, then sighed. "Pride, I expect. Do you think any man wants to admit that his wife's child is not his? And maybe some guilt, too, for having left his wife alone when she must have needed him. Dorinda Wetherell told me he's almost smothered the girl with love and attention and barely lets her out of his sight. He could have sent her off to boarding school or left her to her grandmother to bring up."

"That might have been better for her," I muttered.

We were all quiet for a minute. "I have to talk to her," I finally said. "To *tell* her. If she does have a sealskin, then she should be allowed to decide whether to use it. As it is now, the man she thinks is her father chose for her. She has to be told what she is sooner or later, because what happened tonight will only happen again. What if I hadn't been there and she'd gone to the beach by herself?"

"One of us would have taken care of her," he said calmly.

That didn't make me feel better in the least as I thought of Emma in her thin cotton nightgown. Some of my friends couldn't be trusted around anything female, much less someone as lovely as Emma, and I was damned if I wanted one of them "taking care" of her. "I'd rather that didn't happen. She'd be terrified."

"Would she? I did not get the feeling Miss Verlaine was made of such weak stuff."

"Well, no, she isn't. That's not the point, though. She needs to know what she is!"

"No, Malcolm," Mother put in. "Right now, *you* need her to know what she is."

I opened my mouth to argue, then closed it. They were too good at saying just the right things to make me stop and think.

Was I twisting my desire for her to know into hers?

Well, maybe I was, a bit. But that still didn't mean she shouldn't know. "I still don't see why I can't tell her."

"You have no right to do so," Father said. "She is not bound to you in any way."

"But—"

He held up his hand. "Telling her is up to Professor Verlaine, as her father."

"He's not her father." How many times did I have to say that?

Father sighed. "But *she* thinks he is, Malcolm. Are you prepared to tell her that he isn't?"

"But it's the truth."

"In this case, the truth would hurt even more deeply than a lie, if it is not handled with sensitivity." I paced back and forth some more. "You're the one who said she's strong," I said stiffly, coming to stand in front of him.

"So I did. But this isn't just a matter of strength."

"Malcolm, please be careful with her," Mother said. "You're so intense—and this will all be very strange and unexpected to her. She may be strong, but she's also young and vulnerable. And what if she doesn't believe you? What proof do you have?"

Father nodded. "Listen to your mother. If you wish to hear my counsel, my son, it is this: wait and watch, if you want to help Miss Verlaine. And she will need your help. Keep your wants in check, for her sake." He looked at me sternly. "This will be her trial to face, not yours. Do not try to take it away from her."

"I'd happily take it from her, if it will save her pain!"

"She won't thank you for it. I say again: if you want to help her, let her find out in her own way…and if you have feelings for her, be waiting for her at the end."

That shut me up, of course—how did he know that I had "feelings" for Emma? "Thank you, *mo triath*, for your words of counsel," I said, bowing formally to him and Mother. They bent their head in acknowledgment. But I think they knew I wasn't convinced that they were right.

"Get some sleep," Mother said gently. "You need be up again shortly."

"Yeah, I will. Good night," I said, and went inside.

Oh, Emma. I was desperate to tell her that she wasn't alone any more, that she'd found where she belonged. The question was, how? I needed to know her better, to get her to trust me. After that it would be easy, I was sure.

I was able to snatch an hour or so of sleep before patrolling and before I went to swim with Emma. She seemed subdued when I arrived; I chatted on the porch for a minute with Mrs. Wetherell but examined her out of the corner of my eye. Then Emma's cousin appeared, staggering beneath a beach chair, umbrella, and bag of towels.

"Good morning, Mr. Galbraith," she cooed. "We're all ready for our swim! It's so kind of you to come with us!"

Damnation! Why did she have to tag along? I'd been looking forward to a quiet time with Emma, maybe finding an opportunity to talk...but I wouldn't get one now. There wasn't much I could do about it, so I relieved her of her burdens and we set out across the lawn.

"Are you all right?" I managed to ask Emma quietly just before we fell into single file on the path to the beach.

She nodded. "A little...um, embarrassed."

"Don't be."

Helen glanced over her shoulder at us. I was afraid she would start asking questions, but she didn't open her mouth again till we were on the beach. I set up the chair and umbrella for her and tried not to stare as Emma took off her robe. She looked mighty fine in a bathing suit; I was glad I'd be climbing into the concealing water in a moment.

"How cold do you think the water is?" Helen asked, taking off her robe and tying her hair up in a kerchief. I saw that Emma was looking at her with an odd expression, but couldn't see why.

"Why don't we go find out? Race you," she said to me, and darted down to the water's edge.

Helen followed us more slowly. At the first touch of water on her feet, she gasped. "Oh, jes — um, jeepers! It's icy!"

Emma waded right in. "It's a little cool. No worse than some of the lakes in New Hampshire I've swum in."

"Better you than me." Helen shivered elaborately. "I think I'll sit on the beach and watch."

Emma grinned at me. "See? I told you I'm not a softie."

I tried not to think about just how soft she'd felt in my arms last night. "I never said you were."

"Well, you two are welcome to it. Maybe it will warm up a little by August." Helen turned and swayed back up to the chair under the umbrella, glancing back at us once or twice to see if we — or I — were watching.

I was, but only to make sure she was out of earshot. When I was sure she was, I turned back to Emma. "Are you sure you're all right after last night?"

She gave me a sweet smile. "I'm fine. It took me a while to go back to sleep, but that's all."

"Hardly surprising." I waded further in, and she kept pace with me. "I'll say again what I said last night: everything will be all right."

"I think everything *is* all right." She pushed through the water till it came to her chest, then fell back into it. Her feet promptly bobbed up in front of her. "Oh, that's nice — gosh, salt water *is* different, isn't it? I'm a lot more buoyant. Swimming is going to be a breeze."

It was time to get serious. "Yes, you're more buoyant. But there are things like riptides to deal with that you don't have in lakes. Show me what strokes you know."

She showed me her breast-stroke and side-stroke, then

flipped around for the back-stroke. "This is heaven!" she exclaimed after she'd come up from a dive underwater. The fine ends of hair that had escaped her braid stuck to her cheeks. "And to think I'll be able to do this all summer long!"

I reached out and peeled the strands of hair from her face. I couldn't help myself—I had to touch her. "Sure you can, after you get a little stronger. Can you do the Trudgen?" I demonstrated the over-arm, crawling stroke.

She was frowning when I swam back to her. "I never learned that one. How do you—oh!" She drew in her breath, and I realized she was staring past me.

I turned. Half a dozen sleek seal heads bobbed in the water not twenty feet away, watching us—*her*—with deep interest. I glanced at them again, to make sure there were just seals there. I didn't put it past Luthais or any of my friends not to try to sneak in for a look at Emma, but no, it was just seals.

"It's all right—they won't hurt you," I said, going to move between her and them. If they got too excited, I'd have to shoo them off.

She put a restraining hand on my shoulder. "I know they won't." They regarded each other across the short stretch of water. "They're bigger than they look from a boat. Will they come closer? Hello, you. Have you come to say hello?" she called softly.

I wanted to hug her—that was my brave girl! "Do you want them to?"

"Oh, yes," she breathed.

"*Emma!*"

We turned. Helen stood at the water's edge, shading her eyes and staring at us.

Emma waved and turned back to me. "Can you imagine what it would be like to swim with them? They *dance* in the water. I wish I could do that. I don't want to frighten them, though—no!" she said, sounding anguished. "Come back!"

The seals had disappeared, spooked by Helen's call.

"Emma!" Helen shouted again. "Are you all right?"

Emma ignored her. "I wanted to go to them. Would they have let me?"

She looked so woebegone that I held my hands out to her, just under the surface. She took them as if it were the most natural thing in the world to do. I began to swim backwards, pulling her along. "They might have," I said. They would have, like a shot. "But I don't think it would have been a good idea yet."

"Yet? Then maybe I can, one day?"

"One day," I said. "I promise." I'd gotten a brilliant idea, thanks to the seals.

Helen didn't wait till we were on shore but started scolding while we were still waist-deep. "My goodness, Emma! Are you all right? Those seals were so close—I thought they were about to attack you!"

"As I wasn't wearing mackerel cologne, I don't think it was a concern," she said airily. I smothered a grin.

Helen wouldn't be mollified. "Those are wild animals! I don't like you swimming anywhere near them. George says—"

I stiffened. "What does he say?"

For some reason, Helen reddened. "He says they're sea vermin and should be cleaned out of the waters here. I don't know about that, but Emma, it gave me such a turn to see them so close to you!"

"They weren't really all that close." She took Helen's arm. "It just looked that way from here on shore."

"You're dripping on me!" Helen detached herself with a little grimace of disgust. "Oh, please be careful. I was terrified!"

This was getting to be too much. "No harm will ever come to Emma while I'm here," I interjected.

"Oh, I'm sure." She gave me a saccharine smile. "But if Emma were ever swimming alone…promise me you won't ever go in the water by yourself!"

"Don't be silly, Helen. May I have a towel, please?"

Helen pulled one from the bag, still fluttering and exclaiming. Emma dried her face, then spread the towel in the sand and stretched out on it. I threw myself down next to her, enjoying the view. She'd be sleek and brown as a seal by the end of summer if we kept this up. The thought of it made me want to lean over and kiss her.

"So when will you give me my first lesson?" she asked after a few minutes' companionable silence.

I thought for a moment. "Sunday? I'll need to help get ready for the dance on Saturday—"

"That's right, the dance! I can't wait!" Helen put in. "Won't that be fun, Emma?"

"I'll have to rearrange Maggie's dance lesson, if Saturday is busy for you," Emma said, then brightened. "Maybe I could do it Friday instead? The Red Cross won't miss me, and I can't disappoint Maggie."

Helen looked shocked. "Miss the Red Cross meeting? Aunt Dorinda won't like it."

Emma gave me a sideways grimace. I guessed that the weekly Red Cross meeting wasn't much to her taste.

We sat until Helen began to worry about freckles. I pulled on my old canvas trousers and shirt, and Emma wrapped her loveliness away in her robe.

"Did you like that?" I asked her as we walked up the beach behind Helen. Time to put my brilliant idea into play.

She swung the bag of towels and made a face at me. "It was horrible. Couldn't you tell how I was suffering?"

"I thought so. Would you care for more agony tomorrow in the form of a row with me?"

Her eyes lit up, but she said, "What, no desk duty?"

"The clerks are trained enough, so I'll have a bit more free time from now on," I said, hoping it was true.

"And you promise that you won't push me overboard like Maggie?"

I laughed. "I told you—I only do that when she deserves it. Or asks for it."

"I'll keep that in mind. Yes, I'd love to go for a row with you."

We arranged that she'd meet me at the *Never Late* dock at two, and I left her and Helen at the porch steps. I waited till I was out of sight of the house, then broke into a runout of sheer exuberance. Yes! Tomorrow would be my chance to let the seals start explaining to Emma just what she was.

·CHAPTER THIRTEEN·

EMMA

The next day was warm enough that I wished we were going swimming again instead of out in Malcolm's dory. Yesterday had been wonderful; the water was like swimming in champagne, I'd felt so light and cool. And the seals! If only Helen hadn't scared them away. Maybe when Malcolm gave me my first swimming lesson on Sunday, they would come back.

And I would get to see Malcolm in his bathing suit again. Miss Ayers and I hadn't restricted ourselves to examining just the portraits at the Museum of Fine Arts. I'd had plenty of time to admire the statues of athletes in the Classical Greek rooms; Malcolm would not have looked amiss among them.

Helen had looked spectacular in her suit as well. It had given me a bit of a shock to see how she'd altered it so that it outlined her breasts and waist with a great deal more exactitude than it had in the shop. It was a pity George hadn't been there; he'd have made an appreciative audience. Then again, I was glad he hadn't been.

I was more than a little wilted by the time I had stopped at the post office to mail *another* note to Captain Abbott, then walked to the *Never Late*'s dock. I felt even more wilted when I found not Malcolm waiting for me there, but George and the *Fast Lady*.

"Hello, Emma!" He beamed at me. "Were you going into

Mattaquason? I'd be happy to bring you—we could stop for an ice cream, maybe—"

"Hullo, George." I'd given up calling him Mr. Osborn; he only made a fuss when I did. "Thank you, but I'm not here to catch the ferry." Out of the corner of my eye I saw Malcolm rowing up to the dock, thank goodness. "I know Helen would love to go out in your boat, though." I edged away from him.

He followed me, drat him. "But it's such a nice day—" Then he caught sight of Malcolm tying up at the dock and his smile froze.

"Do stop by my grandmother's—I don't think Helen had any plans for today," I called as I hurried past him to let Malcolm help me into the stern of the dory.

He untied it and stepped lightly in before it could drift away, sitting in the middle seat facing me, and took up his oars. "Are you sure you wouldn't have preferred a spin around the island in Osborn's boat?" he asked in a low voice.

I glanced back at the dock to make sure we couldn't be overheard; George still stood there glaring at us, arms folded on his chest. "Bite your tongue. Those motorboats are smelly."

"And their owners?"

"Miss Ayers told me never to generalize," I said primly. Which was pretty funny now that I thought about it, coming from someone obsessed with reading character from portraits in museums.

He raised one eyebrow at me, and I laughed.

We didn't talk much after that: he was intent on his oars, and I was busy watching him. I could see why he loved rowing so much: there was an inherent music in the actions, a rhythmic pulsing between water and air as the oars moved in and out, forward and back. It would be easy to get lost in that rhythm, once one was expert enough, so that it became a sort of meditation, like some of my governess Miss Nutting's yogic exercises that she'd showed me.

A seaplane flew low over us, scattering my thoughts. I waved at it and it dipped its wings so that I could see the grinning pilot. He flashed us a salute and then climbed upwards into the milky-blue sky.

"It's funny—it didn't take me very long to get used to them," I commented. Living as close as we did to the air station meant getting used to the buzzing whine of seaplanes flying low over us as they took off for patrol or came in to land. It had been more difficult to adjust to the great, ghostly dirigibles, which appeared overhead without warning, blocking the sun.

"You'd never get me up in one of those," he commented.

"Really? I thought all young men wanted to fly."

"I can fly quite well down here." He bent to his oars, sending us skimming across the water.

"They can fly underwater." I nodded back to the small group of seals that had quickly found us, trailing behind. They'd taken turns swimming beneath us in the clear green water, gliding like birds on the wing.

"They do interest you, don't they?" Malcolm asked after a moment's silence.

"I led a sheltered childhood." I grinned. "Yes, they do. I'm a city girl, remember? Being so close to wild animals living free— it's still rather like a fairy story to me. And besides, they're so *adorable*."

He laughed, and we rowed for a few minutes more in comfortable silence. We were quite a way from shore now, off the ocean side of the island. I could see the roof and chimneys of the hotel, looking like a doll's village from here.

"I don't think I've ever used the word 'adorable' in a sentence that wasn't meant to be ironic," he said eventually. "But I am...fond of them too. Would you like to see something?"

"Yes!" I sat up straighter.

Malcolm brought the oars to rest on the sides of the dory— or rather, the gunwales; he had corrected me earlier—and reached over till he could touch the surface of the water. He slapped it three or four times with the flat of his hand, then sat back and waited.

A seal head appeared next to us, then another. Eventually

there were five or six of them, barely an arm's length away, regarding us with their usual inquiring air.

I stared. "How did you do that?"

"They—well, they're sort of pets, in a way. I grew up here, after all." He leaned over and held his hand out. One of the seals rubbed against it like a cat.

Oh...! "Did you train them to do that?"

"No need to whisper—you won't spook them. And no, they didn't need training. They're...friends." The other seals took turns touching their noses to his hand or rubbing against it like the first. It was so sweet—those faces! But also moving; these were wild animals, showing their trust and affection for a human.

"Could—could I—" I couldn't finish, but he nodded. I leaned down and held my hand over the side of the boat, hardly daring to breathe. All the heads promptly vanished.

"Oh, no." I slumped on my seat.

"Wait," he said softly.

I continued to hold my hand out. Below us in the clear water the seals swam in tight circles, staring up at us. Then one surfaced a few feet away, and another. I held my breath, and one of them darted forward, just touching its wet snout to my hand. I managed not to flinch at the sudden move but waited, and then another came up more slowly, examining both my hand and me. Whatever it saw must have satisfied it, for it butted my hand slightly then rubbed its cheek against it.

"You're grinning from ear to ear," Malcolm murmured.

"I know. It's—it's amazing. Hello, mister," I crooned as another seal rubbed against my hand and let me pet its sleek head. "You have very handsome whiskers, you know."

"They use them to sense their surroundings, just as land animals do. They're extremely sensitive to movement."

"How do you know that?" Three or four of them now clustered next to us, trying to reach me. "Wait a minute, you silly things! Here!" I shifted in my seat so that I could reach out to them with both hands. They rubbed against them, shoving their heads under my palms, clearly asking for caresses. "I can't believe this!"

"I can," Malcolm said behind me, so quietly that I almost didn't hear him beneath the splashing water and soft whooshing sounds that the seals made. I half sat up and turned to him. There was something in his eyes — an expression I couldn't quite decipher — though it was making me very aware of his closeness.

"You're getting all wet," he said.

I glanced down; my front was quite thoroughly soaked. Eek! I hoped my brassiere wasn't showing through the white cotton of my middy blouse. "Oh dear. That's enough, everyone. Next time let's do this when I'm in the water with you."

"They'd love that." The seals were circling the boat, still chuffing and making small moaning noises. "Easy, friends," he said to them, and then said something else I couldn't quite hear. They looked at us for a few seconds more, longingly, then ducked their dark heads under the water and were gone.

"What did you say to them?" I asked.

"Nothing," he said, and picked up his oars once more.

He rowed for the better part of half an hour without saying much, which suited me; I was still bemused by the seals' behavior. Who knew that they were so — so *companionable*, like a dog or a cat?

"They aren't always like that, are they?" I asked. "With just anyone?"

"No. Never. You're a…" He took a stroke, then another. "…an exception. Emma…" He hesitated. "I wouldn't talk about it. Other people wouldn't understand."

I thought of Josiah's violent dislike of seals and George's calling them "sea vermin." "I won't," I said. "And thank you. For trusting me enough to show them to me."

The oars slowed. "There's a lot more I'd like to show you," he said.

We looked at each other for a long moment, and I desperately wished I could lean over and take his face in my hands and press my lips against his. I'd been thinking about what it might be like to kiss him for a while now; every interaction we had seemed to draw us closer. I took a deep breath. Something in his eyes said that he would not mind if I did kiss him, and I began to bend toward him—

The sudden sputter and hum of a starting engine made us both look up. I saw a boat maybe fifty feet away, quickly accelerating away from us. With a sinking heart I realized it was the *Fast Lady*.

Malcolm swore. I would have liked to as well, but didn't know any words bad enough to relieve my feelings. Had George really been spying on us? How long had he been there? We'd been so absorbed that we might not have noticed him approach; he'd evidently turned off his motor and drifted toward us on the tide.

"I'm sorry," I said. "I can't help feeling a little responsible for that."

"You're not responsible for Osborn's bad manners," Malcolm said, his expression grim. Then he sighed and gave me a small smile. "It's too bad that cormorants aren't as friendly as seals, or I'd buy the flock that lives near the docks in Mattaquason a bushel of herring and encourage them to roost on his boat."

The image that brought to mind—George's boat plastered with great, smelly streaks of cormorant droppings—made me giggle. "Can't you ask the seals to ask them?"

He smiled. "I suppose I could try."

My feet seemed barely to touch the road as Malcolm walked me home from our row. We paused at the bottom of the drive.

"Will you save me a dance or two on Saturday?" he asked.

I pretended to look surprised. "Why, yes—but I thought you said you avoided dancing?"

He grinned. "And you're completely incorrigible."

"Oh, not *completely*."

"That's open to debate." His grin softened. "I'll see you on Saturday, if not before."

Before sounded good to me. I watched him walk away then started up the porch stairs. The sound of digging over by the side of the house made me pause, though, and I went to see if Gran was there, to let her know that I was home.

It wasn't Gran. It was Josiah, jacket off and sleeves rolled up, shoveling evil-smelling compost between the rows of his enormous vegetable garden. He stopped when he saw me. "Afternoon, Miss Emma."

"Hello, Josiah. Er, I was looking for Gran."

"She's gone up town to play bridge." The curl of his lip left me in no doubt of his opinion of this activity. "I'll be picking her up 'round half past four."

"Oh." I wished he wouldn't look at me the way he always did—as if he were trying to see my mother rather than me. "I think I'll just go down to the beach for a minute. I think we left a towel down there yesterday."

He nodded and went back to his work. I sidled past him and down to the beach. The towel I'd invented on the spot was not there but Helen's chair was, so I sat in it and thought about Malcolm. And George. Avoiding him had seemed like a reasonable course of action to take, but today showed that it wasn't good enough. I would have to do something about him; the only question was what. Oh, why couldn't he have decided to like Helen rather than me? Life would have been ever so much simpler. I would have to tell him, kindly but firmly, that we could never be more than cordial acquaintances—and the sooner I did so, the better.

A buzzy hum made me look up. A seaplane—the same one that we'd seen earlier today?—flew past low, parallel to the shore. It was probably coming in for a landing; they preferred to land on our side of the island, where the seas were calmer than the ocean side. When I looked again at the beach in front of me, I saw that I wasn't alone: three seals were at the edge of the water, erect on their front flippers. Their eyes were fixed on me.

My heart began to beat faster. Were they some of the seals who'd followed us in the boat today? I rose and took a step toward them, then another. "Hello, friends," I said. "Have we met?"

One of them made a soft groaning sound and inchwormed a few feet up the beach toward me. Its two companions followed suit. I walked slowly toward them, holding my hands out. For a second I was uncertain—if only Malcolm were here! But the seals' eyes, anxious and longing, told me that they meant me no harm.

"You really *do* like me," I said. They wiggled closer, their whiskered faces turned up to me. Only another few feet—

"*Hey!*"

The shout made me jump. I turned. Josiah was running down the beach toward me, waving his spade. When he reached me, he grabbed my arm and yanked me up the sand, away from the water's edge. "What the hell are you doing?" he roared.

I heard splashes as the seals made for deeper water and knew that in a few seconds, they would be gone. *No, don't leave!* part of me cried. The rest of me, however, was too busy being furious to watch them leave. I wrenched my arm out of Josiah's grasp. "What are *you* doing?" I yelled at him. "Everything was fine till you came lumbering down here!"

Josiah planted his spade in the sand and loomed over me "Leave those damned seals alone! You and your mother—Laura was just as bad, and look where it got her. I told Professor Verlaine this was a bad idea—"

At the mention of my parents, my anger turned to ice. And curiosity. "When did you talk to my father? How do you even know him? And what did my mother have to do with seals?"

"Never you mind!"

"No. You aren't going to bluster your way out of this. What are you talking about?"

He crossed his arms on his chest and thrust his chin out. "Isn't none of your business."

"It wasn't, until you brought it up. Fine, don't tell me. But don't expect me to take any of your 'warnings' about seals seriously, either, until you do."

That got him. He dropped his crossed arms and gave me a stricken look. "Now see here, Miss Emma—"

I gave him my frostiest look and did not reply. It was like watching a balloon deflate. "I can't say a word," he said, swallowing hard. "I promised."

"Then I guess we don't have anything more to discuss." I turned away from him and, casting one last look at the empty water, stalked back up to the house.

Despite spending all day Thursday knitting a pair of fingerless mittens in addition to my weekly pair of socks, Gran did not let me skip Friday's Red Cross meeting. That meant I also had to endure being in the car with Josiah. I was careful to stare out the side window of the car the entire trip into town to avoid catching his eye in the mirror.

I was still trying to figure out what our argument yesterday had been about. What could seals have to do with my mother? And what about Dad, and why had they spoken about me?

Helen was quiet in the car, too. I hadn't seen much of her in the last few days; she had been out most of Thursday while I feverishly knitted in the window seat in my room—the porch being out of the question as Josiah had been working in the garden again.

"Where were you yesterday?" I asked her when we were established at the church hall with our stacks of bed shoe pieces to assemble. "I hope George took you out for a spree or something."

To my surprise Helen flushed. "Emma, shush!" she hissed under her breath.

"I'm just teasing," I said quickly.

"You should know how easily gossip can start."

Yes, I did. Especially here.

I glanced around us, wondering when it would begin — the whispers about me and my paternity — and caught Gran's eye. She was at the table next to us cutting out pattern pieces and gave me a faint nod. I sighed and relaxed. With her there, no one would be gossiping about us — at least on this side of the room.

I moved my chair a little closer to Helen's. "I'm sorry. About George, I mean. I've been trying to keep out of his way, and when I do see him I always try to talk about you —"

Helen's head stayed bent over her sewing. "It's all right, Emma."

"I wish I could do more." I hesitated. "Helen, are you *sure* that you like him? He seems...I don't know."

She was silent for the space of three or four stitches. "Yes, I'm sure," she finally said. "He's quite...sweet, really, though he doesn't like to show it. You can imagine, with his upbringing, that it's not a side of himself he lets many people see."

I thought of his parents. "I suppose...but he actually followed me and Malcolm in his boat when we were out rowing the other day. That's not a *healthy* way to behave."

"He thinks he's in love with you. When he sees you so clearly prefer Malcolm, it hurts his vanity. He's awfully sensitive about his father not being old money, and about not having gone to the right schools and everything, and he can't help thinking that's why you don't like him."

"That's ridiculous! It's nothing to do with that!"

She shrugged. "You have to feel sorry for him, really."

Just then someone came to drop off more bed shoe pieces, and we fell silent. What Helen said made sense, but it wasn't going to change anything. I *was* going to have to do something about him.

And I was going to have to do something to get away from these cursed meetings. I know the dance on Saturday was supposed to be a social event, but I would definitely buttonhole Captain Abbott there and *finally* talk to him about a job at the air station.

·CHAPTER FOURTEEN·
MALCOLM

If I'd had any doubts about how busy the summer was going to be, they were brutally murdered on Saturday. If this was what May was like, where would we be in July?

Saturday is turnover day: in most cases it's when guests arrive for week-long (or more) stays and, logically, leave when their stays are over. That means we're busy as the dickens with picking guests up at the train station, checking them in and getting them settled into their rooms and into the hotel in general at the same time that we're checking other guests out with just the right air of efficient regret so that they're convinced we'll personally miss them until their next visits and driving them to the train station, after making sure they're given the correct packed lunches they've ordered for the journey. Plus dealing with all the incoming and outgoing baggage, answering questions, taking reservations for the tennis courts, answering the phone…

This morning, Father and I and two clerks were on the go from half past seven onwards—and not only with the arrivals and departures, but with the dance as well. Fortunately Mother was mostly overseeing that, but we still had plenty to do about it around the edges, including my making two trips to the train station just to transport the orchestra from Boston along with their instruments. I was one hundred percent on the job, being

welcoming and friendly and efficient, the perfect junior host...
though it might be more accurate to say I was ninety-nine
percent there, because a small part of me was thinking about the
fact that I would see Emma tonight.

By six-fifteen, the lobby had calmed. Everyone who was
supposed to leave had left, and most of those set to arrive had
done so and were either eating dinner in the dining room or
taking trays in their rooms, resting before tonight's dance. I was
wandering the room, thinking about Emma and generally
tidying up — most of the front staff were finishing setting up in
the ballroom — when someone came sidling in from the front
door, looking nervously around. He wore a pale blue satin
lady's dressing gown, and nothing else. Then he saw me and
hurried over. "Malcolm!"

"Tam!" I took his arm and fast-walked him toward the door
to our apartment by the front desk — which was fortuitously
empty as I'd just let Gus, the clerk on duty right now, sneak
outside for five minutes to have a cigarette. I whisked Tam
through the door and stood in front of it, leaving it half open so
that I could keep an eye on things. "What is it?"

Of course, most selkies don't have human clothes — why
should they? But with the start of our patrols, I'd set up caches
of human clothes at a few places on the beach in case a patroller
had to come up to the hotel to speak to me. I'd used items from
our lost-and-found closet that had never been claimed, which
for obvious reasons included a lot of nightwear. Poor Tam had
no idea that his choice was perhaps not the best one.

"Malcolm," he whispered, when we were safely out of the
lobby. "U-boats. We heard them."

I tensed. "Where? How many?"

"South. Down near the humans' air sta — "

"Is someone following them?" I'd already started to loosen
my tie.

"Yes, three went to see. We weren't sure if there were two
of them or three. I came to tell you. That is what you wanted us
to do, yes?"

"Yes, it is. Good job." I lifted my hand to clap him on the shoulder, then stopped; it's not a gesture that selkies use or understand. "Go back down off the beach and listen and wait for them. I'll be down shortly, after I talk to Father. Here, come this way—it's quicker."

He looked relieved that he wouldn't have to go through the hotel again and let me lead him through our rooms to our private door. I directed him to keep out of sight of the dining room windows, shrugging off my coat as I went, then went to find my father.

Of course as soon as I went back out into the lobby, I met a group of guests at the desk waiting to reserve a tennis court for the next morning on their way into dinner. I ignored their raised eyebrows at my jacketless and tieless state and got them their court. My father emerged from the dining room as they entered it; he greeted them, caught sight of me, and frowned.

"I know, I know," I said as he came up to me. "I'm sorry. Emergency—I need to go find the patrols. Will you call Captain Abbott for me?"

He nodded and headed back to his office. "Which codes?"

Father and I, along with the captain, had created a sort of code to use when we had to telephone each other about patrol matters but didn't want to say anything to rouse the interest of the operators. It consisted of innocuous phrases that stood for things like U-boats seen, directions, distances, and actions.

I trailed after him. "Umm...'multiple U-boats detected' and 'south' and 'off shore.' And 'please investigate' and 'will report.'"

"Very well." He paused in the doorway. "And next time, Malcolm, please keep your clothes on until you're outside the hotel."

I concealed a smile. Good thing he hadn't seen Tam. "Yes, sir."

Ten minutes later, I was jogging down the beach to our thicket. As I ran, I heard the buzzing sound of first one, then another, sea plane climbing into the sky. Good; Father had gotten through to Captain Abbott. Five minutes more, and I was wading into the water, pulling on my skin.

"Malcolm!"

Luthais! We touched noses, then began swimming away from shore, heading south toward the air station. *"What happened?"* I asked. *"I got here as soon as I could."*

"Two U-boats. Struan and I saw them both, and Aodh and Màiri did as well. It was...odd. They were both moving atop the water, with their tops — "

"Towers. Conning towers." I put in.

"Yes — their towers out in the air, where anyone could see them."

"Where were they? Where did they appear to be going?"

"Off shore, not all that far from the humans' air station. They didn't seem to be going anywhere in particular — just meandering around. Could they have been looking for something?"

"I don't know. Were there men outside on the towers, holding things up to their faces and looking through them?"

"No."

Hmm. So no reconnaissance of the beaches. What had they been up to?

Luthais caught my thought. *"If you ask me, it felt...wrong. Like they were trying to be seen by the humans. But why would they want that?"*

"I don't know." I slowed. What were those devils doing? U-boats wouldn't be out just joy-riding; operating on the other side of an ocean from their bases was a dangerous undertaking. There had to be something —

Luthais and I heard it at the same time: the metallic whine of a U-boat's propellers, but to the north above Monomoyick, off the mainland...and miles from the air station in the opposite direction.

We looked at each other and swore. *That* was what the U-boats down near the station had been doing: drawing attention to themselves, so a third U-boat could do...something.

I made a quick decision. *"Go after it. I'll go back and warn the station."*

"No, wait." Luthais hovered, listening. *"I'll go if you want,"* he finally said. *"But I don't think we'll learn much. It's going east, back into the ocean."*

I listened to the receding, thrumming whine; he was right. Damnation! *"Then it's done what it came to do,"* I said glumly.

"Maybe." I could feel his annoyance. *"Or maybe it was a test so see how closely the humans are watching."*

But I knew we were both sure that something had happened—and we'd missed it. *"I'm going to go back to talk to Captain Abbott anyway,"* I finally said. *"He needs to know about this."*

"I am sorry, Malcolm."

"It's not your fault. You all did the right thing. But maybe we need to consider that future U-boat sightings might be diversionary and have plans in place in case." Which would mean trying to train my patrollers to become strategy analysts, when a number of them were just going on patrols for the fun of it.

I left Luthais and made my way back to the beach and to the hotel, threw a sweater over my wrinkled shirt and trousers, and took the Marmon down to the air station; walking would take too long. On the way I passed knots of ensigns and younger officers, hair combed and shoes polished, walking up-island. The dance, of course—curse it, it must be nearly seven-thirty. I would be late, and Emma...but I couldn't think about that right now. Still, I found myself pressing a little harder on the accelerator.

Father had phoned ahead for me, and the guards at the gate waved me in without more than a brief pause, though they did look at me curiously. They were getting suspicious of my frequent visits, I suspected. Another thing to worry about.

Captain Abbott himself opened his office door to me and locked it behind us. "What happened?" he asked.

I told him about the U-boats with their conning towers above water, not even trying to hide, and the U-boat to the north, feeling about two inches tall. He leaned back in his chair, hands steepled in front of his chin, staring fixedly at nothing.

"You're right," he finally said. "Clearly a diversionary tactic. They've pulled one over on us, for sure."

Make that one inch tall. "I wish I could have gotten there faster. I *should* have gotten there faster."

He fixed me with a stern look. "Stop beating yourself up. You did what you could. Without you and your patrols, we wouldn't know anything had happened. As it is, now we know we have to be on our guard."

That was true. But it didn't make me feel any better. "What do you think they were doing?"

He stood up and went to the window. "I wish I knew. It might have been a test, or it might have been something more. There's no way for us to know now." He hesitated for a moment, then said, "You should know that there was some grumbling when I sent those planes up. No one understood why I was doing it until after they spotted the U-boats— and afterward, they wanted to know how I'd known where to send them."

"Were they able to bomb any of them?"

His silence answered me. I slumped back in my seat. "So not even a hit to make it worthwhile. We worried about this— how you were going to explain knowing about U-boats if none of your own people had spotted them."

"I know. It's a risk I was willing to take—and continue taking," he said calmly.

"What do we do about it? And another thing—I'm afraid your people at the gate are wondering why I'm here so frequently."

"That's *my* concern, young man. Just keep doing the job you're doing. I'll say it again: if it weren't for you selkies, we wouldn't know about the third U-boat. Information like what you can bring us is worth a great deal."

"Not that knowing about it did any good."

"Let me be the judge of that." He smiled. "And that's an order."

I sighed. "Yes, sir. Will we see you at the dance tonight?"

"I don't think so. I've talked to the submarine chasing station up in Provincetown and want to be around in case they call back. But you should be getting back to help your father. Is there anything else I should know about while you're here?"

I thought for a moment. "Just one. Do you remember my telling you about Emma Verlaine coming to ask you for a job?"

He chuckled. "How could I forget? I think she's written to me twice a week since the beginning of the month, wanting to set up a time to see me, but I've been just too busy. She's a very determined young lady."

I smiled to myself. Oh, Emma. "When you do finally see her—I know what you'll say about her working on the station. But something else has happened. If things go the way I'm planning, she may be joining my patrols."

He looked startled. "Joining your—you mean, she's...?"

I nodded. "We haven't discussed it yet, but I'm hoping we will soon."

"I see." I could tell that he would have liked to ask about the situation but was refraining. "Thank you for telling me. It will make refusing her, er, request for employment a little easier." He stood up, so I did too.

"Thank you for seeing me, sir. And—I'm sorry."

He clapped me on the shoulder as he walked me to the door. "Nothing to be sorry for. Keep up the reports—and let me worry about how we use them, all right?"

But it was still going to bother me. We'd missed something—I was sure of it. What had the Germans been trying to do—or was it, as the captain suggested, just a feint to see how vigilant the air station was? I needed to talk to my patrollers; while they'd done a good job reporting on the U-boats off the air station, they should not all have then gone down to look for them and left the rest of the shore unguarded. Even I had fallen into that trap.

I wouldn't let it happen again.

·CHAPTER FIFTEEN·
EMMA

I couldn't help gasping when we entered the ballroom at the hotel for Saturday's dance. Great sprays of dark blue irises, red roses, and white carnations seemed to be everywhere, interspersed with American flags and swags of bunting in honor of the air station officers who would be in attendance tonight.

"It looks like the Fourth of July!" I said.

"The Fourth is ten times fancier." Maggie had appeared as soon as we walked in, looking much tidier than I'd seen her before. "You can't move without banging into something red, white, and blue. Annie Goslin has fun with it."

"Annie did this?"

"Yup. You look nice," she added, looking me up and down. "I'm going to get me a frock just like that when I'm grown up."

"You'll probably have one much prettier. Are you dancing tonight?"

Maggie looked glum. "No. I have to leave at nine-thirty and go to bed. I might as well ask for a bottle and to have my diaper changed. And we didn't even get to practice today."

I carefully didn't laugh. "I'm sorry we missed this week's lesson. Maybe when you're out of school we can have them on a day other than Saturday. No dancing on the veranda?" I gestured toward the French doors along the ocean side of the room. They were covered with blackout curtains, jarring with the cheerful lights and flowers within.

"Can't. At least, we can't leave the doors open. But sometimes people go out there to dance 'cause you can still hear the music just fine." She grinned. "Or they go out there to—you know. Canoodle and stuff in the dark."

"We're under strict orders not to canoodle, ma'am." A pair of young men in uniform were beside us. I recognized two of the ensigns we'd met at the Open House on Sunday.

"Good evening, Miss Verlaine. I'm here to collect on my debt," one of them said to me. It was Ensign Gray, who'd arranged for me to talk to Captain Abbott.

"Good evening, Mr. Gray. I always pay my debts." I took his offered hand and let him lead me onto the dance floor. "If this is Officer's Night, is Captain Abbott here?"

"Not tonight. He was going to, but something came up. Poor bas—um, poor chap never seems to get a break. I'll stay a lowly ensign, thank you."

Drat! There went my plan to talk to the captain. But I couldn't take that out on Mr. Gray. "You ensigns are as lowly as roosters on a fence. You forget—I saw all of you crowing about your flying escapades at Visitors' Day."

He laughed. "You've got us pegged, Miss Verlaine. The only thing we like as much as flying is talking about flying."

I thought again of the laughing young men in South Station, and the one I was dancing with, and my throat felt tight. All these young men, so full of life and high spirits...and who knew if they'd be alive six months from now.

While we danced, I tried not to be obvious about scanning the room for Malcolm. I didn't see him among the crowd, which seemed odd. Mr. and Mrs. Galbraith were much in evidence, greeting people; I would have expected him to be doing the same.

As if my thought had summoned him, he appeared a moment later. His hair was wet as if he'd just bathed, and he was adjusting his tie. I saw him go over to speak with Gran, and as soon as my dance with Mr. Gray was over, I made a beeline for them. Malcolm immediately claimed me for the next dance and led me out to the floor. My heart beat a little faster as he drew me to him, and I thought of the night he'd found me sleepwalking.

"I'm sorry I'm late," he said after a moment. "I'm lucky your dance card isn't already full."

"Flatterer. Is everything all right, or were you just avoiding having to dance?"

"Guilty as charged. But then I remembered you'd be here and could be trusted not to step on my toes if we danced. I hate having my toes trodden on."

"I know. You're such a delicate flower—you and the Harvard crew team."

He smiled and swept me into a series of dizzying turns, which was heavenly. But his smile felt forced, and there was a distance in his eyes. Was there something wrong? I wanted desperately to ask him if I could help—but even more desperately not to have him brush me off. So I concentrated on sending him good feelings, as Miss Nutting would have suggested, since I didn't know him well enough to intrude on what might be a private matter. It made me feel like I was doing *something* for him.

At the end of the dance he was about to escort me back to Gran when a pretty, dark-haired young woman in a somewhat out-of-date lavender crepe dress approached us. "Malcolm, wait," she called.

I braced myself; it was probably another hotel guest, come to claim a dance with the innkeeper's dreamy son. That seemed to be corroborated by Malcolm's just barely audible sigh. I was surprised when he stopped and said, "Hello, Izzy. Glad you could make it."

She halted in front of us. To my further astonishment she was looking at me, not him. "Introduce us," she demanded.

He sighed again. "Emma, this is my sister Isabel. Izzy, this is Emma Verlaine."

His sister! I gave her a wide smile, though she wasn't

precisely radiating friendliness. "How do you do, Mrs., er..."
Malcolm had said she was married, hadn't he?

"Isabel will do." She held out her hand. A little surprised, I
took it. To my further surprise, rather than letting it go after a
brief shake, she actually stared down at it for a few seconds
before releasing it. "Hmm. Do you like the island, Miss
Verlaine?"

From behind his sister's shoulder, Malcolm grimaced at me,
the wretched boy. I didn't dare acknowledge that I'd seen him.
"I do, thank you. I've always wanted to stay with my grandmother, and it's lovely here."

"It's better than the city, isn't it?" Why was she looking at
me so intently?

"Umm—"

"Izzy, you're being a pest." Malcolm had circled around to
stand beside me.

"I am not," she said, unperturbed. "I would simply like to
know if she likes the island better than the city."

I was suddenly reminded of Miss Johnson, who had been
governess number eight for two unpleasant weeks before Dad
had politely shuffled her into a job at the university library, and
put into action the one useful lesson she'd taught me during her
short tenure; when confronted by a crank, say whatever you
have to in order to get them to leave you alone. "Oh, I do," I
said, my voice practically oozing sincerity. "Without a doubt."

The effect was all I could have wanted. Isabel's stern
countenance relaxed into a smile, and I realized she was quite
astonishingly lovely. "Good," she said. "How long are you
staying?"

"I...I'm not sure. My father intends for me to go to college
come fall—"

She leaned forward and put a hand on my arm. "Don't.
College *ruined* Malcolm."

Malcolm snorted. "Thanks so much, dear sister." His tone
softened. "Though I wouldn't mind it a bit if Emma stayed right
through the fall."

I felt myself blush. "I — my Dad says —"

"It was interesting to meet you, Miss Verlaine," Isabel said, and turned abruptly away. "Malcolm?"

Malcolm touched my shoulder. "I'll be back in a moment," he murmured.

I watched him follow his sister to the door. How had Isabel ended up as she had with someone as charming and gracious as Mrs. Galbraith for a mother?

It was getting warm in the ballroom. Since we'd finished the dance close to the veranda doors, I decided to sneak out for a moment to cool down. If I left the door open a crack, I could watch for Malcolm's return. I grasped a door-handle and slipped through — and walked directly into someone, stepping firmly on their toes.

"Och, watch where you're going, then!" a voice scolded.

"Annie!" I quickly closed the door. "Is that you?"

"Emma!" She laughed. "I thought you'd be one of those young navy men, out to steal a kiss or two with a town girl."

"I was afraid you were one too," I confessed, and then we both laughed. "What are you doing here?"

"What I always do — havin' a look. It's a bit of a lark, to peek in at the porch and see the lights and the pretty girls in their dance frocks with my flowers. Not so easy to do now, what with the blackout, but I still manage. You try it and tell me what ye think."

I opened the door a crack and peered in. "It *is* lovely from this vantage point," I said. "And much cooler. I would do the same thing, if I were you."

"Aye, I'm not one for the heat. It's why I sit outside to work this time of year. I can make buttonholes and stitch hems outside as well as inside. And see the world go by, to boot."

I peeked inside again, and Annie moved around to the other door so that she could see too. I saw Helen dance by with George Osborn, which made me glad.

Annie made a small noise. "Och, that one again," she said. "I've seen him going by in that wee runabout of his often enough when I'm working outside. I'd wondered if he ever came ashore. Out all times of day, coming and going."

"Really? How strange." I thought of him following us the other day. Was he so enraged by Malcolm that he was—oh, I don't know. Following him when he went rowing? I would have to warn Malcolm. And maybe I could ask Helen if she knew what George was up to. I didn't want to find him hovering nearby next time Malcolm and I were out in a boat together.

"Weel, as I've said before, the strange is common where I live. And there's your young man," she added, poking me. Malcolm had come into view, looking around the room. "Better go in before someone else claims him for a dance."

"You're a tease, Annie." I smiled at her and slipped back into the ballroom—and found myself face to face with George Osborn.

"Emma!" He seized me by the wrist just as the orchestra launched into the opening bars of a one-step. "I've been trying to track you down all evening. Will you dance with me?"

Drat! Where had Malcolm gotten off to? "Oh, I...but...surely you'd rather dance with my cousin. Helen's a much better dancer." I actually had no idea if she was, but right now, I was sure of it.

"I did. But she's not here right now, and you are." He chuckled, as if I were a small, wayward kitten he was humoring, and tried to pull me onto the dance floor.

I set my heels, resisting him. "Except I—I've already promised this dance to someone else."

He looked about him in an exaggerated fashion. "I don't see anyone coming to claim a dance."

I was beginning to feel a little desperate. I did *not* want to dance with George Osborn. "He'll be here in a moment."

"Then we'd better hurry."

That was so awful I didn't answer, but leaned back even harder and tried to extract my wrist from his grasp. And then, much to my relief, Malcolm appeared over George's shoulder. "I'm sorry, Emma—I didn't mean to leave you like that," he said. "May I?" He tapped George on the shoulder.

For one horrible moment, I thought George would refuse. Then, without a word to either of us, he practically shoved my hand at Malcolm and stalked away.

"Well," Malcolm said, staring after him.

"Ignore him," I said. "I try to."

He led us into the dance. I sighed in relief as our steps fitted themselves together, wiping away the memory of George—and then remembered. "Malcolm, I was just talking to Annie—"

"Oh, is she out on the veranda again? My mother always tells her she's welcome to all the dances, but she won't come in."

"I think she likes it better out there. Anyway, she said that she's seen George out on his boat a lot, coming and going at all hours. What do you think he's doing? I hope he doesn't bother us again if we go out rowing."

"At all hours?"

"That's what she said."

"Hmm."

He was silent and frowning for so long that I racked my brain for some way to distract him. "This is how seals would dance, if they danced," I said after a few minutes.

"How do you know they don't?"

"You're right, I don't know. Do they?"

"As a matter of fact, they do. It's not much like this, even allowing for differences between feet and flippers. And they generally don't have dance floors as good as this one. The sand, you know."

I managed to keep a straight face. "I assume, of course, that you've been invited to seal dances in order to have made these observations."

"Dozens of 'em," he agreed. "I'm very popular with that crowd, you know."

"I'm honored that you're deigning to dance with me, then."

His hand tightened on mine, and he drew me a little closer. "There's no one I'd rather dance with," he murmured. "No one at all."

·CHAPTER SIXTEEN·
MALCOLM

A few days after the dance, I was at the train station in Mattaquason with the Marmon to pick up a party of arriving guests. I'd learned to bring a book with me when waiting for the train; Emma's wasn't the only one that had run late these days. If this kept up, we would have to start calling the station for a report; I couldn't afford to waste an hour or two hanging around waiting for trains, especially if we lost another clerk to the army. One of the new ones had given his notice this very morning.

Today's train was running even later than usual, late enough that I finished my book, a John Buchan novel. I checked my watch, sighed, and went into the station.

"Morning, Alves," I said to the young man at the ticket counter.

He jumped guiltily and put down the booklet he'd been poring over. I saw it was a blue-covered Army and Navy recruitment brochure. "Oh, it's you. Morning, Galbraith."

"Joining up?" I nodded at the brochure.

He grinned. "Maybe. Sure beats waiting for late trains here."

"Don't I know it. How late is this one going to be?"

He shrugged. "Word from Hyannis five minutes ago was that it had just crossed the bridge in Bourne."

If it had just crossed the train bridge over the canal separating Cape Cod from the mainland, it wouldn't be here for at least another hour. Which would give me plenty of time to return my book to the library and pick out another. I said good-bye to the clerk—he was already back to his brochure—and went to get the book out of the Marmon. A brisk walk to and from the library would be just the thing; it was a nice day, sunny and not too humid.

Twenty minutes later I'd gotten to the library, found another Buchan novel, and was on my way to the circulation desk when I glanced idly into the Reference Room as I passed and then did a double-take. Emma was seated at a table in the otherwise empty room, poring over an encyclopedia. An open notebook, filled with neat handwriting, lay open next to it.

I grinned to myself and stuck my head around the door. "Hadn't you heard that school's out for summer, Miss Verlaine?"

She looked up quickly, and the expression of surprised pleasure on her face made my day. "Malcolm! What are you doing here?"

"Train's late, so I came over to exchange a book. What about you?"

She didn't answer right away but closed her volume and returned it to the shelf, then picked up her notebook. When she joined me, her face was slightly pink. "I was just doing some research."

"Oh? On what?"

The pink deepened. "Seals. One of my governesses, Miss Talcott—she was my fourth—was an encyclopedia fanatic, and we used to make lists of things we wanted to know more about and went to the library twice weekly to look them up."

I tried not to let my exultation show. "And you wanted to know more about seals?"

"After what you've showed me? Of course I do! I want to know all about them! Not that the encyclopedia entry was very enlightening." She sighed.

"Then I'll just have to take you out rowing again. You'll learn more spending time with them than you will reading an encyclopedia." I didn't care what my father thought. *Something* had to be done about showing Emma what she was, and the sooner the better. "If I didn't have to get back to the station before the train comes in, I'd take you out now."

She waited while I checked my book out, then came down the library steps with me. We paused in the shade of one of the two large copper beeches on the library's front lawn, just above the street. "I have to get to the ferry — Gran's expecting me home for lunch. But I wish we could go rowing now, too," she said, wistfully. "The other day when we were out there with them — it was magical."

If you only knew! "What time do you usually have supper? It's light enough that there's no reason why we couldn't go out for an hour or two in the evenings after I get out of work. That's also when the wind drops and the seas are calmest. Perfect rowing time — I often go out then anyway."

She got a dreamy, faraway look on her face. "That would be wonderful. I'll talk to Gran. Maybe we can pick a day or two every week, weather permit—"

She was interrupted by the blare of a horn and someone shouting, "Emma!" We both looked up.

George Osborn was in his roadster, just creeping to a halt in the middle of Main Street. He was smiling and waving at Emma — until he saw me. It was kind of comical to see him trying to decide whether to glare at me or continue to smile at her.

Emma grimaced and gave him a half-hearted wave in return. "Hullo, George," she called, then said, under her breath, "If we ignore him, do you think he'll go away?"

"Probably not." I waved at him and gave him a big smile. He looked as if he wanted to climb out and have it out with me, but just then another automobile came up behind him and sounded its horn. He was startled, but before he could react the other car had swerved around him and accelerated up the street.

Another car was not far behind; George scowled and gave the roadster some gas, lest another car dare to overtake him.

"Ugh!" Emma exclaimed. "I just can't get away from him, can I?"

"Is he bothering you?"

She sighed. "Not exactly. No more than I can handle. I just wish he'd stop trying so hard. It would be a lot easier to like him if he did. I try to be nice to him for Helen's sake, but it isn't always easy."

I just managed not to lean toward her and kiss away the little frown line from between her brows. Damn that idiot for putting it there. And damn the arriving train that I had to go meet. "I really have to get back to the station. I'd offer you a ride home, but this will be a full load. I'll see you Thursday when you come to give Maggie her dance lesson, all right? We can figure out a time for rowing then."

"All right." She gave me a swift smile and turned to leave. I watched her for a minute, then started back toward the station.

I hadn't gone more than a few feet before, to my irritation, George Osborn fell into step beside me. "Where's Emma?" he demanded.

"Gone back to the ferry," I said, and had the satisfaction of hearing him swear under his breath. By the time he went back to his car and tried to find her to offer her a ride, she'd probably be at the *Never Late*. I didn't say as much, hoping he'd leave.

To my surprise, he kept walking. "See here, Galbraith. You'd better leave Emma alone," he said abruptly.

I almost stopped walking from sheer astonishment. "Excuse me?"

He'd drawn himself up and was trying to look down at me, which didn't work very well as I was at least an inch taller. "You heard me. Leave Emma Verlaine alone. She's mine."

I wanted to laugh, but then I got mad. "I don't recall seeing a 'private property' sign on her anywhere. In fact, she was just telling me that she wished *you* would leave her alone."

He turned a dull red. "She never said that!"

I pretended to sigh. "You're right. Her exact words were, 'I just can't get away from him, can I?' Pardon my paraphrasing—I thought the meanings were similar enough, but concede that the words were not exactly the same." I was suddenly bored with the conversation. "Osborn, stop being an idiot and give her some room, will you? She doesn't like you. Be a man and accept it."

"Why should I believe a word you say about Emma? You—you've been monopolizing her attention since the day she arrived. She hasn't had a chance to get to know me."

I could help a chuckle at that. "Do you honestly think anyone could monopolize Emma Verlaine's attention if she didn't want him to? Why not ask her cousin? I'll bet she'd tell you."

He was silent for a moment, trudging beside me, and I guessed I'd hit home. Emma had said more than once that she hoped the two of them would hit it off. I was willing to bet Osborn was pouring his Emma woes into Helen's ear, poor girl.

I let him think about that for a minute more then said, as we were almost at the station, "Look, I need to get back to work. You know, if you left Emma alone, she might actually like you better." I didn't bother adding that she'd said as much; he'd never believe it.

"Back to work playing chauffeur," he sneered. "I'll bet we pay ours more than you get. Want the job?"

I probably should have just ignored him, but he was getting on my nerves. "No thanks. I like working for my father just fine. Just like you're supposed to be doing. Though I didn't know that making a nuisance of yourself to girls on Cape Cod was vital to our nation's conduct of the war."

"Why, you—" His fists clenched as if he was going to throw a punch, but just then a train whistle sounded, startling us both. I started to turn away—the folks on the train would be anxious to get to the Inn, I knew from previous experience—but he grabbed my arm. "This isn't over," he said in a low, venomous tone.

I shook off his arm. "If you'll excuse me, there's a train I need to meet."

He glared at me a moment longer — then a nasty grin spread across his face. He stepped past me and bent to pick something up, then turned and held it out to me. "There you go, Galbraith. It's just what you deserve." A white gull feather fluttered in the breeze between us. A white feather — the symbol of cowardice, given to men who avoided their duty to defend their country.

I stared at it for the space of a breath or two, and it was my turn to want to hit him. How dared he try to accuse me of shirking my duty when I was out almost daily helping to guard the Cape and keep our waters free from German attacks? He was the one hiding from service under the guise of working for his father.

But no one would ever know what we were doing; the other selkies and I had accepted that. We did it because it needed to be done, not because we wanted anyone's thanks. Still, it rankled when the ones who really deserved to be handed white feathers of cowardice thought they could sneer at us. So I shook my head and made myself laugh.

"Thanks, Osborn, but you'll have to hold onto it for now. I expect it becomes you far better." I moved past him without another glance; the train was just rolling to a halt on the platform behind us.

But he wasn't quite done. "I'd stuff it down your throat if I didn't think you'd run away and complain to the station master."

I whirled. "I'd like to see you try, little man."

He glared at me, teeth practically bared. I met his glare — and then deliberately turned my back to him and sauntered toward the station.

"This isn't over, Galbraith," he muttered again, just loud enough for me to hear.

I didn't bother turning. "It never even started."

·CHAPTER SEVENTEEN·
EMMA

June 19, 1917

Dearest Dad,

I hope the peanut brittle arrived in time for Father's Day on Sunday. Your last letter sounded so forlorn that if I could have fit myself in the box with the candy, I would have. Alas, I'm sure the postage would have been outrageous. I miss you too — so very much. But I'm glad you're doing such important work for our country. I wish I could too.

Well, summer is well and truly here — or at least the thermometer says so, even if the calendar insists it won't be here for a few more days. It's been warm enough for me to have been swimming several times now. Not that cold water has ever stopped me from swimming — do you remember Lake Umbagog, where that man said I must be part penguin? Anyway, I continue to take lessons with Malcolm Galbraith from the Ocean Hotel and am doing my teacher proud, I think. Though honestly, I thought I was a pretty good swimmer to begin with. Our usual audience of the local seals seems to appreciate my efforts, at any rate — they're always on hand (or on flipper) to cheer me on. I do like seeing them here — they make the ocean seem much friendlier.

We also see them when Malcolm takes me rowing. They like to follow his boat for some reason. Malcolm says they're quite intelligent, which I'm inclined to believe as they tend not to come to watch us swim when Helen is with us. I think they sense she doesn't care for them. How she doesn't adore them as I do is a complete mystery to me!

What Helen does adore, I think (and please keep this a deep, dark secret, although on reflection I can't think of anyone you might accidentally tell it to!) is our acquaintance George Osborn, whom I think I've mentioned before. Perhaps "adore" is too strong a word, but she's certainly always ready to let him take her driving in his smart little roadster! All joking aside, I do hope "something" comes of it all. Maybe I was naïve to expect it, but things haven't gone exactly as I'd hoped between me and Helen. Maybe it's the age difference — there seems to be a big gap between my seventeen and her twenty. Or maybe it's just that we're different people. But I don't want her to feel that she's wasted her summer, and falling in love with an estimable young man would go some way toward that. And now I feel like a grandmotherly old matchmaker, wearing a pince-nez and lace shawl and consulting my little notebook. Don't you think the role suits me?

Also in my grandmotherly role, I've been giving dancing lessons to Malcolm Galbraith's little sister, Maggie. She's a funny girl; she's always waiting for me on our Thursday morning classes at the hotel gates, perched on one of the pillars and doing gargoyle imitations. Were those pillars here when you visited the island? It's funny to remember that you've been here too, of course, and not just me.

There's not much else to report since my last letter. Oh, yes, we've received an invitation to a party at the Osborns' house on the 27th. I shall wear my dowdiest dress, to ensure that Helen will shine like the gem she is. And I've sent away for a <u>most</u> *fascinating pamphlet I found advertised in a magazine on raising messenger pigeons for the war effort.*

There's a disused shed here that I could turn into a hatchery, assuming Gran says I can, and I know that the Naval Air Station here uses them. It would let me do something useful beyond sock knitting, though I hope to have good news on that score soon. Girls can help too — or they should be allowed to!

And that's enough nonsense from your loving daughter. Please take care of yourself, since I'm not there to do it — I so wish we could have sent Mrs. Keegan along to watch over you down there to make sure you eat properly and get enough rest and take your pills. She could have done that and reformed the Army in her spare time.

All my love,
Emma

In my mental timetable I'd given Captain Abbott until June 25 to respond to my latest note — that would be number four, by the way. When no reply arrived that Monday, I resolved to go down to the air station the very next day, Josiah or no Josiah. I had been quite patient, but it was time to *do* something.

In fact, it was time to "do something" in many aspects of my life. That's what being an adult was all about, wasn't it? Taking matters into one's own hands and being in charge?

Circumstance seemed to agree with me: on Tuesday morning, Gran asked Josiah to drive her into Mattaquason that afternoon to do some shopping. I sneaked a look at Gran's shopping list and did a quick calculation; with any luck, they would be out of the house for a good three hours, more than long enough for me to walk down to the sir station and back.

As soon as they were gone, I dressed carefully in my gray-blue linen suit — it was the most professional-looking outfit I possessed — chose sensible shoes and a no-nonsense kind of hat, reluctantly donned a pair of gloves, and set out for the air station.

"Where are you going?" Helen asked. She was on the front porch, altering one of her party frocks for the Osborns' party tomorrow.

I thought about fibbing, then decided not to. "Down to ask Captain Abbott for a job. I've been lazing and lounging long enough."

"Oh." She put down her sewing and looked at me. "Are you sure?"

"Yes, I'm sure. I'll be back in an hour or so, I expect. If Gran gets home before I do, please don't say anything. I want to tell her myself."

She nodded. "Good luck, if this is what you want."

"It is," I said fervently.

I took it as a further sign of beneficent fate that on my walk down to the station I met only one group of off-duty sailors, who eyed me curiously but did nothing more than mumble "good day" to me. Evidently my business-like appearance did the trick; I hoped it worked equally well on their commanding officer.

The sentries at the gatehouse were less suggestible, alas. "The captain ain't got time for social calls, miss," one of them said when I produced my card.

I drew myself up. "This is not a social call." I nearly addressed him as "young man," but at the last moment noticed that he was older than me. "I am here on a confidential matter of some urgency."

The first one looked like he was about to tell me what I could do with my confidential matter, but the other sentry shrugged. "You never know, Ed. Cap'n says we need to check with him on civilian callers, no matter what." He took my card and ducked into the guard house, and I saw him pick up a telephone. He emerged a few minutes later, looking surprised. "Captain Abbott says he'll see you right away, Miss Verlaine. I'll take you over."

"Thank you." I nobly refrained from giving Ed a triumphant smirk and followed the sentry through the gates. He brought me to a small clapboard building a few hundred feet up the road from the guard house, and I climbed the stairs and went inside.

The captain's outer office was lined with charts of Cape Cod and the approaches to Boston Harbor and filled with heavy wooden filing cabinets and two desks...both of which, I saw to my dismay, were occupied by young men in uniform. They glanced up at me curiously, but Captain Abbott was already there, waiting beside the door into his office. "Miss Verlaine, I am glad that we finally are able to meet. Won't you come in?"

I followed him into a room with yet more charts and filing cabinets, and he offered me a chair. We eyed each other for a few seconds across his desk before I took a steadying breath and dove in. "Thank you for agreeing to see me, sir. I've wanted to talk with you for a while."

He nodded. "I received your notes, but as you might guess, there are a great many matters vying for my attention. Thank you for taking the initiative."

Well, that sounded promising. "I'm glad to hear that you're busy — it ties right in to why I'm here." He looked encouraging, so I went on. "I am looking for employment on the station, in some kind of secretarial position. I can type" — well, slowly, but I *could* — "and file, and take dictation. I've helped — er, assisted my father for years — he's a geologist and has lots of rocks specimens to keep record of. I can't enlist, which I would have done like a shot if I were a boy. But I can do this. I need to do something to help the war. I'm very trustworthy, and...and punctual, and can work any hours you need me."

That last came out in something of a rush, and I realized I was clutching the edge of his desk and leaning forward. I made myself let go and sit back more properly in my chair. "I have to do *something* to help, sir," I said again, more calmly. "I can knit just so many socks without going nuts."

He smiled. "Never underestimate the value of a pair of new

socks, especially to a soldier in a water-filled trench who hasn't had more than one pair to wear for weeks."

"I can knit in the evenings after work," I countered, but my heart sank. That wasn't what I'd hoped to hear, right after my impassioned speech.

"I'm sure that you could." He folded his hands on his desk blotter and looked at me very kindly. "I don't doubt any of what you've told me, and if I could, I would be delighted to offer employment to you and several other eager young people who have come to me. But the Navy won't let me. I would get into a great deal of trouble if I employed civilians in my office, and that would certainly be of no help to the conduct of the war. As it is, I'm skating on the edge of what's permissible by holding Open Houses, but I think it's important to foster good relations with the local community, so that everyone can help us in our work of protecting the coast from the enemy."

I swallowed, unable to say a word. I'd pinned so much hope on getting a job here, but Malcolm had been right, hadn't he? Why should they hire outsiders, when there were plenty of soldiers to do the work? Only I'd figured they'd need the soldiers for…well, soldiering, and leave the work around the edges for others to do, people who couldn't fly airplanes or take care of dirigibles or—"Captain, I know you use messenger pigeons here—they told us about them at the Open House. Would you be interested in having someone raise them for you?"

I was sure the corners of his mouth twitched, but his voice was perfectly steady when he replied, "Unfortunately, more pigeons is the last thing we need. Our cotes are full to bursting."

"Oh." Well, there went that idea. I was back to square one— or square zero, more likely, because there was absolutely nothing else I could think of to do. The war didn't need useless females like me.

"Miss Verlaine?"

"Hmm?" I flushed and stood up quickly. "I'm sorry, sir. I— was just thinking of something else. I won't take up any more of your time."

"Actually, Miss Verlaine, I was just about to ask —" He cleared his throat. "Have you had a chance to talk to Malcolm Galbraith? There's some special work he does for us that he said you might be able to help him with." He looked at me closely.

I blinked. "He hasn't mentioned it. What kind of work? I'd be happy to help —"

He was shaking his head. "No, I — I probably should not have brought it up. I expect he'll tell you about it soon." He stood up too and moved toward the door to open it for me.

My step on my walk home was considerably less buoyant than it had been when I started out. There would be no escaping the banshees of the local Red Cross. At least Captain Abbott had seemed genuinely sorry that he couldn't offer me — or any other civilian — a job. It seemed to be such a colossal waste — and then I had a brilliant idea: I would write to the Secretary of the Army — and the Navy — and tell them so. I was sure there must be other girls like me, willing and eager to work for their country.

Except for this "special work" that Malcolm was involved with. What could it possibly be — and why hadn't he told me about it when we'd discussed his talking to Captain Abbott about finding me a job? Well, I knew what I would be asking him the next time we met. This would *still* be my week of taking charge.

The weather was beautiful for the Osborns' party the next evening — a cocktail party, which made me feel very mature to think of attending, though I only had a vague notion of what "cocktails" were.

"They're alcohol mixed with fruit juice and other alcohol," Helen explained as we boarded the *Never Late*. Josiah was driving us; George had promised to bring us home again in the *Fast Lady* as the party wouldn't be over till after its last trip. "Be careful — the juice ones taste nice but can be very potent."

"I think I'll stick to soda water, thank you." This past winter

Dad had occasionally allowed me to sip a sherry if we had a guest to dinner, but I can't say I liked it very much.

"That sounds like a good plan." Gran sighed. "I'm too old for this kind of thing. Cocktails." She shook her head.

The Osborns' house was packed. We waited in a sort of receiving line to say hello to Mr. and Mrs. Osborn. Standing with them were George and a dark-haired, sturdily-built man I'd not seen before.

"Delighted you could make it, Mrs. Wetherell!" Mr. Osborn boomed when it was our turn. "You must meet my guest, Herr Keller, all the way from Zürich to visit my little factories. He's an efficiency expert, you know—here to tell me how to be more productive. After all, there's a war on!" He chuckled at his own humor. "Herr Keller, the Wetherells are among our most distinguished friends here on the Cape."

Herr Keller bowed. "It is a pleasure, ladies."

An efficiency expert—that was interesting. It was difficult to hear that German-sounding accent and not bristle a little, but Switzerland was of course a neutral country with many German-speakers. I supposed that life was going on as usual there, even though war raged all around its borders, and people like Herr Keller would continue to go about their business. At least he was here advising *us* and not the Germans.

"How terrifying, to be crossing the ocean this spring," Gran said politely. "You must be very brave, Herr Keller."

"It was exciting at times." Herr Keller gave a self-deprecating shrug. "But there is much work to be done, Mrs. Wetherell. I am grateful for the Osborns' hospitality, and of course for the chance to meet so many of their charming friends." His eyes lingered on Helen. She met his gaze then glanced down modestly.

"You look wonderful," George murmured to me.

"Not as wonderful as Helen," I said brightly, and followed Gran, who'd stepped aside for the next people in line. At least he'd be occupied in greeting people with his parents for a while longer. I was glad Herr Keller had noticed how pretty Helen was, even if he hadn't.

All of the downstairs of the Osborns' house plus the terrace behind it overlooking the ocean were crowded with chatting people. Gran knew at least some of them and was quickly swept into the crowd. Helen and I got our sodas and found an unobtrusive place to stand; we smiled and nodded to one or two ladies we recognized from the Red Cross, but I guessed that the majority of the guests were the Osborns' neighbors here on the bluff, summer people who didn't mix much with the year-round people who were Gran's friends.

Next to me, Helen moved restively. "What do we do now?" I asked her.

"We should go and mingle. Talk to people."

"But we don't know any of them." None of my governesses had taught me about "mingling," which sounded more like a cooking procedure than what one did at parties.

"Oh, Emma, you're such a—" She stopped and bit her lip. "Watch me. It isn't hard." She left me, paused at the edge of one chatting group and appeared to listen for a moment, then somehow seamlessly melded into a second group not far away. How had she done that?

Well, if Helen could do it, I could at least try. I scanned the room, looking for a likely group to join and caught George's eye. Before I could look away, he was striding toward me. I sighed and prepared to be nice to him for Helen's sake. Maybe she'd see us and come over, and I could escape.

"Emma!" He leaned over me and I caught a whiff of—well, of cocktail breath. I wasn't familiar enough with the types to know what he'd been drinking, but I guessed he'd already had plenty. "Can I get you something to drink?"

I held up my soda. "No, thank you, I'm fine. Er...what a nice party."

"Dad likes to have a few every summer. He thought Herr Keller might enjoy meeting some Americans during his visit. Interesting chap, Keller."

"Is he? How nice." I scrambled for something else to say.

"Er, how long will he be—"

"Let's go outside," George interrupted. "It's too warm in here." He took my elbow and steered me through the crowd toward the French doors leading out onto the terrace. I didn't complain; several people in the living room had been smoking, which made my eyes smart. Once on the terrace, I took a deep, relieved breath.

George nodded. "Filthy things, cigarettes. I'm glad you don't like them. I think it's unwomanly for girls to smoke."

I shrugged and made a mental note to warn Helen of the fact. "I think they're smelly no matter who's smoking them."

"Yes, but there's something particularly off-putting about girls—"

"Oh, what is that?" I interrupted. Past the gray flagstones and a stretch of green lawn edged with evergreens blown into odd shapes by the wind was a wooden balustrade on the edge of the bluff. I hadn't noticed it the last time Helen and I were here.

He followed my look. "The stairs down to the beach. Want to see it?"

"Stairs? Really? How high is the bluff here?"

"Only about sixty feet."

I hesitated. I *would* like to see the beach, especially since it meant I could leave the party without actually being rude. But it meant being alone with George. "I'm sure Helen would like to see it too."

"I'll get her," he said. "Don't go away." He went back inside. A moment later, he emerged. Alone.

"Where's Helen?"

"She'll be along in a moment. She said she wanted to powder her nose."

"Oh." That was all right; she probably wanted to touch up her lipstick so as to appear to her best advantage. I was all for *that*. I put down my glass and followed him to the stairs.

"I'll go first," he said, turning to me when we reached them. "Don't be afraid."

Oh, *honestly*. The stairs weren't at all rickety, and heights had never bothered me after clambering around the hills of New Hampshire with Dad, who called me a mountain goat. "I'm fine, thank you," I said, ignoring the hand he held out to me. He looked disappointed.

"Do you keep your boat here?" I asked as we descended.

"No. There's no shelter for boats. But it's a nice view. You'll see."

The bluff wasn't sheer, but dropped down to the beach at a slope. The wooden stairs were anchored to it with iron rods driven into the bluff's face. I hesitated at the bottom. My shoes weren't meant for walking in sand, but I wasn't going to let that stop me now.

"Emma?" George was holding his hand out to me again.

"Oh, it's lovely!" I said, pretending not to have seen it. The beach wasn't very wide here, but being tucked into the foot of the bluff gave it a secluded, castaway feel that might have been romantic if I weren't here with George Osborn. "Do you come here much?"

He shrugged. "Not really. I'd rather be out in the *Fast Lady*. Do you know, this is the first chance I've had to be alone with you?"

"I can't think why you'd want to be." Where was Helen? I moved away from him, towards the water's edge, and tried to peer up the stairs without being too obvious. "I'm not very interesting."

He followed right after me. "I think you are."

I was almost at the edge of the waves, so I began to walk down the beach, parallel to the water. It was chilly down here away from the sun, and I shivered. He noticed, drat him, and tried to put his arm around me. I quickened my pace. "I—really, I'm nowhere near as nice as Helen. In fact, she admires you a great deal—"

"I don't want to talk about Helen. Why don't you like me, Emma?"

Off the beach ahead I saw the dark head of a seal appear in the low swells, and then three or four more, their faces all turned toward me. I smiled at them and mentally squared my shoulders. If Helen didn't get here soon, I'd have to say something to George. In fact, now might the right time to do so, while I had my friends nearby for moral support. It was "take charge" week, after all.

I took a deep breath and turned to face him. "I don't *dis*like you. I'm grateful for the way you came to our assistance the day we arrived." I still refused to say *rescued*.

"But…while I'm sure you're very nice, I have no interest in being anything more than acquaintances with you."

He frowned. "Why not? You've hardly given me a chance."

Why did I have to "give him a chance?" Wasn't that *my* decision? But I quashed my impulse to snap at him. "I like to think I know my own mind. And truly, I'm sorry if it hurts your feelings." I turned away to walk up the beach, away from him, looking at the seals who'd swum closer in. They gazed back at me, I swear, with sympathy.

"Emma!" He put a restraining hand on my arm. I stopped and gave it a frosty glance, then looked up at him. He had a strange, determined expression on his face, and before I could decipher what it meant, he'd put his arms around me and pushed his face toward mine. I realized with horror that he was about to kiss me.

I'd read about enough first kisses in Miss Blunt's novels to have formed a picture of what mine would be like, though I hadn't really expected choirs of angels singing in my ears or fireworks erupting around me. But this wasn't even remotely pleasant because it was George, and I really, *really* did not want him kissing me. His mouth was unpleasantly wet and hot and tasted of alcohol—and suddenly I was mad—no, enraged—that my first kiss was turning out to be so *awful*.

"Stop it!" I tried to say, but his mouth was covering mine in a horrible, suffocating way and I could only sort of gurgle the words. I squirmed in his grasp, trying to free my trapped arms, and tried to scream. And suddenly, much louder noises re-sounded behind me—splashing, and then a terrifying, barking bellow very close by that seemed to echo against the cliff and redouble.

To my immense relief George let me go and staggered away. I took a gasping breath and scrubbed my hand across my mouth, trying to erase the feel of his lips.

"Call them off!" he demanded, staring fearfully at me.

Or past me. I turned and saw what had made him release me. The seals that had been keeping me company had surged up the beach. As I watched they surrounded me, one in front and two to each side. Their posture was unmistakable: if they'd been dogs, they would have been growling and baring their teeth at George.

"You knew," I whispered. "You knew I needed help."

The seal in front turned long enough to give me a look that clearly said, *"Did you expect anything else?"* then resumed his hostile stance.

"Emma!"

I didn't bother trying to conceal my relief. "I don't think they'll bother you so long as you keep your distance."

"But we need to talk!"

I stopped rubbing my face. "No, we don't. I certainly don't have anything I wish to say to you. Except maybe, 'don't you dare do that again.'"

"I—I got carried away." He stared at the seals and then at me. "How did you call them?"

I thought about spinning him a story, then shrugged. "I didn't. They just came."

He continued to stare between me and them so long that I began to get impatient. "Look, I would like to go back, and I don't think my friends here will let me go unless you leave first. So if you don't mind…"

He took a step backward but said, "I love you, Emma."

All at once I was incredibly tired. "Don't. Just don't."

He opened his mouth then seemed to think better of it, eyed the seals around me once more to make sure they were staying put, then hurried toward the stairs.

The seals stared sternly after him. When he was out of sight, I counted to one hundred, then sighed. "I think he's gone. Thank you for coming to my rescue." I took a step toward the stairs, then another. The seals spread out around me, but rather than turning back to the ocean they wriggled their way down the beach with me, an ungainly but stalwart honor guard. When we reached the stairs I paused and held my hands out to them, a little nervously. One of them—the leader?—delicately touched his nose to my fingers while the others bobbed their heads, then watched me as I climbed the stairs. I was relieved that they didn't try to ascend them with me but waited below, watching. If there had been any sign of George, I was willing to guess they would have done their best to squirm up after me. Malcolm was right, they *were* smart.

At the top of the stairs I hesitated, but no one on the terrace seemed to notice I was there. I made my way to a wrought-iron chair on the terrace's edge, collapsed into it, and stared at the lengthening shadows of evening, wriggling my toes to try to get the trapped sand out of my stockings.

Helen found me there a little while later. "There you are! I wondered what had happened to you."

I stood up. "What happened to *you*? George said you'd be right down."

"Down where?"

"To see the beach. You were going to go powder your nose first, remember?"

She looked at me blankly. "I have no idea what you're talking about."

He lied. He'd *lied* to me, the skunk. I clenched my fists. "I'll kill him."

"Emma, what are you talking about?"

In a low voice I told her an expurgated version of the events on the beach, leaving out my rescue by the seal cavalry. She pursed her lips but only said, "Well, what did you expect? He's nuts about you, and if he'd had a few drinks, it's no wonder he made a pass at you. Come on, Aunt Dorinda is ready to go. If we hurry, we can catch the last ferry."

"Good. The last thing I want is to go anywhere on George's boat. In fact, the last thing I want is to ever lay eyes on him again."

"Good luck with that," she said skeptically. "You're far too straight-forward and guileless, you know. You need to cultivate a little dishonesty in your soul."

I couldn't answer because we'd gotten to the front door where Gran was waiting. She looked at me with a furrow in her brow. "Are you all right?"

"Just tired," I said.

"Did you thank the Osborns? I couldn't find you when I was taking leave of them."

"Yes, Gran." There. I'd cultivated a little dishonesty. But there was no way I could thank George for a lovely time; my guileless soul would not have been able to take it.

I was glad that Gran and Helen found plenty to chatter about as one of Mattaquason's two cabs took us to the *Never Late* and we settled in the foot passengers' seats. I was simply too tired to talk and let their conversation wash over me.

Drat. Why hadn't my first kiss been from Malcolm?

·Chapter Eighteen·
Emma

Friday was the Red Cross, as usual. It was a warm day; we were almost into July now, and the heat was getting more humid. All the seats near the open windows in the church hall were taken when Gran, Helen, and I arrived, so we were forced to sit in the center of the room, away from the light breeze that occasionally made its way inside. Several ladies were evidently not in the habit of using deodorant, which did not improve the atmosphere.

The heat seemed to dull conversation, and only a few murmurs could be heard as we sewed—flannel bed-shirts today, Helen and I sewing on the tapes which were used to fasten them in back instead of buttons. I began mentally composing the letter I was going to write to the Secretary of the Army (with a copy for the Secretary of War as well as the Navy) about their poor utilization of women's labor: it seemed like an appropriate use of my time here and got my blood moving on this hot, sleepy day.

It got my blood moving so much, in fact, that it was hard to sit still and sew. When we'd finished a stack of shirts, I jumped up to carry them to the storage room where they were held until enough had been accumulated to send to Red Cross head-quarters.

There were people in there talking. I could just hear the rise and fall of female voices, committee ladies settling down for a really good gossip, protected by the mostly-closed door. I started to rebalance my load so that I could knock, but an overheard word made me stop and listen first.

"The girl does look awfully like Laura," one voice said thoughtfully. I'd come to know them well enough to recognize it as belonging to one of Gran's bridge-playing friends, Mrs. Simmons. "Has anyone seen her with Josiah Barnes? Any resemblance there?"

I just managed not to gasp, but it wouldn't have mattered if I had. A chorus of muffled titters followed her question.

"Oh, really, Sarah!" someone else said. "You don't possibly think Laura would have — you know — with Josiah!"

"Why not? He's the one who had the most opportunity. You may not remember, but they were all over the island together in their teens. I'm amazed Dorinda allowed it."

"Well, maybe so — but after Laura was married? Do you really think so?"

"I don't know. The husband was a good deal older. Maybe she preferred someone closer to her own age — and if they were already in the habit—"

This was quite enough. If I'd been able to face George down, I could do the same to these harpies. I just managed to keep myself from throwing the bed-shirts on the floor — they were for Our Boys, after all — and instead shoved — well, kicked, actually — the door open.

Five women were crowded into the small, shelf-lined room. I'd hit one of them with the door; she was rubbing her shoulder with a peeved expression that dissolved into shock when she — and they — saw who stood there.

"Here are some completed bed-shirts." I thrust them at the nearest woman, who just happened to be Mrs. Simmons.

"Th-thank you." She took them from me, her face reddening.

I recognized two of the others as members of Gran's church and gave them a broad, false smile. "My, you ladies have been busy in here, haven't you?"

Most of them found it convenient to look elsewhere than at me. I took a deep breath and let my rage out. *"Haven't you been busy?"*

"Now, dear—" one of Gran's friend started.

"You know, some of us are actually working rather than hiding in closets and stirring up dirt. Is *this* your idea of how to help the war effort?" My voice had started to rise. I let it, using all of Miss Nutting's breathing exercises and Mademoiselle Renard's (governess number nine, French and elocution) training. "Gossiping about a dead woman—a woman who died in the saddest way a woman can?"

The room behind me, which had been quiet to begin with, now became perfectly still.

"Because if it is…well, I don't want any part of it. I can sit at home and knit socks in a much more comfortable chair than I get here, and I wouldn't have to listen to small-minded hypocrites tearing my mother to shreds—my *mother*. How would you like to hear strangers talking this way about *your* mother"—I pointed at Mrs. Simmons—"or yours, or yours?" I fixed them all with what I hoped was an accusing glare. *"Shame on you!"*

Mrs. Simmons drew herself up. But before she could say anything, I turned my back on her and stalked to the row of hooks where we left our hats and purses, taking off the white smock that someone had thought we should all wear because it would make us feel more official, and dropping it on an empty chair. I jammed on my hat, and only then looked over at where Gran and Helen sat. Helen's eyes were wide; Gran's face—I glanced at her then looked away quickly, took my purse, and left.

I hadn't gone more than a few yards before I heard footsteps hurrying after me. I didn't turn as Gran and Helen joined me, and we walked without speaking along Main Street and down the dusty road to the *Never Late*. We crossed in silence and again walked without speaking through Monomoyick village to home. The entire time, I could hear Mrs. Simmons's voice in my head, saying those hateful words.

When we got home, Josiah was in the garden. He saw us walking up the driveway, dropped his hoe, and came over to us. "What're you doing here? Committee end early? You shouldn't have walked in the heat like this, all the way from town," he said sternly to Gran. "I would have been down to get you in an hour or so."

"Emma...that is—we had to leave," Gran said, a little faintly. "I think I'll go inside."

I steeled myself to look at Gran for the first time since that quick glance in the church hall. There was such sadness in her face that I felt my righteous indignation slip several notches.

If I'd conducted myself a little differently, Gran might not have had to know what her so-called friends were up to in the storage closet. They deserved the public shaming I'd given them, but I'd dragged her and every other person in the room into it as well. The gossip about my mother would be nothing compared to what I'd started. "Gran, I'm sorry."

She shook her head and smiled at me, but it was a bleak kind of smile. "It's not your fault, dearest. I should have known something like this would happen."

"I'll apologize to her—to all of them—"

"No," she said firmly. "They don't deserve that. It's just..." She sighed.

"Come on, Aunt Dorinda. We'll make you some tea and you can put your feet up," Helen said soothingly, putting her arm around Gran's shoulders.

"I'd rather have a manhattan, thank you," Gran said tartly, but let Helen draw her into the house.

That left me and Josiah, me on the porch, him staring up at me accusingly from the foot of the stairs. "What'd you do?" he demanded.

"*I* didn't do anything," I said, stung. "They started it."

He gave a derisive snort. "What is this, the playground? You must have done something or your grandmother wouldn't be so upset and you wouldn't be offering to apologize."

"Fine!" I snapped. "Gran's lovely friends were all discussing just who they thought my real fa—" Too late I remembered who I was talking to, and clamped my lips together, my face reddening just as Mrs. Simmons's had.

But he'd heard enough. "Who your real father was," he finished. His voice was grim.

I turned away from him toward the door. "I have to go to Gran."

"It weren't me, Emma," he said quietly.

I stood still, my back to him and one hand on the doorknob, unable to say a word.

"Much as I would've liked—" He cleared his throat, paused, then continued, "I worshipped her—your mother—even when she...even though she didn't notice that I did. But I never laid a finger on her. Guess I loved her too much to want to do her any harm. I know those old tabbies your grandmother calls friends like to drag out that tired old story, but there ain't no truth in it."

I was shivering now, even though I wasn't cold.

"Go in now, chickie," Josiah said, and his voice was kinder than I'd heard it for a long time. "You've had enough for one day."

His words seemed to loosen my paralysis. I turned the doorknob and went into the house, but paused and looked back before I shut the door. Josiah still stood at the bottom of the stairs—I could just see his upper half from here—and I was struck by the sadness in the droop of his shoulders and head. Just like what I'd seen in Gran's face.

I knew I should go in to Gran and Helen—I could hear them in the library—but instead I went up to my room—Laura's room—and huddled on the window seat, arms around my knees. Had she sat here like this when she was sad?

I'd made a complete mess of this week, first with George and now with the female population of Mattaquason, under the mistaken apprehension that I was taking charge of my life.

Taking charge, ha. What was I going to ruin next? Could this week get any worse?

That Sunday, Gran looked troubled when I came down to breakfast not in a going-to-church dress but in an everyday shirtwaist and skirt. Did she really think I could go to church and keep a straight face when people like Mrs. Simmons were there, pretending to be decent human beings? God would understand. I couldn't imagine he'd like the gossiping ladies of Mattaquason any more than I did.

If Gran wanted, I would apologize to them. But I was not going to do it on my own account. And to be honest, if she asked me to apologize and I did, I wasn't going to mean it. My ire hadn't subsided over Saturday; if anything, it had increased, especially in light of what Josiah had told me. I was glad he'd spoken. It seemed to at least partly clear the air between us. Not that I'd really thought my mother and he had...had done anything.

To make myself feel better I'd written a long letter to Dad first thing that morning, remembering all the things we'd done together when I was growing up and telling him how I appreciated what a good father he was. Hopefully it would cheer both of us up; he'd let slip in his last letter that he still felt low and tired. I had asked if I could come down for a visit to take care of him and spoil him a bit, but he'd vetoed that by return mail; he would not have me traveling all the way to Washington alone on a train. I wondered if officers at headquarters got leave; it would be wonderful to have him come up here for a few days' rest, and I wrote him that too—Gran's gossipy friends be damned. In fact, I couldn't help wishing that he'd brought me to visit Gran on the Cape years ago; seeing us together might have silenced the gossips. But it was too late now. And I didn't want a word about any of what had happened at the Red Cross meeting reaching his ears. There was no reason for poor Dad to feel badly…and I didn't want him to worry about me any more than he already was, for whatever reason.

Then I'd started my pair of socks for the week and, feeling virtuous, decided I'd also knit a helmet, the pattern for which I'd found in one of Gran's magazines. No one was going to be able to say I wasn't doing my bit, even if I weren't going to Red Cross meetings.

And since doing my bit wasn't going to happen at the air station, I was going to ask Malcolm about that special project both he and Captain Abbott had mentioned. He would be over shortly after Gran and Helen left for church with Josiah because I'd called the hotel yesterday and left him a message suggesting that if it was convenient for him to give me my swimming lesson in the morning, he could come then. For a few minutes I'd wondered if I'd done the right thing: look how "taking charge" last week had turned out. But I wanted to ask him about the special project, and that would be best done when we were alone. Besides, I wanted to see him.

"No Helen today?" Malcolm asked as we started for the beach later that morning. I'd been waiting for him on the porch with my towel.

"They're at church."

He nodded. I was glad when he didn't ask any further questions. Instead, he smiled at me. "Probably a good thing no one's around. I've started feeling like I'm here under false pretenses. You hardly need swimming lessons any more. To be honest, you didn't to start with, but I needed to make sure you didn't."

"Yes I do. You still haven't showed me how to do the Trudgen." I pretended to look sad. "Unless you're getting tired of teaching me."

He tweaked the braid hanging down my back. "Quiet, you, or I'll toss you in the water like I do Maggie."

I laughed. How was it possible to be so in step with another person—so deeply *comfortable*? I wanted to take his hand as we walked down the path to the beach, but didn't. What if this feeling was all in my mind, not his?

The sun on the sand was a pale morning colorand the water a lighter blue than I was used to seeing it in the afternoon. It was low tide, so we had to walk out to find deeper water to swim in. Seals soon gathered, watching us with their usual eagerness. Were they the ones who rescued me from George? I wanted to suggest we swim out to them, but Malcolm was suddenly all business.

"Since you mentioned it, we'll work on the Trudgen," he said, pausing when we were waist-deep. "You already know half of it—it's done with a scissor kick, like the sidestroke. You'll just need to learn the arm motions and put them together. Watch."

He bent over from the waist and began windmilling his arms in a forward motion. I giggled, and he looked up, eyebrows raised.

"I'm sorry," I said. "That looks silly."

He grinned. "Don't laugh too hard. It's your turn next."

"Yes, sir. I think I can manage the flailing well enough, but how do you face forward to do that while doing a sideways scissor kick?"

"You twist from the hips." He launched into the water and swam away from me a few dozen yards, then back. "See?"

"Um…no, not really. It's fast, but I couldn't really see what your legs were doing while your arms were in motion."

He thought for a few seconds. "Let's go into shallower water. I'll show you."

When we were thigh-deep he came to stand close behind me. "Think about the rhythm of a scissor kick—up, open, close, up, open, close. Now let me move your arms for you while you picture your legs moving. Ready? Say it—open, close."

"Up, open, close." I obediently followed his chant, feeling somewhat silly. His arms slid over mine, hands atop my hands. I could feel his chest lightly touching my back, cool at first from his wet bathing suit and then warm, so warm, and his right cheek against my left ear...and any thought of learning how to do the Trudgen completely left my mind.

"Up, open, close. Up, open, close." He moved my arms for me in time to the words, but I couldn't say them anymore; I was too busy comparing this with how I'd felt on Wednesday when George kissed me. There wasn't any comparison. Why had he done that and ruined my first kiss for me?

"Up, open, close. Up, open, close."

Except...except I hadn't kissed George back. So while it had been the first time a boy had kissed me, *I* hadn't kissed one.

Yet.

"Up, open, close—Emma? Are you getting this?"

"Almost," I said, and then turned my head and felt the side of his mouth against mine, halfway through a word. I didn't try to eat his face the way George had done to me; I closed my eyes and brushed my lips gently but decidedly against his once, twice.

He drew in a startled breath. I decided to take further advantage of the element of surprise and, extracting my hands from his, twisted around in his arms to face him then kissed him again. And again.

By the third time, his arms had come up to encircle me properly. "Emma," he whispered into my lips.

I opened my eyes and met his, so close. "I'm sorry...up, open, close. Is that what you were going to say?" I put one hand on his shoulder and allowed the other one to slide up into his damp, curling hair.

"No. *This* is what I was going to say." And then he kissed me, and George was forever erased from my memory. I closed my eyes again and let my other senses take over—touch, yes, and taste, oh yes...

When he finally drew back, I opened my eyes. Maybe

taking charge didn't always turn into a disaster after all. "What were you saying about the scissor kick?"

"Blast the scissor kick," he said, and bent his head to mine again even as he began walking us backward into deeper water. I clung tightly to him to keep from falling until he tipped us both over into the waves. He placed small kisses all over my face until I ran out of breath and struggled to rise. He promptly righted us and we stood in the waist-deep water, breathing hard, still wrapped in each other's arms.

I leaned my head on his shoulder. That had been beyond Miss Blunt's angelic choirs and fireworks. It had been beyond *anything* I might have imagined...and I'd been trying pretty hard. Beyond the sheer deliciousness of it was the emotion: I'd been so wrapped up in *us* that nothing, no one else existed in the world...and it had felt wonderfully *right*. I kissed his throat and, tentatively at first, let my fingertips trail down his shoulder and across his chest. I'd admired his figure for weeks now; actually touching him, feeling his skin and the smooth muscles beneath them was ten times better than just looking. I wanted to take his bathing suit off just so I could explore all of him, every single delicious inch. "You feel so good," I couldn't help murmuring.

"So do you," he whispered into my mouth as I lifted my head and kissed him again...and then his hands were on me, running down my back, dipping in to skim my waist then further down over my hips, pulling me tight against him. I thought I'd collapse back into the water because my knees had stopped working. It was almost—almost—a relief when he folded me in his arms again and went back to kissing me.

"We have company," he said a moment later. He sounded as dazed as I was.

"What? Where?" I lifted my head and looked guiltily toward shore. Helen wasn't back from church already, was she?

But then I heard the soft calls from the water beyond us and turned. The seals were still there, watching us with bright-eyed interest from not far away.

"Not now, my friends," Malcolm said. "We're busy." He

tilted my chin up and bent his head to mine once again.

When we came up for air (figuratively, that time), he leaned his forehead against mine. "Where did you learn to kiss like that, Miss Verlaine?"

I let my hand drift down to trail over his chest and heard his intake of breath. "Count Tomaso Benedetto de Longhi, mostly," I said.

"What?" Malcolm pulled away and looked at me with consternation.

"He's the hero of *Her Outlaw Love*, by A. M. Spruce. A plucky English girl on a sketching tour of the Apennines is captured by banditti led by the brooding, embittered Count de Longhi, who is in disguise after his father the duke disowns him due to an enormous misunderstanding, but they fall in love at practically first sight — the heroine and the count, of course — and she learns a lot more than the regional dialect from him. The descriptions were very enlightening."

The corners of his mouth were twitching. "And where else?"

"*The Loveless Laird* was good, too. The heroine is won by the brooding, embittered Lord MacRae in a card game with her gambling-addicted father who had killed his father in a duel, but in the end she tames him with her sweetness and innocence. Well, innocence isn't perhaps the right word," I added after a moment's thought. "That was one of the ones my governess thought she'd hidden, but she could be forgetful and left them out sometimes. Oh, and there was *Captured by the Pirate*, but that one was a bit much even for Miss Blunt, and she kept it under lock and key instead of just in the bottom of her wardrobe."

He was shaking his head and smiling. "Emma —"

"It's true, you know. She did keep the especially 'seasoned' ones there — that's what she liked to call them."

He laughed and leaned his forehead against mine. "Emma," he murmured. "I was afraid I'd never find you."

"How did you know I even existed?"

"I didn't. That's what makes this so incredible." His arms

tightened around me. "There's so much I have to tell you — so much we have to talk about." I felt him smile. "I want you to show me what else you learned from those books."

I laughed. "It was all variations on the same theme."

"That's fine with me. I like this theme a lot."

That was something Miss Blunt's books had never touched on: how shared laughter was just as important — and intense — a way to express emotion as anything involving physical contact. I drew back so that I could kiss him again, then leant my head against his shoulder with a sigh of contentment. "I'm just glad you never met any Radcliffe girls who'd read *Her Outlaw Love* while you were in college."

"I may have met dozens of them who'd read any number of novels. But none of them were *you*."

Oh, he was a darling, wasn't he? "You can keep right on saying things like that. I promise I won't get tired of hearing them."

"No, I'm serious." He drew back to look at me. "I don't think that there's another girl like you anywhere. If you only knew — "

"You can tell me now, if you'd like." Speaking of which... "You can tell me about your special project, too. Captain Abbott told me to ask you. I didn't have a chance to tell you, but he won't — can't — let me work there."

"I know. He told me." He was silent for a long minute, staring at me and stroking my cheek with his thumb. "Yes, that would work," he finally said. "It makes sense, to do it all at once."

"To do what all at once?"

"Ssh." He silenced me very effectively, and by the time he was done, I could hardly remember my name, much less what we'd been talking about.

A seal's bark, followed by a splash, brought us back to the here-and-now. I turned and saw that they'd disappeared, only a thin ring of foam marking where they'd been. At the same time I heard someone call, "Emma?"

Malcolm and I released each other quickly. Helen was standing on the beach, shading her eyes and waving at us. Our enchanted morning was over.

"I knew it was too good to last. We don't have to go back in right away," I added hopefully. "Lunch isn't for another hour. Helen will leave in a moment, I'm sure."

But Helen was showing no sign of leaving. "Emma!" she shouted again. "Please!"

The "please" got me. I sighed and waved to Helen to let her know we'd heard her.

"I hope everything's all right," Malcolm said as we made our way back into shore.

"I'm sure it is," I said, then of course thought immediately about what might *not* be all right. Gran appeared perfectly healthy, but she was nearly seventy. The morning was warm and humid; what if she'd been overcome in church, where the ventilation wasn't the best, and collapsed?

As we waded through the shallow water, I saw that Helen still wore her Sunday shoes and stockings, which worried me even more—whatever it was couldn't wait while she changed her shoes. "Is Gran all right?" I called, hurrying up the sand to her.

She handed me my towel. "She's fine. It's—" She bit her lip. "Come up to the house. She'll tell you."

Now I was frightened. "Helen, what happened?"

Malcolm put my robe over my shoulders, then his arm around my waist. "Come on, Emma," he said quietly.

I was grateful for the warmth of his arm around me as we hurried up to the house. Gran was waiting on the porch for us. She looked white-faced and somber.

"Gran!" I thumped up the stairs. "What is it? What's wrong?" She looked so pale—had something happened to one of my uncles?

"Dear child." She held her hands out to me. "I'm afraid there's some bad news about your father."

I stared at her as the world began to crash around me. Not

Gran, or Uncle Robert or Sam. Daddy. My dad.

" —a heart attack, early this morning—"

"Is he dead?" I whispered.

"No, darling. But he's very ill."

I sagged where I stood. Only Malcolm's hands under my elbows kept me from sliding to the floor. I leaned against him, not much caring what Gran or Helen might think.

He put his arms around me. "Do you want to sit down?" he murmured in my ear.

I shook my head. "Tell me," I said to Gran.

In answer, she held out a slip of yellow telegram paper. I took it in shaking fingers and read:

CAPT VERLAINE SUFFERED HEART ATTACK THIS AM STOP CNDN SERIOUS BUT STABLE AT WALTER REED HOSP STOP MORE LATER STOP MAJ OLIVER FULL STOP

"It's all we know, dear—Mr. Grover at the telegraph office knew we'd be at church and was waiting for us at the door when the service let out," Gran said. "It being Sunday, I don't know if we could phone this Major Oliver—"

"He's the head of the section Dad's working for," I said automatically. Dad had mentioned him a few times in his letters. "I have to go to him. When's the next train to Boston? Or maybe I can get one straight to New York and change there for Washington—"

Gran was shaking her head. "Emma, you can't. Traveling from Boston to Cape Cod is one thing—taking a Pullman to Washington is another. And where would you stay? From what I read in the papers, the hotels in Washington are simply bursting...and they wouldn't give a room to a young girl on her own."

"Why not—oh." Damn the double standard that meant the world thought nothing of a young man staying in a hotel alone but would see a young woman doing the same thing as highly inappropriate. "Can't you go with me?"

Gran looked at me sadly. "I think we should wait until tomorrow and phone the hospital. Then we'll know if we ought to make plans to go down to him. Rushing down there without knowing exactly what his condition is might worry him and make him worse. I know how concerned you are about him, dear, but we have to think of what is best for him first."

I closed my eyes. She was right, of course, but that didn't make me feel any better. This was *my father* we were talking about. Had he forgotten to take his medicine down in Washington without me to remind him?

"I hate this. I hate not being able to *do* anything!" I burst out.

"Emma," Malcolm murmured, and pulled gently on my arm to turn me toward him. I buried my face against his neck and started to cry. He kissed the side of my head and tightened his arms around me.

"I sh-should have gone with him. He needed me to t-take care of him," I sobbed.

"I don't think so." His voice was calm and measured. "My guess is that he needed you to be here while he did his job. Your grandmother's right—rushing down there before you know anything just might make him think he's worse than he actually is."

I nodded because I couldn't manage coherent speech just then. Malcolm held me, stroking my hair until I cried myself out. Eventually I fished a handkerchief out of the pocket of my robe and mopped up as well as I could. He gave me his when mine was too sodden to be of use, smoothed my hair back from my face, and touched my cheek. "Will you be all right?" he asked.

"Not until I know how he is." I took a deep, sniffling breath. "But I'll manage."

"Of course you will," Helen said heartily.

I turned. Helen and Gran were watching us, Gran with not-very-well-concealed surprise. Helen only wore a slight smile.

Malcolm let go, retaining my hand. "I'll phone tomorrow to

see if you have news. And maybe Tuesday we can talk. About the project and — things." He squeezed my hand at the mention of talking. I remembered as if through a haze the happiness of the earlier part of the morning and nodded. I did want to talk...but only once I knew more about Dad.

After he left, Gran looked as if she wanted to say something but changed her mind. "Go and bathe," she said. "I know you probably won't want lunch, but you should have a little something."

"I'll try, Gran." I guessed she probably wouldn't appreciate a hug from me in my wet robe and bathing suit, so I settled for touching her hand. "Thank you."

She smiled and gestured me into the house. I went in and began to climb the stairs, and realized Helen had followed me. I went into my room. She paused in the doorway and watched as I started to unbraid my hair.

"I'm sorry about your dad, Emma. I know how much you love him. But I'm sure they're taking good care of him down there," she said. "It must be an important hospital if it's in Washington."

My fingers faltered. "Yes, I'm sure they are."

"Malcolm was very kind to you."

I looked up at her, wondering what she meant by that, but only read sisterly concern and sympathy in her expression. What exactly had she seen from the beach? Malcolm and I had been a fair way out because of the tide, but if she'd been there for a while, watching —

Well, what if she had? We had done nothing to be ashamed of. If Gran asked, I would tell her so. But I didn't really want to talk about it right now, even with Helen. Thinking about Malcolm would mean I wasn't thinking about Dad, which seemed disloyal.

"Yes, he was," I replied.

She nodded, watched me for a minute longer, then left.

·Chapter Nineteen·
Malcolm

I walked home more or less on air and spent the next hours while working the front desk—we were already down a second clerk—thinking about Emma: how she'd felt in my arms, her mischievous expression when she'd talked about her governess's novels, the touch of her mouth on mine. It was a good thing it was a quiet afternoon and no one wanted much from me, because I wasn't more than half-attending to what I was doing. I wished I could have taken my skin and gone for a long swim to think about it all.

I was sorry the news about Professor Verlaine had arrived when it did—sorry he was ill, of course—but even more sorry that Emma was so upset. I felt a little bad that I was so happy when she was not; I wish I could have done more to comfort her, but I think Mrs. W. was taken aback as it was by my holding Emma when she cried. I would have done anything to make her feel better, just as I'd chased that moron Osborn away from her on the beach at their party the other day. I hated to see anything upset my girl.

My girl.

"Pleasant thoughts, Malcolm?" my mother said, pausing at the desk with an armful of flowers. She and Maggie had gone to Annie Goslin's for tea.

"You were grinning like a hyena," Maggie said. "I'll bet he

was thinking of Emma," she added to Mother. "He was swimming with her this morning."

I scowled at Maggie and turned back to Mother. "She got some bad news about Professor Verlaine this morning. He's been taken ill."

"Is that why you were smiling?" Maggie pretended to look shocked. "The poor man! Wait till I tell Emma!"

"Stow it, Maggot." Evidently this was one of my sister's three-year-old days.

"Mother! He called me a maggot again!"

"Margaret, will you please go put Annie's flowers in water before they wilt? That would be a shame, as she picked them at your request." Mother handed them to her. Maggie looked like she wanted to argue but took the flowers and stomped into our apartment.

"What happened?" Mother asked when the door had closed and Maggie's footsteps had progressed down the hall.

"Heart attack. They got a telegram. Emma's pretty upset."

Her voice softened. "Of course she is. She loves her father very much."

I frowned. "He's not really her —"

"He's the only father she's ever had, Malcolm. Don't forget that. I'll call Dorinda and see if there's anything I can do." She turned to our door.

"Mother, wait," I called after her.

She paused and looked at me, then came back. "Yes?"

I hesitated. This was personal, but it was important to others besides me. "Emma — she and I..." I took a deep breath. "I love her."

Mother's mouth did not so much as twitch into anything approaching a smile, I was glad to see. This was too serious for that. "Does she return your feelings?"

I felt a grin stretch across my face. All right, maybe a smile was permissible under the circumstances, at least for me. "She started the whole conversation, actually." I'd be daydreaming about when she turned and kissed me for a long time.

"Well." Mother's face was still serious.

"You do like her, don't you?" I couldn't help asking.

"Yes, I do like her. We all do. I'd guessed that none of the girls Isabel is always bringing to meet us would do for you—"

I should have known Mother would figure out what Izzy had been up to. She was pretty smart that way.

"—but I wouldn't assume that it's all decided, no matter how strongly you feel about her. There's a lot more than your feelings to be considered."

"I know. That's why I've already decided that I'm going to talk to her Tuesday about what we are. What *she* is."

A crease appeared between Mother's brows. "Are you sure that's wise?"

"The sooner she knows, the better, don't you think?" I certainly did. She would love being a selkie. I pictured her delight with her new world; I couldn't wait to hear what she would say about it all. We would swim together as selkies, then lie on the beach together as humans and talk and laugh and kiss—

Mother's voice brought me back to earth. "Not necessarily. Do you remember that I warned you to be careful with her? Not to overwhelm her?"

"But—"

"She's not only dealing with finding love—which can be both wonderful and painfully intense—but with her father's illness. It might be better to wait to bring up the question of her being a selkie at least another few days, until she knows Professor Verlaine is on the mend."

Wait a few days...I supposed I could. But why deprive Emma of the wonders I would show her? Wouldn't it help her with her sadness? "Her being a selkie is not a question; it's a fact," I said. "A few days won't change that."

"But a few days might change how she accepts that fact."

I still had an ace card up my sleeve. "I want to talk to her before the next full moon, which is this Wednesday. You remember what happened to her last month. If it happens again, that would be even more upsetting, don't you think?"

She sighed. "You're determined, aren't you?"

I grinned at her. "Yup."

"Malcolm, I think you're making a mistake. But she's your love, not mine. You have to do what you think is best." She went up on tiptoe and kissed my cheek, regarded me seriously for a moment, and followed after Maggie.

I went back to my dreaming about Emma. What would it be like to bring her to one of our moonlit gatherings on the beach? Maybe this month I could…but I wasn't sure I wanted to, not yet. I didn't want any other selkies trying to woo her away from me.

I was at Emma's promptly at one on Tuesday, after making my preparations. My sealskin was in my leather kit bag concealed under the beach rose shrubs at our changing place. I'd be there in less than an hour…and so would Emma.

I'd called yesterday to see if they'd heard anything. Emma had answered the telephone, her voice full of suppressed excitement. "Wetherell residence!"

"Emma, it's Malcolm."

"Oh."

Disappointment flattened her voice. I tried not to mind. "Any news? How is your father?"

"I don't know. We're still waiting to hear from the hospital."

"Then I won't keep you." I hesitated. "I hope you're still going to come for a walk with me tomorrow, so that we can talk."

"Y-yes, all right. If we've heard from the hospital by then. We *better* have," she added.

"I'm sure you will. Tomorrow—it's important, Emma. I wouldn't ask you if it weren't."

"Uh, I really shouldn't be tying up the line much longer…"

"I'm sorry. I'll see you tomorrow, then. Around one?"

She'd said yes and hung up quickly. I guessed I shouldn't be surprised, but her lack of enthusiasm had stung for a second. Maybe Mother was right and I should wait until she wasn't so preoccupied. But the next full moon was coming. She needed to know by then.

Today she met me at the door looking somber and puffy-eyed. I gave her a quick kiss on the cheek after we were safely in the front hall. "Any word?"

She nodded. "We got through to someone at the hospital around three yesterday. Dad — they said he's all right, under the circumstances. Weak, of course, but he's been restless — agitated was the word they used — so they're keeping him sedated so he can sleep. They said rest and calm is vital, so as not to put any undue strain on his heart."

"That's good news. It sounds like they know what they're doing."

"Yes," she agreed, but it sounded half-hearted. "I just wish I knew what he was agitated about," she burst out. "It's not like him. Was it why he had the heart attack? He's usually the calmest person in the world. If I could *go* there — but I can't, and it's driving me crazy."

I glanced around to make sure we didn't have any company, and put my arms around her. "You know I'd take you if I could."

"Oh, Malcolm." She rested her forehead on my shoulder. "I know you can't, but thank you."

I couldn't resist stealing another kiss. "Let's go for that walk, instead. You need to get out of the house and think about something else for a while."

She stiffened and pulled away. "What else should I be thinking about right now?"

For a moment, I hesitated, again hearing in my head Mother's warning to give her more time. But no — Emma needed to get away and think about something else. And wouldn't what

I was going to tell her be so amazing that it would help her feel better? I'd see how she was, once we'd gotten out of the house and down on the beach, and make my decision then.

"Come on, Emma. It'll be good for you. There isn't anything you can do for your dad by sitting next to the telephone all day. Besides, we have some important things to discuss. Remember what we talked about on Sunday?"

She sighed. "I...yes, I guess you're right. Gran's on the back porch—she'll hear if the telephone rings," she said, more to herself than to me.

"Then let's go tell her we're going." I stole another kiss, and she finally smiled.

Mrs. Wetherell was on the porch, knitting and reading aloud an article in the newspaper to Josiah Barnes while he shelled peas. Emma waited till her grandmother paused and looked up at us inquiringly. "I'm going for a walk with Malcolm," she said. "Could you listen for the phone?"

"Where're you walking?" Josiah demanded, glowering up at us from his peas.

"Malcolm won't get lost. Don't fuss," Mrs. W. admonished him. "Of course I will. Have a nice walk."

"Getting lost ain't what I'm worried about," Josiah muttered. "Bad enough that grandniece of yours is away more often nor not."

"Is Helen out too?" Emma asked. "I didn't know. I haven't been very good company for her lately, have I?"

"She went for a picnic with the Osborn boy." Mrs. Wetherell frowned at Josiah. "They're young women now. You can't put them in a box and tie it up with twine and sealing wax, you know."

Josiah muttered something under his breath, and Emma gave her grandmother's shoulder a quick squeeze. I hoped we wouldn't bump into Helen and Osborn, wherever they'd gone for their picnic. I doubted any of us would enjoy that.

"Where are we going?" Emma asked as we turned down the road away from the village and the hotel.

"Down to the beach below the hotel. It's quiet and no one will bother us."

She got a flash of that mischievous expression that I loved. "Shouldn't you be entertaining young lady guests at the hotel? I thought that was one of your duties."

I sighed. "It is, but there aren't any pretty ones staying right now. So I figured I'd come see you to pass the time."

"Pass the time, huh?"

Instantly I wrapped my arms around her. "Only with you," I said, and covered her mouth with mine. After a second's hesitation, she melted against me. I think I could have spent the rest of the afternoon kissing her, but I made myself stop after a few minutes; we had things to discuss. But I was glad I had: the tightness around her mouth and forehead had relaxed. I'd been absolutely right to coax her out today and take her mind off Professor Verlaine.

We walked on in silence after that, our hands entwined. I led her past the last house on the road, then across a heath of beach plum thickets and cedars. It was a perfect July day, sunny but not too hot and with a nice breeze blowing from the south-west. On the beach below, the sand would be warm and the dune grasses would sway and hiss their soft music in the wind — the perfect accompaniment to our talk. Someday years from now I would remind her of today, and we'd smile at each other and remember. I squeezed her hand, and she looked at me inquiringly.

"Just thinking," I said.

"I'm trying not to." Her forehead had creased again.

"How about if I make you think about something else?" We were on a path through dune grass now, almost at the beach. Not too far down the sand, my skin waited for us.

"Like what?

"Like what you can do to help Captain Abbott."

"I'd almost forgotten about that, what with Dad." She took a deep breath. "Yes, tell me. If I can't go to him, I need *something* to do."

There—I *had* been right to do this. I knew it.

But now that it was actually time to tell her, I wasn't sure how to begin. I led her down to the sand and took my own deep breath in turn. "First, this is—I guess you'd call it top secret," I said. "It's so secret that the captain doesn't have anything about it in writing. Though if anyone knew about it, they probably wouldn't believe it."

Her brows drew together. "You're being awfully cryptic."

"Yeah, it's...it's a little hard to explain." I hesitated, then plunged in. "There's a group of us here on the island and further up the coast all the way to Provincetown who keep watch on the waters around the Cape, just like the boys at the air station do. Only we're not doing it from the air."

"Where are you doing it from?"

We were almost to the beach rose thicket on the edge of the sand where my skin was hidden. I answered, trying to keep my voice casual, "From the water."

"Oh." She was frowning. "But I don't know the first thing about boats. Why did Captain Abbott think I could be useful to you?"

"We—well, we don't use boats."

"You swim? Is that why you were so intent on making sure I was a strong swimmer? But...really, how can people swimming do a better job watching for U-boats than airplanes or dirigibles? You can't go very far from shore—"

"Yes, we swim. But..." This was it. It took me several seconds to bring myself to speak, the selkie habit of secrecy was so deeply ingrained. "You've heard of selkies."

"Yes, of course. I had that dream—" She stopped and looked at me. "You aren't saying that...or you're teasing me—"

"I'd never tease you about this." I turned her to face me and took her hands in mine. "Selkies are real. They're here—*right here*," I added, squeezing her hands and smiling at her. "Oh Emma, I've been wanting to talk to you about this ever since I realized—and now we'll be able to look for your father—your real father—"

"My *what?*" Her hands jerked out of mine.

I hesitated, then decided to forge on, recapturing her hands and drawing them and her closer. Once she'd heard everything, she'd understand. "Your real father. You're a selkie—or a half-one, anyway—and so are we Galbraiths. Maggie was the one who figured out about you, and she's right. The only question is, what happened to your skin? Even half-selkies are often born with a sealskin, my mother says. Have you ever seen it? If Professor Verlaine did anything to harm it—but no, that would have hurt you too, so he must have hidden it somewhere—"

"*What are you talking about?*" Her voice was low and calm, but there was a sharp edge to it, and she was trying to pull her hands away again.

I wouldn't let them go. "Emma, listen. We know it's true. Your mother—she must have—have been in love with one of us, and you're their child." I skirted away from a less delicate description of what her mother had done. "But your sealskin—we have to find it. Have you ever seen anything that might be it—"

"This is ridiculous." Emma wrenched her hands away and took a step back, breathing hard. Her eyes were bright with tears. "Don't tell me *you're* going to start too. Dragging my mother's name into the mud, just like those harpies at the Red Cross and—and everyone else on this b-blasted island! Or is this supposed to be a joke? If it is, it's in rotten taste. My father—my FATHER—is lying sick in a hospital practically a thousand miles away, and now you're—"

This was not going as I'd expected. "Now, Emma," I began reasonably. "Washington's not a thousand miles away, and he's not really your fa—"

"Don't you *dare* say that again." The tears overflowed. "I can't believe—you too—I thought you loved me!"

"I do." I reached out to touch her face. "You don't know how happy I am that I found you—that you should be a selkie too—"

"I am not!" She swatted my hand away. "There's no such

thing as selkies!"

"There damned well is!" Now I was getting mad. "I can prove it to you." I stalked past her and around the clump of beach roses to where my bag waited with my skin. It wasn't there.

My skin was gone.

"God damn it!" I didn't care who heard me. "Margaret Galbraith, get over here and give me my skin back." I'd seen Maggie hanging around the lobby when I'd told Father where I was going. She must have overheard and got here first, to play a trick—she *must* have... "Maggie!" I turned around, cupping my hands at my mouth to shout. "I'm going to murder you if you don't get over here in the next five seconds with my skin!"

Emma had followed me, still scowling. "Maggie's not here. What are you—"

She had to be. Who else would have known it was here? "My skin. She took my skin. *Maggie!*" I turned back to Emma. "I was going to show you, to prove it to you—damn it, selkies are real! I'm one, and so is my little sister who is going to regret the day she was born if she doesn't appear with it right *now!*"

The only answer was the hissing of the dune grass—no longer musical, but mocking—and that's when I began to panic. If Maggie wasn't here—if she hadn't taken it as a joke—then *where was my skin?* I had put it here barely an hour ago and gone straight to get Emma...who now stared at me like I was something a gull had dropped on her shoulder.

"Don't look at me that way." I held my hand out to her. "You've got to believe me. I'm a selkie—truly I am—and you are as well—"

"No." Emma was backing away. "I'm not. I don't know what you are, but I'm Ernest Verlaine's daughter. I am *not* some imaginary creature, and as soon as I can manage it I'm getting off this island to go see him, and if I never see Monomoyick again, or a seal, or *you*, I will be perfectly happy." She scrubbed at her mouth with the back of her hand. "I can't believe I wanted you to kiss me—"

"Emma," I said, but the word came out in a hoarse whisper. "Emma, I love you —"

But she'd turned away and was running up the beach to the path that led to the road.

"Emma," I whispered. And then I was crouching in the dune grass by the beach rose, staring at the spot where my bag had been. I could see the outline in the sand where it had rested. Should I have pointed that out to her? But no. She wouldn't have believed me.

My skin — one half of me — was gone. And so was the girl I loved. I wasn't sure which loss hurt worse.

·CHAPTER TWENTY·
EMMA

All that miserable walk home, I barely felt the road under my feet; I think my anger kept me hovering above the ground like the zeppelins dropping bombs on London.

Why had Malcolm said all those ridiculous things about selkies? And even worse, what had possessed him to repeat that unforgivable, awful lie about my mother and father? He said he loved me…but there was no way I could believe that.

He was wrong. They were *all* wrong. I knew they were wrong, but their lies were there now in my head, and I could never un-hear them.

The first thing I would do when I got home was compose a telegram telling Dad I was coming to him because I could not spend a day longer on this island than I had to. I would catch the first ferry to Mattaquason in the morning and send it. With any luck, I could be out of here by the day after tomorrow.

By the time I reached Gran's I had calmed down a little, but it wasn't a relief. Grief and loss were filling in the spaces that anger had vacated. Why had Malcolm done this? Why did he have to ruin this — this fragile new thing between us? *Why?*

I made it up to my room without seeing anyone and threw myself onto my bed. *Why — why — why* pounded an insistent rhythm inside my head like hammer blows until I couldn't stand it any longer and curled into a ball on my side and let myself cry. Miss Blunt had said that a good cry always made things better, that tears would flush out the bad feelings. But no number of tears seemed capable of flushing out this hurt. I shed enough to figure that out.

Gran didn't force me to come down to dinner. In fact, I must have slept through it, because the next thing I knew it was dark in my room. I sat up groggily and felt for the light by my bed and turned it on. The glare made me wince and screw up my eyes, so I didn't notice for a moment that Helen was sitting on a chair drawn up to the foot of my bed.

"There's a plate of dinner in the oven for you, if you want it," she said, calmly rising and going to the windows to let down the blackout curtains.

"No" My voice came out in a croak. I cleared my throat and squinted at her. "What are you doing here?"

"Waiting for you to wake up. Great-aunt Dorinda thought I should." She came back to her chair, pausing next to it as if suddenly unsure. "Are—are you all right?"

I thought about that. "No," I finally said.

She sat down and folded her hands in her lap. "Do you want to talk about it?"

"No."

"Your grandmother was a little upset when you told her to go away."

"Did I?" I lay back down, trying to remember. Someone had been knocking on the door and wouldn't leave me alone to die. "Was that Gran? I'm sorry. I couldn't talk."

"Can you talk now?"

"No."

"Was it Malcolm?"

I rolled over so that my back was to her. After a long time, I said, "Yes."

"I thought it might be."

We were both silent for a while. I thought about drifting off to sleep again, but the lamp was shining right in my face.

"What are you going to do?" she asked, after a while.

"Leave. I need to send a telegram to Dad tomorrow."

Thank heavens she didn't try to contradict me. Instead she said, "Would you like me to take your telegram into town?"

"Yes. Thank you." I'd thought about that. Taking the telegram myself to Mattaquason would put me in danger of bumping into Malcolm. All I really wanted was to stay right here in bed until it was time for me to get on a train.

More blessed, cool silence. Right now, words felt like burning coals in my ears. Then she said, "What will you do if your father says not to come?"

I hadn't—didn't want to—think about that. "I don't know." Go to one of my uncles. Or maybe my last governess would let me stay with her. Miss Nutting was still in Boston. Maybe she'd let me visit until—until I went somewhere else. As much as I'd resisted the idea, there was a place at Bryn Mawr waiting for me come September.

"Well, maybe they'll send your father home to recover."

I sat up again. "Oh, do you think so?" That would be best of all—for Dad to come home to Boston, for us to pick up our lives where they'd left off in May and go comfortably on as we always had.

Except I wasn't sure we could do that anymore. I'd been cursed by this place, so that from now on I would be unable to look at my beloved father without remembering. There was no magic scouring powder that could remove that taint even though I was certain there was nothing to the story. I lay back down again. "Thanks, Helen," I said, but my voice sounded listless, even to me. "Maybe they will."

She stood up. "Here. Let's get that cable written, and then you can get properly ready for bed. I promise I'll take it to Mattaquason first thing, all right? I really do think you could use a couple of weeks away from here."

I took the pad and pencil she handed me and managed to compose something to send Dad that would convey my desperation to come to him without worrying him (I hoped), and got undressed and into a nightgown. Then I drank the glass of sherry that she'd snuck up from the decanter in the library, and I slept.

Unfortunately, sleeping meant I had to wake up again.

Gran brought me breakfast on a tray the next morning. She sat down in the chair Helen had left and looked at me anxiously.

"I could have come downstairs. I'm not ill," I said, gruffly, because the words I really wanted to say wouldn't come to my tongue.

"I know. But occasionally a lady needs some time alone in her room," Gran said, and I wanted to cry because she was being so wonderfully, delicately understanding, even though she had no idea what had happened. I did cry, a little, as I nibbled my toast with beach plum jelly, but she didn't seem to notice. When I was done she took my tray, kissed me, and started to leave the room.

"Gran? Has there been any news from Dad?"

"That nice Major Oliver called yesterday. He's still resting comfortably. They want to keep him sedated for another day or so until they judge he's stronger." She gave me an encouraging smile and left me alone again.

I managed to bathe and dress, but that exhausted my initiative for the day. I wished I could be sedated for a few days, like Daddy, until I felt stronger too.

I spent the afternoon sitting in the window seat in my room trying not to think, and succeeded pretty well, staring out without seeing the lawn, the path to the beach, the shining water. I definitely didn't want to think about the last time I'd been down by the water—

And then it all rushed over me in a horrible, dark flood. Malcolm—his mouth on mine, his hands pulling me close, so delicious, so right—then his words, stripping my father from me. I pulled my knees up to my chest and buried my face against them, trying not to howl.

"Emma!"

I ignored it, but the call was repeated. I lifted my head and told the door to go away.

"Emma! Down here!"

I looked out the open window. Maggie Galbraith was on the lawn, her long braids practically bristling with tension. When she saw me looking down, she didn't smile, but gazed at me solemnly. "They wouldn't let me up to see you," she said in a stage whisper.

"Go away, Maggie." I leaned my head against the window frame and didn't look at her. The last person I wanted to see was anyone named Galbraith.

"Uh-uh. Not until I tell you what I have to say."

I didn't move, hoping she'd give up and leave. I should have known better; this was Maggie, after all.

"Emma, I didn't do it. I didn't touch Malcolm's—his—his you-know-what. I wasn't anywhere near there. I don't know who did, but it wasn't me."

I didn't move.

"Anyway, I wanted to tell you that. I didn't want you to think I was a horrible person. I—I miss you. I wish you would come see us. Malcolm—he's really upset—"

"Here! I thought we told you Miss Emma wasn't feeling well?" Josiah's voice, sounding very cross, approached from the victory garden side of the house. "You take yourself home right this minute, Miss Pain in the Rear!"

"I had to talk to her," Maggie's voice replied stubbornly, but in retreat from Josiah's. "I miss you, Emma. AND I DIDN'T TAKE IT!" A patter of running footsteps punctuated her last shout.

Something—a faint, questioning, *Could it be there really was something to take?* welled up in my thoughts, and then sank out of sight in my darkness.

There was a dance at the hotel that night. I'd forgotten it was the Fourth of July. Gran and Helen went, though Gran didn't want to leave me. But I roused myself enough to tell her I would be far happier at home and that they shouldn't worry about me. I didn't want to think about girls in party dresses twirling around in the arms of handsome boys or going out onto the porch to watch the fireworks that would be launched from the beach out over the water, superimposed on the full moon rising up from the ocean. It would be glorious. No German U-boats would be sneaking around Cape Cod tonight with all that light—and then memory caught up with me like another razor to the throat. When I was done crying, I went to bed.

I suppose it was inevitable that I should dream that night—or maybe it was a nightmare. I was running down the beach again as I had from Malcolm the day before (Was it just the day before? It felt like eternity), but this time it was night, and the full moon shone down, making the sand gleam coldly.

And then, up ahead, I saw them—thirty or forty figures, maybe more, in a circle, while others stood round, watching. The figures in the circle were dancing. I heard something that sounded round and silvery, like flutes playing in harmony.

"No," I said, my steps slowing. I tried to make myself stop, turn around, but my feet wouldn't obey me. They carried me right up to the edge of the watching people, men and women and children, the children running and weaving in and out of the crowd in their own dance. None of them wore any clothes. I looked down at myself and saw that I still wore my nightgown, thank goodness.

An old man a few paces away seemed to notice me then. His silver hair shone in the moonlight, and he limped slightly as he approached me.

"Well, young woman. So you found us," he said, pitching his voice under the music. A short distance away I saw the flutists, three of them, two women and a man, their eyes smiling above their puffed cheeks as they played.

"I don't particularly want to be here," I said. It sounded rather rude, but this was a dream. What did it matter if I was?

"No?" He smiled. "And yet here you are. Sometimes fighting is more trouble than it's worth. Besides, why fight this?" He gestured up at the moon-flooded sky, the gentle breeze, the laughing, beautiful people circling and swaying to the music.

"It's my dream. I can fight it if I want to."

"Ah, a dream, is it?"

"What else could it be?" I folded my arms across my chest. "You're all supposed to be selkies, right? Doing your dance-on-the-beach-by-the-light-of-the-moon thing. Of course I'm dreaming about that. I wish I weren't, but I am."

"Why do you wish you weren't? You could accept it and join in instead. It's a lot of fun. I rather miss it, myself, but at my age and with this leg…" He shrugged ruefully.

"What happened to your leg?" I wondered what explanation I'd come up with; it was an interesting detail to add into a dream. My governess Miss Ayers had read Dr. Freud's book on dreams and decided we should both keep accounts of our dreams for a few months. None of them had made any sense; this one was much more coherent.

"Nothing interesting. I'd rather hear you say why you'd rather not dream about us."

"I don't have to explain myself."

"Well, no," he said, rubbing his nose reflectively. "As a matter of fact, I already know why. I can't say I fully understand, but I know. He loves you very much, by the way."

"No." I turned away. I would not put up with being lectured in my own dream. I stepped away and almost bumped into another man, a young one.

"Why, a newcomer!" His eyes gleamed under dark brows, and his smile was wide and ever-so-slightly predatory. "A very fair newcomer. But wearing far too much for a dancing night. Come, my lovely one." He tugged on my nightgown. "Come join your steps with ours—or perhaps would you like to walk with me under the moon to a place where we could dance our own dance, just the two of us?"

"Enough." The older man was beside me in an instant. "This one is not for you to entice with your charming ways, Struan."

"*She* hasn't said that." The young man reached out to take me by the shoulders, but my silver-haired friend had captured my arm and started to lead me away.

"Go back now," he said. "This isn't the place for you after all, not when you're alone. There are too many sharks here who would happily devour you." A derisive laugh trailed after us. "Go, and sleep well and dreamlessly. You need the healing that sleep will bring." He touched me once, twice, just above each eye, and the dream faded. I rolled over, fluffed my pillow, and slept like the dead the rest of the night.

I made it to the back porch on Friday and completed the pair of socks I'd begun last weekend: some poor soldier on the Front should not have to do without socks because I was unhappy.

I forced myself to think about every stitch so that my mind couldn't wander. Wandering minds were dangerous things; for heaven's sake, I couldn't even trust it in sleep—look at that crazy dream I'd had. I wished Helen had been around to keep me company; she could chatter inconsequentially about clothes, which was an excellent way to occupy my wandering brain. But she'd vanished again, off on her own business.

We'd still not had any word directly from Dad, though Helen brought me the receipt from the telegram she'd sent for me. Major Oliver called and said that his doctors had decided to let him fully wake up over the weekend, to see if he seemed calmer. I clung to that thought as I knitted away. Maybe they *would* let him come home on leave to recover. I would take the next train home to Boston to open up the house if they so much as hinted at it.

At least thinking about Dad and planning how I would take care of him kept me from thinking about—about other things. I could just barely recall the existence of the Ocean Hotel without wincing, but that was as far as I'd gotten. I cried only four times over the course of the day. That was progress.

But at night…that's when the thoughts would ambush me. Just as I fell into that state between waking and sleeping, I would remember Malcolm's eyes smiling at me, remember talking and teasing him, remember his arms around me as we danced, his mouth warm on mine when we kissed—and jerk awake, heart pounding and aching. I wanted to wail like an abandoned child then, but I didn't.

·Chapter Twenty-one·
Malcolm

I'm not quite sure how I got through the days after Emma ran from me on the beach.

When I made it back to the hotel and told my father what had happened, he had paled—and then sent me down to the delivery entrance to accept a shipment of wine from our supplier in Boston. The same sort of thing happened the next day, and the day after: my parents still expected me to pull my weight in the running of the hotel despite the fact that my life had been all but ruined. At first I hated them until I noticed the worry in the depths of their eyes when I caught them looking at me.

So I went through the motions, and in a way it helped: I could check guests in and out, give them their mail, reserve their times on the tennis courts, answer their questions, all with a polite smile on my lips and nothing at all in my head. I was blank, void...until the rage and grief and fear overwhelmed me and I had to get out of the hotel and take myself far down the beach, away from everyone, where I could beat the sand with my fists until my hands hurt.

Had Emma not really loved me after all? Had I just been someone to pass the time with over a dull summer until she went to college? Occasionally I could almost convince myself of that...but it never lasted for more than a minute or two. She hadn't been bored here—I knew that. And those kisses she'd given me on Sunday hadn't been faked. And then I was back to pounding the sand...without even the solace of putting on my skin and escaping into my other world. Bits of that last encounter on the beach kept replaying in my mind like a damaged Victrola record skipping back to play the same phrase over and over—mostly when she'd said, *"if I never see Monomoyick again, or a seal, or you, I will be perfectly happy."* And every time, it felt like a harpoon in my heart.

I couldn't imagine never seeing her again. Maybe if she would talk to Maggie, who could prove that we were selkies...but I wasn't going to ask my eleven-year-old sister to try to get my girl back for me. Besides, Maggie wasn't talking to me because she thought I'd hurt Emma.

That *I* had hurt Emma. That was rich.

I certainly wasn't able to go out on patrol (oh, *gods!*), but I continued to wake up at 3:30 a.m. anyway. Habits die hard with selkies as much as with humans.

Rather than lying in bed and trying not to think of Emma, I got dressed and wandered into the hotel lobby. A light shone from Father's office. He often got up as early as I did in order to have an hour or two to himself before things began stirring at the hotel; much past seven he couldn't call his soul his own during the summer months. I tiptoed past his mostly closed door, but it didn't do me any good.

"Malcolm," he called.

I sighed and stuck my head around his door. "Good morning, sir."

He was cradling a cup of tea in his hands, probably one of Annie Goslin's herbal blends. She made one with seaweed that he was especially fond of. "Why are you up so early?"

I shrugged. "Couldn't help it."

He continued to look at me. "Sit down for a minute."

"I don't want to disturb you—"

"You aren't."

I sat. He sipped his tea, then set his cup down and said, "I have asked the clans to spread the word about searching for your skin. All the beaches of the Cape will be scoured. If it is anywhere outside, it will be found." He cleared his throat. "Are you sure you saw no one on the beach that day?"

"I'm sure."

"Or at any other times? Someone on the beach who should not have been there?"

I looked down at my lap and shook my head.

"Is there anyone—human or selkie—whom you might suspect of stealing it?"

That made me look up. "Gods, no," I said. I could not even imagine a selkie taking another selkie's skin: among us, it was worse than murder. And anyway, I didn't have any enemies—at least none who hated me like that.

And as for humans...yeah, there was one human who probably hated me that much. But as far as I knew, George Osborn didn't spend much time on the island. At least, I'd never seen him here aside from at hotel dances.

Father sighed. "Your mother and I have searched all the guest rooms under the guise of checking the plumbing for a leak, as well as the staff rooms, offices, and outbuildings. Nothing has been found."

I swallowed. It had only been two days; they were moving fast. Before the trail went cold? I shivered. "What if it's never found?"

He gazed at me bleakly, and I knew he was thinking—and fearing—the same thing. How could a selkie be a selkie without his skin? What would become of me, already being trained to follow in his wake as a leader of the selkies, if I could no longer venture into our true home?

Would I even be a selkie anymore?

Some, like Isabel's husband Muirfinn, would no doubt

laugh and say I deserved it—that I had already stopped being a true selkie. If my skin were never found, I would have to leave here, before the sight of an ocean I could no longer enter drove me mad…except abandoning my home would destroy me too.

"Maybe losing my skin is a good thing after all," I said bitterly. "Emma would probably like me better if I can't change."

"Malcolm." His voice was stern. "I did not intend to speak of Miss Verlaine. But I hope you have no intention of trying to see her again."

"That won't be hard. I don't think she has any intention of seeing me." Not that I hadn't fantasized about every possible ploy to get her to see me, from lying in wait in the hydrangeas outside her house to climbing in her window in the middle of the night.

"I cannot say I blame her. You did not handle her well, my son. If you truly love another, you must endeavor to give them what *they* want and need, not what you want her to want and need. Even when they are not the same."

A spark of rage flamed through me, and I half-rose from my chair…and then fell back as the truth of his words hit me.

I *hadn't* given her what she wanted and needed on Tuesday—a listening ear, a shoulder to have a good hard cry on, a comforting hug. I'd been too intent on giving her something she had no room in her head to accept right now—forced it on her, to be honest. I hadn't known about the gossip she'd been hearing at the Red Cross meetings; Mother ran a weekly knitting circle for guests and staff at the hotel, rather than going to the meetings in Mattaquason. If I had, would I have had the wisdom and patience to wait until she was less worried about the professor's—all right, I would stop being stubborn—about her dad's illness?

I didn't know. But I was afraid I wouldn't.

"I know I ruined everything," I finally mumbled, and before my father could say another word, I rose and almost ran from the room.

Isabel came to see us a day or so later, to my mother's joy. I was less overjoyed; she was the last person I wanted to talk to about any of this. When I heard her voice in our apartment, I hurried through the lobby to the veranda. It would be a longer walk to the beach, but I didn't care; escape was escape. I couldn't face her false sympathy over Emma; in another day or two she'd probably be trying to throw me together with another of her friends. Except none of them would probably be interested in me now—a selkie without his skin.

It didn't do any good. Before I was halfway across the front lawn, she'd caught up with me. "Malcolm!" She seized my arm. "I want to talk to you."

"Hello, Isabel," I said wearily. Calling her Izzy seemed like too much trouble. "I was just going out—"

"Where?" she demanded, and I winced. There was nowhere on the beach for me to go to—not any more. She must have caught my expression, as her face softened. "I am sorry, brother—so sorry. For all of it. Please, may I speak with you for a few minutes?"

My sister was sounding almost human. The thought nearly made me smile. "Yeah, all right."

She steered me over to a pair of chairs near the stairs down to the sand—the same chairs Emma and I had sat in a hundred years ago. My heart seemed to twist inside my chest.

"Malcolm." She turned her chair so it faced me and leaned toward me. "I really am sorry. I can't imagine what you're going through right now. We're all doing everything we can—we've searched every inch of the island, and up around Mattaquason as well."

"Thank you."

"We've been talking about it, of course. No one of us would ever have done such a despicable thing, and most of us are convinced that it had to have been a human who stole it. Maybe someone was out walking and saw you putting your bag under the rose bush." She sighed. "You know how humans are about 'souvenirs.' It wouldn't surprise me in the least if it were a guest from the hotel, maybe. Or one of those boys from the air station."

"Could have been," I finally said after a moment. Because what else could I say? I had no idea who'd done it. It could well have been one of those.

"You don't think" — she leaned closer. "You don't think that Emma might have had something to do with it, do you?"

"What?" I lunged out of my chair.

She drew back, alarmed. "I heard that she and you had had words — that she…well, it makes some amount of sense, doesn't it? Maybe you were wrong about her. Maybe we all were, and she isn't really a — "

I turned away and stalked up the lawn, ignoring her indignant "Malcolm!"

The week just kept getting better and better. When by Friday my skin had still not been found, I forced myself to go down to the air station to tell Captain Abbott what had happened.

"Stolen!" He stared at me over his desk.

"We think so, sir," I said. Amazingly, my voice only shook a little. "We're doing everything we can to search for it, but in the meanwhile I can't go on patrol. My friends will still be out there, though. I hope everything will continue to run smoothly even if I'm not there."

"I'm sure it will." He shook his head. "Who could have done such a thing?"

"I don't know." The fact that it had been unsupervised for only an hour still preyed on my mind. That made it feel deliberate, not just a random theft.

The captain frowned and drummed his fingers on the blotter. "Would you like me to make inquiries here on the base? If someone found it by accident…"

"Thank you, sir. I'd appreciate that."

He made a note on a pad then stood up, came around the desk, and put a hand on my shoulder. "I'm not a man of much imagination, but even I can guess a bit of what you're going through. If there's anything I can do to help—"

"I'll let you know." I stood up too, because I had to get out of there. That had been harder than I'd thought it would be. And while I appreciated his sympathy, I also couldn't handle much more of it. This is how everyone in my world must view me now—as only part of myself, like an amputee. Sooner or later that alone would be enough to drive me away from here. The human world would at least see me as whole, even if I forever bled from an invisible wound.

I went back to the hotel the long way around, via the beach. Father had given me the morning off to call on Captain Abbott; I guessed he knew it wasn't going to be an easy thing to do. The blue-green water, today just lapping the sand with gentle wavelets, was both beautiful and painful to look at. On any other day with the morning off I would have been under those waves, not walking beside them.

My throat grew tight, and I had to blink a few times. I should have gone by the road.

A few dozen yards off the beach, a dark head surfaced. The seal looked at me, hesitated, then swam straight for shore. Before it had paused in shallow water, I knew who it was and waited for Luthais to shrug off his skin before I went to meet him.

We clasped hands silently, then stood there not quite looking at each other. He was the first to break the awkward silence. "So…how are you?"

I looked at him then, and he flushed. "Sorry. That was a stupid question."

"Yeah," I said drily. We looked at each other again, and

both broke into crooked smiles. He embraced me awkwardly, and then things were better. He fell into step next to me, and we walked up the beach.

"How is everyone?" I asked. I just realized that I hadn't talked to any of my friends since—since *it* happened.

"Oh, fine. Struan said something completely rancid to Dugal yesterday, though…"

We fell into familiar lines—we'd always had conversations like this whenever I was home from college, and Luthais was a good storyteller. Not that there was much for him to tell. It only *felt* like I'd been away for months.

"Mostly, we've all been busy searching," he concluded. "Your sister's barely let anyone rest."

"Izzy? Really?" I might have to forgive her for what she'd said the other day. "Captain Abbott at the air station said he would as well, in case someone there found it and took a fancy to it. And my parents have checked the hotel."

"That's…that's good." He hesitated. "It sounds like they think the same thing as Isabel, then."

"What do you mean?"

"That whoever took your skin was human."

I sighed. "Yeah, probably. I can't think of any selkies who dislike me that much."

We were quiet for a moment. Then he said, "A lot of us are pretty angry."

There was an off note in his voice. "What is it, Luthais?" I asked, standing still.

A long pause. Then, "The patrollers have quit."

"*What!*"

He winced; I'd shouted almost in his ear. "I told you: they're angry. They can't see why we should be helping the humans, if this is how the humans repay our help."

I stood still. This wasn't happening. It couldn't be. "But— they can't. This is *important*. The Germans—"

"It's hard for them to care about the Germans, Malcolm— *they're* not a threat to us. Some human stealing the skin of one of our leaders is." He looked unhappy. "I probably shouldn't say this, but I'm kind of relieved they're so upset. There was a lot of grumbling that you'd become too human, going off to live as one for four years then falling in love with a human girl and all—"

"Emma isn't human. Her father was a selkie," I said absently, because most of me was still reeling. No patrols were happening. A U-boat could sneak in and torpedo the *Never Late* or lob a few shells at Mattaquason or the air station and no one be able to do anything about it till they were back out to sea and it was too late.

"She's a *what?*" He grabbed my arm.

I shook off his hand. "Ask them—*beg* them for me. We can't stop patrolling—"

"She's a selkie? Are you sure?"

I smiled bitterly. "Yes. But it doesn't matter, she hates me now." I'd destroyed that part of my life already; I had to save the rest of it. "Look, I'll come and talk to them myself—this evening, right here—"

"This is getting too complicated," he muttered. "They'll be glad to see you if you come, so I hope you do. But it won't do any good."

I made myself speak as calmly as possible. "If the Germans should attack anyplace on the Cape, we won't be safe. We'll get even more humans down here than we already have at the air station, and none of us want that. And—what the Germans are doing is wrong even if we aren't directly affected by it. There's such a thing as a greater good."

I might as well have saved my breath. Luthais shook his head. "I'll keep at it—I know this is important to you. Maybe one or two others will, too. But I don't think most will. I'm sorry, my friend. But I thought you should know." He touched my shoulder gently and went back into the water.

I stood watching long after he'd put on his skin and disappeared under the waves. That was it, then. I'd have to go back to Captain Abbott and tell him that no, the selkies would not help him and he was on his own. He would take it calmly because that was the kind of man he was. Me, on the other hand...

And now I might as well get on a train for Boston and enlist and let them send me to the trenches. There really wasn't anything left for me here.

·Chapter Twenty-two·
Emma

On Tuesday, I'd just finished casting on a new pair of socks after lunch when I heard the telephone ring from where I sat on the back porch. I leapt up, dropping my needles and yarn and probably a few stitches, and raced inside to the front hall.

Gran was already there. She smiled and nodded when she saw me. "—so pleased to hear that, Ernest!" she was saying. "You don't know how worried we've been. Poor Emma's been a trooper, though you can imagine how upset she's been—"

Poor Emma had been anything but a trooper, but I didn't care about that now. I hovered next to Gran, practically hopping from one foot to the other. "Can I talk to him?" I mouthed.

"—what was that, Ernest? Oh, yes, very. She's right here and will probably explode if I don't let her speak with you. Here she is." She handed me the mouthpiece and receiver.

I took them carefully, because my hands were shaking. "Dad?" I quavered.

"Emma, my dear." He sounded weak and even more quavery than I did, but it was *him*. "How are you?"

"I'm fine! How are you—we've been so worried—you don't know how hard it was for me not to jump on the next train to Washington!" I was babbling, but I knew he wouldn't mind. "Do you—hurt? Are they making you comfortable?"

"They're spoiling me terribly. It's just this confounded

weakness. I'm afraid I won't be doing the job Uncle Sam asked me to do for a while yet."

"Would they let you come home? I could go back up to Boston and get everything ready for you—"

"I don't know, child. The doctors haven't decided yet, They mostly stand around my bed looking like stalagmites, stroking their stalactite beards."

I laughed. If he could make geological jokes, he must be feeling better. "Maybe I need to have a word with them. I can tell them I'll take good care of you—"

"I'm sure you would." He paused, as if to muster his strength. "Emma, my dear," he finally said. "You don't know what a comfort your last letter has been. I just read it yesterday—I was too groggy before. I—I'm glad you've had such a happy life with me."

Oh, the letter I'd written him last Sunday, before... everything. "I'm glad you liked it. It's true, every last bit of it. I love you, Daddy." I didn't care if every telephone operator on the eastern seaboard was listening.

"I love you too." He paused again, as if talking was winding him. "Your letter—it helped me decide. Is Josiah Barnes there? I would like to speak with him."

"Josiah?" Why should Dad want to talk to Josiah? Then I remembered that Josiah had let slip that they'd discussed something before I came here. Hmm. "I don't know. Gran?"

She'd withdrawn to the library, but came hurrying at my call. "Dad wants to talk to Josiah," I told her. "Is he here?"

Her eyebrows shot up just as mine must have. "I think he's in the garden. I'll get him."

Josiah came clumping in a moment later, looking mystified. I held the telephone out to him. "It's my father. He wants to talk to you."

He wiped his hands on the bandanna hanging out of his pocket, a grim expression on his face, and took it from me. "Barnes here, sir," he said, and jerked his head at me, toward the library door. I pouted, but left.

However, it seemed Josiah had only one volume for speaking on the telephone. I joined Gran in the library, took a casual seat in a chair near the door, plucked a book from the nearest shelf for protective coloration, and heard everything he said perfectly. I wasn't ashamed of eavesdropping. Sometimes you had to out of sheer self-preservation, as Miss Lansing, my sixth governess, once said.

For a while, Josiah said nothing. That meant Dad was talking, and I hoped he wouldn't tire himself out. Then Josiah said, "Are you sure you want to do that?"

More silence. "Well, of course I can. I'm just not sure it's a good time—no, I suppose there ain't any such thing. Where is it?"

Another silence, longer. "All right. I'd rather not be the one to do it—I think it should more properly come from you, sir. But under the circumstances...yeah. Probably can't get there for a couple days though, so don't be fretting. She won't thank me any, I can tell you that. But I said I'd help back then, an' I'll keep my word. Hold on a minute; I'll get the missus."

My ears had pricked up like a bird dog's. She? Who was "she?" Me? Gran?

Josiah looked around the door. "You're wanted back on the instrument," he said to Gran, gave me a long look, and followed after Gran back into the hall. I did, too.

Dad only spoke with her a moment, but Gran looked very surprised at what he said. "Why, yes, I—I don't see why they shouldn't, if you want them to. No, don't worry about that; I'll take care of the tickets. Yes, here she is." She held the telephone back out to me.

"Dad?"

"Emma." He was almost whispering. The poor dear sounded exhausted. "I—I have to hang up. I just wanted to say—listen to Josiah. And remember that I love you."

"I know you do, Daddy; I love you too."

"Listen—to him. Promise me."

"I will. I promise."

A pause while he caught his breath. "We'll…talk soon. Good-bye, my dear."

"Good-bye, Daddy." I hung up the receiver and turned to Josiah and Gran.

"He sounded well, under the circumstances," Gran said, cautiously.

All at once my legs felt weak and rubbery beneath me. I tottered over to the stairs and sat down. "He did. He sounded…he sounded like my Dad." I looked up at Josiah. "I'm supposed to listen to you. What about?"

"Your father wants you and Josiah to pay a visit to your apartment in Boston," Gran said. She frowned at Josiah, who was scribbling something on a piece of paper. "He wants you to go as soon as possible. I have no idea why." She ended on an inquiring note, waiting for Josiah to explain.

He didn't. Instead he remained stubbornly silent while he finished writing, then folded the paper into his waistcoat pocket. Gran sighed and rolled her eyes at me.

"He wants us to go now?" I asked. "Why? What are we supposed to do there?"

He coughed slightly. "Can't really say, right now."

Well, that was very strange. What could Dad possibly want? But at least it would get me off the island and thinking about something else. "All right. When should we go?"

We left Friday, on the mid-morning train. The trip had taken on odd undertones: Josiah had been taciturn all week, and almost bit Helen's head off when she offered to come with us to keep me company. When I scolded him for it later on in private, he got a mulish look on his face. "She's trouble, that one," he muttered.

"Josiah! Helen is no such thing! What makes you say that?"

He shrugged. "I been around long enough to see a thing or

two. I don't trust her farther than I can throw her."

I snorted. "You're being nonsensical. Helen's a dear, and nothing you say will convince me otherwise."

He'd stomped away in silence and maintained that silence now that we were on the train, not looking out the window but staring straight ahead, as if out over a bleak landscape. Wearing his second-best suit and a shirt with a collar might have been the source of his discontent, but I didn't think so.

A train journey is a good time to think, and with Josiah so stonily silent, it looked like I'd have plenty of time for it. Part of me wanted to think about why Dad had insisted we make this trip and why Josiah was so grumpy about it. But the rest of me kept slipping back to what—or whom—I'd been resolutely not thinking about these last few days.

I'd so longed to be able to go for a walk with Malcolm— there, I'd said his name, at least to myself—even while being so very angry at him. It wasn't only because I ached to feel his arms around me once more; I hadn't realized how much I'd come to need him as a confidante—much more than Helen, I saw now. As he'd come closer to me, she'd grown more distant. Had that been my fault? Had I neglected her for Malcolm?

And I was no closer to understanding what had happened. I was a scientist's daughter—did Malcolm really expect me to believe not only that selkies were real, but that the head of a U.S. Navy air station used them to patrol for U-boats? Maybe it had all been a joke—that he'd decided after all that he didn't want me helping with whatever he was doing for Captain Abbott and had hit upon this way to put me off. That made some sense: he might have heard the gossip about my mother—I'm sure the hotel was quite the clearinghouse for gossip—and put it to good use. Even Maggie's visit fit in: she came to tell me she hadn't taken his—his sealskin, because she hadn't. Because it didn't exist.

Or maybe, once he'd gotten to kiss me, he'd decided he'd had enough—or had had a bet with someone that he could— what was the term? Get to first base with me? College boys did that sometimes, I'd heard. Except that I had kissed him first and made it easy for him...

I shuddered. Perhaps I had been the summer's entertainment while he was stuck on the island with nothing else to amuse him. Only I'd turned out to be less entertaining than expected, and this was his way to end it. Or maybe this selkie thing was just an attempt to derive a little more amusement from the situation...

I was sure if I kept at it that I could come up with four or five more of these and make myself even more miserable than I was now.

What would I do for the rest of the summer? Red Cross meetings were out, and I would do everything in my power to avoid the Ocean Hotel. And then there was George Osborn—but he seemed finally to have gotten the message. I'd heard his car a few times this week when I was on the back porch knitting and licking my wounds, but he hadn't tried to come in, nor had Helen invited him in. That was one thing to be grateful for.

It looked like I would be doing a lot of knitting. And swimming...but this time, alone. And if the seals came to watch, I—I didn't know what I'd do. They were inextricably linked with Malcolm in my mind now, and he'd taken away the pleasure I found in their presence.

I realized that I was staring straight ahead of me, my face a stone-like mask, just like Josiah's.

We didn't get into South Station until nearly six; troop trains kept delaying us the closer we got to Boston. Josiah insisted we find some dinner before we went home, so I made him take me to Durgin-Park, which I thought he might like. But neither of us seemed to be terribly hungry; we just picked at our chicken pie and broiled cod, not talking much.

It felt funny, unlocking our front door and walking into the dusty silence of home. The rugs had been rolled up and tied and lay on the floor like giant sausages; drop cloths covered the furniture in the front parlor, and the air was stuffy and still.

"Shall I uncover the furniture?" I asked Josiah. He was looking about him with the air of a person who very much wishes to be someplace else.

"Nah. Won't be here more 'n the one night." He looked dubiously at the sheet-covered couch. "I'll kip there, I guess." It had taken Gran an hour yesterday to convince him to even stay in the house with me; he'd been all for getting a room at the YMCA for the night.

"Or you could stay in the guest bedroom, like a normal human being," I said tartly.

He shrugged.

I wasn't sure I wanted to be here either, all at once: it was my house, but it felt like the "home" part of it had leaked away while I'd been gone. Going up to my room would be like visiting a girl I once knew but hadn't seen in a long time and had lost touch with. Where was home anymore?

I dropped my small carpetbag next to the stairs. "Now that we're here, can you tell me why we came?"

He got his stubborn look again. "Tomorrow," he said shortly. "There ain't time enough tonight. I'm tired."

"You don't look particularly tired. And besides, we're supposed to catch the 1:30 train back to the Cape tomorrow. It doesn't sound like there'll be enough time then, either."

"It'll do." He sat down gingerly on a sheet-covered chair, as if he expected something to be lurking beneath the cloth, and ignored me.

"You're afraid of something, aren't you? Well, *I'm* not."

That nettled him, as I knew it would. "I ain't afraid."

"Then why do we have to wait? Come on, Josiah." I went to him and knelt on the floor by his chair. "Why did my father want us to come here? Why are we putting it off? The only logical answer is that you're afraid of something about it."

"I ain't afraid," he repeated, then added, meaningfully, "At least, not afraid for me."

That made me pause. "Why are you afraid for me?"

To my surprise I saw that there were tears in his eyes. "I— oh, damn it all, there ain't any putting it off, and I'm a fool to try. Where's the cellar?"

"What?" I blinked. "Is that where Dad told you to go?"

"No, but it's past eight and we're going to want lights. Water, too. Your Dad said they got turned off when he left. I'll go turn 'em on, and then we'll—we'll do what we came for."

I found him a flashlight, showed him the door to the cellar from the kitchen and then paced impatiently around the front parlor while he puttered around down there. His heavy tread climbed the stairs and crossed the kitchen. Then he was in the hall. He cleared his throat. "We need to go to your father's room."

"It's upstairs." I turned on the wall sconces lining the stairwell even though there was still enough evening sun coming through the fanlight over the door to see by. Suddenly lots of light seemed like a good idea.

At the door to Dad's room, I paused then stepped inside, flicking on the lamp by his bed since the heavy curtains were drawn across the windows. Here at the back of the house no sounds penetrated from the street, and I hoped Dad's room at the hospital was as quiet. There were no dust sheets and rolled-up carpets here; it felt as if he had merely stepped out for a moment. Only his brushes missing from the mahogany bureau and the lack of geology journals and unbound monographs stacked on his bedside table bespoke his absence.

Josiah followed me, reaching into his waistcoat pocket and pulling out a scrap of paper which he consulted briefly, then looked around the room. His gaze fixed on the wardrobe by the door and he stared at it for a moment, then squared his shoulders and approached it. He opened the doors and stood on tiptoe, reaching for something on the top shelf.

"There's nothing there but blankets," I said, but just then Josiah grunted and strained to catch hold of something. The something turned out to be a large, sturdy pasteboard box that I'd never seen before, bulging against the lengths of heavy knotted twine sealed with wax that held it closed. It looked like one of Dad's specimen boxes, but a much bigger one than I'd ever seen. Josiah pulled it down and stared it for a moment with an unreadable expression on his face, weighing it in his hands.

"You might want to sit down 'fore you open this, chickie," he said, his voice a little rough. He cleared his throat and held it out to me.

"For me?" I took the box from him, set it down on Daddy's bed, and began to pick at the wax.

Josiah touched my shoulder. I looked up; he was holding his pocket knife out to me. "Don't think you'll be using that again," he said, jerking his head at the box.

"Why? Do you know what's in it?"

He nodded.

I wasn't sure if that was reassuring or not. Surely whatever this was couldn't be too horrible if overprotective Josiah could stand by and watch me open it. I took the knife and sawed at the twine till it fell free, then lifted the top from the box.

Layers of blue tissue paper crackled and whispered as I folded them back, revealing something brown and sleek and furry. I stared at it, then looked up at Josiah. "What is it? It looks like a fur coat."

He didn't say anything. In fact, he didn't appear to be breathing. He glanced up at me then reached out and touched the furry thing with one finger.

And I felt it. I felt a pressure on my right shoulder, just beyond the shoulder blade...and when Josiah lifted his hand, the sensation went away. I gasped, though my mouth suddenly seemed to be stuffed with dust.

"You felt that," he whispered. It wasn't a question. He touched it again in a different place, a little further over, and I felt that on the middle of my back.

I swatted his hand away and seized the thing in the box. It hung limp in my hands—was it a cape of some sort, with a hood? Or—or—it looked a lot like a seal's skin—the rounded head with a pointed snout, dead-looking now with the whiskers hanging limp…the sweeping back leading into powerful flippers at its end—

No. No, it wasn't. It couldn't be. I threw it back into the box and slid to the floor, burying my face against my knees. "No," I heard myself say. "No."

"Oh, Emma." Josiah winced, and I knew he'd dropped to his knees next to me. "Emma, don't. It's just—it's just what it is."

"No," I said again. It felt like the solid floor beneath me had buckled and shifted, and now I had no idea where it was safe to put my feet. The tears started then, and I let them come. I could just let them wash over me.

But I couldn't stop thinking, because nothing was what it was—or what I'd thought it was—and everything I'd unquestioningly accepted as truth was in fact a lie. There was no denying it; Josiah's tentative touch on the sealskin in the box had destroyed the lie forever, no matter how much I wanted to continue to believe it. My mother…my father.

My *father*.

And then I did stop thinking, except for the hurt. Those two words wouldn't stop resounding in my head, over and over again, until they became meaningless—just as they always had been. And I hadn't known it. The man in the hospital bed in Washington—the man who'd coddled and cared for me, kept me safe by his side for my whole life, been both mother and father…my dearest, beloved Dad—*wasn't* my father.

I don't know how long Josiah let me cry, but at some point I felt something cool and wet touch my hand and realized I'd stopped. I lifted my face from my arms. He was holding a damp washcloth out to me. I stared at it stupidly, so he leaned forward and wiped my face with it, both carefully and clumsily.

"That's better," he said as if he hoped it were true, then held out a glass of water. I took it from him and drank; the water was warm and a little metallic-tasting, but I swallowed it anyway. Then we just sat.

"He still loves you, you know," Josiah finally said. "More than anything, I expect. Just because he didn't father you don't mean he ain't still your dad."

"How did you know?" My voice rasped with unshed tears—how could I have any left?

"Because I was there when you were born. Helped deliver you, actually. Me and your—and the professor." He sounded faintly apologetic.

That was unexpected, and I actually looked at him. "Why? Where was the doctor?"

"There wasn't any time to find him, and I'm glad we didn't because there wouldn't have been any easy way for us to explain...that." He jerked his head behind us at the sealskin in the box.

My sealskin.

I felt my head begin to whirl again but his voice drew me back. "Laura—your mother—she knew it was time for you to be born, and she went to find...them. The selkies. Your father's people. She left the house in the middle of the night and walked as far as she could down island, on the beach, wearing only her nightgown and a shawl. When we realized she was missing come morning, we all lit out fast as we could—your grandparents went one way, and me and the professor the other. I heard her crying in the dunes, just over the wind—it was March, and damned cold for it. We were going to bring her back—we had the wagon—but you were already on your way. We had blankets, and we got you born somehow. And you were wearing that thing. I knew what it was, and why you had it. I knew the stories too, and I knew about your mother and who she'd been meeting. I'd seen them." He looked down at his hands. "I told you once I was nuts about Laura. Always was, from when we were kids together running around the island like wild things. I couldn't stop loving her, even after she was married. When she came home that summer and started going off on her own, I...well, I was jealous, and I followed her. Spied on her, I guess. And I saw them—him and her—lots of times.

Mostly on the beach way down island where the air station is now, away from everyone, talking and holding hands and—and other things. I know she was fond of your—of the professor, but I expect she married him to get away from being the proper young lady she'd always hated being forced into pretending to be. But her selkie—they were in love. I didn't think any two beings could love like that." He sighed.

Her selkie. My mother had fallen in love with a selkie. At least they had loved each other. It didn't make me hurt less, but somehow made things a little more comprehensible. "My dad— he knew, then. Why I had that…thing."

"I told him, but he'd already guessed you weren't his. He— well, he was all for chucking your skin into the dunes and forgetting it existed, but I wouldn't let him. If something bad happened to it, I wasn't sure that it wouldn't hurt you too. So we kept it hidden and brought you and Laura back home in the wagon. Laura was in a bad way. A beach in mid-March is no place to have a baby, and she'd been in a state ever since she'd come home. She was missing her selkie. I think she'd planned on running away with him—that's why she wanted to have you born on the island—but he never came for her. Maybe he didn't know she was bearing his child—she didn't know it herself till after she'd gone back to Boston in September. Or else he realized he couldn't take a human woman to live with him as his wife and thought it kinder to leave her with her people. She tried to take care of you—she held you constantly and talked to you and nursed you—but a couple days later she was sick with the pneumonia. I think she died of grief as much as anything, myself."

I had started crying again while he spoke. No one had ever spoken of my birth; I'd assumed Laura had died while having me. But to hear she'd held me, and *known* me—had actually mothered me, if only for a little while…it suddenly made losing her hurt a lot more.

And Dad—he'd known I wasn't his. But he'd taken me anyway. And cared for me and loved me as if I were. Was that why he had held on to me so tightly—because I *wasn't*?

"Why? Why did he do it?" I sniffled.

"What, the professor?" He sighed and handed me a clean handkerchief. "Because he loved your mother, and felt responsible for you—for your being born, I mean. He thought he'd failed Laura and wasn't going to fail Laura's daughter, even if she was another man's. 'Least that's what he said—he and I talked about it. He tried to make me keep your sealskin because he didn't want it in the house with you, but I wouldn't take it. It was part of you, and if he was taking you for his, he had to take it too. So I washed it, and he folded it away in that box and said he'd keep it safe. I don't think he ever opened it, from the looks of it. Funny—" He reached up, and I felt him lift my skin. "When you were born, it was just a little thing, all spotted like seal pups are. And here it is now, just like a full-grown seal's. It was ready to bust the box open." He held it out to me.

I stared at it, my arms still wrapped around myself. The fur shone in the light from the lamp, warm brown highlights glinting. If I reached out and took it, in some way that would mean I was accepting that I wasn't who I'd thought I was...and I wasn't sure I was ready to be that other girl yet. Who *was* I?

"Take it, Emma," Josiah said gently.

I didn't move. "Why did you try to keep me away from the seals earlier this summer?"

He sighed again. "Because your fa—because the professor asked me to. He was afraid that this would happen—that if you came to the island you'd somehow learn the truth, and he—he didn't want to lose you. But I suspicioned he wouldn't be able to hide it from you forever. Nature would win. You would have come to the island sooner or later—he couldn't forbid you to visit your grandmother when you were a grown woman, even though he managed to keep you away all these years. And I knew in a hurry that there wasn't going to be any keeping it from you after the Galbraith boy started sniffing around you."

Malcolm...oh God, Malcolm! "He's—he really is—?"

He nodded. "You hear the stories, and you pay attention,

and —" he shrugged. "Don't make no difference to anyone — the Galbraiths bring a lot of money to the island with the hotel and employ a lot of people, both on the island and in Mattaquason. Ain't our business what they are underneath."

His tone was matter-of fact, as if we were discussing the tides, and I knew — really *understood*, then — that this was all real, and that I couldn't pretend any longer.

"Why now?" I asked. "Why did Dad" — I stumbled over the word a bit — "tell you to do this *now*?"

Josiah rubbed his chin. "Ain't sure, but from what he said on the telephone, I think the heart attack scared him. He didn't want you to know the truth, but he's a good man, and I think he decided he couldn't *not* tell you, either. If he died, there'd be only me who knew, and I think he thought telling you should be his responsibility even though I'm the one who's doin' it anyway." He smiled a little sourly. "He said something about your letters, too — he knew the island was getting to you, he said — and then something else about you telling him what a good father he'd been, and I guess he decided it was about time."

About time...or was it too late? "Does Gran know?"

"I don't know. I didn't tell her when you was born because the professor swore me to secrecy, but I don't know how much she's figured out on her own. She's a smart lady, though, your grandmother." He held the skin out to me again. "Take it, chickie."

I swallowed. He wasn't going to let me avoid this. Ready or not, I steeled myself and made my hand reach out and take the skin from him, trying to hold it between two fingers like a dirty dust-rag. But it was too heavy for that, and I was forced to reach out both hands to hold it. A peculiar sensation went through me, a weird sense of relief from some tension I'd not known I carried until it was lifted. This was mine. I couldn't deny it.

I laid it across my lap and touched it hesitantly. So sleekly smooth...it seemed to warm under my fingers as I ran my hand down its length. We sat there without talking for a long time while I tried to put my world back together, like a jigsaw puzzle whose pieces had suddenly changed. I was half a selkie; the sealskin in my lap attested to that.

But what did that mean? How was my life different now that I knew that I was some kind of magical, legendary creature—or at least half of one. Could I put this skin on and turn into a seal? Or was that too much for a half-blood? Was I still Emma Verlaine of Boston, or someone else?

And Malcolm—if I accepted that I was a selkie, I had to accept that he was one too...and I'd told him I never wanted to see him again. He must hate me now after the things I'd said to him. I cringed, remembering, and drew my skin up against my chest. The sensation was oddly comforting.

What had happened to his sealskin that he'd been about to show me? If it hadn't disappeared, how differently the last few days might have gone...or maybe not. Would I have believed him even if he had turned into a seal before me? I was too tired and wrung out to decide.

But one thing I did know: I would have to tell him what I knew now as soon as we got back to the island...and apologize to him. He might not want to hear it, but if I didn't, I wouldn't be able to live with myself. And I needed to tell Gran too, because she deserved to know, and I knew she would keep my—our—secret. After that, I had no idea. I'd been so sure of myself once, ready to march off to be a nurse in France or become Captain Abbott's secretary. Now, instead of an indefatigable modern girl, I was something...something not quite of this world. It would take some getting used to.

I'd be boiled in oil before I apologized to the Red Cross ladies, though. They might have been right, but it still wasn't any of their business. In one of Miss Blunt's novels, it said the truth would set one free and make everyone saintly and forgiving. Well, I would never be a saint. I was going to have a hard enough time as it was just being myself...whoever that was.

·Chapter Twenty-three·
Malcolm

Early on the morning of the fourteenth, eleven days after I last saw Emma (yeah, I was keeping count), I—and most of the hotel, probably—was awakened by my little sister's shrieking, "Malcolm! Come *quick*!"

"What?" I sat up in bed. It had sounded like Maggie was outside; she sometimes liked to get up earlier than anyone else and pretend she was the only person in the world. I stumbled out of my room and down the hall to the door that led to our porch. It was open, and she was out there in her nightgown, staring at something I couldn't see. When I came to stand next to her, I saw what it was.

My kit bag sat on the railing of the porch—the kit bag I'd last seen stowed under a beach rose thicket on the beach.

"I came out just now, and there it was!" Maggie tried to cling to my arm, but I was already past her. I grabbed the bag and yanked it open, and there was my skin. I snatched it up and held it, my hands shaking. I would no longer be half of me.

"Is it whole?" Mother had taken a moment to put on a wrapper, but she was right behind me.

"Yes," I whispered. It was undamaged, and *back*.

"Let me see." Father emerged as well. I gave him my skin and he ran his hands over it, a faraway expression on his face. "It seems to be all right. I do not feel any maledictions or curses on it." He handed it back to me, but there was still a frown between his eyes.

I hadn't even thought about that. All I could think about now was storming down to Emma's and showing it to her. If she knew I was telling the truth about that, then maybe it would be easier for her to believe it about herself. And then I'd go to the beach and put on my skin and start resurrecting my patrols. Or maybe I'd do that first, and then go to Emma's—

"If you want to see Emma, she's not there." Maggie had recovered from her surprise. "She went somewhere with Josiah yesterday. I saw them going to the train station, and his car's still there."

Maggie was better than a Special Agent sometimes. I looked at Mother. "Do you think they might have gone to Washington to see Professor Verlaine?"

"I expect that if they had, Dorinda would have gone, not Josiah—"

"Emma and him just had little bags, so I don't think they'll be gone a long time," Maggie interrupted. "Are you gonna go see if she's back?"

I was suddenly so happy, I didn't care that Maggie was being nosy. "Right now, I'm going for a swim."

Father cleared his throat. "Right now, we will have break-fast and then spend the day getting ready for the dance this evening. Margaret, I expect our guests would rather not see you in your nightclothes."

She squinted at me. "*He's* in his pajamas, but I can tell when I'm not wanted." She stuck her nose in the air and went inside.

Father shook his head, but I caught the twinkle in his eye. It faded when he turned to me. "I am concerned by this sudden reappearance of your skin, more or less delivered to your doorstep, as the saying goes. It feels—contrived."

Mother raised her eyebrows but didn't disagree.

"You mean, you think someone stole it and has returned it for a reason?" I asked.

"Perhaps." His frown deepened. "I assume I cannot request

that you stay close to home for the next few days—"

"No, you can't. I have to get the patrols going again. And I—*need* to go."

He sighed. "I'd expected that was what you would say, and I understand. But please, be careful for the next few days."

"I'm always careful," I said. "Especially on patrol." He should know I took that very seriously. Still clutching my skin against my chest, I went in to get dressed.

With today being Bastille Day, Mother had thought it would be fun to give tonight's dance a French theme in honor of our allies and sent a special invitation to Captain Abbott and everyone at the air station. The officers and men who hadn't been able to come to the dance on the Fourth of July would be there, and Mother had hired a band from Boston that I'd heard at a party at the Copley Square Hotel, so the music would be top-notch.

But that meant a lot of work setting up. I helped hang tricolor buntings and French and American flags around the ballroom, fetched Annie Goslin's flower arrangements as she finished them and set them in place, made a trip to the print shop in Mattaquason for the dance programs, then helped Mother and Maggie tie two hundred tiny gold pencils to them with fine white silk cords, went to the train station to pick up the band members, and a dozen other errands. And all the while I was inwardly grinning to myself: I had my skin again...and the chance to regain Emma.

About six, we were done: the last details would be handled by staff. I grabbed a quick sandwich and escaped to my room, folded my skin into a spare pillowcase since the kit bag just didn't feel right anymore, and left the hotel quickly via our porch. A squall last night had blown the humidity out and given us a beautiful day, and tonight would be fine and starry, with only a sliver of waning moon showing. I'd have to check the blackout curtains in the ballroom windows tonight once it was full dark.

Since it was getting on toward evening and most of the

guests were having dinner before tonight's dance, I thought about not bothering to go all the way down to our usual spot, then decided that was poor discipline and went there anyway, but didn't bother going up to the rose bushes to hide my things. I'd taken off my shirt and was just unbuttoning my trousers when of course I spotted someone approaching from the hotel side of the beach. I groaned and pulled my shirt on again and sat down, hoping they were out looking for some solitude and would turn back when they saw me, but the figure kept on coming. After a minute, I realized who it was.

"Damn it, Maggot, what are you doing?" I yelled when she was close enough to hear.

She broke into a run. As she got closer, I saw she was clutching her school-bag. "You shouldn't be here alone. Father said so," she said accusingly, after she'd halted in front of me and caught her breath. "So I came too."

Counting to ten when confronted with Maggie was rarely enough. I made it to twenty-three and was still mad as hell at her. "You mean you were eavesdropping."

She crossed her arms on her chest. "So?"

"Aaand," — I drew the word out because I knew it would annoy her — "You're going to do *what*, precisely, to keep me safe from whatever might be out to get me?"

"Father said you shouldn't be alone," she repeated doggedly.

"Thanks, Dad," I muttered to myself.

Maggie giggled, and I had to smile too. The incongruity of calling our father "Dad" was too much to keep a straight face at. "All right. You can come with me."

She was already unbuttoning her dress. "Are you patrolling? You said I could start learning."

I finished undressing, pulled out my skin, and bundled my clothes into the empty pillow-case, making sure I left it well above the waterline. There was nothing worse than coming back from a swim and discovering your human clothes had been carried away by the tide. "No. I just need to get out in the water for a while. But we can talk about it."

I went down to the water's edge. Maggie scampered after me, already swinging her skin up to cover her head. "By the way, I thought you weren't talking to me," I said to her.

She slowed, scuffling her feet in the damp sand just above the waves. "I wasn't. But if you're going to be nice to Emma again, I guess I'll forgive you."

I started to open my mouth to explain that I'd been perfectly nice to Emma, then closed it, remembering what my father had said to me. If—no, *when*—I got my second chance with her, I would do it differently—and this time, I would wait until she was ready for it.

When the water hit my waist I reached up, took a deep breath, and settled my skin over my head and shoulders…and felt the familiar, comforting sense of my selves becoming one as it enveloped me, the jar as my senses shifted from human to seal, the release from gravity and the change from living in two planes to three as the waters closed over me. Oh gods, how I'd missed this over the last days! I shot forward into deeper water with a few hard strokes of my hind flippers, tucking my front flippers against my sides and rotating as I went, just out of sheer exuberance.

"*Hey!*" Maggie struggled to catch up. "*I'm supposed to be guarding you, remember?*"

"*You're just slow.*" I waggled my tail at her, then put on another burst of speed.

After a few more minutes of goofing around, we settled down to a more sedate pace. The setting sun was shining from an oblique angle behind us, but we could still see well; seals have excellent vision under water, even in low light. But our sight was nothing compared to our senses of hearing and touch—we could feel even small movements in the water with our exquisitely sensitive whiskers. I swam straight out to sea, listening. I could hear the distant cries of some humpback whales conversing well off-shore. Closer in, a small shoal of mackerel shivered through the water. And closer still— "*There.*

254   MARISSA DOYLE

Do you hear that?" The whining hum of a boat propeller was north and east of us.

I could feel Maggie's mental shrug. *"It's a boat. I know what a boat sounds like."*

"Yes, but if you're going to think about joining the patrol, you have to be able to know what kind of boat it is just by its sound. Different engines and propellers make different noises. Let's go have a look."

We followed it, traveling fast under water, just barely surfacing to grab quick breaths. I was startled when the sound suddenly ceased and came up to the surface to have a look, Maggie following me.

It was still a few hundred feet away, but I recognized George Osborn's flashy little mahogany runabout at once. *"He's a mainlander,"* I said to Maggie. *"Kind of a silly ass. He was chasing after Emma for a while. Let's see what he's doing."*

We dove and surfaced again maybe twenty yards away. I could see Osborn and another man, a stocky, fair-haired stranger. They both held fishing rods—out for an evening's bit of sport, apparently—but something didn't feel right. Fish seemed to be the last thing on their minds; they were both gazing out to sea.

"Where are they?" I heard Osborn say. His tone was nervous, and I was tempted to dive and bite on his line just to see if he would fall overboard. I was about to suggest to Maggie that we leave, when the other man spoke.

"It is too light yet for them to risk surfacing. Relax and catch a fish, why don't you? It's a good evening for it, *ja*?" He waggled his pole.

Surfacing? And that carelessly dropped "ja"...what was going on here? *Wait here*, I said to Maggie, and eased closer to the boat till I was only a few yards away.

"I thought you said they'd be here around seven? We're far enough offshore that no one can see us."

"And what if a seaplane should be flying home late from patrol and happen by? Stop complaining, boy." The other man's voice had slid from cheerful to contemptuous.

I felt as if my insides had turned to ice. There was something serious going on here, and it was happening now, when I had only my little sister with me—

"—don't know these waters very well at night, is the problem, Keller. I don't want to run us aground," Osborn was saying. "Dammit, why didn't Dad warn me about this? I don't know how you're forcing him to do—"

"Your father has a great deal of history with us that he would rather not become public knowledge. He was delighted to be able to do us this little favor…and it's *Herr Fregattenkapitän* Keller to you, boy. You American youth are spoiled—useless! We will crush you, when you finally arrive at the front and join the fighting. Now listen to me. If you run us aground before we make it to the air station, I may have to shoot you, and your father won't be able to say a word."

"You can't do that! This is America!" Osborn sputtered, but something else had caught my attention. I dove, and the water was full of another sound, a sound I'd heard on several occasions already, and my heart sank.

A long, narrow shape moved slowly through the water, coming up from below. I surfaced as it did, and saw something that looked like a squat garden shed with a couple of projections sticking out of it gliding along the face of the water. I wanted to attack it, to pound a hole in its hull or something, but of course that was ridiculous. All I could do was watch and learn what I could, then high-tail it to the captain. Damnation! Why did this have to happen *now*?

As I watched, it glided to a halt, and a hatch opened at the back of the garden shed—the conning tower—and four men emerged from it. One waved at Osborn's boat.

"Ah." Keller smiled. "Perhaps you would be so good as to put away your fishing tackle and go to meet my colleagues?"

Osborn fumbled with his pole and nearly dropped it while reeling in his line, and for a moment I almost felt sorry for him. He was an ass, but it appeared that his father was much worse—

an American industrialist was aiding and abetting his country's enemy…and had embroiled his son in his treason.

Osborn got his motor to turn over after a few false starts, and the runabout put-putted toward the U-boat. I followed them.

"That's as close as I dare get," Osborn said, sounding sulky.

"It will do," Keller said shortly and motioned to the men to approach. They jumped into the water and swam the short distance over. One of them towed a small raft loaded with boxes. He brought it alongside Osborn's boat, and he and one of the men clambered aboard and unloaded it while the others stayed in the water to keep it steady. When it was empty they swam it back to the U-boat, where two more figures took it from them.

"What's that?" Osborn asked, craning to get a better look at the boxes.

"Nothing that's any of your business," Keller replied. "*Alles in Ordnung?*" he asked the man who'd towed over the raft.

"*Ja,*" the man said. He'd taken a dark shirt and trousers from a bag and was putting them on. "*Herr Kapitänleutnant* Feldt sends his compliments," he added in English.

"He can do so in person once we have completed our task," Keller replied. "Are Erich and Walther back? Ah, there you are. Quickly, now! There—let us—"

"Wait!" Osborn put in. "You mean you're not coming back with me? But my father was having a dinner for you tomorrow night—"

"Your father is a fool. And I very much doubt your dinner will be taking place tomorrow, whether I'm there or not." He smiled thinly and turned back to the men, who were dressing and smearing some sort of black goo on their faces, and began to converse with them in a low voice.

Something bumped into my side as I hovered there, and then Maggie surfaced next to me, nose high in the air as she looked at the boat. "*What's happening?*"

"*I told you to stay put!*" I said angrily. I should have told her to go home. *"Be quiet and stay out of sight. I need to listen."*

"Well, fine!" Maggie dove, flipping her tail in my face. It made a small splash.

"What was that?" Keller swiveled toward me. "Oh, just a seal. Go away, *Herr Seehund*. No fish for you here." He suddenly seemed to be in a very good mood. "Or maybe it was one of your seal people someone was telling me about—what are they called? Selkies? Yes, selkies."

"A seal? Where?" Osborn nearly threw himself across the boat to stare at the water.

"Tscha! It's nothing." Keller had already turned away.

But Osborn had spotted me. His face twisted in rage, and he reached into his jacket pocket and pulled something from it. It took me a second to realize that it was a gun.

"No, idiot!" someone—Keller?—shouted. "Are you trying to bring the world out here? It's just a seal."

"Might not be," Osborn muttered, and pulled the trigger.

I had flipped around to dive, but before I could submerge something slammed into me. I rolled with the force of the impact and then dove, pushing hard with my back flippers. I think I managed to put twenty or thirty yards between me and the boat before I noticed pain like a hot knife slash across my back, behind my head. I swam anyway, fast as I could, front flippers drawn in tight. He'd shot me—the bastard had shot me! I had to get to the beach—had to get home and phone Captain Abbott—

"Malcolm!" Maggie was suddenly there next to me. I could feel her rising panic. *"What happened? You're bleeding!"*

"Listen to me." I slowed because it was hard to think and swim at the same time with that pain. *"Follow the boat. Tell me what direction they're going. Don't let them see you."*

"Did one of them shoot you?"

I ignored her question. *"Do it, Maggie. I can get to the beach. When you're sure you know where they're headed, come find me. Be careful. Very careful."*

"But—"

"Do it!" I hated to send her into danger, but we had to know where that boat was going.

I felt her reluctance, but she swam away. I kept going, hoping that shoal of mackerel I'd heard hadn't drawn any sharks in. A throbbing had joined the burning sensation in my back, and every movement hurt—ah gods, how it hurt...

I don't know how long it took me—part of the time it felt like I wasn't there, even though I knew I was still swimming—but eventually the bottom came up to meet me, and then waves breaking gently on shore rolled me for a minute, the gravel biting against my back making me groan. Thank heavens there wasn't a heavy sea running, or I'm not sure I could have made it out of the water. I gritted my teeth and gave a wrench—and blacked out for a minute, I think, because the next thing I knew, I was lying face-down, half in the water, my skin next to me and that searing pain across my upper back.

I lay there for a while, enjoying the sensation of not having to move, except something was niggling at me, more insistent with every passing second, telling me that I *did* have to move. I had to get up, go back to the hotel, and—and—

A gun. Men in black clothes with black-smeared faces. A U-boat...

"Get up, Galbraith!" I muttered and pushed myself up. If I had to crawl, I would—but the pain across my shoulders sent me quickly up to my knees to take the pressure off my arms. I swayed for a minute, but now I remembered: I had to find Captain Abbott.

One leg...then the other...and I was standing. I blinked owlishly around me. I'd managed to home in on where Maggie and I had entered the water; selkies were good at that. I could see the pillowcase with my clothes, a little way up the beach from me. The sun was low enough that it just touched the dunes at the top of the beach. We hadn't been out there more than half an hour.

I stared at the pillowcase, trying to think. Thoughts dripped slowly though my head, like raindrops trickling down a pane of dirty glass.

Pillowcase.

Clothes.

I would have to get my clothes out of the pillowcase and put them on if I wanted to go back to the hotel.

Put them on...where was my skin? I had taken it off, right?

I looked down, and there it was in the sand next to me. I had to bend down and pick it up...and suddenly wasn't sure if I could, not without falling down again.

But I couldn't lose it to the outgoing tide. If I lowered myself into a squat instead of bending over, then maybe the fire raging across my back wouldn't break into fresh flames.

I steeled myself to bend my knees, to reach down for it— and the black waves that had been lapping at my brain surged higher, pulling me down into darkness.

·Chapter Twenty-four·
Emma

I didn't sleep much that night in Boston. I don't think Josiah did, either; I heard him pacing downstairs. I suppose I should have gone down to him, but I think we both needed to be alone with our thoughts. So I sat huddled in a chair in Dad's room, holding my sealskin.

What did it mean, this skin? I held it up before me to look at it, as I'd already done at least a dozen times. Could I put it over my head right now and turn into a seal, the way Annie said selkies did? I let it fall in my lap with a sigh. Right now, I didn't have the courage to try it.

But what if, when I was finally brave enough to place it over my head, nothing happened? This morning when I got up, I was a human. At some point in the near future, I might find that I was neither human nor selkie. I wondered what it would be like to lose that identity that I hadn't even known I'd had before today. Would I be less than I was now?

If only Malcolm was here...I felt tears start to my eyes again and let them fall unchecked onto my sealskin. There was something else I'd lost—and I knew full well that it had been mine and that I'd driven it away.

Malcolm's skin—what had happened to it? He said he'd hidden it in the bushes, but it had disappeared...which could only mean that someone had taken it. I cringed when I remembered how I had accused him of faking his distress. To a selkie, losing one's skin must be about the worst thing that could happen. I could maybe begin to understand that now.

We arrived at Mattaquason station around five-thirty that afternoon after another long, silent train ride. Josiah clucked and grumbled at the dust that had accumulated overnight on his precious car and we drove through town and, to our surprise, joined a queue waiting at the ferry to cross to the island.

"What's with this?" Josiah asked one of the deckhands when we finally drove onto the *Never Late*.

"Dance at the hotel tonight." The deckhand shrugged.

A dance, tonight? How had I not known that?

Let's see, Emma. Maybe it's because you cut off all contact with the Galbraiths, who have been remarkably kind to you since you arrived...

Ouch.

We finished the crossing and rolled up the shell road out of the village toward Gran's, and I gave way to a sudden impulse. "Josiah, if you don't mind, I'll get off at the hotel."

He slowed and looked at me from the corners of his eyes. "You sure?"

"Yes. Tell Gran I'll be along in a little while. I—have to do this now, before I lose my nerve."

He didn't say another word, but turned at the hotel gates and drove me right up to the entrance, ignoring the cars clogging the drive. "You be all right?"

I nodded, clutching the bag I'd held close all day on the train. "Josiah?"

"Yeah?"

"Thank you."

He looked away, but nodded. I stepped away from the car, and he drove off.

As I approached the front doors of the hotel, Annie Goslin emerged from them. "Why, 'evening, Miss Emma," she said. "Havena seen ye for a cuppa in a long time. How's your dad getting on, then?"

I wondered if she was one of the ones, like Josiah, who knew the Galbraiths' secret. Based on our conversations, I'd guess she was. "He's on the mend, thank you, and I know I haven't been to see you in a while. Maybe I could stop by next week?"

"You do that, dearie. The door's always open. Och, it was a day in there." She put a hand on her lower back and grimaced. "Big dance tonight, for Bastille Day." She pronounced it *bastilly*. "You going to be there?"

"I don't know, Annie. I'm just getting back from a quick trip to Boston—in fact, I haven't even been home yet. But I'll try to sneak a look at your flowers before I go."

"Weel, they're not too bad. I may be back to sneck a look maself, to see how it all does." She went off, a small smile playing at the corners of her mouth. I watched her go then took a deep breath, straightened my shoulders, and went into the hotel.

The lobby was quiet, but the clink of glassware and cutlery and a hum of conversation came from the dining room. I hesitated before turning to the front desk: would Malcolm be sitting there?

It wasn't Malcolm but his mother who was on duty this evening. She glanced up from the sheaf of papers she was reading and started. "Emma!"

"Good—good evening, Mrs. Galbraith. Is Malcolm here? I— it's very important that I speak with him."

She put down her pencil. "No, he isn't. He went for a swim before things got too busy this evening. I think most of the air station will be here for the dance tonight."

"A swim? But I thought—" I bit back my words. Then he'd found his skin again!

"Yes, a swim." She gave me a long, appraising look. "If you

want, you could go down to the beach and look for him." There was a faint questioning uplift in her voice.

I thought quickly. It would make me late for dinner, but I could explain to Gran later. "Yes, I—I think I will. I have... something that I want to show him."

For the first time, she smiled. "I'm sure he would very much like to see it. You know where to go?"

"Yes, I think so."

"Good. You can go out through our apartment. Leave your shoes and stockings on the porch, if you like. It's...easier, I think you'll find."

"Thank you." I could see that there wasn't much point in wearing shoes and stockings on a long walk down the beach. Especially if one was eventually going to take them off.

"And if you happen to see Maggie, send her home, won't you? I think she might have tagged after him."

That made me smile. "I will. Thank you, Mrs. Galbraith."

She came out from around the desk, eyeing my bag, but didn't comment. She unlocked the door and motioned me through—but first, put a hand on my shoulder. "I'm glad you're back, dear."

I wanted to hug her, but it didn't feel quite right to do so. "I'm glad too."

I stopped in the Galbraith's sitting room to remove my stockings, rolled them up and stuck them in the toes of my shoes, and hurried out the door to their porch. There was a private path from here to the beach, winding through hydrangea bushes. The sun was westering, and its early-evening pink-tinged light made the clumps of blossoms on the bushes glow. I made it to the sand, which also glowed pink, and started walking south.

Would he be in—in seal form, somewhere out in the water? If so, I'd never find him. I remembered the leather kit bag he'd placed in that clump of beach roses; I'd keep an eye out for that. Or maybe he'd be on the beach, and I—well, I didn't know what I would say to him until I could gauge his reaction to seeing me again. I hoped he'd forgive me, at least long enough to let me tell what I'd learned.

The sun set further, and the pink tinge faded into the paler mauve of twilight. I walked faster; if I couldn't find Malcolm, I didn't want to have to find my way home in the dark.

Would Maggie be with him? That might make talking awkward—or maybe it wouldn't. If he were still angry with me and wouldn't listen, then she might—

Wait. There was something—or someone?—down the beach, far enough away that I had to squint to confirm its existence. It was standing by the edge of the water, and my heart began to beat faster. Might it be Malcolm, just setting out or even returning from his swim?

There was something not-quite-right about the way it stood so stiffly, not moving—something unnerving. As I got closer, I saw that it was definitely a person—and definitely unclothed. I hadn't thought about that: if it were Malcolm just back from the water, he'd be naked. I would have to do my best not to blush and stare. And if it weren't Malcolm but another selkie, what would I do?

I hurried my steps and kept watching, and I think I somehow knew it was him before the rational part of my mind said, *"yes, that is he."* I don't think he'd seen me; he hadn't moved or acknowledged my presence. I hesitated; was this the cold shoulder treatment I'd feared? But then I saw him sway as he stood there. Something was very wrong.

I dropped my bag and ran. "Malcolm!" And as I reached him, I saw what was wrong: blood ran down his sides and back, dark in the fading light. "Oh my God, you're bleeding! What happened? Where are you hurt?"

He finally seemed to see me then and opened his mouth, but no sound came out. I reached for him, and he almost toppled into me. I was afraid to put my hands on him till I knew where the blood was coming from, but managed to hold him upright by just being there for him to lean against. We both stood, breathing hard, while I fought back panic. What should I do? What had happened to him? How could I get him back to the hotel?

"It's really you," he muttered.

"Yes, it's me. Where are you hurt?"

"Back, up high. Hard to know — whole thing feels like fire. He shot me."

"Someone shot you!" My panic escalated. I forced it down and tried to remember the First Aid course I'd taken. Had he been hit in a lung? His spine hadn't been touched, or he wouldn't be standing, and no internal organs had likely been hit either. A flesh wound, then? Not that flesh wounds couldn't be horrible. "Can you walk, if I hold you up? Just a little way up the beach so you can lie down and I can have a look at things?"

He didn't answer for a moment. When he did, his voice seemed stronger. "I think so."

"Good. Lean on me. I'll back us up the sand a bit. Ready?"

"My — skin. It's there. Don't leave it."

I glanced down and saw a length of sleek, gleaming-wet fur by our feet. So like mine...but I couldn't think about that now. "Let's lay you down, and then I'll get it. It won't take a minute if you stop being such a chatterbox and distracting me."

He actually gave a weak chuckle, and my spirits rose. I felt him tense against me, and I took a short step backwards, then another. I counted twenty steps and decided we were far enough up into dry sand, so I helped him kneel, then lie face down. "Wait a minute," I said, and ran for my bag. It was a small carpet bag; I upended my skin out of it and lifted his head to slide it under his cheek to serve as a pillow, then bent over to look at his back.

It was a gory mess, with what looked like a jagged rip across it. I couldn't tell if the bullet that had made it was still inside him.

He sighed and opened his eyes. "My skin."

"Yes, of course." I rose and went back to the water's edge, hesitated, then lifted up his skin. It was warm; I gently ran one hand down it and heard Malcolm groan softly, and remembered what had happened when Josiah had touched mine. I hurried back to him and laid the skin next to him, against his side. "I'm sorry. Did I hurt you?"

"No. Emma—" He started to lift his head.

I wondered if I'd broken some selkie taboo. Was it unacceptable to touch another's sealskin? "I—I'm sorry. I didn't mean to—"

"It's not that. Why—why are you here?"

Panic started to bubble up again. "Let me see what I can do, now that you're comfortable." I had no idea if he was comfortable; it was merely babble. I stood up, thought for a moment, then hitched up my skirt as discreetly as possible and wiggled out of my fine cotton petticoat. I folded it and laid it gently across his back, to stanch some of the blood.

"My things—they should be here somewhere." He'd closed his eyes again.

"Good. Maybe I can use your shirt to help hold this in place for now." I looked around and finally spotted a pale sack—no, a pale sack and a scuffed school-girl's book-bag —a short distance up the beach. I fetched them both and went to work, folding the sack—a pillowcase!—into a pad on top of my petticoat.

"Emma—" he began again, after a moment.

I thought fast to forestall him. "Where's Maggie?" A horrible thought struck me. "Is she all right? Did she—"

"I hope so. I—I sent her—find out where they were going."

"The people who shot you?"

"Yeah." He tensed and lifted his head. "We've got to get back—the hotel. I have to…call the captain."

"We're not going anywhere until I get you tidied up," I said firmly as I started to twist his shirt into a binding to hold on his makeshift bandages.

"Emma, no—it was Germans. A U-boat. Osborn…meeting them—"

I stopped. "George Osborn? Meeting *Germans*?" Was he delirious from blood loss?

"In his boat with another man—Keller—"

"Keller?" That had been the name of the Osborns' guest whom we'd met at their party a million years ago. What was going on here?

"Mmm...pretending to fish, but waiting—and a U-boat came, and four men got out—they brought...something to Osborn's boat, and got in...and Osborn saw me and shot me."

"Good heavens!" This was unbelievable...except that it was Malcolm. I felt a surge of rage at George. "What about Maggie?"

"I told her to stay—watch where they were headed, then come back." He swallowed. I wished I had some water to give him. "Go back to the hotel. Tell my father. He'll call them—warn them—

"Malcolm—*Emma!*" Maggie was scurrying up the beach, waving her skin. "You came back!" she shouted and threw herself at me.

I was so relieved to see her that I didn't mind that she was a very soggy little girl just then. I returned her hug. "You're all right?"

"I'm fine." She detached herself from me and bent over Malcolm. "Is he dead?"

A smile lifted the visible side of his mouth. "You wish, Maggot."

"Oh, good. They're going south. I think I heard one of them say something about the air station, wanting to know how far it was."

The air station! Why were Herr Keller and his German friends wanting to go to the air station? Malcolm had said they had unloaded boxes into George's boat. *What was inside those boxes?*

He was struggling to raise himself on his forearms, and I knew he was thinking the same thing. "Emma, go. You've got to warn them."

My thoughts were racing. "Maggie should go. She can run faster than I can."

She was already reaching for her bag and yanking out her dress. "I can run like anything. Should I go to the air station?"

I hesitated. That would be the most direct thing to do...but would the guards at the gate let a bedraggled eleven-year-old girl in to see the captain, no matter how insistent she was? "No. Go home and tell your father. He can telephone the captain, and then you can lead him back here to Malcolm afterwards. Your mother's worrying about you, anyway. Can you do that?"

"'Course I can!"

"Good girl! Go quick."

She finished haphazardly buttoning her frock and slid her skin into the bag, then paused. "Are...are you our friend again?"

"Yes," I said firmly. "Now, go!"

She nodded, then lit into a run and galloped up the beach. I watched her until Malcolm cleared his throat. I looked down; he was watching me, and I knew he was thinking about Maggie's question and my response.

"Tell me why you're here," was all he said.

My first instinct was to put him off. "Oh, that's not important right now —"

"Yes, it is."

I sighed. After a moment I said, "I—learned something, yesterday, up in Boston."

"And?"

"And—" I took a breath to steady my nerves. "I was given something that—that belongs to me. Something I—that I was born with."

"Ah." He was silent for the space of several heartbeats while I tried frantically to decipher what that monosyllable might mean. "Is it here?"

This was it. I turned around and picked up my skin, which I'd unceremoniously dumped on the sand so that I could give him my satchel as a pillow. I held it for a moment, trying to draw some courage from its furry warmth, then turned and placed it on the sand next to him where he could see it.

Neither of us spoke. Then carefully, his face wrenching in pain as he moved, he reached out and ran his hand down it. I closed my eyes and felt his touch reverberate through me like the peal of an organ.

"It's beautiful," he whispered, his hand warm on it—on *me*. This was me. And yet, right now I felt as empty as it was.

"I don't know if it will work." I hated the quaver in my voice. "If I can—you know—wear it. I'm—I'm only a half a selkie—"

"You aren't *only* anything," he snapped. "You're Emma. I don't care about anything else, so long as you're you." The last word came out in a whisper.

"But I care," I said, and took another big, steadying breath. "I didn't want to believe any of this. But now I have to, and I'm scared. And...and yet I want this. I was born with it. It's time I took what's mine."

He closed his eyes. I bent over him, worried that he'd fainted from blood loss, but he opened them again, and I saw they were bright with tears. "You want this? Truly?"

"Yes."

We were both silent for a moment, but it was a good kind of silence that oddly seemed to fill some of the emptiness inside me. But I wasn't done yet. "Malcolm, I need to say—I mean, I'm sorry. I was so very horrid to you. My dad—he—"

"Emma," he said softly, and stroked my skin again. I shivered, but felt steadier. "Don't apologize. I was...far more horrid, and completely selfish." He spoke slowly, with pauses between phrases. I wanted to tell him not to talk, to save his strength, but knew he wouldn't welcome that. "I did it all wrong...made it worse than it had to be. I'm sorry, too."

I touched his hand where it lay on my skin. He turned it and held onto mine tightly. I clutched at it and felt the rest of my emptiness filled till there was none left.

"So can we start again?" he whispered after a while.

"Yes." I leaned over to kiss his cheek, then laughed shakily. "As soon as you don't have enormous wounds on you any-where."

"The one...in my heart...is pretty much healed," he said, the corner of his mouth turning up, but then he sighed. "Drive me crazy…not follow those Germans. Someone should watch them…until Capt'n Abbott…gets them."

My poor darling. I could see how it would drive him crazy. I wished there were something I could do—

Wait. I took a deep breath. This was probably ridiculous, but—"What about me?"

"What?"

"Why shouldn't I follow them?"

He gripped my hand. "No…too dangerous."

"You sent Maggie after them. I hope you'd trust me as much as you do a child."

"I'm not hoping…to spend the rest of my life… with Maggie." He withdrew his hand and started to push himself up, then gasped and fell back again.

I scrambled to my feet. "How long would it take you to swim to the air station from here? Or would going by the road be quicker?"

"No, swimming's faster," he said, then frowned. "Emma— you're not—what're you doing?"

I reached up behind me and started to unbutton my dress. "Taking off my clothes. I gather it's what you do before you put on your sealskin."

"Abs'lutely not!"

I paused. "Why not?"

"Osborn isn't…only one with a gun."

I suddenly felt insanely cheerful. "Of course not. They're German agents. I expect they're armed to the teeth. Or,"—I deflated somewhat—"Or is it that you don't think I *can* go after them?"

"No!" His voice was anguished. "This isn't…not for your first time. I want…be there, help you…show you—"

"It isn't what I'd planned either, but there's not much I can do about it. We don't even know if I *can* change, but I have to try. You don't need me—your family will be back for you soon, based on how fast Maggie was running. Maybe I can do some good in the meanwhile."

"Emma." He spoke through gritted teeth. "I. Forbid. It."

I stopped. "Would you like to reconsider that statement?" I asked in a very quiet voice.

He closed his eyes, and after a minute's pause, sighed. "I'm sorry. If anything…happened to you, I—I'd—"

"You won't have to do anything, because nothing's going to happen to me." My dress was off; my petticoat was already gone, covering Malcolm's wound. I bit my lip, then unfastened my brassiere and stepped out of my drawers. I wasn't sure which was stranger—undressing on a beach, or in front of a boy. But this was no time for silly modesty. Lives might be at stake. And anyway, it was mostly dusk now—I doubted he could see much of me.

I bent and picked up my skin. "What do I do?"

"Emma—*are you sure?*"

"I have to do it," I said. My very first governess back when I was six, Miss Antrim, told me something that had stuck with me all these years: if you see a task that needs doing, don't wait for someone else to take care of it; do it yourself. Malcolm certainly couldn't do this, and Maggie, despite my optimistic words to Malcolm, might not be back for a while. This was *my* job. "What do I do?"

He looked up, and I saw something on his face I'd never seen before: fear. I knelt again and kissed him gently. "I'm not going to get hurt, and I'm going to come back. Someone has to keep you entertained and away from a pair of oars while you convalesce."

He smiled unwillingly. "Go out…'bout waist deep. Put your skin…over your head. Like a hood. It should happen."

And if it didn't, then… I shoved that thought aside. "Anything else?"

"Call for others."

"Other selkies?" I hadn't thought about that. It would be less lonely if there were other selkies with me, but I wasn't sure I was ready for that yet. "How?"

"Like this." He closed his eyes.

I waited. "Um, Malcolm?" I said, after a long minute.

"Didn't you hear?" he asked, opening his eyes.

"Did you say something?"

"I called you...the way selkies do." He frowned. "Damn...didn't hear me before either, did you?"

"Have you tried before?" This was fascinating! "Does it work far away, or do you have to be close?" I remembered the way he and Maggie seemed to know each other's thoughts. Now I understood why.

"Doesn't work over much distance. Close is best. Mother said you might not be able to hear, because..."

Because I wasn't a full selkie. I swallowed. "I'll just have to do the best I can on my own, then." I draped my dress over his legs to give him a little warmth until they came for him from the hotel and gave him another kiss; he turned his face up slightly so that our lips met. Then I stood up and walked with my skin down to the water's edge. When the water lapped around my waist, I took a deep breath, closed my eyes, and lifted my sealskin over my head.

•CHAPTER TWENTY-FIVE•
EMMA

Nothing happened.

"No!" I cried in disappointment. In that moment, I realized just how much I wanted this thing, this other existence, that I'd denied so vehemently at first. And how much I wanted to be able to share it with the young man on the beach behind me. If I couldn't change, would that truly ever be possible?

For some reason, though, my cry came out as a strange, inarticulate groan—and then everything—the sky, the water—tilted sideways. I fell *sploosh!* into the water, which was funny—I wasn't dizzy or anything, but...but something was not right. Sputtering, I tried to stagger to my feet—and realized I didn't have any. Or rather, they were different. I stopped struggling and found that I was floating in a whole new world.

It had worked. My skin had worked.

I was swamped with sensation. The dusk was suddenly much brighter, like someone had dialed back the sun by an hour, only I couldn't see the colors of sunset. In fact, the world looked like a photograph, black and white—and yet there was such richness in the nuances between darkness and light that color would have felt like a distraction. I turned and saw Malcolm on the beach, painfully lifting himself and straining to look back at the water—at me. I wanted to yell at him to lie back down before he disarranged my makeshift pads on his back, but it came out as a sort of "*a-rooo!*" At least it sounded fairly annoyed and might get the message across.

I heard him laugh and then sigh. "Be careful, my love," he said, and let his head fall back onto my satchel. My hearing was more acute as well, much more so: he had whispered those words rather than spoken them. I longed to go back to him and stroke his hair and hold his hand until his father came for him.

But I couldn't. I turned back to face the sea spread before me—and froze. As a human, I could paddle and splash in the shallows close to shore. But now I had to enter the ocean as one of the ocean's creatures. And it suddenly seemed very big indeed, and I very small.

One step at a time, soldier, I said to myself and did a sort of roll call through my body. My legs and feet were good for one thing now—providing the power to move me through the water. I gave them an experimental kick, which was awkward until I realized it wasn't just them but my entire lower body that helped me move, almost like a fish. My arms—fore-flippers, rather—could help with that, or I could just keep them tight to my body and soar, like a Fourth-of-July rocket.

And if I was going to catch up to George Osborn's boat, I'd better start pretending I was a rocket. I took a breath and slipped under the water.

To my surprise, I could see just as well under the surface as above it. But I was overwhelmed by the rest of my senses. Strange and incomprehensible sounds assailed my ears, and my entire body seemed capable of...of *feeling* what was going on around me, especially my face. I wanted to curl up into a ball and sort out all these sensations, but I couldn't. I came back up for breath though I hadn't really needed to, just to stop the rush of information that I could not quite parse flooding my brain. But I would have to get used to it eventually. Another breath, and I made myself swim away from shore.

After a few minutes, I started getting the hang of paying attention to one sense at a time. Maybe eventually I'd be able to use them all at once the way I used my human senses on land—

integrating them all automatically—but that wouldn't be happening here and now. I concentrated on hearing and heard some very strange moaning, wailing cries from what seemed like a distance—and closer in, a deep, whining hum that I desperately hoped wasn't the U-boat Malcolm had seen. George's boat was evidently too far away for even a seal's ears to detect, but I knew where to go. Clumsily at first, I set out.

I wasn't sure how long I'd been swimming—my sense of time didn't feel the same—when I realized I wasn't alone. Three?—no, four shapes were pacing me, a short distance to my left, just far enough away not to feel threatening but close enough to keep tabs on me. They were watching me with what appeared to be deep interest, and I wondered if they were seals or selkies. Not that I could communicate with selkies, shy of taking human form and talking to them. I wish I'd asked Malcolm if he could speak with seals mentally, too. There was so much for me to learn!

Somehow—I think it had to do with my whiskers?—I could sense the shape of the island to my right by the way the water moved and felt when I'd reached the southern tip. I glided closer to shore and followed it westward—the air station had been set on the southwest edge of Monomoyick, angled away from open ocean, to give it some protection against storms—and paused to listen for boats. There was nothing; George and his companions must already be on shore.

After another distance, I surfaced and took my bearings.

I'd never seen the air station from the vantage of the water before, but even in what was now nearly full dark, my seal eyes could clearly make out the outline of the great hydrogen storage tank and the hangar for the dirigibles; closer by were the concrete bulwarks and the great ramp leading to the hangar for sea planes. I could just see some of the other buildings as well, but all seemed strangely dark—no windows had lights showing. I pondered that, then wanted to slap my forehead: of course no light was showing—the station itself would have been supremely careful with maintaining blackout at night. Slowly, cautiously, I swam into shore, and sensed my companions follow behind me.

Anchored in just a foot or two of water, I saw George Osborn's boat. I swam as close as I dared; thankfully, it appeared to be deserted. Then all the Germans had gone ashore, taking George with them. I would have brought him too, if I'd been them; I would not have trusted him to actually wait for my return. I wished I could have climbed up on the boat to see if any of the boxes Malcolm had seen were there, but I certainly couldn't do so in my present form...and then it hit me: I had no idea how to take my skin off. Why hadn't I thought to ask Malcolm that before I dashed off?

A quiet "*mraaaa*" made me start. One of the seals/selkies was only a foot or two from me, looking at me with such an inquiring air that words were unnecessary...except they were, if I was ever going to learn anything. I stared at it hopefully; maybe it was a selkie, about to instruct me in proper skin shedding technique. But after we'd stared at each other for a while and it didn't change into a person, my hopes sank. This would have to be up to me. I lifted a flipper toward my head, as if to lift my skin from my head. But a flipper is not a hand, and all I succeeded in doing was swatting my nose. That annoyed me.

Come off! I said to myself, and gave an impatient, twisting squirm—and then I was standing in water—really standing, on two feet—and my skin had slipped from my head. I snatched at it and held it close, trying to get my human bearings once again. It was disorienting, shifting from one form to another.

All four seals who'd followed me now clustered around me in a circle. "Er, hello," I said, and waited for them to take off their skins as well. None of them moved. Well, that explained matters.

The seals looked at me anxiously. What was I supposed to do? I couldn't talk to them in my head, so I'd have to use words—if, that is, they could understand me. "Um, thank you for coming with me. I'm very new at this, and you made me feel safer. Since no one's taking off their skins, I'm assuming you're seals."

They watched me raptly. I took a deep breath and said, "Look, if you can understand me—if you know what I'm saying—please, go find some selkies and send them here. And send a couple to Malcolm too, where I left him on the beach. He's been hurt, and I'd feel better if someone were with him. But I have to find out what's going on here, and—and a little help would be...helpful," I finished lamely. "Please." Politeness counted, even with seals, as all twelve of my governesses would probably have agreed.

They watched me a moment longer. Then, without ceremony, they backpedaled into the water and disappeared.

"Well," I said, exhaling. I had no idea if they'd understood a word I'd said, or if they'd decided I was boring and had left in search of better entertainment. I waded carefully into shore; my legs felt shaky, as if I'd just run several miles—which I supposed I had, in a way. As I stepped up onto the sand and into the soft night air, another revelation hit me.

I was naked.

I was naked, and I was about to march through a Naval air station staffed with three hundred healthy young men and tell them to be on the lookout for Germans. Why, oh why, had I not thought this through more thoroughly?

I held my sealskin before me like a towel. It covered what it needed to in front, but there was nothing keeping my backside from being viewed by all and sundry. Would I be able to go more than ten feet, even in the dark? Would they bring me to Captain Abbott, or arrest me, or...or worse?

I would have to be stealthy, then. Could I sneak up to his quarters, evading sentries and chance passers-by—not many of those at this hour, but one never knew—without being seen?

I would have to try.

I picked my way carefully up the beach, wishing I had my seal vision again as night had fallen and no light came from the crescent moon low in the sky. Every long, matted drift of dried eelgrass at the high tide line looked like a body—say, a German agent lying in wait in the sand. I was afraid a real German agent would look like a drift of eelgrass and that I'd step on one, and had to remind myself that they would not be lying on the beach like that. I hoped.

At the top of the sand I paused, reviewing what I could remember of the station's layout. Most of the working part of the station—the huge hydrogen storage tank for filling the dirigibles, the even huger dirigible hangar and the one for seaplanes with its track to the water, the ordnance magazine, and many of the maintenance shops and the power plant were here near the beach. Captain Abbott's office and quarters were, of course, three or four hundred feet away across a broad, open field.

It wouldn't be easy. I set out.

I scared myself half to death only five or six times tripping over a tussock or losing my footing in a rut. But I didn't bump into any sentries, even after I recalled that there was a nicely graded dirt road leading to the top of the station, perfect for sentries to make their rounds on, and snuck over to it.

It took me a few minutes to find the officers' quarters. It was dark—not even a glimmer of light showed from the edge of any window—and silent as well, which was even spookier. I made myself tiptoe up the stairs and press my ear to a window: nothing. The administration building, a short distance away, was also dark. Even the large double building that made up the enlisted men's quarters seemed quiet. Where was everyone?

And then I remembered. They were at the Bastille Day dance at the hotel—Mrs. Galbraith had said they would be turning out in force tonight. But surely the entire base hadn't gone—they would never leave it unguarded. Yet I hadn't seen a living soul.

So what should I do now? Probably the only thing was to go back to the beach, hide myself somehow, wait for the Germans to return, and see if I could learn anything that way. I sighed and began the trudge back.

I was back on the beach not far from George's boat, trying to think of where I could hide close enough to be able to hear and see what might happen, when I heard voices. For a moment I froze; was it soldiers from the air station, or George's Germans? Should I hide, or call out to them? Recollection of my condition made me drop to my belly in the sand by a long drift of eelgrass and pull it over me, and a moment later, I was grateful that I had.

A small group of people were approaching from farther down the beach. I wished again for my seal vision, but I could just make out their shapes as they approached. Two of them appeared to be carrying something—a crate of some kind?—between them. I listened carefully…and yes, it sounded like the voices were conversing in German. I knew the barest rudiments of that language—*hello, good-bye*, and *where is the train station, please*. Fortunately, it seemed George didn't speak German either.

"What about the hotel?" I heard him say above the others. "It's a hotel. What do you want me to say about it?"

"Don't be more stupid than you need to, boy."

I recognized that voice—it *was* Herr Keller, the "Swiss industrialist" whom we'd met at the Osborns' cocktail party—and I felt a flare of anger. Posing as someone from a neutral country was pretty despicable.

"How large is it? What is the layout? Where will most of the station personnel be?" he continued.

"How the hell should I know?" I'd heard that sulky tone before from George. "There's a dance, so I guess they'll be in the ballroom."

"And can you tell me where this ballroom is, or does your family not deign to attend functions there?"

"I've had just about enough from you, Keller—"

I heard a slap and cringed. *Don't be an idiot!* I thought very hard at George. *Keep him talking!*

There was silence for a minute, during which I heard the soft splashing of people walking in water, and then a grunt and *thunk!* They must have put what they were carrying on the boat.

"It's on the ground floor." George finally said, still sulky, but I heard the fear, too, in his voice. "Next to the dining room. To the—to the left, as you look at it from the beach. There's a veranda along the whole ocean-facing side as well."

"That's better. How long would you say this ballroom is?"

A pause. "I don't know. Eighty or ninety feet, maybe."

"And that length is along the veranda facing the ocean?"

"Yes."

"Ah, good. That wasn't so hard, was it? Walther!" Herr Keller's tone became brisk.

"*Ja?*"

"*Die Amerikaner sind bestimmt im Ballsaal. Er ist dreißig Meter lang auf der Seeseite. Hast du genüg Dynamit?*"

A pause. "*Ja, wir haben gerade genüg, um diese Hurensöhne in die Hölle zu jagen.*"

"*Gut.* All right, boy—" I assumed he was speaking to George. "Let's go."

I expected George to complain again, but he didn't—though his tone was still surly. "Fine. Get your boys to push us off while I start the engine."

While they were pushing the boat into deeper water, I thought furiously, most of all about one word I'd heard Herr Keller say: *Dynamit.* Dynamite...down the length of the ballroom. That's what the box they were carrying must hold. But wait: Malcolm said they'd loaded several boxes into George's boat, and now they had one left. Which meant they'd used most of it here.

They were planning to blow up the air station—*and* the hotel.

Oh God, what should I do? The hotel and the air station were at opposite ends of the island—and there was only one of me. I had no idea where on the station they'd planted the dynamite. And meanwhile, they were on their way to the hotel to blow it up, along with Captain Abbott and his men and all the local people who'd bought tickets to the dance...and Maggie and her parents—and possibly, by now, Malcolm.

I made myself take a deep breath before I panicked. I could beat them there if I left now—a seal could swim faster in the dark than George could run his boat. But that meant leaving the air station to be blown up, leaving the busy shipping lanes south of Boston unguarded.

Explosives could be set with timers—I'd been on enough of Dad's field trips to know that dynamite was sometimes used to uncover outcrops and so on. I assumed they'd used them here to give themselves plenty of time to get away before the explosions started. But how long would they have set them for? Was there enough time for me to warn everyone at the hotel and for the captain to come back here to search the station? No wonder the Germans had planned this for the night of the dance, to ensure that the station would be minimally manned.

George had finally gotten his engine started, and the boat had begun to move slowly away from shore. It was just me left here, trying to make a desperate choice—

"Hey!" The shout from the boat made me sit up. That had sounded like George. "What the hell do you think you're—"

The angry words ended in a loud splash. A jeering laugh drifted through the night. "You seem to dislike our company," I heard Herr Keller call. "So we'll leave you with the seals. Maybe one of them will rescue you—except no, you shot at one. Not very good at making friends, are you, boy? *Auf Wiedersehen!*"

There was the sound of an engine accelerating; it moved quickly away into the night. They'd thrown George off his own boat.

A bit of me was glad—served him right for helping them! Then frantic splashing made me stand and peer into the darkness. What if he couldn't swim? Reluctantly, I put down my sealskin and waded into the water. I didn't particularly want to help him, but I couldn't just let him drown. "George! Are you all right?"

The splashing continued. I swam toward it and soon saw him flailing awkwardly in the water. He wasn't drowning—but he wasn't swimming very well.

"George!" I called again, treading water. "Do you need help?"

"Wha—who's that?"

"It's Emma Verlaine."

"Emma!" The splashing resumed. "Where are you? What are you doing here?"

I swam closer. "Do you need help?" I repeated.

"What? No, of course not."

I should have guessed. "In that case, I'm going back to shore." I still needed to think about what to do—darn it, having to deal with George Osborn on top of everything else was simply the outside of enough.

The splashing became frantic again. "No, wait! Don't leave me here—"

"You're only about sixty feet off the beach. Keep swimming toward me."

"But I can't see you!"

"Listen for me, then."

I managed to guide him back to shore, thank heavens—I really didn't want to have to swim out and rescue him. I was waiting on the sand with my skin held close when he finally trudged out of the water. "Emma?" he said uncertainly, looking around.

"I'm here," I said. "Are you all right?"

I heard his sharp intake of breath as he came up to me. "Emma! You're not—"

I sighed. "Not wearing any clothes. Yes, I know that."

He reached a hand toward me. I stepped back smartly. "Don't you dare touch me!"

His sulky voice was back. "I wasn't going to do anything."

All my anger at him burst out like a geyser. "I don't care what you were or weren't going to do. I'm simply sick to death of you. Are you proud of yourself for shooting a seal, by the way? Were you aware that it wasn't a seal? Malcolm's on the beach with a gunshot wound in his back, thanks to you."

I waited in vain for any sign of contrition. "But—that was him? He can't have found his skin! I locked it in my—" He closed his mouth abruptly.

His skin! "You stole Malcolm's skin? You—"

I started toward him ready to—what? Punch his face? Throttle him with my bare hands? Sanity returned, along with an icy calm. "Be glad your aim wasn't any better, or he'd be dead and you'd have even more trouble on your hands. I wouldn't have left him, except I had to follow you and your German friends here to find out what you were up to. Serves you right that they threw you out of your boat. Aiding and abetting the enemy and attempted murder, all in one evening. That's quite... *impressive.*"

He was making peculiar sputtering noises, as if trying to decide what to respond to first. "You—you heard them do that?"

It figured he'd fix on that. "I heard all of it."

"Then you know it wasn't my fault! I didn't want to help them—I didn't even know Keller was a German. My father—they're blackmailing him over some little foolishness. I had to do it, or they'd have ruined him—"

"Where did they set the dynamite?" I didn't want to hear any more, and we were wasting valuable time.

"The—you know about that too?" he asked weakly.

"Oh, honestly! Yes, I know about it. I want to know where it is."

"I don't know."

"Don't add lying to the rest of your—"

"I *don't* know!" he burst out. "They tied me up and left me lying on the ground while they did whatever they were doing!"

More humiliation; no wonder he was writhing. Still, he must have heard where they were hea—

"Halloo?" a voice said from somewhere behind me, and I jumped, spinning around.

"Who—who's there?" George quavered.

Then I heard a liquid sound and realized that whoever it

was, they weren't coming down the beach, but walking in from the water. Which could only mean—

"I'm here!" I said, starting toward them.

"Emma, stop!" George made a grab for me. "You don't know who this is—"

But I had a fairly good idea. There were three figures, maybe twenty feet away, just at the water's edge. A chuckle came from one of them. "Ah, I think we've found her. Or has she found us?"

I took another step toward them. "You're selkies?"

"Oh, aye," the voice said easily. For some reason, it sounded familiar. "Are you?"

I hesitated. "Yes. I think so. Mostly."

"What?" George said behind me. "Emma, what did you say?"

"Well." The voice sounded decidedly amused. "I reckon we've come to the right place."

"Yes!" I said, starting forward to meet them, till I remembered that I was naked apart from my skin clutched to my front. I was going to have to get used to this nudity business—not only mine, but others'—in short order, and gave myself a mental shake. "Please, I need your help!"

"That's what we came for."

The trio walked up to me, and I realized why the voice had sounded familiar. "I dreamed about you!" I said to the silver-haired one who walked with a limp—the older selkie I'd spoken to in my dream last week.

He gave a small, deprecating cough. "Not quite, lass. But I'm glad I've already made your acquaintance. We were told you would be here and that you seemed to be in some distress. You're Malcolm's Emma, yes?"

"Yes, that's right—*oh!*" Oh heavens, that *hadn't* been a dream—I'd really been to the beach and seen the selkies dancing. In another minute, my head would explode—along with the air station, if I didn't keep on task. "Did the seals tell you I was here?"

He smiled. "As well as they could. We've been waiting for the humans to leave. They're planning bad things for the station, yes?"

"Yes." I hesitated. "Malcolm's on the beach below the hotel. He's hurt. Can one of you go to him until his father comes?"

The selkies looked at each other, then one of them turned back to the water. The silver-haired one nodded to me. "He'll go to Malcolm — they are old friends. Now, what do you wish us to do?"

"Emma!" George had gotten up the courage to come over and tap me on the shoulder. "You shouldn't be — be out here like this." He made a furtive gesture toward me.

"I'm a selkie, George." Saying those words out loud gave me a strange feeling, but I didn't have time to figure out what it was. "This is what happens when a selkie takes off his or her skin. Bathing attire is not an option."

He opened his mouth but no words came out, so I turned back to the two selkies and tried to explain what was going on. Did selkies know about things like dynamite? At least they would understand about the dance at the hotel...

"But I don't know why it's so quiet," I concluded when I'd told them everything. "There should be guards — sentries — and there aren't any. And someone has to get to the hotel and warn them before the Germans start setting explosives there."

The other selkie — he was somewhat younger than his silver-haired companion, maybe Malcolm's father's age — spoke. "So you wish us to find these things that will make great fires and stop them, yes? Where are they?"

"I don't know," I began...and then I *did* know. It only made sense. "They'll be around the big tank there and the dirigible hangar. And maybe around the ordnance magazine and the seaplane hangar." But my bet was on the tank and the dirigible hangar. All that hydrogen, just waiting for a source of ignition...

"And him?" The older selkie nodded at George.

"The Germans made him bring them here. I would *hope*" — I fixed him with a glare — "that he will help us if he wants to have the least chance of redeeming himself before Captain Abbott—or a court of law."

"Yes," he replied weakly.

We hurried down the beach, then up a gravel road toward the tank. The gravel bit into my bare feet, but the discomfort couldn't distract me from thinking about what might happen if the Germans had set their timers—I'm sure they had used timers, or things would have already been exploding—to go off, say, a half hour after they'd set them. That would soon put us in a very unpleasant position indeed.

"Emma," George, at my side, muttered. "I can't believe that you're one of those...*things*!"

I kept a firm hand on my temper, but it wasn't easy. "Yes, I had a hard time believing it myself, at first."

"But the Wetherells—you're not really one of them—"

"I am very much a Wetherell," I said. Just...not a Verlaine. Oh, Dad... "Not that it should matter in the least to you. That's all you cared about, wasn't it? That I was a Wetherell."

"You never even gave me a chance," he said resentfully.

"Where is the rule that says I had to?"

"You thought you were better than me because of your family—"

Once again, I'd had enough. I took a deep breath and said, "It's worse than that, George. I never thought of you at all."

He recoiled. "You—you—bitch!"

"Call me whatever you like. I honestly don't care." I hurried to catch up to the two selkies. Poor Helen—and she *liked* him.

A few yards from the tank, Sim, the younger of the two selkies—they'd introduced themselves as we'd walked as Sim and Aonghas—swerved to one side. "This may be why you saw no guards," he called to us, and we hurried over.

A young man lay on the ground, unconscious, gagged, and handcuffed. I yanked the gag from his mouth for fear he'd suffocate.

"He was struck hard," Aonghas said, rising from a quick examination. "Your Germans are good at their job."

"They're not my Germans!" George exclaimed.

"You'd better not have helped them do this," I said to him. So this was what had happened — they'd lain in wait and taken down the sentries. "Will he be all right?"

"Aye, I expect so. A sore head, for sure — maybe worse, but there's no way to tell now." Aonghas's voice was sober.

I stared down at the limp young man. "Poor thing — oh!" A flashlight lay just beyond him. He must have been holding it when he was attacked. I picked it up; my thumb found the switch, and to my relief it turned on, though the lens cap was cracked.

Aonghas was delighted when I held it up to show him. "A rod of light! That is something we can use!"

We found our first dynamite bundle just a few yards away at the base of the metal cagework that housed the hydrogen tank. I shone the flashlight on the dozen brown sticks, four large batteries, and clock — the timer — all wired together.

The others stared at it as well. "And that will cause a great fire?" Sim asked dubiously.

"If we leave it here, it will."

"How do we stop it?"

Thank heavens for Miss Ouimet, my fifth governess, who'd thought that girls should learn something about sciences other than botany. "If we pull the wires out so that it's no longer all connected together, it won't be able to explode. It's their working together that makes the explosion. These," — I pointed to the batteries — "supply power to set off the actual explosives." I indicated the dynamite. "The clock sets what time it will happen." I had no idea what time it was now, but they were set to go off at ten.

George looked at his wrist, then held it up to his ear. "My watch has stopped."

When he took his unexpected bath, no doubt. "What time does it say?" I shone the flashlight on it. Nine-ten. That had been...what, fifteen minutes ago? Twenty?

We had half an hour to find all the dynamite on a three-hundred-acre air station.

I handed the flashlight to Aonghas and, crouching next to the bundle, began unwrapping the wire connecting the batteries to the dynamite, then, for good measure, the one connecting it to the clock. Oh for a pair of wire cutters right now — or even a sturdy pair of kitchen shears. But I didn't have them; this was what I had to do.

We found another unconscious sentry and another flash-light, which let us split up into pairs. Aonghas attached himself to me, and we crept along the base of the tank, shining the light around the base and up into the iron cagework in case they'd set it higher as well.

"So you're accepting it now, are you?" he asked.

There wasn't any need to ask what he meant by *it*. I couldn't help feeling a bit defensive, though. "Since my skin had been kept hidden from me until yesterday, I think I had an excuse not to before."

"Eh." He shook his head. "Bad thing to do. You shouldn't have been kept from yourself like that."

Kept from myself — that was a neat way to phrase it. I was going to have to talk to Dad, to work through both of our pain — and happiness, too — around this. I hoped some of the happiness could be his as well, eventually. "Well, I'm here now."

"You are, lass, you are." He smiled to himself.

We met up again with Sim and George; altogether, we'd found five more bundles set around the periphery of the tank and disconnected them all. Then we started on the enormous dirigible hangar, again in pairs. We'd found one bundle and disconnected its wires before it hit me — wires!

"Can you keep looking for these without me?" I asked Aonghas.

"What will you be doing?"

"I'm going to try to get into the captain's office and use the telephone to call the hotel." Why hadn't I thought of it before?

"Ah, the telephone. I have seen that instrument." Aonghas nodded wisely. "Go."

This time I didn't bother trying to be stealthy. I draped my skin around my neck like a scarf and ran straight up the road that circled the station to the Administration building, wishing all the while that a sentry would appear. None did. Once there I stood half bent-over, waiting for the stitch in my side to ease, and regarded the locked door for a moment. Then I went over to the neat, brick-edged flower bed in front of it.

"I'm sorry, sir," I muttered to Captain Abbott, and used a brick from the flower bed to smash one of the panes of glass in the door. I reached in and unlocked it, then used the brick to scrape aside the broken glass and went to the desk I'd seen occupied by a young man in uniform when I called on the captain. I picked up the telephone and clicked the hook briskly to get the operator's attention.

Silence.

I tried again, but I'd already guessed: Herr Keller's Germans must have cut the telephone wires first thing. I should have figured that out before, drat it! Did that mean Maggie's warning, relayed by Mr. Galbraith, hadn't gotten through? Probably not, or the station wouldn't be deserted. Which might mean that Captain Abbott was on his way back here from the dance…but maybe not yet. I had to get to the hotel.

I hurried back and found Sim and George near the front of the dirigible hangar. "We found two more guards," Sim told me. "One in the same condition as the others."

"And the other?"

"He is dead."

I swallowed hard, glad I hadn't seen the poor man — or boy; all the others sentries had been young, probably recent recruits. It made me angry all over again, then resolute. "The telephone wire was cut, I think — at least, it's not working. I have to get to the hotel and warn them."

Sim nodded. "Do you wish one of us to go with you?"

That would be much less scary, but— "No. Keep searching. And be careful."

"You be careful as well, Malcolm's Emma. The seals will go

with you." Sim touched my arm.

The seals. I had them, didn't I?—at least, the comfort of their presence. "Thank you. And you—" I frowned at George. "Help them. And keep a lookout for Captain Abbott or anyone returning from the hotel and tell them what's happening."

I turned away toward the beach. Before I'd gone a dozen steps, I heard George call, "Emma—wait."

"I don't have time right now," I said, not stopping.

He caught up with me. "I know. I just had to say—I'm sorry."

I stopped and closed my eyes. It was horribly, laughably inadequate. But it was a start. "I'm glad to hear that. If you're really sorry, go make sure the station doesn't blow up."

·CHAPTER TWENTY-SIX·
EMMA

It was much easier this time, when I wasn't worried about whether or not it would actually *work*, to put on my skin and take seal shape. I knew what to expect—the sudden changes in my body, the alteration in senses and perception—but I didn't have time to think about them this time: I had to get back to the hotel. I wasn't sure how I'd find it with the blackout in effect, but all I could do was try.

Again, I was quickly joined in the dark, velvety water by seals. Perhaps they sensed that I was unfamiliar with their world and needed watching over—or maybe they were just nosy, as Malcolm had once said. I didn't much care which it was; once again, their presence was comforting. I would take any scrap of comfort I could find right now.

In the end, it didn't matter that the hotel's blackout curtains were all properly in place; as I approached the hotel I could clearly hear the music from the dance drifting out into the night. Then the little striped tents on the beach confirmed matters. I headed in to shore.

I'd decided that I'd go to the Galbraith's apartment first; Mr. or Mrs. Galbraith would surely be there with Malcolm by now, and one of them would be able to find Captain Abbott or round up enough hotel employees to guard against the Germans. Besides, they would not be surprised when I showed up with only my sealskin to cover me. It would be an exquisite relief to hand this whole thing over to someone else to deal with — and to be with Malcolm. Even through my preoccupation at the air station, the worry for him had always been there, quietly gnawing. Now it was licking its chops and getting ready to really take a bite.

I passed George's boat anchored just off the beach and paused but detected no motion on it. The Germans were probably all ashore, the thought of which made me shiver. I wanted to run up the beach, shouting warnings, but knew I couldn't — in fact, I would have to be very, very careful. I slid out of my skin — a little less awkwardly this time — waded out of the water as quietly as I could, then zigzagged up the beach from one tent to another, hoping to maybe find a forgotten towel to wrap myself in one of them (no such luck.)

In the last tent before my final dash up to the hotel, I tried to read the night the way I had the water as a seal. The sky was dark and dappled with stars, the Milky Way a filmy scarf trailing across it. The air was mild, with just a breath of breeze to stir it. The music from the hotel was too loud here for me to hear anything like the stealthy movements of saboteurs planting dynamite, but at least I knew — or hoped I knew — that they would not set the dynamite to explode immediately. How long had they been here? I had no way of knowing. Time…oh please, give me time!

Finding the path through the hydrangeas up to the Galbraiths' porch took longer than I wanted. When I finally did I hesitated, then started up it at a stoop, trying to keep my head below the tops of the bushes so as not to be seen. When I reached the porch stairs — my shoes and stockings where I had left them, neatly side by side — I hurried up to them and went to the door.

It was locked.

I raised my hand to knock, then stopped and stepped back. There were no seams of light — no blackout curtain was completely perfect — visible at the edges of any of the windows or at the bottom of the door. No one was there. My stomach knotted; surely they'd found Malcolm by now, but why weren't they back yet? I could wait...

But no, I couldn't, much as I wished otherwise. Every minute mattered, and for now, this was my job and I had to see it through.

I tiptoed back down the stairs, back down the hydrangea path, and around to the edge of the lawn in front of the veranda to figure out what to do next. There had to be any number of alternate routes into the hotel — service entrances and side doors and so on — but I didn't know where any of them were. I could go around to the front of the hotel where the Germans wouldn't be, go in through the lobby, and tell the desk clerk that it was vital I find Captain Abbott. Easily done...except for the fact that a stark-naked girl clutching a piece of fur and wanting to see the captain would probably get short shrift, no matter how insistent I was. It looked like my only choice was the direct route: across the lawn and up the stairs. Going over the top, just like our boys would soon be doing in the trenches Over There. The thought steadied me; if they could do it, I could too.

I kept close to the bushes at the edge of the lawn, moving in a semi-crouch with my sealskin over my right shoulder to hide my white nakedness. No wonder the Germans had been wearing black; I would do anything for a black cloak right now. Then I scuttled to the first of the staircases leading up to the veranda, climbing them as lightly as possible. The music was very loud here, but it was something sweeping and waltzy, and it wouldn't conceal the vibrations of a heavy tread. Taking a seal's shape had made me very aware of vibrations.

At the top of the stairs, I hesitated then went quickly to a group of chairs and huddled behind them. No shots rang out; no dark-clad men jumped out at me from the shadows. I waited till I was sure my trembling legs would carry me and sneaked over to the next group of chairs, and the next.

Just beyond where I crouched was one of the French doors leading into the ballroom. I squinted at it, thinking furiously.

The doors were open on the other side of the blackout curtains, which swayed gently in the soft breeze. Could I poke my head around the edge of the curtain and get someone's attention without revealing my state of undress?

All I could do was try. I settled my skin firmly against me and sidled up to the curtain, then grasped its edge and stuck my head in the door—and into a man's shoulder.

"Hey!" the man turned...and to my immense relief, I recognized Ensign Gray. Thank heavens *something* was going right!

He recognized me too; his surprised and slightly indignant expression relaxed into a smile. "Miss Verlaine! I'd hoped you'd be here tonight. Will you give me a dance?" He held a hand out to me.

I backed away, just enough to avoid his hand. "Mr. Gray, please—you've got to find Captain Abbott and bring him here, right now. Or Mr. or Mrs. Galbraith—but the captain would be best. Tell him I sent you—no, tell him Malcolm Galbraith sent me."

His eyebrows rose. "Is everything all right? Can I help you?"

"No, it's not—but I can't talk right now. It—it's a matter of life and death. *Please!*"

He frowned. "I probably shouldn't say this, but the captain stepped out a few minutes after he got here, along with a few other officers—something came up back at the station, it seems. We juniors had the word passed down to keep smiling and dancing." He looked at me closely. "Is this something to do with that?"

"Quite possibly," I said. So the captain *had* gotten the message and gone back to the air station. "How long ago did he leave?"

He glanced at his watch and considered. "Not sure. Forty, forty-five minutes ago—maybe a little more. I didn't actually see him leave, so I can't say."

I thought quickly. Would that be enough time for him to get

to the station, talk to Aonghas and the others, and come back here? It was impossible to know; too much depended on chance. "What about Mr. or Mrs. Galbraith? Have you seen one of them?"

"I think I saw Mrs. G. not too long ago. You wait here, and I'll go look for all of 'em." He stepped aside and made to pull aside the curtain to draw me in.

"I'll wait outside," I said, again pulling away. "Please, hurry!"

"'Life and death,'" he said, smiling.

I didn't smile back. "Yes. Go!"

His smile faded. "You're serious, aren't you? All right, I'll be back with someone as quick as I can."

"Thank you." I withdrew my head from the curtain and closed my eyes, waiting for my vision, dazzled from the light in the ballroom, to adjust to the darkness once again. In a minute I'd take cover behind the chairs and hope to remain unseen until Ensign Gray came back, bringing Captain Abbott with him—

A hand clamped over my mouth from behind, jerking me backwards. I fell hard against something—no, someone—and dropped my skin. Before I could struggle, I felt something press against the side of my throat, something cold and narrow and metallic. It didn't take much imagination to guess that it was the barrel of a gun.

·Chapter Twenty-seven·
Emma

"And what have we here?" a voice murmured against my hair in lightly accented English. "I think it is a little selkie who seems to know more than she should."

It was Herr Keller.

I didn't move. I could barely breathe, with his hand covering half my face. He must have heard me begging Mr. Gray to get the captain. How long had he been watching me? Long enough to see the sealskin I held against me, evidently.

"Good girl," he said approvingly. "Struggling will not get you far. It will only get you dead." He pushed the gun a little more firmly against my neck. "I wonder what you know, little selkie? Maybe I should have let that stupid boy shoot you when we saw you. I should not like you talking to anyone else while my friends are busy, so I think we are going to go for a little walk. Do you think you can do that? I should hate to shoot you if you're about to faint, under the mistaken assumption that you're trying to escape. Nod your head if you can."

I hesitated. *Think, Emma!* For one thing, he knew about selkies. What would happen now? Keller probably *didn't* want to shoot me here—too close to the ballroom, even with the loudness of the music. No, he would want to get me away and then try to find out what I knew and if I'd warned anyone beyond Ensign Gray. And then he would either tie me up and leave me somewhere while he and his men finished setting the dynamite, or just shoot me out of hand—no, probably not that. It would be easier and less dangerous for them to just leave me tied up next to a bundle of dynamite and let it deal with me for them.

What could I do? If I tried to escape, screaming warnings, that would at least drive them away from the hotel. It would also leave me dead…and anyway, I was so terrified right now that I wasn't sure I *could* scream.

"I don't have all evening, girl," Herr Keller said, and prodded me again with the gun. I shut my eyes and nodded frantically.

"Good. We will walk backwards for a few paces. You may rest that pretty backside of yours against me, yes?" His voice smiled, loathsomely. "I wish I could examine that skin of yours—how does it work?" He nudged my skin with his toe, and I shuddered at the touch.

His arm tightened over me. "Ah, but you're like a *nixe*, a magical creature. It's not for men to know your secrets, eh, little selkie?" He took a step backwards and another, drawing me with him. I tried to guess how many steps it was to the nearest set of stairs, but I had no idea where they were; it was all I could do to make my legs continue to hold me up.

We inched backward, and every step seemed to take a week. I kept my eyes shut and tried to hold myself away from his body, but he used his elbow to draw me back against him. I guessed he was enjoying my discomfiture.

"Another few steps, my selkie," he murmured in my ear after an eternity had shuffled past, one step at a time. "We will go down the stairs sideways, you and I. Are you why we have had no lovely explosions down at the air station? Well, we will just have to make up for it here, won't we?"

I wanted to collapse again, but this time in relief. It had to be well past ten by now—and nothing had happened at the air station. It was safe; Aonghas and Sim and George had done their jobs—

"Here we go. I shall turn us—ah." He froze and muttered, "*Scheiße!*"

My eyes flew open. We stood sideways to one of the flights of stairs down to the lawn, just at its top. Several men in white uniforms stood on the grass below us, guns trained on us. At their front was the captain. I heard running footsteps and grunts and scuffling from elsewhere on the veranda through the music from the ballroom. My legs wobbled under me, weak with relief. It looked like there would be no explosions interrupting the dance tonight.

"Let her go," Captain Abbott said. His voice was tight and clipped.

Keller hesitated. "No, I don't think I shall do that. I think the little selkie will stay with me while we go to the beach if you will be so kind as to move away. Unless, of course, you don't mind my shooting her."

Captain Abbott didn't move. "You can't get away that way. One of your men has already gotten back to the boat and left with it. There's no escaping now."

Herr Keller snorted, and his hand tightened against my mouth. He was breathing hard, exhaling into my ear so that I could hardly hear. "Then we will wait here, you and I, until one of us gives way. You may have the advantage of numbers, but I have *her*. I don't think your hotel guests would like to see her blood spattered all over the stairs here, would they?"

An explosion sounded from somewhere behind and to my left. I cried out against Keller's hand—*the dynamite!* But the gun against my throat jerked away, and Keller shouted as well—then collapsed against me. His weight knocked me forward; I thumped and banged down the stairs as a spray of something hot and wet spattered me. Herr Keller fell too, moaning like an animal. It hadn't been dynamite, I realized through my daze. Someone—I had no idea who—had shot him from behind us, from the veranda.

"Halt!" Captain Abbott shouted, leaping toward the stairs. "Don't move!"

"Och, dinna raise such a fuss over *him*," a creaky voice said. I raised my head, and Annie Goslin appeared above me. She held a gun—the pearl-handled revolver I'd seen in her cottage years ago, it seemed—and as we watched she tucked it into the purse on her arm.

"I never could abide a bully," she commented.

◆Chapter Twenty-eight◆
Malcolm

Someone was calling me.

"Wha—?" I opened my eyes, trying to blink away the blear. Where was I?

Then I moved, and the pain across my back reminded me of where I was and why. I groaned.

"Lie still, man!"

"Luthais!" The sound of my old friend's voice startled me into clarity. I lifted my head, or tried to, anyway—I was too dizzy and sick-feeling to move it more than an inch off Emma's bag. "What are you—where's Emma? Is she—did she—?"

He clasped my hand. "She's who sent me here."

"Was she all right?" I didn't care if I threw up all over him; I lifted my head right up then. "Where'd you see her?"

"I said lie down, idiot!" He shoved my head down, but not ungently. "Yes, she's fine. We found her down by the air station. She asked someone to come here to be with you." He hesitated. "She swam down there alone? In the dark?"

I was afraid I would burst from pride. "Yeah. It was her first swim."

"Well." He was silent for a moment. "Then I guess you were right. About her, I mean. She's—she *is* something special."

"I know." I knew Luthais would tell the others what Emma had done—and what she was. I relaxed onto the makeshift pillow in relief. I think I dozed off again, because I suddenly heard my father's voice — and when I opened my eyes, Maggie's face was an inch from my nose.

"Still not dead?" she asked, sweetly.

"I'm not, but you might be at some point if you keep it up," I mumbled.

"If you can catch me—" she began, and then she wasn't there. Father was beside me instead.

I tried to focus on his face, but it wasn't easy. "Th' captain?"

"It's all right, Malcolm. I tried calling him as soon as Maggie told us, but the lines were down. Your mother is waiting for him to arrive for the dance—I expect he's already been and gone back to the station by now."

"Oh," I closed my eyes again. Then everything would be all right. And Emma—she was probably already on her way back to us. To me.

"Luthais and I have to lift you onto a stretcher and carry you home," he said. "I'm afraid it won't be pleasant."

"'S'all right," I said.

But it wasn't all right. It hurt like hell, and I think I yelled a couple of times. Maggie trotted beside me as they carried me home, reaching over occasionally to pat my foot. I think she was trying to be comforting.

Eventually, they got me back to the hotel and into our apartment and set me down on the sitting room floor. The sand on the beach had probably been more comfortable, but I didn't care. I was *home*.

"Malcolm." Mother was there. She knelt beside me and washed my face with a warm wet cloth. It felt like heaven. "The surgeon from the base is here," she said in a calm voice. I had never been so grateful to have such an unflappable mother. "We'll have to clean your back to begin with. I'm afraid it won't be very comfortable."

The next bit was worse—far worse—than the trip home. The doctor had something to numb the sensation, which helped some as he dug the bullet out of the back of my shoulder and cleaned the wound. But I didn't want him to give me anything to knock me out completely. I wanted to be awake when Emma came. I think I hurt Mother's hand, gripping it too hard; she held it oddly for the next several days.

Some minutes after he started, we all heard a loud report like a gunshot, very close by. I flinched, and the surgeon harrumphed at me. "Lie still, son!"

"I'll go see what it was," Maggie said, from somewhere across the room.

"I'll go," Mother said firmly. I realized that Father wasn't there and wondered what had happened to him...and then I just *endured* while the surgeon kept on working.

"Some muscle damage here," he said cheerfully as he started sewing me back up. "We'll have to hope for the best—I can see you've been in the habit of using them."

"Rowing," I said, through clenched teeth.

"Not for the rest of the summer, you won't. I'll give you exercises to do once you've started healing."

I wouldn't be on patrol for a while, it looked like. Mother had whispered that my skin was safe in my bedroom and that Father would take it to Aonghas's wife for healing tomorrow. I wondered what the surgeon would do if I asked him to stitch it up as well, and actually smiled a little.

Maggie plonked herself next to me. "Is Emma coming back here?" she asked me.

"Hope so," I muttered. Why wasn't she here already?

The surgeon dragooned Maggie into bringing him more hot water then, and I went back into endurance mode as he did his work. He'd finished stitching and was bandaging me up when we heard our front door bang and voices growing louder as they came down the hall toward us. The surgeon swore under his breath, and I felt him drape a towel over my bare backside. I heard the footfalls of several people—four or five, at least—heard them come into the sitting room. And then the voice I most wanted to hear said, "Oh, Malcolm," and Emma dropped to the floor next to me.

"Weel, he looks a right mess," someone said.

Annie? What was Annie Goslin doing here?

"You should have seen him before!" Maggie said gleefully.

"Dr. Cook, if you're almost through here, we have another patient for you," Captain Abbott's voice said. "Gunshot wound to the elbow. It—I don't think the arm can be saved. He's being held in a room off the lobby."

I twisted my head so that I could see Emma. "Are you hurt?" I demanded, reaching for her with my good arm.

"A little bruised," she said. "But nothing broken. Or shot," she added with a quaver to her voice, and burst into tears. I heard or felt my mother, my sister, and Annie all cluster around her, murmuring, but she held fast to my hand. Evidently something *had* happened—something bad—while I was out of commission. Damn it, I should have been there!

The surgeon left with Captain Abbott and Father. Mother brought a blanket to cover me and a thin pillow and sent Maggie to put the kettle on once again, this time for tea. Emma and I held tight to each other's hands, though the others tried to coax her up. I shifted my head to get a better look at her and saw that she was wearing a white naval dress blazer...and nothing else. Her skin was clutched in her other hand.

"What happened?" I asked, as gently as I could.

"Ssh. In a minute," my mother said, bustling back into the room. She made Emma stand up and take off the blazer, wrapped her in what looked like one of Isabel's old dressing gowns, then washed her face as gently as she had mine. I could tell that she had been hurt—something other than the bruises she'd admitted to. Or maybe the bruises were somewhere that couldn't be helped by aspirin and a warm washcloth.

When Mother let her go, she sat down beside me again, then lay down, right on the sitting room floor in front of everyone, and huddled close to me. I carefully lifted my arm and put it protectively over her. It hurt, but it would've hurt worse not to.

"What happened?" Mother answered me, as if there had

been no interruption after my question. "Just Emma saving the air station from the Germans. *And* the hotel."

"The *hotel?*"

Next to me, Emma began to shiver. "I heard them, at the air station," she whispered. "They wanted to blow up the hotel too. So I followed them back here to warn everyone."

I kissed her because I couldn't find words enough to say what I felt.

We heard the door open again. This time, I recognized Father's tread and, after a minute, Captain Abbott's. The captain came and squatted next to us. "Will you be all right, Miss Verlaine?" he asked, not sounding at all surprised at her posture.

"I don't know," she said after a minute. Her eyes were closed, and there were tears on her eyelashes. "I mean, I...I don't know what I mean."

"What about the German swine?" Maggie asked, her voice avid. "Did he croak?"

"No, he didn't, and he won't. He'll be on his way to Boston as soon as it's light, for questioning and a nice uncomfortable jail cell. Along with his friends."

"Aw." Maggie sounded disappointed. "Annie, you should have pegged him right in the heart."

"As Miss Emma was blocking the way o' that, I'm fine with winging him in the elbow," Annie said, unperturbed. "I didna think the captain would be any pleased if I'd killed him outright. It's hard to ask questions of a dead man."

What? "Will someone please tell me what happened?" I demanded.

Eventually, they did. I held Emma close and listened as everyone related their part of the story—all except Emma. Annie's account, however, smoothed over that gap.

"What were you even doing here, Mrs. Goslin?" the captain asked.

"Och, that." I could picture Annie's shrug. "I often coom over on a dance night to see the ballroom. Miss Emma knows aboot that. I like looking in at the decorations and the dresses. But I always take my gun when I go. No telling when one might run into a footpad or some other creature o' the night."

"Of course," the captain said gravely.

"You'd be surprised, young man. So I was coming nigh on the veranda, listening to the music as I walked, and I heard sneckin' and shufflin' a-coming up the lawn. I stopped, and saw those Germans creeping up on the hotel, but I didna ken they were Germans, then. I did m'own sneckin' up the stairs and hid in the shadows and watched. It almost startled the breath out o' me when Miss Emma came up out of the grass and crept right past me. She talked to someone at the door. I couldn't hear it all, but it was plain there was something wrong—verra wrong—and I wanted to stay hidden in case I was needed."

"You were very definitely needed," Mother murmured.

"I was, wasn't I? When that horrid man grabbed our Emma from behind, it was all I could do not to shout and pop him one right there."

Emma stiffened against me. I pretended no one was watching and kissed her softly until she relaxed.

"But I didna know how many more of them were around," Annie continued, "and wasn't wantin' to attract their attention. He began to drag her off, and I followed. Their backs were to me, so I felt mostly safe. When the captain appeared, I hoped that would be it, but it wasn't. A desperate man is like a snake— it'll strike no matter what, because that's its nature. I feared our Emma would be hurt, and soon, so I shot him."

"Just like that," Father said. He was having difficulty concealing a smile, I could hear.

"His elbow stuck out like a sore thumb, just asking for it," Annie explained. "I told maself it was a groundhog, like in my garden, and that was that."

It was almost comical the way Annie told it, but oh, my poor Emma. What she must have felt, being attacked like that— and I hadn't been there to protect her. If George Osborn ever dared show his face on this island once I was healed, he would regret it *deeply*.

"Ma'am, if my boys could hit groundhogs as well as you do, we'd be guarding the President, never mind the Cape," Captain Abbott said.

There was silence for a few minutes. Then Mother asked, "And the other Germans?"

"We got them all but one," the captain said, sounding frustrated. "One got away in their boat. But all the dynamite has been safely disposed of."

Father said, "I should not be at all surprised if something happens to him and his boat. And the vessel that comes for him."

Emma stirred. "The Osborns," she said, then pushed herself up on one elbow. "Captain Abbott, it was Mr. Osborn — he was the one who agreed to help them."

"I've already set guards to watch their house, Miss Verlaine. Mr. Osborn won't be going anywhere before I talk to him in the morning. His son is at the base for now, in protective custody. He seems glad enough to be there, away from any possible contact with Germans. He says that he had no idea what was going on with his father and Herr Keller — or *Fregattenkapitän* Keller, I should say — until this afternoon."

"But what about him being out in his boat all the time? He must have been looking for U-boats to plot with." Maggie said. "I'll bet that's how Keller got here."

"Nothing so romantic, I'm afraid. Keller has a Swiss passport — or what looks like a Swiss passport — and arrived here in an ordinary liner. We've put a cable in to the Swiss embassy in New York to ask for, ah, clarification of his citizenship."

"Rats." Maggie sounded disappointed. "You don't think George picked him up off a U-boat?"

"I am inclined to believe his story, for now."

I sighed. "Yeah, I think he's telling the truth." I told them briefly what I had seen and heard before he'd shot me.

"No, George didn't know," Emma said. "The Germans stole his boat. And he did help us get rid of the dynamite."

"Hmm," Captain Abbott said. "Based on your word, I won't hold him accountable for now. I will see what I think after I speak to his father."

"What will happen to Mr. Osborn?" Mother asked.

"It depends. He might have a great deal of useful information for us if he is willing to cooperate. And his factories are providing essential war matériel. But even if he doesn't go to prison, he'll still likely find himself taking an early retirement and selling out—at not too much of a loss, if he's fortunate."

Next to me, Emma sighed. "Oh, poor Helen," she whispered. So that was why she'd defended George—for her cousin's sake.

Father stood up. "I ought to check on the dance," he said. "Thanks to Emma and the captain, no one knows that anything happened here tonight."

"No one heard Annie's gun?" Maggie demanded. "We sure did in here!"

Captain Abbott cleared his throat. "Unfortunately, it seems that one of my boys had a touch too much to drink and decided to try some target practice out on the veranda to impress his friends. He and they have been severely reprimanded."

"Oh." Maggie sounded disappointed but held her tongue.

Father and the captain and Annie left then, the captain offering Annie a ride home in his own car, which she graciously accepted. Mother made Maggie go to bed, and then knelt beside us.

"I called your grandmother earlier to warn her you'd be late," she said to Emma. "She made me promise to call when you were ready to come home. Josiah evidently won't rest until you have."

"I've got her clothes!" Maggie piped up from the doorway. "Her shoes got kinda wet from being out on the porch in the dew, though. And her petticoat's a *mess*."

"Thank you, Maggie. You may leave them on that chair and go to bed—*really* go to bed this time." I felt Mother looking down at us. "I'm going to run you a quick bath, Emma dear," she said gently. "I think it would make you feel better. And I'll call your grandmother and tell her to send Josiah in three quarters of an hour. Will that suit you?"

"Yes," she said, and sighed again. "Thank you, Mrs. Galbraith."

Mother left, and then it was just me and Emma. "His blood is still all over me," she said, suddenly.

"What?"

"Herr Keller's blood—from when Annie shot him."

No wonder Mother was running her a bath before she went home. My poor darling. "I wish she'd gotten him in the head," I said, and tightened my arm. Whatever the doctor had used to numb my back was starting to wear off. But I didn't care.

"I'm not. It would have been worse, to have him die on me. This was bad enough." She started to shiver again.

"You won, Emma. You got here in time. You saved everything—and everyone."

Her voice was very quiet when she finally replied. "I know. I know that with my—my thinking brain. But I can't get rid of the feeling of his hand over my mouth and his gun against my throat. And the way he touched my sealskin with his foot, like it was—like—"

I held her while racking sobs shook her. When she seemed to have cried out the worst of it, I kissed her. "I guess I'm going to have to keep doing that until that's the only feeling you remember on your mouth," I whispered, and carefully shifted my hand till I could stroke the side of her throat with my thumb. "And touch you here, and everywhere, till the other feelings are gone. But I...I don't think you should forget. Not completely. Sometimes, remembering the bad things that happen is good—if you remember that you beat them. Because then you'll know you can handle any other bad thing that might come down the road. But I'll promise you this: it won't be a damned German spy with a gun." And I kissed her again and didn't stop kissing her till my mother came back into the room and cleared her throat.

I drew back and looked at Emma. "So…is that better?"

She looked at me, and a tiny smile blossomed in her eyes. "I don't know. You may have to do a lot more of that to really make it work."

"I will, gladly, after you have that bath." The sight of that nascent smile made my heart swell.

She touched my cheek, then got up and went with my mother. I lay there feeling, under the circumstances, not altogether too bad, till Mother came back into the room.

"The surgeon wanted you to take these," she said, kneeling beside me.

I saw something cupped in one of her hands, and a glass in the other. "What is it?" I asked suspiciously, lifting my head.

"Aspirin." She popped them into my mouth before I could protest and held the glass to my lips. I gulped at it to get the bitter taste washed down and didn't notice till I'd drunk the rest that there was something mixed in with it, something chemical and smoky-tasting.

"Traitor," I muttered.

"It was just a chloral hydrate draught. Dr. Cook wants you to sleep."

"But Emma—"

"Emma is having her bath and is quite well," she said firmly. "Even young men who think they're invincible have to sleep. Especially if they plan to keep up with young women who truly are."

That made me smile. "Will she be all right?" My eyelids were already getting heavy.

"She'll be fine. She's quite a girl, Malcolm. Be sure that you deserve her."

"I know. I will." I closed my eyes. I wasn't sure if I dreamed it or not, but at some point, I felt Emma kiss me, and then I slid the rest of the way into dark, cradling sleep.

•Chapter Twenty-nine•
Emma

I probably would have slept past noon the next day if Helen hadn't come into my room around nine, flung open the curtains, then come to stand over me.

I looked up at her, blinking and shielding my eyes. "I'm not going to church, remember?"

"Neither am I. Not today, anyway. Probably not ever again," she added, almost to herself. She surveyed me for a minute; there was something tense about her, as if she were holding her breath—her entire self—in anticipation of some enormous event. Then she pulled a chair over and sat down. "How was your trip?"

It took me a minute to decipher what she was talking about. "My—oh, uh, fine. Just—fine." I evidently wasn't going to get any more sleep this morning; I yawned and sat up.

"Good." She got up suddenly and walked back to the windows. It was a sunny day, but she didn't seem to actually see anything beyond the glass. "You might want to get out of bed soon and get dressed. We're going to have callers," she said, not turning around.

"Who?"

"Mr. Osborn. George too, I should think. I don't know if Mrs. Osborn will come too."

I took a breath, and another. What should I say? "Um...I—

that is, I—I might not expect the Osborns to be paying social calls today."

"It's not a social call." Then she turned, frowning. "What makes you say that?"

I made a show of turning to fluff my pillows, to buy myself time to think. I knew she liked George a great deal. But things had changed, and even though I had decided against warning her about him, it might be that the Osborns would be leaving Mattaquason shortly, whether they wanted to or not, and she deserved to have some previous notice of it.

"I expect Mr. Osborn is busy talking to Captain Abbott right now," I said.

She came back and sat down again. "Why?"

I steeled myself. "Because it appears he's been collaborating with the Germans."

"Good God." She stared at me for a moment, then shook her head. "No. They'll come. Mr. Osborn will manage it somehow. It's too important."

"What is?"

She took a deep breath. "Arranging our wedding."

Huh? "Um, Helen—he's already married."

She snorted. "Don't be an idiot, Emma. My and George's wedding, of course."

I didn't—couldn't—think of anything to say. That casually dropped 'idiot' from my usually kind cousin had stung. "I don't understand," I finally said.

She sighed. "Yesterday afternoon I sent Mr. Osborn a note informing him that I am reasonably sure that I am expecting a baby, and that it will be—is—his grandson."

I stared at her, at her sweet, round, Ivory-Soap-ad face and folded hands, and blurted, "You're *pregnant*? With George's baby?"

She shrugged. "Maybe. I'm not sure yet, but it's not something you can wait very long on to be sure. And yes, if I am, George is the father."

Oh. I slumped back against the pillow while the last weeks

rearranged themselves—Helen's frequent absences, the feeling I got that she was miles away. When I assumed she'd gone for a walk or into Mattaquason to sew for the Red Cross, she must have been with George. "Helen, this is—this is very bad. Mr. Osborn might be under arrest at this very moment. For helping the Germans try to—to do a very bad thing."

Helen closed her eyes and reached up to rub her temples. "Honestly, I don't much care what they've done. I just want to get married. Why do you think I even *came* to Cape Cod?"

I blinked. "I don't know."

"To find me a husband. I wasn't going to find one where we live in New York. I came here so I could find a rich man to marry."

"But your job in the fall—you're going to be a career woman—"

She laughed grimly. "Emma, you're such an innocent. I lied to you. I don't have any job lined up, unless I want to go work in a mill or walk the streets. My father's ready to throw me out if I don't start bringing in some money, so when Aunt Wetherell invited me here, I knew what I'd have to do. All kinds of rich folks come to stay on Cape Cod in the summer, right? I just had to snag me one."

"Oh, Helen—"

"Don't 'oh, Helen' me. You've had a doting papa stuffing you with sugar plums all your life. I haven't." Her gaze changed, grew distant. "My, I thought I'd fallen in the cream, the day we arrived: Malcolm Galbraith with that big hotel, and George Osborn and his daddy's factories, and that was before we'd been here an hour. I wasn't very happy when they both decided they liked you better."

"I'm sorry," I whispered.

"Oh, I figured out quick enough that you only had eyes for Malcolm, which left George for me. Besides, the more I thought about it, the more I knew I didn't want to live here and help run a hotel, no matter how posh it was. I just had to figure out how to call George to heel."

"I *tried*," I had to say. "I did my best to get him to pay more attention to you."

Her expression softened a little. "I know you did. You're not a bad kid, Emma. Problem was, a lot of the time it backfired and just made him more interested in you. Men are stupid that way sometimes."

I wasn't quite sure how to respond to that. "What—how—did you—"

"Call George to heel? I became his best friend, instead. I let him cry on my shoulder about how you were being taken in by Malcolm, who obviously meant you no good. God, he hates him. He made me spy on you two, and just on Malcolm, when I could." She hesitated. "That's how I found out."

Oh. Oh, *no*. "Found out what?" I asked, trying to sound not very interested.

"It's no use, Emma. I know what Malcolm is. I've seen him…change. I'm assuming you know too?" Her voice went up questioningly.

I couldn't look at her. More pieces fell into place. "And you told George," I said quietly. "Did he take Malcolm's skin?"

"You knew about that."

"We knew somebody had."

She was silent for a minute, thinking no doubt about my use of 'we.' "I took it. I didn't want to—George made me. He was convinced Malcolm was plotting something—that he was trying to help the Germans somehow. It made it easier to hate him—easier than to just admit he was jealous of him. He'd planned on revealing it all to you at some point so you'd fall into his arms."

"Except you'd already done that."

She flushed a little. "Yes, I had. It was so easy—and besides, you didn't want him."

"Helen, how…how could you fall in love with someone like that? He shot Malcolm—did you know that? Shot him in cold blood. And some German saboteurs nearly succeeded in blowing up the air station last night with his help." I shook my head. "Malcolm's been helping to guard the air station *against* the Germans, not helping them."

"It has nothing to do with love—I told you that." Her face had gone pale and set. "There was nothing else I could do. I'm sorry Malcolm was hurt—is he all right?—but I don't think George shot him knowingly because he didn't know I'd given Malcolm's skin back to him. I didn't see any point to keeping it, so I left it on their porch early yesterday morning—it was a lot easier to sneak out since both you and Josiah were gone. And I doubt George was in cahoots with the Germans—I'll bet it was all his father. George would never have been able to keep something like that from me. He liked to talk too much about what a big man he was, or would be some day." She swallowed. "Now what will happen?"

"I don't know. The Germans are in custody, and Captain Abbot was going to see Mr. Osborn today." I hesitated. "In the end, George helped us save the air station, so maybe they won't be too hard on him. I told the captain that."

"Helped *us*?" She looked up at me keenly. "How are you mixed up in this?"

I couldn't meet her eye. "I'd rather not say."

She waited, but I remained silent. "Well," she finally said, and stood up. "In that case, I'd better plan on paying the call myself, rather than waiting for him to come here. I'm sure that Captain Abbott and his men will let me in to see them, once they know why I'm there."

And here are the Wetherells, I thought, providing the good women of Mattaquason with yet another subject for gossip for the next twenty years. "Helen, how do you know it's a boy?"

She was already at the door but hesitated, then turned and smiled without humor. "I don't. I don't even know if it's real. But it's just what you say to men like Mr. Osborn, in this situation." She slipped into the hall and was gone.

After Helen left, I thought about going back to sleep but doubted I'd be able to. Anyway, there was something I had to do. I dressed quickly and went downstairs to the telephone, picked up the receiver, and clicked the hook to call the operator. "Information, please," I said when she came on the line. "Washington, D.C.—Walter Reed Hospital." I wrote down the number she gave me, clicked the hook again, and gave the connecting operator the number.

I wondered what had gone through Dad's head as he lay in his bed after we'd spoken last week. I hoped he hadn't been fretting, waiting for us to go to Boston...waiting for some response from me. I would write him a long letter later today. But I needed to do this now.

"Walter Reed Hospital," a voice said.

"May I please speak to Dr.—um—Major Oliver, please?"

"One moment, please."

I waited one moment, then several more. Finally, a new voice came on the line—a masculine one. "Oliver here," it barked.

I jumped. I'd expected to reach a secretary, not the man himself. It knocked me off balance. "Um...good morning, sir. I'm Emma Verlaine—you're taking care of my father, Professor—umm, I mean Captain—Verlaine? Ernest Verlaine? I'm really sorry to bother you, but I had to. It's important or I wouldn't do this," I blurted. "I need you to tell my father something."

There was a pause. "Miss Verlaine," the bark said, only it wasn't a bark any more. "I'm glad to hear from you. Your father's mentioned you several times, and I know something is troubling him. I suggested he telephone you again, but he refused. I think his recovery would progress more rapidly if his mind were quiet." There was a faint question in his voice.

Yes, he would have refused to call until he heard from me first. "Could you give him a message for me?"

"Certainly. Give me a moment to find a pencil—all right, I'm ready."

"Please, tell him—can you use these exact words?" I took a deep breath. "Even though some things are different, one thing that hasn't changed is that I love you, Dad. And I always will."

There was a pause, and I heard the faint scratching of a pencil on paper. "Got it," he said. "Is that all?"

Was it? There were dozens of other things I could say—things I longed to say—but they all boiled down to the same thing: that no matter what, he was and always would be my Dad.

"Yes, it is," I said. "Thank you."

When the doorbell rang a little while later, I was sure the Osborns had managed to get away from Captain Abbott. But when I peeked out the library's bay window, I only saw Maggie, finger poised to ring the bell again. I hurried to the door to let her in.

"Nope, not coming in," she said. "I'm under strict orders to bring you back to the invalid's bedside so you can mop his fevered brow."

I gasped. "Malcolm's running a fever? Did someone phone the doctor at the air station?"

"Oh." She giggled. "No, he's all right. I was taking—um, you know, drama—dramatic license. He just wants to see you."

I pressed my hand against my quickened heart and frowned at her. "Maggie Galbraith, don't scare me like that!"

She looked impressed. "Gosh. You really do like him, don't you?"

"Yes," I said shortly, and went to tell Gran where I was going.

"So did you hear?" Maggie said, before we were halfway down the driveway. "They found the other dirty rotten German. He was floating face down in the water, near the boat they stole. Father *told* Captain Abbott we'd take care of it."

"No, I hadn't heard." I couldn't help shivering, even though I was glad.

"Uh huh. Serves him right, too. And they're gonna have to chop the other one's arm off—the one who tried to kidnap you. Dr. Cook said he couldn't save it, and he doubted they'd be able to in Boston. He's already left on the train with the others."

"Where did you hear that?"

"I eavesdropped." She grinned. "Captain Abbott came over this morning. He wants to talk to you again, he said." She blinked at me, suddenly solemn. "Are you going to marry him?"

"What?" What had put it into her head that I would want to marry Captain Abbott?

"Are you going to marry Malcolm?"

Maggie was making me dizzy this morning. "I—don't know. He hasn't asked me."

"Oh, he will," she said confidently. "As soon as we get back home, prob'ly. He was asking for you the minute he woke up. But I don't want you to marry him. I mean, I do want you to. Just not yet."

I smiled; I couldn't help it. "All right. When do you want me to marry him?"

"After you've gone to college." She looked up at me. "It's only *fair*—he went, didn't he? So he could see the world of humans and learn something about it? You should, too. And besides, if you go, they'll have to let me go too, when it's my turn. Right?"

I laughed out loud then—the first time in forever, it felt like—and some of the weight of the last few days seemed to lift from my shoulders. "Right," I said.

My heart began to thump uncomfortably and my palms to sweat as Maggie and I climbed the front stairs of the hotel. Was this how it would always be from now on—had last night poisoned the place for me forever? I couldn't even imagine going out onto the veranda—especially not at night. I'd thought I was fine after last night, but maybe, like Malcolm, I had my own healing to do.

Fortunately, we didn't go there but to the Galbraiths' private porch, where Malcolm lay, on his stomach, of course, on a sort of couch. With him were Mrs. Galbraith and, to my embarrassment—after all, he'd seen me without any clothes last night—Captain Abbott.

"Emma, my dear." Mrs. Galbraith embraced me warmly.

Captain Abbott has risen as well. "Miss Verlaine, I hope you've begun to recover from your exertions last night."

But my attention was riveted on Malcolm, who had started to push himself up. "Don't you *dare* try to get off that bed, you!" I said sternly.

"Here." Maggie appeared with a footstool and set it next to her brother. "He's not gonna let you go sit on a regular chair."

I sat. He caught my hand and kissed it. "You were taking too long."

"I don't care. I warned you I was going to make sure you stayed in bed until the doctor says you can get up, even if I have to sit on you." I smoothed his hair off his brow. His voice sounded normal, but he was pale under his tan and there were dark circles under his eyes. "Were you able to get any sleep last night?" I asked, more gently.

"Some, before the drugs wore off." He grimaced.

"Miss Verlaine, I assure you that this young man's recovery is of the utmost concern to the Navy. Dr. Cook will be in shortly to check on him," Captain Abbott said. "And I hope you'll make use of the doctor's services as well, if you feel the need. I don't take my officers' health and welfare for granted."

It took a moment for what he'd said to sink in. "Your *what*?"

There was a momentary silence—but Mrs. Galbraith was smiling, and Maggie looked to be on the verge of explosion. "What?" I repeated, because I *couldn't* have heard him correctly…could I?

"You mean my sister didn't spill the beans on the way here?" Malcolm said. Maggie stuck her tongue out at him.

Captain Abbott was smiling as well. "Miss Verlaine, thanks to you and the selkie patrollers, a tragedy was averted last night.

Hundreds of servicemen and civilians might have been killed and a huge blow dealt to our country's defenses and morale if you had not stopped those saboteurs. I didn't think there was any way I could adequately express my gratitude for your bravery and resourcefulness, but I believe I might have hit upon one."

I was probably cutting off the circulation to Malcolm's fingers, I was squeezing his hand so hard. "Sir?" I whispered.

"I spoke briefly this morning with an old friend who coincidentally happens to be the Assistant Secretary of the Navy." His smile widened. "Mr. Roosevelt appreciates — ah, *unorthodox* solutions to problems even more than I do, which is why he's given me carte blanche to establish a formal selkie intelligence unit — a secret one, that is — supported as needed by the resources of the Monomoyick Naval Air Station. I've asked your young man here to lead it and recruit as he sees fit, but there's one candidate I felt I personally needed to invite. It makes me glad I wasn't able to give you an office job, since I can now offer one much more suited to your talents — Midshipman Verlaine."

I tried to say something, but all that came out was a squeak.

"Gee, he said I could only be a Seaman, and not till I'm twelve." Maggie sounded impressed. "You're *lucky*, Emma!"

"It's no sinecure, young lady," the captain said to her. "I'll expect selkie patrollers out from before dawn till well after sunset, every day, until the war is over. Are you ready to make that commitment?"

"Oh," I said, stricken, and began to rise. "I left my skin at home. I can run there and be back in a few —"

Malcolm pulled me down again. "My other patrollers are back on duty. You get forty-eight hours leave to recover from last night." Though he was smiling, his eyes were somber. "And a few more beyond that to learn how to be a selkie. It's killing me that I can't get out there with you for weeks yet."

I squeezed his hand. "I can wait."

"No." He shook his head. "You've waited long enough. I'm

not going to hold you back. Not that I think there's anything that can, really."

For a moment I could only sit there and blink back tears. Finally—*finally*—I would be able to do something important, something that *mattered*, even if no one would ever know that I'd done my bit for the war too…and not just by knitting socks.

"No, I don't think there is," I said.

- The End -

Thank you so much for reading *What Lies Beneath*! If you enjoyed it, please consider telling your friends who might also enjoy it or posting a review on the site where you purchased it or on your favorite book social media sites such as Goodreads or LibraryThing.

If you would like to sign up for my newsletter and get the latest information on new releases, sales, free stories, and other fun stuff, visit https://eepurl.com/bVDwlf

·Author's Note·

All right, dear readers, here's the fun part (at least for me—you may think otherwise!): where I get to talk about what's historical in *What Lies Beneath* and how I played with it to create the fictional bits.

It's a given that the United States entered World War I in April 1917 after a series of events that reads more like an international spy novel than fact, complete with intercepted messages, code-breaking, and more. I suggest picking up Barbara Tuchman's *The Zimmermann Telegram* if you'd like to learn the whole amazing story.

But what did entering the war mean? It meant the usual things—training soldiers to send to Europe to fight, gearing up industry to create the war materiel those soldiers would need, and so on…but in addition, there was a huge media campaign to encourage the rest of America—especially women—to support the war effort. That meant—you guessed it—knitting socks and hats and other comforts for the troops and rolling bandages and sewing and growing gardens and conserving food and fuel and and and. I managed to track down dozens of women's magazines from the spring and summer of 1917 that are chock-full of knitting patterns and recipes for food conservation, and I hope that I was able to convey the flavor of the time in which Emma lived. The one thing I did kinda-sorta make up was using blackout curtains. While they were definitely widely used during World War II, far fewer locations used them in the earlier war, most notably areas in Scotland that were being bombarded in zeppelin raids. But it didn't seem out of the question that an intelligent navy base commander in a highly vulnerable area like Cape Cod wouldn't have hit upon the idea as well, so here we are.

As for the place where Emma lived...

Cape Cod is, of course, real: on a map you can see it sticking into the north Atlantic like a skinny arm trying to show off its biceps. But Mattaquason and Monomoyick Island are invented terrain, though based on real places on the Cape. Also invented is the naval air station on Monomoyick where Emma longs to get a job, though it too is based on reality: there really was a naval air station on Cape Cod in World War I. The Chatham Naval Air Station—complete with dirigibles and sea planes and hydrogen tank and offices and barracks, was established to guard the approaches to Boston harbor and the local shipping and fishing industries, as described in the story. Though it no longer exists—it was dismantled not long after the war—you can still see concrete walls and bases for its docks on a beach in Pleasant Bay, on the Cape's elbow. I fudged a bit with the timing and a few other minor details—the real station wasn't fully operational until some months after the summer of 1917—but other than that, my Monomoyick station is a fairly faithful representation of the real thing. I am fortunate that an exhaustive study, *Wings Over Cape Cod: the Chatham Naval Air Station 1917-1922* by Joseph D. Buckley, enabled me to create a convincing facsimile.

You might be asking if German submarines really were nosing about around Cape Cod, and the answer is yes, indeed, they were. In fact, in the summer of 1918, a U-boat surfaced off the town of Orleans, just above the Cape's "elbow." It was likely there looking for the underwater communications cable that stretched from Orleans to Brest, France, in order to cut it. But a tugboat towing some barges and a schooner happened by, and U-156's captain decided to open fire on them with its deck guns. As it was a Sunday, the captain of the tugboat had brought his wife and small son along for what should have been a pleasant day's outing...and instead the family was forced to abandon ship when the tug was heavily damaged and the barges and schooner sunk by the U-boat. They and thirty-two crew from the barges and schooner were rescued (amid heavy fire from the U-boat) by a gallant US Coast Guard surfboat. Two Curtiss HS-2L flying boats took off from the Chatham air station and tried to drop bombs on the U-boat, but the bombs either didn't explode (a common problem, it seems) or the airmen weren't deploying them correctly. The U-boat tried shooting at the sea-planes but missed, instead landing shells on the Nauset marshes and beach before slipping away. As a result, the "Battle of Orleans" (yes, that's a tad tongue-in-cheek) has the distinction of being the only time the United States mainland was fired upon during the war. U-156's subsequent career was not a long one; it disappeared in September 1918, likely while traversing a minefield in the North Sea.

The Ocean Hotel also has one foot in real life: it is based on actual resort hotels on Cape Cod in this period, almost none of which are still standing today, alas. Coincidentally, the (no longer extant) Hotel Chatham which I used as a model for the Galbraiths' inn was located on some of the land that would one day—some thirty years later—become the Chatham Naval Air Station.

As an author, I get to play make-believe with locations and history...but I can't make stuff when it comes to, yanno, actual languages that people speak. So a hearty thank you is due to Dr. Jonathan Green for the German translations in Chapters 23 and 25; any errors are purely my fault.

Hearty thanks are also due to friends who read and made invaluable comments on earlier incarnations of this story, including Rose Green, Larissa C. Hardesty, Robin Lemke, and Holly Westlund. Beth Campbell and Sherwood Smith performed their editorial magic and made me make it so much better than it originally was, for which I am forever grateful. And copyeditor Tamara Kaupp reined in my wayward commas, brought back my skipped articles, and made the manuscript very shiny indeed.

Thanks also to my colleagues at Book View Café for their support and assistance with many aspects of this book, in particular Sherwood Smith, Jen Stevenson for her work on the e-book edition, and Pat Rice for her masterly touch with blurbs as well as everyone else who works behind the scenes to keep bringing out top-notch books.

Continued thanks are also due to my dear Shenaniganizers: Jen Clark Estes, Larissa Hardesty, Ena Jones, Katie Kennedy, Robin Lemke, Cindy Marko, Deena Lipomi Viviani, and Holly Westlund for support moral and immoral, for hand-holding when needed, and for laughter at all times.

And lastly, thank you as always to my family for brainstorming, read-throughs, and general understanding, support, and tolerance for living with someone who has all these people living in her head. I love you all so much.

Connect with me
(because I love hearing from readers!)

Website: https://www.marissadoyle.com

Blog: https://www.nineteenteen.com

Facebook: https://www.facebook.com/marissadoyleauthor

Twitter: https://www.twitter.com/marissadoyle

Pinterest: https://www.pinterest.com/mdoyleauthor

Bookbub: https://www.bookbub.com/authors/marissa-doyle

Sign up for my newsletter
for news of upcoming releases:

https://www.eepurl.com/bVDwlf

See what else Book View Café has to offer:

https://www.bookviewcafe.com

·About the Author·

Marissa Doyle graduated from Bryn Mawr College and went on to graduate school intending to be an archaeologist, but somehow got distracted. Eventually she figured out what she was *really* supposed to be doing and started writing. She's channeled her inner history geekiness into a successful young adult historical fantasy series and is now also happily writing fantasy of various types for teens and adults. She lives in her native Massachusetts with her family, including a bossy but adorable pet rabbit, and loves quilting, gardening, and collecting antiques. Oh, and coffee.

Please visit her at her website, https://www.marissadoyle.com, and at her history blog, http://www.nineteenteen.com.

ABOUT BOOK VIEW CAFÉ

Book View Café is an author-owned cooperative of professional writers publishing in a variety of genres, from fantasy to romance, mystery, and science fiction as well as select non-fiction.

Book View Café authors include New York Times and USA Today bestsellers; Nebula, Hugo, and Philip K. Dick Award winners; World Fantasy Award, Campbell Award, and RITA Award nominees; and nominees and winners of multiple other publishing awards.

Since its debut in 2008, Book View Café has gained a reputation for producing high quality e-books, and is now bringing that same quality to its print editions.